Mad for the Marquess

by

Jess Russell

Reluctant Hearts

Mad for the Marquess

Cover Art by *The Wild Rose Press, Inc.*

The Wild Rose Press, Inc.
PO Box 708
Adams Basin, NY 14410-0708
Visit us at www.thewildrosepress.com

Publishing History
Second Edition, 2025
Trade Paperback ISBN 978-1-5092-6211-3
Digital ISBN 978-1-5092-6212-0

Reluctant Hearts
Published in the United States of America

Dedication

To the women in my life who bear me up.

Acknowledgements

Many thanks to:

Ash, Veronique, Mary, and my family for weighing in and giving me the thumbs up;

My fellow writers Amber Belldene, Collette Cameron, Julia Tagan, and Mary Beth Bass—you inspire me with your heart and tenacity;

To Dianne Cooke, Helen McIver, and Rose Blue, who I have yet to meet but who have been uber supportive in my writing journey;

And on that note, to Kate Mercial Nelson, because every writer needs a steadfast (and patient) fan;

To the Beau Monde Chapter, and most especially Laura Mitchell and Susan Pace, who answered a gazillion questions about C-section;

With deep gratitude to Cynthia Young, who I rely on utterly and who is always there for me;

To Nicole D'Arienzo and The Wild Rose Press;

And finally to Bliss Bennet, Laurie Alice Eakes, and Judith Laik—the "Three Graces" or alternately, "The Three Witches" (depending on the feedback they are giving) but either praising or criticizing, I know they are striving to make my story better. Thanks, ladies!

Praise for Jess Russell

"Engrossing, emotion-packed, hard-earned happily-ever-after you won't soon forget."

~Collette Cameron

~*~

"Dev and Anne are exquisitely drawn, complicated creatures who linger long after the last page has been turned."

~Julia Tagan

~*~

"Reminded me of Kinsale's Flowers from the Storm."

~PFTH judge

~*~

"Rich, vivid description! It unfolds like a movie."

~*~

"Everything in the book is excellent—the tension, the setting, the secondary characters, the dialogue—everything."

~Shelia Judge

~*~

"A compelling and intensely emotional story with complex and flawed characters I really cared about."

~Rakes and Rascals

~*~

"In my top ten books for this year. If you enjoy exciting, emotional stories with damaged heroes and heroines, this is the perfect one for you."

~Long and Short Reviews

Chapter One

The Scottish Highlands, late March 1863

Ballencrieff Hall crouched upon the crag like a wary giant, its arm-like towers thrust up as if to hold off the heavy clouds that threatened its battlements.

Anne Winton took in a draft of cold foggy air. Ignoring the sick feeling of dread lodged deep in her belly, she bent her head into the wind and made her way up the last of the stone stairs, stepping onto the castle's portico.

A huge brass phoenix hung fixed to the door, wings spread, talons at the ready, its red eyes daring her to enter.

She turned back toward Ballencrieff's massive gates, now far below. Like a broom, her too-long cloak marked her progress through the thin dusting of snow and up the steep drive.

A stiff wind blew, blurring her trail. Soon it would be swept away altogether.

She squeezed her eyes shut. There was no going back. Her fate lay within the walls of this madhouse.

Straightening her shoulders, she caught the stray hairs that lashed her cheeks and tucked them beneath her bonnet. She met the glare of blood-red eyes. "I want this." She reached up to lift the curved beak that served as the door's knocker.

"Ahhhhhhh!"

The scream from within sent her jumping back. Her foot caught the hem of her cloak, nearly sending her to her knees. Hesitating only a moment, she pressed the heavy iron latch expecting—hoping—it would not yield, yet the massive door swung open with nary a sound. She stepped inside.

The gloom of the outdoors was nothing compared to the cavernous dark of the great hall.

"Hallo?" Her greeting echoed as if the darkness was a living thing. She pulled her cloak more tightly about her.

Twin heavily-carved staircases hugged the stone walls like corded vines before meeting at the gallery above. Enormous pillars soared as if straining toward the light, whose pale beams washed the hall's timbered ceiling, but had no chance of penetrating to the dark below.

Hoping to find a living being, she headed to the back of the hall. Halfway across the room, a burst of color bloomed at her feet. Startled, she looked up.

Tiny panes of colored glass flashed and winked within a raised cupola. The sun, which she had not seen since crossing the Scottish border, must have momentarily breached its prison of clouds. She spread her arms, her drab woolen cloak transforming into a jeweled robe.

"You will not geld me!" A deep voice shattered the quiet. "I will not bow to your will to become some managed thing!"

The bright spangles of light jumped and shuddered as if the voice and light were one.

She leaped into the safety of shadows, searching for

the owner of that desperate voice.

Then she saw him.

He flew across the gallery. Head thrown back, arms spread wide, his shirt tails streaming like a shooting star. Taking three or more steps at a time, he fled down the farthest stairway.

A gaggle of women followed in his wake.

Unaware he stood only a few feet from her, he paused within the dappled circle of light, then, like a showman, he turned and made an elaborate bow to his audience.

Startled, the women stopped halfway down the staircase, seemingly uncertain how to proceed.

He laughed when they clucked in confusion.

Anne touched her fingers to her mouth, as if she might catch his joy.

The jeweled kaleidoscope melted away as more clouds must have moved in. His limelight lost, the man ran past her, his shirt a bright flash as he dashed up the opposite staircase.

Yes. Yes, get away. Damp wool filled her hands as she grasped the edges of her cloak.

Two large, dark shapes skidded to a halt at the top of the gallery. His keepers?

The beautiful man threw a long leg over the balustrade.

"No!"

Only when his gaze locked on her did she comprehend it was she who had cried out.

She should duck her head and retreat, leaving keepers to do their job. But she found herself stepping toward him, caught in the warmth of his gaze.

"No sense runnin', ya devil!" One of the shadows

moved forward.

Her breath caught as both keepers moved in.

The man tossed his head, pitch-black hair whipping his pale face, and then slid down the banister, hopping off, light as an acrobat.

She backed under the stairway, praying he might somehow escape into the depths of the castle, or perhaps out the front door, which still stood open.

Only he didn't. He came straight to her.

Hot breath blew against her brow and eyelashes. A musky smell filled her nostrils—*a man's smell?* Utterly foreign. She should move away, but his gaze, so tender and alive, had her heart knocking at her breast and her tongue darting against her teeth.

Heavy boots slapped on the stairs above. The keepers. Closer now.

The man never flinched, seemingly oblivious to the oncoming threat.

Go! But the word froze in her mouth.

Dear God. What was happening to her? She must look away. She must at least step away.

She groped for the wall behind her. Cold rock pressed at her back, framing her in a curved niche. But he only stepped closer, his body radiating heat.

What did this beautiful madman seek? She closed her eyes to gather her own light, her powers of healing. Perhaps she might bring him comfort.

If only she could quiet her fluttering heart and chaotic breath. His scent filled her nose. A distraction. But soon familiar tingles coursed through her body. She took in more air and then raised her hands to touch him.

Rough fingers bracketed her cheeks, as heavy hips pinned her to the wall.

She flinched. Something hard pressed against her belly, but when she looked down, his fingers cradled her chin, asking her to meet his gaze. He frowned, cocking his head, his mouth now a soft smile, his eyes shimmering pools of silver. "You..." The feather of breath fanned over her lips.

He seemed at a loss to say more. Instead, his fingers wove into her hair, knocking her bonnet sideways. His breath came hot against her lips, his mouth so close.

Like a young child seeking to hide, she closed her eyes as if the darkness would be enough to conceal them. Bracing herself, she waited for the touch of his lips against hers—her first kiss.

Nothing.

Cold rushed in, and she blinked her eyes open. *Please...* Her hands pulsed with healing power, but now she wanted only the touch of his lips against hers. She reached to pull him back just as the keepers tore him away.

Her gaze snapped up to see the smirk on the larger jailor's face.

Oh, dear God. What had she done?

Her cheeks and neck flared hotly as horror and shame surged through her body. A hundred times since learning she was to be sent to Ballencrieff, she had imagined this first introduction. Always calm, assured, in control. What must they think? A silly, naïve girl, breathless over a madman. But just as she thought to drown in her disgrace, the beautiful man smiled.

Oh...Bless Bess. Perfect white teeth, one corner of his lips hitched up a fraction higher, his eyes crinkling to crescent moons. She could not look away. He seemed to pour himself into her, filling her with—

She had no inkling. But one word bobbed to the surface. *Yes.*

Her reply rose from her very center, over her belly, surrounding her heart, moving past her constricted throat to finally spill from her lips.

"Yes," she whispered. Whatever he wanted, her answer was yes.

He smiled wider.

Someone thrust a lantern between them, and her answering smile froze.

Held fast now, the keepers jerked his arms up. Light spilled onto his hands and wrists. They were smeared with something. His cuffs and shirt front were also soiled with red and black. Soot, she thought, and—*blood?*

"I say, miss, did he harm you?" A woman's profile appeared at the edge of light.

Harm? She touched her cheeks. His blood?

The man's smile hardened. And his beautiful eyes iced over.

No, this was wrong. "No—Wait—I—"

He jerked his head, snorting like a shying horse.

The woman touched her shoulder. "Truly, are you well?"

"Yes. Yes, I am…" But she shook her head despite her words and pulled her cloak about her. If only it were magical and she could disappear.

"Now you've had enough fun, your lordship. Sent us on a merry chase, you have." The older keeper's voice rang within the small niche.

"Do not harm him!" The words were not hers, though they echoed her prayer. A golden-haired man burst through the clump of bystanders and came to the bloody man's side. "Unhand him!"

"Nothing for it, Lord Austin." A nasty scar twisted the keeper's upper lip. "Your pardon sir, but Doctor Hives' orders. The marquess has to learn. Can't have them other unfortunates seeing this behavior and thinking to follow suit, now can we?"

"Mr. Macready, I do realize Lord Devlin is not the only patient here at Ballencrieff. However he is a marquess and our father the Duke of Malvern. You'd do well to remember that."

Lord Devlin? James Drake, The Mad Marquess? The girls at Ardsmoore had spoken of him in hushed tones calling him *Handsome as the Devil.* But in the same breath, *Butcher and Murderer.* She could not imagine this man willfully harming anyone. As to handsome, she had only seen a handful of men in her sheltered life, but even with his angelic-looking brother standing next to him, she could well believe Lord Devlin the handsomest man in all of England.

Lord Austin dropped his head and squeezed the bridge of his nose. "How did he get out this time?"

"Esther and I came with his porridge and—well…" Mr. Macready rose up on the balls of his feet, eager as a boy for his first taste of treacle. "Let's just say the marquess was very busy in the wee hours of the morning. While I was calming Esther." Lord Devlin snorted and Macready jerked his lordship's arm up sharply behind his back. "He slipped by us and threw the bolt."

Lord Austin turned to the woman. "Doctor Hives has not yet returned?"

"No, your lordship. He is still in Edinburgh. Then with the upset over Major Cummings…"

The marquess' frozen smile cracked, his entire body seeming to draw in on itself. He wheeled on the keeper and spat.

"Why you damned—" Macready swiped at his face and then pulled back his fist.

"Enough!" Lord Austin stayed his hand. "Take him away. Do as Doctor Hives prescribes, but nothing outside the usual treatment. Do you understand me, Macready?"

"Aye. I understand *you* perfectly, my lord." He jerked his wrist from his lordship's grip.

Lord Devlin shifted his features from a grimace into one of boredom. But the pain in his eyes as he turned to her and performed a courtly bow made her want to weep.

Oh, why did you not run when you had the chance?

And what was this treatment that lay before him? Her hands still throbbed and burned, so ready to ease his pain.

"Enough gawking. You all have your duties. Get on with them." The woman made a shooing motion. The keepers jerked Lord Devlin away, and the group of servants began to disperse, further blocking him from sight.

"You must be Miss Winton, from Ardsmoore School." The woman offered her a handkerchief.

She took the linen napkin, taking care not to touch the woman's hand, as hers still burned hot. "Thank you. Yes, I am Anne Winton." She wiped her face and then folded away the blood and soot into a tidy square. Would that she could fold her emotions away as easily.

"Well, I am Mrs. Coates, matron at Ballencrieff. Hobbs did not meet you?"

She shook her head. "Once I determined the direction, it was not far."

"In this weather? Useless boy. Couldn't find a rock

8

in a quarry, that one. Or lock the door, apparently." Mrs. Coates sucked her teeth and signaled to one of the lingering women to go and secure the door. "I am sorry for your introduction to the place, but I'm afraid I cannot say this scene, or the weather for that matter, is all that out of the ordinary. Though, I am pleased to know you are not squeamish. The last girl from Ardsmoore was a hopeless ninny. Spouting Bible verses with her every breath, afraid of her shadow."

Mrs. Coates seemed more concerned with Anne's comfort than censuring her for unseemly behavior. But then, the matron had not been inside her body and could not know its turmoil.

Lord Austin coughed.

"Oh, excuse me, your lordship, I am forgetting my manners. May I present Miss Winton?" Mrs. Coates nodded to her. "She is come to be a general companion to Lady Tippit and Mrs. Nester."

"Miss Winton." He nodded. "I must apologize for my brother. Despite Mrs. Coates's assertions, he is not usually so…charged."

She curtsied. "Lord Austin."

"He did not hurt you, did he?"

"No, my lord—that is, I—no, he did not."

"If you will excuse us, sir." Mrs. Coates snapped closed the watch on her chatelaine. "I am short staffed what with poor Major Cummings"—she shook her head—"I must make sure every patient is accounted for and then deal with the marquess' room."

"Mrs. Coates." Lord Austin released a heavy sigh. "I would like to see my brother's room now."

The matron looked toward the gallery, then at the floor, and back to Lord Austin. "Your lordship, sir, there is a great deal of…damage. If you will give me an hour, I can get someone to clear up the worst of it."

Having no wish to sit about mulling her shame, or worse, imagining Lord Devlin's near-kiss, she ventured to speak. "Mrs. Coates." A long loop of hair grazed her cheek. It must have escaped when Lord Devlin's fingers wove their way into it. Ignoring another flush staining her already heated cheeks, she straightened her bonnet and pushed the lock behind her ear. "Perhaps, if you have no need of me, I might assist with the cleaning?" The older woman shook her head, but Anne pressed on. "I would like to be of service, ma'am. I know this kind of labor will not be part of my regular duties, but I assure you I am used to all manner of work and would be up for the task."

Once again the matron sucked her teeth. "Well, if Lord Austin is agreeable, then I suppose I will not look a gift horse in the mouth." The frazzled woman turned to his lordship.

His gaze raked over her, and she resisted the urge to stand taller than her scant five feet. "She will do very well, Mrs. Coates." He nodded. "Thank you, Miss Winton."

"I will have Esther bring water and such as soon as I can calm the girl." Mrs. Coates spied Anne's bags beside the now closed door. "Is that all you brought?"

Anne nodded and went to retrieve them.

"Do not bother yourself. I will see they get to your room. Eventually," she muttered.

"Thank you, ma'am." She slipped the soiled handkerchief into her pocket and turned to Lord Austin. "Then I am ready, sir."

His long strides had her picking her skirts up nearly

to her knees to keep pace as he ascended the far staircase.

"Sir." He did not stop. "Lord Austin!"

He turned impatiently and she almost collided with him. "What is it?"

"I believe the marquess, your brother, might have a weapon." She swallowed. "Will he be punished for that?"

"A weapon?" He glowered. "Impossible." He started back up the stairs.

"I felt it."

He wheeled on her. "You felt it? Where?"

"I believe he had something hidden underneath his…fall."

Lord Austin frowned, shook his head, and then laughed. "Miss Winton, you are truly an innocent."

"I am not afraid. I am only concerned for others. And for him, the marquess."

The man swiped at his eyes as if trying to school his features. "You should be afraid, Miss Winton. What you perceived is a weapon—one Dev is all too adept at using—but it will not kill." He turned away, shaking his head. "Perhaps slay, *a la petit mort*, but not kill."

Little death? Her rudimentary French did not help. "I am not used to riddles, sir. I am afraid I do not understand."

"No. Better you don't, Miss Winton. Much better you don't."

He continued leading her through a warren of passages, rooms, and staircases. She pressed a hand over the stitch in her side. They must be at the very top of the house. A massive door stood partially open at the end of a long hallway.

As they drew nearer, the beautifully carved wood

shone with a patina honed over years of regular oiling. However, an incongruous, heavy-looking bolt bisected the door, an, just at eye level, a crude hatch had been cut into the wood. As Lord Austin pushed wide the larger door, the smaller hatch swung open revealing a grill of thick, black bars.

She released her aching side and took a deep breath. The room she was about to enter was no common chamber tucked away in an ancient Scottish castle. For all her fanciful, romantic flutterings, this was a cell for a madman.

His lordship stepped over the threshold, ignoring a huge rat that lapped at a bowl of spilled gruel. Anne covered her mouth, lunging back as the vermin scuttled down the hallway.

"Merciful God." Lord Austin had stopped just inside the room. "Perhaps you should leave, Miss Winton. I can manage well enough on my own."

His wide shoulders blocked her view, but she would not shirk her duty. "I am not afraid." Not precisely the truth, but she needed to get used to this new world. And quickly.

Her calm outward manner must have convinced him. He stepped aside and gestured her forward.

Oh, dear Lord.

"It is his blood," she whispered.

Chapter Two

The chamber's walls had been used as a huge canvas. Black coal leapt out against the stark white, punctuated with wild swipes of brownish-red. Even the ceiling had not escaped Lord Devlin's artistry.

Anne spun round, trying to take it all in. It seemed to be a full-length self-portrait, but the body was dismembered. His head—the face quite beautifully drawn—had huge horns. The skin at the hairline was flayed back, held by tiny demons, exposing twisted coils of what must be the brain. The arms were spread wide, very like the crucified Lord, only they were slashed open, showing bone and muscle. His chest was cracked wide to reveal a blackened, bloody heart.

Just to the left of this last painting was what looked to be a tower painted entirely in the brown-red color. It leaned as if about to fall, its peaked roof spewing a fountain of black. Situated in the middle of two low lying hills—no… *Legs? Part of his body?* But it was far too big and too… This could not possibly be—

Her gaze shot to Lord Austin.

Sure enough, he had been watching for her reaction, but blessedly, he turned away to move farther into the room.

Inhaling sharply, she spun away as well, her mouth gaping like a simpleton.

Clamping her lips shut, she stole another look at the

"tower." Not a total innocent, she knew what the male anatomy looked like. Alison Pierce had received a book on Greek myths from her aunt one Christmas. Always on the periphery, Anne had just managed a peek over the shoulders of the other girls when, drawn by the brouhaha, Mrs. Abbot had swooped in declaring it to be "Heathen trash," and took the book away. But not before Anne had gotten a glimpse of the utterly nude Apollo.

The golden-haired god had filled her dreams both day and night. But in the book his member had been small, a few inches at most. And it hung limply against the sack behind. Nothing as large as the weapon-like thing that had pressed hard and heavy against her belly.

"Dev is a genius, really," Lord Austin's voice startled her. "A sort of Leonardo da Vinci, if you will. Ran off to study anatomy with Barton Wainwright, mostly to learn musculature, but I suspect he relished the thrill of poaching the bodies just as much as the actual science." Lord Austin traced one of the painted arms. "If he weren't heir to the Malvern duchy, my brother would have made a very fine surgeon…" He tilted his head upward.

An angel hovered over them, its wings spanning more than half the ceiling. Though Lord Devlin's palette of color was obviously limited, she would swear this Lucifer had golden hair and a face very like that of Lord Austin. It also had horns and a forked, snake-like tongue. The perspective so keen, she would swear that tongue could lap her up in a trice. Where the other images were fascinatingly gruesome, this devil-angel made her flesh crawl.

"Da Vinci, however, had discipline. My brother possesses many gifts, but self-control is not one of them." Lord Austin's smile never reached his eyes. "Still, he should not be shut up like this. Our father is not…a liberal thinker," he said with a shrug and then bent to inspect something under the bed.

At one time this room must have been quite lovely. But it had been stripped down to nothing. Only the beautifully inlaid floor and a few moldings remained of its former opulence. Even the fireplace, where he must have fished for his coal, was walled off by ugly iron bars.

A huge chair stood away from the wall, looking as if it had been unearthed from a medieval torture chamber. Against its back, at the head, chest and waist, leather straps lay in U-shapes, their ends disappearing through slots where they must be cinched. The chair's legs were bolted to the floor, and heavy chains ending in iron and leather manacles lay pooled there. Chains and manacles also dangled from its age-blackened arms. Arms that were stained with whitish crusts—old food? And then darker spots…

"They will not bleed him? Will they?"

Lord Austin straightened from kneeling by the cot. "Honestly, I do not know, but I would think he has done a right job of that himself."

A knock at the door startled her. When had his lordship closed it?

He went to answer. "Just leave everything outside in the hall, Esther. Miss Winton will fetch it later. You may go now."

The door closed again.

She had never been alone with a man, never mind such a well-favored one. Still, she wished he had left it open.

"I am impressed, Miss Winton. I confess I was not

sure you were up to this task."

She said nothing as he took stock of her.

"You were at Ardsmoore?"

Panic, slick as a silver fish, darted in her belly. How much more did he know? She nodded.

"For how long?"

"Five and ten years, my lord."

"You must have arrived as quite a young girl?"

"I am not yet twenty, sir."

"Ah. I have not been to that particular school, but if it is anything like its boys' equivalent, Ackermoore, then you are to be pitied. I am afraid your lot has not improved by coming to Ballencrieff."

Terrible images crowded her head. Madge Barrow frothing at the mouth, raising up and pointing an accusing finger. The horror in Headmistress Abbot's eyes, and finally, Mr. Harlow's shock as he pulled Anne away. All a carefully orchestrated act wrought by a jealous girl. But one that had nearly ruined Anne's life.

She swallowed. Ardsmoore was behind her.

"I am hoping to be of service, sir." Simple words that could never convey her need to make this place a home.

"*Hmm...* Yes. You might very well be, Miss Winton. You might very well be."

She held his gaze. His blue eyes were beautiful, but they left her cold. So different from his brother's warm pewter.

"Well, I must leave you. I am going to try to see my brother before catching the train back to London. I presume you will be well enough on your own? There is a proper ladder outside and plenty of water and lye soap."

She nodded and then remembered to curtsy.

"Welcome to Ballencrieff, Miss Winton."

Lord Austin's footfalls sounded farther and farther down the hall until all was silent.

The tiny devils' mouths, open in frozen screams, mocked the utter quiet. At Ardsmoore there was never such cold, empty silence. In chapel, Marion Peebles wheezed, Agnes Bromley constantly fidgeted with the pages of her Bible, and any number of girls could be heard sniffling and coughing.

Even the wind had stilled now. This was how death would be. Heavy and palpable.

Enough. She untied her bonnet and then stripped off her cloak and threw it over the gruesome chair.

Lucifer would go first. He hovered above her, his hideous tongue just waiting for her to put a foot wrong so he might lap her up. Good thing he had not been in the great hall when she'd arrived…

After situating the ladder and the various buckets and brushes, she found herself drawn to that dark red column—a man's sex. How could it grow so big? So hard? Lord Austin did not dispute it as a weapon. She touched her belly, where it had pressed against her. Closing her eyes, she tasted her lips.

****

Red against white. Blood red against pure white.

The contrast of color beat like wings against his brain.

Red—white—red—white—red—

Dev could not feel his body. The devils had his head. They pricked him in his throat, behind his eyes, even his gums. They whispered in that deep red color on his chalk-white brain. He would scrape them off just as he used his palette knife to clean a bit of canvas, but he could not feel his arms.

Ah, the strait-waistcoat again.

Even without the confining vise, he did not think he possessed the energy to raise an eyebrow, much less a limb.

They must have dosed him again. The devils always came in droves when he was given the stuff. Poison, he was sure.

The small room was familiar—and the smell. So thick with dank must you could carve it off the walls. He had been here before. Many times. But what had he done this day?

Blood, the devil whispered.

He shook his head trying to knock the word from his mind.

Blood, it whispered louder.

"Blood," he echoed, now taking it in. Now understanding. His blood against her pale, calm cheek. Her perfectly winged brows streaked with red. And the eyes beneath those brows that spoke so clearly of awe and mercy. He inhaled sharply.

The girl.

He had wanted to kiss her.

Seeing that innocent warmth in her eyes, he had wanted it for his own. He had wanted to steal it from her and push it deep within so it might kill the cold, blank emptiness inside him.

He had blighted that pure creature with his vileness. Shock had come over her face when he had pressed against her, but it had not diminished its openness, or the hope that lay behind her deep sable eyes.

And, merciful God, she had wanted to kiss him

18

back.

He shivered despite the strait-waistcoat swaddling him from chin to cock. The freezing dunking pool had taken care of his erection. *Jesu,* he must be truly mad to have got so stirred over such a mouse of a girl. No, more like an owl, shrouded in her dull brown cloak. Small mouth. Pointed chin. Huge, luminous eyes. A common brown owl had his cock stiff as a pike. *Yes, I must be mad.*

"I hope to God at least the bloody moon is full."

The voice out of nowhere startled him, yet it seemed familiar. The moon?

"Why?"

The word jolted him. He squeezed his eyes shut, wanting to block it out. Wishing to think instead of a small, warm, feathered owl, her wings softly fluttering against him.

"Devlin. Dev, look at me."

The sound persisted no matter how hard he tried to snuff it out. The warped voice focused itself into a face. The face of his brother, Austin.

"Why did you do it?"

His brother's features shifted with his words, floating like feathers in the air. He could not catch them. Could not pull them into his brain to make them into sense. Do what? He knew better than to answer before knowing the game.

"I don't know why I bother. Honestly." His brother's hands dug through golden blond curls. The hair sprang back to angelic perfection. "I thought we had begun to make some progress." Austin wheeled and began another circuit of the small cell.

Dev closed his eyes to make the world stop

spinning.

"Cost me five pounds to Macready this time. I swear I'll end a pauper at the rate you are going."

Something touched the place below his pounding head. The devils moved though his body now, a heap of limbs cobbled together by the heavy linen of a lunatic's waistcoat. His hands prickled wanting to defend himself, but he couldn't make them move.

"Be easy, Dev."

Warm breath fluttered against his cheek. A cloth swiped his chin. A bitter taste on his tongue. His breakfast. Macready at work again. No wonder he felt so muddled.

He opened his eyes to his brother's frowning face. "Poison." He tried to form the word clearly.

But Austin only shook his head, his attention now on Dev's belly. He followed his brother's gaze. Red seeped through the stiff waistcoat. Blood.

Images began to fall into place. Last night the moon had tormented him with its brilliance as it moved freely against the sky. He had broken the window pane to smother it, to squeeze it between his fingers and crush its luminous light. But he could not reach so far. The moon-face still hung to mock him and his bleeding hands.

"You did not do this to yourself because of Major Cummings, did you?"

Red pain flared. He reared away from it, cracking his head against the stone wall. Not now. Please don't make him think of that. He shook his head despite the pain.

"Good. It is well you do not dwell on what cannot be undone." Austin stood. "I must get back to Father now."

Father? Austin was leaving? But he had just arrived. Dev reached out, but he had no arms. They lay locked and bloody against his roiling stomach. He smashed his head again.

"Stop that!"

Hands bracketed his face forcing him to meet Austin's eyes.

"Harming yourself will do you no good. I must go. Dev, Father is worse. The post came yesterday. I showed it to you. Remember?"

He strained his memory but could not remember. Yesterday was gone. A gray wash without a hint of color.

"Useless. Nothing stays in that head of yours." Austin's hands slipped away, and his face grew smaller—farther away now. "The duke is ranting about an heir again…"

There was a question he needed to ask Austin, something vital—if only he could remember.

"…this latest incident…stress his weak heart further…next time you plan such antics."

Stop. Stop talking so I can hear myself.

"I only pray Hives will see reason…if it gets back to Father…not want that on your head as well…make a trip up to speak to Hives himself, but that won't be possible now. I have a letter—"

"Stop!"

Austin's gaze jerked toward him.

Concentrate. Say it now. "If I could only paint." He prayed his words transcended mere thought to be intelligible.

"What?"

He opened his mouth wider, forcing his thick tongue to make the words. "My. Paints!"

"Paints? Paints! My God, you are the heir to a dukedom and you talk of paints? Your bloody paints have brought you to this. A shivering lunatic huddled in a dank, dark cell."

"I must have them, Austin. I must!"

His brother shook his head. "I cannot understand you. Utter gibberish. If you are to get better, you must try harder, Dev. After all, you are the heir."

The heir. The word rushed over his brain. *The Mad Marquess…the heir…*

"See that his hands are treated." The door yawned open spilling light into the cell. Austin disappeared into the light.

Yes, the light. He would follow him. Must get his feet under him. Must stand.

"Right you are, Lord Austin. Don't I always see to the marquess right and proper?" the devil said.

Panic flared in his breast. He blocked out the voice, concentrating on reaching the light. His muscles screamed in protest as his legs drove his body upward. Must get out. Get away.

But he was too slow. A shadow filled the doorway blotting out freedom. "Where do you think you are going, guv?"

"I must…" But the dark was coming closer. He tried to push it away, but the devils would win. They always did.

Chapter Three

"I am sorry Hobbs was not there to meet the mail coach." Mrs. Coates apologized again as Anne stowed the now empty bags under the bed in her room.

Blistered feet and aching shoulders were nothing to the balm of having this snug little chamber, with its very own coal fireplace where she would no longer have to share a bed. Originally a dressing room, she supposed, it connected Lady Tippit and Mrs. Nester's bedchambers. Oh, to shut the world away, if only for a moment or two.

A beautiful, pale face with searching pewter eyes and lush lips slipped past her thoughts of solitude to invade her new haven.

Stop, Anne. She closed the door. If only her action might lock out the memory of Lord Devlin's smile.

"We are usually not so lackadaisical, but what with the major…and the doctor away…" The matron opened the next door with one of her many keys. "This is her ladyship's room."

Anne took a few steps into the bedchamber.

"Matilda Tippit was originally sent here by her father, but when he summoned her to return home, she refused." Surprised, Anne turned to the matron. Mrs. Coates simply shrugged. "Her ladyship has been here ever since."

Who would choose Ballencrieff Hall over the comfort of a real home and family? The spare room offered no answers. An armoire dominated one wall, then a narrow bed, and opposite stood a plain vanity with a small mirror above.

Anne had only seen her reflection in the silver used on the church altar and in the basin where she washed herself each morning. What would it be like to see herself in a proper mirror? Her waist and skirt appeared in the glass. A simple bend would reveal her face. Turning, she rejoined Mrs. Coates.

The matron locked the door. After testing the lock, she handed the key to Anne who slipped it onto her own ring.

"Major Cummings was a great favorite among the servants and patients alike. Came back from the war blind with but one arm." She moved to the door on the other side of Anne's. "Mrs. Phoebe Nester's room."

Anne peered over the woman's shoulder. This room was even more austere: a small cupboard and no mirror above her dressing table.

"Mrs. Nester—came to us in mid February—has endured three miscarriages, and as a result suffers from hysteria. She is now five months along in her confinement."

Anne took a second key. Several questions bubbled within her, but Mrs. Coates had moved on.

"I shall miss our major. So quiet and gentle he was. Never caused a lick of worry. Never had one visitor, poor soul. Though I suppose someone must have paid for his care. Lord Devlin took it very hard. They used to play chess together."

"Was the major ill?"

Mrs. Coates stopped and turned to her. "Oh, heavens you wouldn't know, would you? He hanged himself."

The woman hastily made the sign of the cross. "Truly, he seemed in better spirits of late. We never thought…a man with but one arm could manage…" The older woman sucked in her cheeks with her indrawn breath. "I suppose his death was the reason the marquess went wild like he did. Well, that and his paints being taken away."

Oh the despair one must feel to end one's life. Even at her lowest, she always had a glimmer of hope. "Have patients—that is, does this happen often?"

"Only once before, that I know of. Mr. Macready would recall as he was here then. A woman. She jumped from the gallery in the great hall."

The picture of a broken figure dappled with jeweled light leapt from her mind's eye to lodge in her breast. She quashed the vision only to have it replaced by the vivid images of the body parts she'd so recently scrubbed out.

"The marquess, he is not allowed to paint?"

Mrs. Coates shook her head, and they started back down the hallway. "Uses his talents to paint evil, says Doctor Hives. Terrible, wild pictures. Devils. Well, I don't need to tell you." She stopped again. "I am sorry you had to see that—a green-girl nearly fresh from the schoolroom." Mrs. Coates made another turn into a narrow hallway. "I'll not soon forget the service you did me today. I'll put in a good word with the doctor. You are here on trial, but I have a feeling you'll stick."

"I assure you, I want to remain."

"*Ack,* I can't imagine why. A young girl like yourself, shut away from the world in a place like this. Well, perhaps it is better than Ardsmoore?" Mrs. Coates *humphed* and seemed to need no answer, thank goodness. "A shameful place. I do not mean to disparage the Methodist ways or the duke's generosity in funding these schools, but I must own, some of the practices employed are more suited to a nunnery than a place of learning."

True, Ardsmoore had never been a home, but it had been a refuge—until it wasn't. Madge Barrow had seen to that. But her lies could no longer touch Anne here at Ballencrieff. That horror was over.

After wending their way through a warren of hallways Mrs. Coates stopped in front of a door. "Her ladyship is the one you need to impress. She goes through companions like a tippler through gin. Mrs. Nester will follow Lady Tippit." The matron knocked, and Anne followed her into a room.

She blinked at the sudden opulence. Papered in cream and gold, the walls with their scrolls and flourishes, reminded her of Mr. Harlow's vestments during Easter. But on closer inspection, large squares were brighter than the rest—the shadows of paintings long since removed—giving the room a muted patchwork effect. A hodge-podge of mismatched furniture from a bygone era stood in haphazard groupings. Beneath her feet a carpet of pastel flowers and swagged garlands festooned a background of more subtle latticework. But it too had seen better days, many places showing through to the weft, and the fringes eaten away.

"Lady Tippit, Mrs. Nester, this is Miss Winton, your new nurse."

A lady, seated before the fire, rose briefly and then sat again, her gaze darting to a large arm chair. There a nest of hair shifted forward to reveal another lady as she peered around the wing of the chair.

"Where is everyone?" the older woman in the

26

elaborately powdered wig said. "I have been ringing for I know not how long. That useless girl came running through the chamber screaming as if the very devil were at her heels. I attempted to engage her to assist with the tea service, but she ignored me, spouting some nonsense about a bloody fiend and how she will not stay in a place full of devils."

Her gaze shifted to Anne, and she pursed her lips. "I do not require a nurse, Mrs. Coates. I require a proper lady's maid who knows how to dress hair and maintain my wardrobe. I am seriously displeased to have my toilet disturbed, and now my tea. How am I to entertain suitors in such *déshabille*?" Her wig now listed precariously to the side with the force of her tirade. "You there, girl, stop your gawping and attend me."

Seeking direction, Anne looked to Mrs. Coates who then motioned her forward. *A lady's maid?* Bless Bess. Though the daughter of a gentleman, and therefore a lady by rights, her education at Ardsmoore had not included anything about the needs of a lady.

"Mark my words, Coates," her ladyship barked, "Hives will hear of this shoddy service." She turned to dismiss the matron, but not before her wig toppled into Anne's waiting hands.

A cloud of powder enveloped her. She dare not breathe. Or cough. Please. She ducked her head and retreated a few steps to regain her poise.

The woman did not even acknowledge the loss of her hair as she squinted up at her.

"Come closer, girl. Though I am not short-sighted, Mrs. Nester is not so fortunate."

Unsure what to do with the wig whose powder was no doubt soiling her best cuffs, she approached, bearing the frizzled hair like some bizarre offering.

"Closer. I want to see what they've sent us this time." Despite vowing she had no trouble with her sight, she produced a quizzing glass. "Ballocks! Mrs. Coates, this—person—does not possess any of the feminine arts. Why look at her hair, black as ink with not a curl to soften a stubborn jaw line." Her gaze narrowed. "I do not approve of a stubborn jaw. I vow she would not know a powder from a pomade." She snapped her glass shut. "No, I reject her."

Dear God, Lady Tippit had the right of it. Anne's tenuous world shifted. How to play the part of a lady's maid? Once again the dream of working as an actual healer slipped farther away.

The younger woman poked her head forward and sniffed delicately. "My dear Lady Tippit, I care not so much for my appearance as for my safety. She does not look nearly strong enough, to my mind. What if one of those unfortunates was to fly into a mad rage? What if Lord Devil were to come at me again? I would have no hope with her as sentinel."

Lord Devil?

"Mrs. Nester," said Mrs. Coates firmly, "that confrontation is all in your mind. We have discussed this before. Lord Devlin has never come within ten feet of you."

"But he is the Mad Marquess! We all know he butchered that young girl to study her—parts." Mrs. Nester cradled her belly. "It was in all the papers. And that poor soul was with child, just as I am!"

Oh, dear God, they had to be wrong. Lord Devlin could not possibly be such a monster. But his paintings… Those tiny demons holding back his exposed brain mocked her defense.

"Now, Mrs. Nester." The matron sighed. "Miss Winton has only just come. We do not want to fill her head with tall tales."

Anne knew firsthand what it was like to be the brunt of malicious gossip. Still, the dissection of a young and pregnant girl was heinous. But surely this story could not be true.

"They are not tales!" Phoebe Nester insisted. "Mr. Nester says the girl was found at Lord Devil's lair on Greene Street, and he was covered in her blood!"

"Enough, Mrs. Nester." Mrs. Coates cut her eyes to Anne and shook her head. "You will upset the babe."

The woman gasped, clutching her belly, she wilted into a nearby chair.

Whilst her companion was in the midst of her lamentations, Lady Tippit had pulled something from beneath the cushion of her chair. It flashed, and Anne almost dropped the wig.

Only a mirror.

"You know the Marquess is—was—quite well-known as a painter before his unfortunate troubles." Her ladyship held up the mirror and frowned tilting her head one way and then the other as if she knew something was missing but could not pinpoint what it might be.

Mrs. Nester half rose from her seat like an eager student. "Mr. Nester swore Lord Devil was painting famous beauty, Nora Havermere, when he lost his mind," she hissed at Mrs. Coates as if to say, 'so there.'

"The old Earl of Havermere's countess?" Lady Tippit shook her head. "Hardly likely. From what I hear the poor girl was never let out of the house." Her ladyship smiled to expose large, yellowing teeth. She frowned, and then promptly snapped her lips closed, giving the woman in the mirror a stern look. "One could not name a more heinous viper than Lord Havermere. My poppa knew him…" She abruptly hiked up her skirts and shoved the mirror between her legs, back into its hiding place under the cushion.

Mrs. Coates only sucked her teeth and rubbed her back.

"Mr. Nester admires Lord Havermere greatly and longs to cultivate a friendship with him. My husband says the earl has much sway in Parliament," Phoebe Nester spouted this information as if reciting her times tables.

"That's quite enough about your husband, Phoebe," her ladyship said rising. She adjusted her rumpled skirts and proceeded to meander from one flower cluster on the carpet to another, like a bee seeking honey. "Lord Devlin is famous for his love of feminine beauty, you know." Her fingers grazed her neck as if she were fondling a beloved necklace. "Loves to touch, as well as look, I'll be bound." Whereupon Lady Tippit dipped her hand into her bodice and squeezed her breast.

Alas, this time the wig could not be saved. As it hit the carpet, a cloud of powder rose. *"Ah-choo!"*

Mrs. Coates smiled tightly. "Yes, well…ladies, if you will excuse me, I must meet with the staff."

"What?" The older woman spun around. "Are you leaving us with this inferior person?"

"Ladies, I am sure you will find Miss Winton more than capable. I ask you to give her a chance."

Eagar to demonstrate her commitment, she bent to retrieve the wig.

"Coates, mark my words, if she is anything like that

nervous, feather-headed chit who abandoned us, Hives will hear of it! I am of a more stalwart nature, but Mrs. Nester, in her delicate condition, cannot tolerate silly hoydens without a jot of sense disturbing her peace."

"Trust me, Lady Tippit, if Miss Winton does not suit, she will be sent packing. There are plenty of girls anxious for a position here at Ballencrieff."

Had the matron forgotten her promise already? But Mrs. Coates was already halfway to the door.

"Yes, I daresay there are." Her ladyship waved her free hand. The other, as if forgotten, still lay within her bodice.

Mrs. Coates bolted out of the room.

What a picture this odd group presented. Herself, holding the enormous beehive of a wig as if it might truly be full of bees; Mrs. Nester, cowering behind a gilt-edged chair clearly waiting for some directive, and finally, balding Lady Tippit, her arm half-way down her bosom, staring daggers at Anne.

The tableau broke when Lady Tippit moved to sit. "Come," was all she deigned to say.

This was her moment. She must make these women easy and comfortable. She must make herself indispensable. Only then would Ardsmoore be in the past.

Concentrating on her hands, the familiar pulsing started in her wrists and then fingers. She approached her ladyship.

Eyes now closed, the woman gestured for Anne to set the wig upon her head.

The hair might resemble a cloud, but in fact it was quite heavy and wearing it surely took a toll on her ladyship's neck and shoulders.

Taking a great chance, she set the wig aside and then gently brushed her fingers over the woman's frail shoulders. Lady Tippit jerked and hissed with an intake of breath. Used to such reactions, Anne did not flinch. Gently, she began to knead the older woman's cramped muscles.

"What? Oh, heavens..." The woman's lips parted.

Mrs. Nester sat straighter in her chair.

Anne closed her eyes willing the tightly knotted muscles to loosen and release their coiled strain. She imagined spinning wool into long, soft, looping threads as she worked over the lady's neck and shoulders.

Lady Tippit sighed. "So...soothing." Her head tilted slightly. "What is your name, girl?"

Relief washed through Anne's body. "Winton, your ladyship. I am Winton.

Chapter Four

The room appeared just as it had been before his…tirade. As if his time—two weeks—in that cold, dark cell had been a dream.

Had it? Panic welled. No, a different smell. Lye soap sharp in his nostrils. And darkness over the windows. Shutters. No view. No sun. And, blessedly, no moon.

A scuffling noise in the far corner made him wheel around. He threw his arms up, ready for the bastard.

Not Macready. This man loomed twice his size. This beast could easily squash a man like a beetle. Perhaps, better the devil you know…?

"Welcome to my corner of Hell." Dev bowed, and then wished he hadn't, his ribs still smarting.

The man frowned and then, pointing to himself, said, "Ivo."

"Ivo?" The man nodded. "I am pleased to meet you—I hope. I am Lord Devlin. Or Lord Devil, or sometimes The Mad Marquess, depending on my mood or who you talk to." So much effort to assume this false bravado. A wave of despair rocked him.

The giant looked down at his feet, his mouth working as if he wanted to say more. Finally he sputtered, "Lor Aus sent."

"My brother, sent you?"

The big man grinned like a monkey, exposing a

graveyard of teeth.

By God, could Macready be gone? Maybe the tide had turned. Maybe he would finally have an ally in this hell.

Ivo moved like a prizefighter, his balance forward on the balls of his feet like he had to take a wicked piss, his hands half-raised as if to protect his body. A lantern jaw held a mound of pudding that was his face—small pig-like eyes above a smashed nose, fleshy cheeks pocked with scars. Dev would have bet a wad of blunt on this fellow in any boxing ring.

Where had Austin unearthed such a hulking puppy? He bowed deeply, this time holding his aching ribs.

The giant bowed back even deeper, his huge head nearly touching the floor.

"Whoa, lad, easy. Don't want to topple over."

Suddenly the hulk straightened. Grabbing his pocket, he spun away.

Right. Maybe too hasty in his assumptions. Dev backed away. What was the man hiding? Macready always carried a set of brass knuckles.

"Can you show me, Ivo?" Best not startle the lad. "Can you show me what is in your pocket?"

He looked as if he wanted to and then swung his melon of a head side to side.

"Very well. I will not press you. Just as long as you do not decide to murder me in my bed." Good God, this man is barmier than me. One madman sent to mind another.

Being sure to keep the giant in his sights, he turned toward his cot. Would the night terrors come tonight?

And his laudanum. Had Austin brought more? He dare not check under the loose floorboard. Not until he sorted out where this newest keeper stood.

Besides, he must wean himself from taking the stuff if he were to have any hope of getting free of this place.

The door latch rattled. His new keeper retrieved Dev's dinner tray from some unseen minion.

The familiar gray gruel littered with chunks of tasteless mutton had his stomach heaving. Hives had called him paranoid. *Lord Devlin, your meals only contain tinctures to balance your humors, nothing more.*

Wet lumps on his tongue. Tasteless. He swallowed. No bitter tang. No poison? A few more spoonfuls. Still nothing. He made himself take more to fill his hollow belly. But the spoon shook as his body cried out for sleep. He laid it down and used the back of the chair to hoist himself on to his legs. The giant hovered by his side, ready to catch him or club him, he did not know.

Gruel rose in his throat as he lay down. How much longer? How much longer could he endure before submitting to despair like poor Cummings?

The new white wash had obliterated his tally of ticks on the wall. No matter; they were wrong anyway. No way to tell, with entire days lost to oblivion. Eight months at least in this hell. Of that he was sure. Could it be April? Today might even be his birthday for all he knew. That meant four until he might be free?

He would never make it.

The giant loomed over him.

He raised his arms. After an incident, the doctor always prescribed more stringent measures, both wrists and legs shackled.

Ivo's lower lip protruded as his brow furrowed. The keeper did not seem to like using the restraints.

Something to file away.

Despite their thickness, and the lack of light, the giant's fingers were surprisingly adept as he secured the manacles.

A moment later he snuffed the light, and the room plunged into darkness.

A soft sing-song crooning filtered through the quiet. Was the man singing? Hell, maybe this bruiser was religious and at his prayers.

Steeling himself, he waited for the numbness. The seeping raw weather got into his bones, behind his teeth, and under his fingernails. It would leach its way into your very heart, if you stayed still enough.

Bits of memories ticked over his brain: the smell of brandy and burning flesh, a sharp cry, a knife, blood, so much blood. He shook his head, but the action only made the fragments shift and warp, teasing him with the possibility of recognition. The moon? No, the face. The white face with its sea-green eyes. Those terrible staring eyes…

"By God, this time you have gone too far, sir." Nora's words rang over his drink-sodden brain.

His delectable mistress had certainly gotten herself into a stir. What had he done this time?

"Undoubtedly I have, madam." He tried to smile, but he couldn't seem to make his face work. "Too much of too much." He hiccupped and licked his parched lips. "But in for a penny, in for a pound, I say." He started for her hoping a quick tumble might put her to rights.

His feet somehow tangled in the carpet, and he fell to his knees.

Nora scoffed and brushed past him.

He caught her ankle and grinned. "Very well, I am foxed. Is that such a crime that you must play the wounded lady?"

Then he saw the girl.

She stood at the top of the stairway and seemed to float toward him. Her face and then her belly became huge and swollen like a full moon. Her white gown bloomed with blood—

"Noooo!" He pushed the face away.

Bands of iron held him down." No, no more!"

"Shhh. Shh."

He jerked awake. A monster stared back at him.

The leather cuffs bit into his wrists, and his breath came like a bellows as sweat ran into his eyes.

"Shhh." The giant loomed over the bed, huge hands engulfing his own.

He blinked. The new keeper—Ivo. Not a fiend.

Just another nightmare.

Bracing himself, he waited for the blow. Macready would have landed him a good one by now. Good ol' Ned Macready never liked a fair fight. Or to have his sleep disturbed.

But the blow did not come. The huge man only cocked his head as if confused about what he should do. Gently, he took one of Dev's hands and placed a finger against his lips.

"Shh," the man said, putting his own finger to his lips like a child sharing a secret. Then he laid Dev's hands in his lap, palms up. Ivo turned and delved into his pocket.

Dev jerked his hands up to shield his face.

The giant frowned and once again patiently placed Dev's hands open and waiting as if he might be about to receive the holy host.

Very well, he'd gamble.

He held still as Ivo dipped into his pocket and pulled something out. Reverently cupping it in his hands, and with a shy smile, he deposited the thing into Dev's waiting palms.

Tiny *skritching* feet scrabbled against his flesh. Soft fur brushed his thumbs and a moist quivering nose found the cleft between his fingers.

Relief gushed from his lips. A mouse. That was all. Just a plain mouse.

God, he wanted to howl with laughter, but the keeper stood with his mouth hanging half-open, a look of such wonder in his eyes. And just like that, Dev's laughter turned to tears. This tiny mouse was the most precious thing this man possessed. Dev knew it as sure as he knew his own name.

He stroked the soft fur and looked up into the giant's eyes. Ivo grinned.

By God, this sweet brute must truly be daft if he believed Dev worthy of such a gift.

Perhaps the tide had turned.

Chapter Five

Doctor Hives spared Anne a glance when she entered his office and then continued scanning a letter with an impressive golden seal.

If only she could gauge his mood, but all she could say with any surety was the man took prodigious care in arranging the few curls on his otherwise shiny head. He did not offer her a seat. She resisted the urge to adjust a hair pin slipping loose to tickle her neck. Instead she smoothed her perfectly ironed apron.

Mrs. Coates said the doctor was often gone and could appear without any forewarning as he had this morning. Nearly two weeks after her arrival, he'd entered the gold withdrawing room while she had been kneading Lady Tippit's shoulders.

The massage had become part of their daily routine. She found it best not to interfere when the woman touched herself inappropriately, simply ignoring the behavior, as if it were normal to dip a hand between the legs or fondle a breast. Mrs. Nester followed her lead, and her ladyship indulged less and less.

Thank goodness Lady T's hands had been quietly folded in her lap when Doctor Hives had stepped into the room. Beyond introducing himself, he'd remained silent, only observing. After several endless minutes, he left, and she had been summoned to his office by Mr. Macready.

The keeper stood just behind her, his hot breath stirring the fine hairs on the back of her neck. He had certainly taken full advantage when the doctor was away, strutting about, barking orders as if he were lord of the manner. She had not seen Lord Devlin once since that first day. Servants whispered about him but clammed up when she came near. Once, she had sneaked up to his room and even opened the small hatch in the door, but she could see no one within the narrow view the window provided. No sounds either.

Only yesterday she had secretly followed Mr. Macready down a set of narrow and twisting stairs. He disappeared through a low door. She had pressed her ear there until her neck ached but again heard nothing. When she went back later, the portal was locked. She'd nearly jumped out of her skin when the keeper caught her coming back up the stairs. When questioned, she had said she had lost her way.

Had he mentioned her snooping to Doctor Hives?

"Miss Winton." Doctor Hives pushed the letter aside. "I am sorry I was not here when you arrived, but I am at the mercy of my benefactor. When he requires my attention, I must comply."

"Yes, sir."

Hives' small head, snub nose, and thin lips reminded her of her old turtle, Tobias. A thick woolen cravat, wound round and round the doctor's neck and chin, only added to the comparison. Indeed, his eyebrows, drawn sharply upward, seemed to be the only thing keeping his mouth from being swallowed up.

Tobias had been her only friend that first year at Ardsmoore. Would Hives be a friend?

"Mr. Macready, you may leave us now."

Hot, fetid breath pulsed heavy against her neck as the man crowded closer before turning and quitting the room.

"Now Miss Winton, are you clear on your duties?"

"Yes, sir. I am to assist the ladies with their toilets and dressing, accompany them to morning prayers, read from prescribed books, supervise their diets, take them on short walks when the weather is fine, attend tea when asked, make sure they take their various medications, and generally see to their comfort." She pulled a small book from her pocket. "I have kept copious notes, sir."

Not a healer so much as a glorified lady's maid.

"Let me see." He gestured for the book.

She handed it to him. Were her observations helpful? Too much detail? Not enough? She felt like a dangling boot lace.

The doctor opened it and began scanning pages.

"If all goes well, you will be with us for quite some time, I believe, Miss Winton? Paying off your debt?"

"I am contracted for four years, sir." No way to know how much Mr. Harlow had revealed to the doctor. The hair pin slipped down her back, and her bun loosened.

"I understand you are an orphan, and the vicar, Mr. Harlow, did a great deal for you in settling you here at Ballencrieff?"

"Yes, sir, Mr. Harlow has shown me every kindness. I owe him much."

"Indeed." The one word held a world of meaning but nothing she could decipher. "You were a bit of an…oddity at the school, weren't you?"

She smoothed her apron uncertain how to answer.

"Yet Mr. Harlow urged me to take you on despite—

rumors." Doctor Hives narrowed his already beady eyes. "He assured me your "talents" were wasted in teaching, and you could be more useful here." The doctor turned another page, his gaze remaining fixed on her. "Ballencrieff is a place for re-birth and second chances. I hope I will not be disappointed, Miss Winton."

She tried to smile. "I am very eager to be of service, Doctor Hives, sir," she said, with less assurance than she intended.

"We will see, Miss Winton. We will just have to see."

Please allow her to do some good somewhere. Her gift was a blessing. Surely she could prove it if he would only give her a chance.

"We will meet formally every odd day of the week after tea when the ladies are resting. Of course, if anything dire should arise before then, you will come to me immediately."

Taking her first real breath, it seemed the inquisition was over. "I understand, sir."

"Mrs. Nester had another nightmare last night?"

"Yes, Doctor. However, if you'll note." She leaned over, directing him to the correct page. "I was able to get her settled and back to sleep in a much shorter amount of time."

She had just turned out her lamp when the moans started. Once again, Phoebe Nester had been clutching her belly, so sure she had lost yet another child. After an earlier spell, Anne had found the poor woman huddled over her chamber pot convinced she'd seen a bloody mass. It had taken most of the night to settle her fears.

"Mrs. Nester's hysteria seems to have improved since your arrival." The doctor looked displeased despite the good news. "We were accustomed to coping with her terrors on a nightly basis. I am told you have a calming effect on her." He looked up as if he might catch her out. "Indeed, Mrs. Coates informs me many of the patients here at Ballencrieff seem to have benefited from your presence in the short time you have been with us." His eyes narrowed, and his lower lip brushed the top of his neck cloth.

"I try to help where I can, sir." She must tread carefully if she was to be of any use in her new life. Mrs. Coates said Hives fancied himself a forward thinker, but it would be a mistake not to test the waters first. "If you'll pardon my saying, Doctor, I do not see all that much difference between these patients' infirmities and the rest of the world. Yes, they have their idiosyncrasies, but don't we all?"

"Idiosyncrasies?" The doctor smiled, which was not a smile at all. "Granted, this is not a home for extreme lunatics. It is more of a way station toward entering back into the world, a haven if you will, where patients may recover without prying eyes."

Haven was not a word she would ever use to describe this place.

"However, while Ballencrieff Hall is no Bedlam, Miss Winton, do not be lulled into complacency. We must provide a strict routine where these unfortunates cannot indulge in their ravings and fantasies."

Not so forward a thinker as she'd hoped.

"Which brings us to Lady Tippit." He sat back in his chair, steepling his fingers together in the general area of where his chin might be located. "Where did you learn this 'massage'?"

Finally, the sticky wicket. "It is not learned, sir, it is

something I have always remembered doing. My hands seem to bring comfort. I do not know why."

"Yes, your talents. I see it is not mentioned in your notes."

"No sir, it is something I have been trying. However, I do believe—"

"You believe? You are very free with your opinions. Is there something I have missed? Do you have medical training?" His eyebrows rose to meet the arranged curls high on his forehead. "Excessive touching is contrary to the therapy I have set out for her ladyship. She must have less tactile interaction, not more. You will desist immediately."

Disappointment pricked, and she took a step backward. "Yes, sir."

"I am sure you mean well, but we cannot be lax, Miss Winton. These unfortunates need strict discipline, much like naughty children. You will report any unseemly behavior immediately. Time is of the essence. Lady Tippit must learn to associate certain actions with punishment." He paged through the book until he came to her last entry. "I see no cold plunges were ordered? No restraints? Am I to understand that her ladyship has indulged in no aberrant behavior these last thirteen days?"

She said nothing.

"Believe me you will do her no good service by omitting her failings." He closed the book and handed it back to her. "We cannot indulge her fancies. As her nurse and companion, I rely on you in this regard. Do I make myself clear, Miss Winton?"

"Yes, Doctor Hives." *Too soon.*

For now her light must remain under a bushel.

Punishment and even the threat of the madhouse had hung over her those early years at Ardsmoore when she had felt so lost and alone. But slowly the tide had turned, and she'd become almost accepted. Until a jealous, spiteful girl wiped her world away in one fell swoop.

"You must be vigilant and always on guard. Make no mistake these patients can become unbalanced in the blink of an eye." He sat back in his chair. "I believe you saw that behavior demonstrated by Lord Devlin when you first arrived?"

"He did not harm me," she hastened to say. She did not think anyone had seen their brief intimacy, tucked as they were within the niche under the stairway. And he had already been drawing away from her when Macready arrived. She, herself, could not believe Lord Devlin had sought her out. So why would anyone imagine a marquess, who had apparently enjoyed the company of the most celebrated beauties, would ever bother with plain Anne Winton.

But deep in the most secret place in her heart, she could not squelch the peculiar stirrings within her body. Or the feeling of reciprocity. Lord Devlin *had* noticed her. There had been a palpable vibration between them that had shocked her. She tried to dismiss the moment a hundred times, but like a vivid reoccurring dream, it would not die.

If only she could look in his eyes, she might be reassured he could not be a murderer. And she might also put her inexplicable fantasy to rest. Surely this pull toward him was only his affliction, drawing her to help him.

"I have been thinking of the marquess' case ever since I arrived." She shifted her feet. "I wonder if I might offer a thought, sir?"

The doctor's neck stretched up a fraction, his upper lip protruding, but he did not say no.

Heartened, she pressed on. "After seeing Lord Devlin's room, and on further reflection, I wondered if perhaps the marquess uses painting as a way to exorcise his demons?"

"What an extraordinary notion, Miss Winton. This is precisely why you must leave the therapies to the experts who have studied these cases." Doctor Hives adjusted a fold in his cravat and cleared his throat. "I was most displeased Mrs. Coates allowed you to enter the marquess' room. However, she assured me you did not seem fazed by his...artistry."

She considered how best to answer. "I will not lie. I was shocked, but seeing his pictures allowed me a glimpse into his world, if only through a small window."

"His world is narrow, Miss Winton. Lord Devlin has lost crucial memories. Recouping these memories is vital to his cure; however, he must recover them in his own time."

"Yes, certainly, Doctor Hives."

"And, thus far, my efforts at hypnosis have not proved efficacious. So, we move on." The doctor traced the golden seal on the letter in front of him. "You are not the only person to broach the subject of the marquess painting again. Lord Austin has been hounding me with his own ideas. Would that I could do as I saw fit without a passel of laymen to muck up my work. But I am dependent on others for my living and the running of this place, so I must bow to them. At least for now."

Doctor Hives hefted himself onto his legs and waddled to the window, pulling aside the curtain to look out at the rain. "I do not like this painting idea. The marquess turns excitable and his humors become…disturbed. However, Lord Austin believes if his brother can produce a work of calm beauty, it can be used as a kind of testament to help win their father over. The idea has some merit as Devlin's lewd and almost pornographic paintings were part of the reason he came to be confined here."

"I also understand there was a—event that traumatized his lordship?"

He dropped the curtain and turned to her. "Has Mrs. Nester been gossiping again? That incident is none of your concern, Miss Winton. Do I make myself clear?"

"Yes, Doctor."

"The Duke of Malvern is not well. It is now vital that I make progress with his son. His Grace wants to secure the succession before his demise, and he is pressing me to find Lord Devlin *compos mentis*. However, in good conscience, he will not go so far as to release a lunatic into the world. So for now, I still hold the reins."

He seemed to require an answer of her. "Of course, Doctor."

"Believe me, Miss Winton, I would like nothing better than to deliver the duke a viable heir. Do you imagine I wish to remain here at Ballencrieff, tucked away in an obscure corner of the Highlands? I have important work to do." He stared off into space and seemed to have forgotten her existence.

She cleared her throat and his gaze jerked back to her. "Miss Winton, we have a window here, and you must help me open it wide enough so I may provide a cure for his lordship." He adjusted a wilting curl that had the audacity to slip lower on his forehead. "I have laid out a whole new regime for the marquess." Hives lowered his voice. "Macready has been replaced as Lord Devlin's keeper. And we will try this painting. In accordance with my instructions, the marquess will paint his brother. He will depict Lord Austin's pristine, classical beauty. We will see if it proves a panacea."

A beginning, at least.

"I wish to see how far your *talents* go. I will observe you with Lord Devlin to determine if you have a similar effect on him as you have on the other patients. If so, I believe it might be advantageous that you attend these sittings."

Her stomach flipped. She would see him again.

"I trust you will be unbiased and will alert me the moment Lord Devlin becomes the least unbalanced or lewd. Of course, I do not believe you pose any kind of fleshly temptation, but how he behaves with a woman, will be yet another indication of his character."

She knew she was no beauty, but to be dismissed out of hand still hurt. She stood taller.

"Do not engage him with too much talk. I find the patients reveal far more when they are forced to hold up the conversation. I will be concealed in the next room, observing from a spy hole in the wall, however, Lord Devlin's new keeper will be there should you require him."

Anne nodded. "Yes, sir," she said, firmly.

"Lord Austin, while well-meaning, is prejudiced and not likely to report small infractions. I do not need to tell you, Miss Winton, we all have much at stake with this experiment."

"You have my full cooperation, Doctor Hives."

"Very well, you will attend the marquess in his room tomorrow just after prayers."

Chapter Six

A key rasped in the lock, and Ivo stopped sucking the grime from beneath his nails to stand at attention. A small white hand came around the door and then the hem of a dark skirt. Dev's breath hitched uncomfortably. A woman? He schooled his features.

The little owl.

The air he'd been holding released in a hush as the door swung shut. She turned to it, startled, as if the noise sealed her doom.

"Ah, Miss Owl." He stood awkwardly—being bound in this damned strait-waistcoat often played havoc with his balance. The manacles around his ankles clunked against the oak floor, music to his ineptness.

She flinched.

He'd forgotten what a shock seeing his restraints could be to an innocent. Covering his ire, he made a reasonably elegant bow.

She swallowed and dipped into a curtsey.

"You have flown into my cage."

Her eyes darted to the spy hole in the wall just to the left of the fireplace. The one he was not supposed to know about, but which was as obvious as a whore in church.

"Or perhaps you have been thrust inside? A mousey tidbit to bate the tethered falcon?" He did not really expect an answer but wanted to gauge her reaction—to divine her allegiances. Austin had written of Miss Winton's concern for him and of her help in scrubbing his room back to its present dead white. "But, as you see, you are safe. I am sporting my jesses for the occasion." He indicated his bindings, though any fool could not fail to see the grotesque chains and shackles. He nodded to the only other chair in the room. "Please sit down."

She perched on the very edge of the chair as if she might fly away at any moment.

He felt remarkably well considering his recent confinement in the hands of Macready. Still, he shifted his eyes away from her. He did not want to chance her seeing the devils who often used his eyes as windows. He would thwart the bloody bastards. Let them do their evil work within him, but by sodding Satan, he would not let them get a glimpse of her beauty. They would steal her from him—make her afraid of him. That, he could not stand.

"I am told by Dr. Hives I must apologize for my rude behavior when we met. Is he correct? Do I owe you an apology?" He risked a glance at her. Her cheeks were pure cream now, but he could still see them streaked with his blood. He swallowed the burn of guilt. "The moon was full, and I was not myself that day."

The girl's hands fluttered in her lap, but she clasped them together and then shook her head. Cream cheeks turned red again, but this time, a charming blush.

"Ah, good, I do so loathe apologies." He sat. "Forgive me. I am unused to female company. I must dredge up my manners and my polite conversation." The injuries on his hands itched beneath the bindings. He shifted, trying to get comfortable. "Let's see… The weather is always a safe beginning, is it not? How do you find our Scottish spring, Miss Winton? It is Miss Winton?"

She nodded again but remained mute.

"What, are you not authorized to talk to me? Do not engage the lunatic?"

Again she turned toward Hives' spy hole.

Sharp disappointment pricked him out of nowhere. "They send me fools and ninnies, Ivo, with not a thought of their own."

He sucked in cold air and expelled slightly warmer. "Yes, the weather continues bone chilling and dreary, do you not agree, Lord Devlin?" he mocked in a slightly higher pitched voice. "Oh yes, Miss Winton, I must concur. The Scottish weather is certainly something to be relied upon."

Her winged brows drew together. She did not seem to appreciate his little *tête-à-tête*.

He ground his teeth. They had sent this girl as some sort of test, and old Polonius Hives was squirreled away to see if he passed.

Again, no bitter taste in his breakfast porridge, best take advantage of this lucidity. Perhaps the devils would leave him be today. "Let's see, the weather exhausted, what else is there to say?" His voice was too loud. He crossed his ankles, his chains dragging. "My days are so full I hardly know where to begin. Up at six, put into my stylish waistcoat while Ivo shaves me. Can't let me have anything sharp you know. But surprisingly, Ivo here has proved a very credible valet."

Her gaze went to the boarded up window.

He gritted his teeth against another stab of humiliation. This young innocent a witness to the aftermath of his poisoned mind.

The devils be damned. He focused on her calm beauty. She did not seem repulsed. Could the fiends be frightened of this little bird?

"Where was I?" He scrambled to play the gallant. "Oh, yes. And then I break my fast—the good doctor allows me to feed myself now. Not much damage one can do with a spoon. Very good porridge today, Ivo. I think the cook must be doing something a bit different. Perhaps a bit less salt?" He stared at Hives' spy-hole.

"Next, I while away the hours, sometimes doing mathematical equations in my head, sometimes, I do…other things." He favored her with a rakish grin. She only blinked. *Humph.* Served him right, trying to get a rise out of a naïve virgin.

However, he could just imagine Hives scribbling that little jewel down. A tidbit to masticate over in their next session.

"Let's see, what else to amuse myself? I used to breathe against the glass and play noughts and crosses, but as you see that luxury is no longer afforded me." He jerked his head toward the boarded up window. "Then dinner is more porridge, this time, with yummy mutton. And when I am a very good boy, I am dressed up for tea and paraded before my fellow lunatics. Needless to say, I have not seen them in a long while."

Her silence enveloped him. Too intense. Somehow too personal. He wanted to fling himself at her feet. Or out the boarded up window. He could not be sure which.

"I am forgetting my manners once again and dominating the conversation. How are you getting on, Miss Winton?"

To be fair, she did look as if she wanted to answer him, but obviously thought better of it, continuing to sit like some Madonna, her hands open, one folded on top of the other as if expecting the Christ child to drop into her lap.

Hives be damned—or maybe the devils had finally slipped into his brain—but it was time to get a rise out of her. He leaned forward and whispered, "I must say I thoroughly enjoyed our first meeting. It seemed you did as well, despite my having a weapon."

That did it. He was rewarded with another blush even short-sighted Lady Tippit could read. And, blessedly, Anne Winton's wholesome gaze slipped to her lap. Most ladies would have flown up into the boughs in outrage. But, by God, he gave Miss Winton full marks for not turning tail and running.

"Don't be such an owl." He prodded her again, partly because she was so delightful wreathed in blushes. "You had to know Austin would share that juicy morsel. I get so little entertainment."

She recovered, looking him straight in the eyes.

He sat back. "Come now, you must have at least one question wedged behind those huge sable-brown eyes. Let's have it and then perhaps I can stop concentrating on you and what you are not saying, and go back to contemplating the walls. This distraction is becoming tedious."

"Why devils?"

The low, richness of her voice surprised him as much as her question. "Pardon?"

She licked her lips and sat up straighter. "Why do you paint devils?"

He stepped away from her words as surely as he would flinch from a crumbling precipice, taking shelter in mockery. "That's it? That is your burning question?

The question that has been brewing these last endless minutes while I have rattled on?"

She said nothing.

"You disappoint me, Miss Owl. I would have thought perhaps you might ask why my sire can stand by—or rather lay low, I am told he is ill—while his son and heir is imprisoned in this hellhole? No interest?" His head suddenly pounded. "Or perhaps you might want me to elaborate on some of the antics that have brought me to this fateful place?"

She frowned and bit her lip.

"Ah, I see you must have heard some of them. I'm sure those cackling crows you attend have more than filled your ear with my evil deeds?"

He paused to give her an opportunity to refute him, but she didn't. He spent an uncomfortable moment wondering what she had heard and if she believed the drivel. Blasted ballocks, he couldn't remember a shred of his past.

"How about why God is so cruel as to bestow the venerable Malvern duchy on the evil, mad son instead of the angelic, perfect one? No? No interest in that one?"

She shifted on her seat and tucked her feet completely under the hem of her skirt, but remained mute.

"Shocking. I must own I find myself deliberating that particular thorn over and over in my mind. I confess I am always confounded when it isn't foremost in others' as well."

He had a terrible urge to push harder to see when she would fly away from his onslaught of rudeness. Or perhaps she was simply a dullard and not worth the effort.

God, he despised himself. When had he become such a loathsome toad?

Focus, damn it. He didn't know why yet, but he needed this woman. She had drawn him to her like a sea siren that first day. But why was she here now?

Hives must be testing her as well. Whatever the reason, Dev wanted this girl near him if only to gaze into her beautifully clear eyes.

"But I digress. You are desirous of an answer, and I cannot bear your quiet and oh-so-solicitous waiting." He tried out his most charming smile. After all, it had worked beautifully at their first meeting. Nothing. "Pardon, I sound very like that bag of wind, old maid Tippit, rattling on without a rejoinder in sight."

He waited hoping she might favor him with some remark, or perhaps an answering smirk?

"Right. Why do I paint devils?" He glanced at the spy hole. "The answer is simple, Miss Winton. Any good painter paints what is in his heart." He felt suddenly exposed, as if he had come into a room without any clothes. He rushed to fill that empty yawning space—to cover himself. "There, not so exciting or illuminating, is it? The truth rarely is."

"I do not believe that is your truth," she said without hesitation.

"Ha!" Her jaw line twitched. His expletive a harsh smack against her softness. Served her right. "Well, well, you presume to know me—my heart even—after so little time? Astonishing, considering I hardly know myself these days. Very well, I will play, my little owl."

He stood and strode to her, his chains snapping taut.

Ivo jerked forward, no doubt startled into action by the clank of chains and sudden movement. The henchman glanced nervously at the spy hole. Miss Winton did not. Bless her.

"Since you are so wise…" He pointed his chin to his breast. "Tell me what lies here."

She hesitated only a moment before rising and, without breaking eye contact, made a staying gesture to Ivo who looked like a cur on too short a leash. She took the three steps to close the gap between them, this girl-woman with her soulful liquid-brown eyes and quietly elegant bearing. His head throbbed, and his nerves ratcheted up until he thought his heart might burst through its cage of bone.

She raised her hand, her gaze burning into his breast.

Swaddled in his strait-waistcoat, he had no way to defend himself against this tiny woman with her huge presence, so he made himself into pillar of rock.

She too seemed to freeze. Her hand hovering in the pulsating air, her eyes wide as her lips opened in a silent "oh." Her gaze flicked up to his. Astonishment reflected there. Dear Satan, he had the terrible urge to kiss her again. But her gaze had already dropped.

She touched him.

Involuntarily he jerked, shocked by the sensation of her small palm and the pulse which radiated out her fingers. They stung. Even through the thickness of the strait-waistcoat, he could not tell if they were burning hot or freezing cold—the feeling was the same. Intense cold-fire. But whichever it was, warmth began to spread into his cold stone body just as it had during their earlier encounter. His heart seemed to want to migrate into that small, comforting hand, to be cradled in her soft-petaled fingers.

Used to his cock jumping to attention at every

fantasy he concocted in his demented mind, after all, he was relatively healthy—at least that part of his body was. Certainly it had risen to the occasion when he'd first met this girl, but his heart? No, that particular organ had not stirred for some time now. No wonder he felt raw, as if his skin had been turned inside out—

He bucked her hand away, disgusted with his vulnerability, and retreated a few steps.

"You are naïve and not so wise if you think this rather tame outward package reflects what lies within," he whispered. But he was lying. For other than his wildly beating heart, he had never felt so peaceful inside. So warm. Perhaps his devils had been burned by her fire.

They would be back. He would not be lulled into thinking they would be vanquished by a tiny woman with huge eyes and the trick of heat within her hands. Hives was just toying with him.

"Surely you've heard the truism, 'do not judge a book by its cover'?" He turned away to his blocked up window. It was far easier to wax philosophical than to meet her quiet challenge. He squeezed his eyes into fists because his hands lay useless and trapped within the lunatic's coat.

Lord, this encounter had not gone at all as he wanted. He took a breath, his best smile in place.

When he turned back, all he saw was the swish of her dull brown skirts licking the doorway as the door swung closed.

Damn. What had she thought of him? The devils had not come, and his breast still held the heat of her touch. Who was this magical girl? And would he ever get another chance to find out? He could still hear her lovely voice.

Why did he paint devils?

Chapter Seven

April's mantle of blue-gray frost ebbed and then disappeared to be replaced by the glistening wet and new-green earth of mid-May, and still Lord Austin did not come to sit for his portrait. Each delay sorely taxed the marquess whose shouts could be heard throughout the castle. Anne's own frustration with the mundane routine of tending her charges echoed Lord Devlin's.

Fittingly, Lord Austin arrived as spring finally touched the highlands. After more than a month, he came bearing smiles, painting supplies, and more importantly, he brought hope.

The summons came to attend Lord Devlin and his brother in the marquesses' cell.

Armed with knitting and a Bible, she slipped inside and took a seat in the far corner closest to the fireplace.

Lord Devlin stood in the middle of the room tethered to that hideous chair. He touched his brushes as if they were living things. He stroked them over his cheeks and lips. He feathered them down his neck—his eyes closing in a kind of private ecstasy. The humming feeling within her body could be nerves, but she knew deep down it was more than simple anticipation. It was being in a room with him. Hadn't she felt the same feeling, only more acutely, during their one-sided interview when she had been brazen enough to rise and touch his chest—to feel his heart beneath the swaddling he wore. And her heart had answered his. She had never felt so alive, every fiber of her answering every fiber of him.

As it did now. His gaze locked on her.

Her heart jolted as her knitting needles stilled. She ducked her head desperately stabbing the last loop of wool. Fingers shaking, she cast the thread too wide. The yellow yarn snarled.

Stop. She must stop this line of thinking. Of feeling. This beautiful man would never be interested in her outside the walls of this madhouse. She was nothing. Besides she could not lose her position.

Even now, she could feel his smile on her as she wrestled with her tangled mess.

"Ah, Miss Winton," Lord Austin spoke. "How nice of you to provide our entertainment."

A blush stole over her as she pressed herself into the back of the chair.

The marquess now rolled vials of paint between his long fingers, his wicked smile still on her. Next, he took up a beaker and unstopped it. She felt the sting in her nose, the oily taste on her tongue, even from across the room. But the marquess inhaled deeply, smiling through his cough. It must be turpentine.

"Dev, enough." Lord Austin lounged, as well as one could, in the straight-backed chair. "You know that stuff is not good for you. And stop staring. You are frightening Miss Winton."

But Lord Devlin did not seem to hear, or, if he did, did not care. Finally he relinquished his hold on her, and satisfying himself that all his tools were in place, he took up a charcoal and faced a large square of paper.

Once again she took refuge in her knitting, trying to look industrious, but stealing a glance or two when she thought him immersed.

"Turn to the right." Lord Devlin ordered his brother. Lord Austin shifted. "No, your other right. That's it. Now, head down. More. More…there! Yes, just there." He began to furiously sketch.

Her knitting needles stilled.

He was a ballet of movement, so forceful and energetic. His black hair had escaped its queue and brushed his shadowed cheeks. Chin tucked, his unflinching gaze raked over his brother, his lush lips pulled into a firm line. Every part of him wholly focused on his subject.

What would it be like to be the object of such intense concentration?

"Blast, Austin, you've moved again." The marquess strode forward to adjust his brother. The chain links snapped taut, and he stumbled.

Both she and his brother half rose from their seats.

Lord Devlin made a staying motion. Closing his eyes, he took a deep breath. He rose, dusted his knees, and then sat. "Austin, would you kindly settle your arm thusly." He dangled his hand off the arm of the chair, so effortless, the curve of his fingers so full of grace.

"I will try, Dev. But I warn you, I must have entertainment. Either you must talk with me or Miss Winton must provide some relief from this tedium."

She dropped her knitting and bent to retrieve the Bible from the bag on the floor next to her.

"It must be Miss Winton then, for I have no energy to spare you."

"Very well." Lord Austin turned to her.

She stood, Bible in hand. "Lord Austin, you mustn't move—"

"Blistering Hell!" The marquess threw his pencil and ripped the sheet of paper from his easel.

****

"Well?"

Anne smoothed her skirts as she stood before Doctor Hives to give her report. "I do not believe Lord Austin is the best choice of model for the marquess."

The doctor raised his eyebrows and made an impatient gesture for her to continue.

"Lord Devlin seems to require absolute stillness in his subject. I am not sure his brother is capable of such quiet. And neither of them seems to appreciate my reading from the Bible."

"Did the marquess become violent?"

She did not hesitate. "He threw his pencil, ripped up—several—pages, and once stood upon the seat of his chair."

Doctor Hives nodded slowly, dipped his pen, and made a few notes. "I suppose one must allow for the artistic temperament?"

"The sketches seem to be going well. He is so beautiful—" She stopped herself.

Doctor Hives looked up from his notebook. His eyes narrowed as he gazed at her. "Yes, I'll warrant half of England is in love with Lord Austin Drake," he said, with more than a bit of disapproval. Or perhaps jealousy? "But unfortunately he is not the heir."

Happy enough to let the doctor think she had been speaking of Lord Austin instead of his brother, she said nothing.

"What of the marquess? Is he agitated? Does he pace or stare for long periods at nothing?"

"Yes, to all. But I do not think it goes outside the

63

perimeters of being in the throes of creation. His frustration is mostly with his brother. And the light."

"The light?"

"Yes, I am surprised Lord Austin has not spoken to you about it. The marquess must have northern light, and a lot of it. Apparently it is imperative before he begins the actual painting. Besides, sir, if I may offer an observation." She waited for the doctor to nod. "I do not think it is good for Lord Devlin to sleep in the same room with the smells of turpentine, especially with only one small window for air."

****

To give Doctor Hives credit, the very next day the marquess' studio had been moved to the North Tower. One could almost see the village to the west, curls of smoke from its chimneys lashed the clouds, and if the wind was right, one might hear the toll of the church bells. And to the east lay higher mountains still laced with snow. There were no bars on these windows. If one chose to escape they would not do so and remain alive.

Several pieces of furniture had been brought in, a large table, several chairs—one that actually looked comfortable. Lord Austin would perhaps use it when he posed. A fainting couch and a screen in the corner concealing the chamber pot completed the furnishings. Opposite the windows, a blaze crackled and spit in the firebox.

"Why are you here at Ballencrieff?" The marquess stood well away from his easel, his brush dangling uselessly from his left hand.

How long had he been watching her?

Yarn snagged and then tangled. She fumbled and the inevitable happened, she dropped a stitch. Now two.

"What did you do to be punished so?" he said frowning.

She looked down hoping to catch her lost stitches. Useless. She lay the ruined knitting in her lap. The door stood open just as Lord Austin had left it when he went in search of food. He had declared if he was to be subjected to such torture, he must at least have nourishment. Ivo lounged against the wall intent on the mouse he kept in his pocket.

"Surely someone as good and virtuous as yourself could have secured a more favorable place." The brush flicked like a testy cat's tail against his lordship's thigh. The muscles rippled as his feet shifted.

To buy time she made a show of marking her place in her stitches.

"Miss Winton?" the marquess repeated.

"It was time to go." *Where was Lord Austin?*

"Hmmm. To leave the nest? I am sure there is a story behind that answer."

She forced herself over hurdles of memories that sprang up, leaping beyond one of happiness, another of pain, reducing fifteen years into a few carefully chosen words. "I was tired of teaching." Not a lie.

"Tired of teaching? So you consigned yourself to a house for the insane somewhere just south of the Arctic Circle? Perhaps you are the one who is mad. I cannot imagine Lady Tippit and Mrs. Nester provide much stimulation."

"No." She stared down at the yellow tangle of yarn meant to be a cap for Mrs. Nester's coming babe. How to remedy this mess?

He went back to his work, giving her a reprieve.

Her life was indeed a tangle. No opportunities for

real healing, a terrible attraction for a marquess who would never return her feelings, and nowhere else to go in this wide world. In four years she could have paid off her debt to Ardsmoore School with a little nest egg to try to study, perhaps in Edinburgh. But Madge Barrow had put those dreams to a sure death.

"Would you care to watch?"

She ducked her head caught staring. Again.

"I do not mind. Some painters do, but I suppose my ego is such that I enjoy an audience."

Rising, she pulled her chair around to the side of the canvas, making sure to be well out of his way.

"I will not bite. And as alluring as those knitting needles are, my chain only goes this far." He took three steps toward her until the chain lengthened out over the floor. "You see? Even if I were to lunge,"—he did so— "I can barely reach your boots peeping out from beneath that hideous frock."

She nearly pulled her feet beneath her. He would only laugh. Though on second thought, she would like to hear him laugh, a real delighted laugh, not the raw bark he would make when he deemed something worthy of humor.

She'd situated herself perfectly. She could see the painting, but also view his face. Emotions flowed over it, like ripples in a pond; down into his body and into his arms and then into his hands which held multiple brushes. A furrowed brow or a jump in his jawline would translate to a staccato jab of his brush. Next, chin up, eyebrows raised, lips slightly pursed and a most delicate flick of his wrist. Then, a long sweep where his whole body and sometimes even tongue would follow.

"What?" he said to the canvas.

She shot up straighter in her chair, unsure if she was meant to respond.

"What are you thinking?" He turned to address her. "You are distracting me with those bewitching eyes of yours."

Bewitiching? She did not like to be teased. She stood to move her chair away.

"No!"

The chair *thunked* to the floor. Ivo grunted and shuffled to his feet.

"Damnation." He raked his hands through his already wild hair. "Why must you act like some scared rabbit? Pardon." He took in a long breath. "What I meant to say is please do not go away, I would very much like to know your thoughts."

Settling again, she allowed one of the questions rolling in her head to tumble out. "How do you see those colors?"

He looked back at the painting. "Where?"

"There, the wall." He had been working on the white of the wall which made up part of the background. "It is white. I would paint white, and it would be dead and utterly cold. But you have not painted just white. You see beyond the thing that it is into what it holds; all its possibilities. How do you see that there is lilac and green and even blue?"

"Because there is," he said simply as if anyone could see those extraordinary colors.

She bit her lip. "You cannot know how illuminating your wall is to me."

"You know, little Owl." He cocked his head, an odd look on his face. Had her question displeased him? "You are a bit like the color white. At first glance white is thought to be inconsequential and even plain. But that is wrong. White is never just white. White contains all the colors in the rainbow. It is the queen of color."

He must be teasing her again, but when she glanced up, he did not look as if he were jesting. Warmth stole over her entire body like a hand sliding into a pocket.

The door slammed closed. "You both look as if you have a secret. Have I missed something?" Lord Austin had returned.

Chapter Eight

Hives certainly was stepping up the game—whatever it was. First the painting, then providing a studio in the North Tower. And now Dev, dressed in his finest was to be exhibited before Ballencrieff's more benign menagerie. Austin stood next to him just outside the door to the withdrawing room where the doctor would be analyzing Dev's every twitch and fart.

Very well, he'd play, put on his best manners and perform like one of those drugged and dulled tigers. *A tamed pussy cat, that's him.*

For the twentieth time, he pulled at the hideous vest, another kind of strait-waistcoat, only in cheap brocade instead of heavy canvas. God, how he despised wearing these castoffs.

Hobbs, who acted as footman on the rare occasion the Hall needed such a person, waited by the door. At Austin's nod, he opened it, announced in a rather theatrical voice, "Lord Devlin and Lord Austin," and then stepped aside, ducking his head.

They all looked like a bunch of startled peahens. Well, all except his Owl. She was a study in calm. Though, on second glance, she did fidget with the keys at her waist. Maybe not so cool after all.

He could not wait for the afternoon. To pick up his brushes, smell the paints, mix the perfect shade of green. But mostly, to see Anne Winton again.

Austin, as a subject, did not necessarily inspire. And to be fair, his brother clearly had no wish to spend hours posing. But knowing his Owl sat tucked in the corner of the tower, her knitting needles tick-ticking away, or her calm, fluid voice spouting Bible verses, the world seemed somehow right; her serenity spilled from her, flooding the room with an almost liquid calm. Hives would do well to bottle and sell it if it were only possible to capture her charm.

A gasp pulled him out of his reverie. Phoebe Nester, who shared the settee with Miss Winton, nearly leapt upon her nurse's lap, as she took up a large pillow and attempted to hide behind it. No small task as the woman must stand at six feet. By Jove, the silly chit was defending herself against his person.

Dr. Hives rose and came to her side. "Now, settle, Mrs. Nester. You are among friends, no one will harm you."

The woman clutched her pillow all the more tightly.

"Lord Devlin!" Horace Beauchamp emerged from behind the drapes by the farthest window. His hands flapped at his sides like a fledgling bird about to leave its nest. He blinked continually behind thick spectacles as he nearly hopped across the room to make his bow.

"Mr. Beauchamp." Dev nodded. "How goes the project?"

"Oh, your lordship is very kind to remember my work. You are the true scientist, sir. To have been bosom beaus and worked alongside Sir Barton Wainwright—well, I cannot imagine such ecstasy."

Dev ground his teeth. *Wainwright.* He should know the name. He should know the man. He was sure he had spent many hours in the fellow's company, but even though he felt so much stronger of late, try as he might, this black hole in his memory would not heal.

Austin touched his arm. He shook it off with a contemptuous shrug any Frenchman would have admired.

Hives had perked up anticipating some slip.

By God, he would not give the man satisfaction.

"And your planned journey, Mr. Beauchamp?" He pressed, making his words calm and measured.

"Well, I am progressing in spite of the endless hurdles put before me." Beauchamp's over-loud and strident voice provided a perfect foil to his own quiet. And just to bring that fact home, he smiled at Hives.

"We men of art and science must forever be mired in the petty business of lesser men." Mr. Beauchamp glared at Dr. Hives. "I tried your suggestion of using Newton's formula, f=ma to ascertain the rocket's thrust, and I believe it will prove fruitful. If only I were allowed a bit of powder and a proper launching area, I am sure I could be on my way in no time."

Dr. Hives raised his shoulders, his shirt points now flirting with his ears, as he clasped his hands behind his back and rocked up on his toes. His face, as usual, provided no insight into his thoughts. "Mr. Beauchamp, the conservatory is still being repaired after your previous experiments. The glazing of the windows aside, I would not wish to be in your shoes should Mrs. Coates' orange trees, which had to be moved to the south drawing room, perish."

"Pish!" The agitated man flapped. "What was I to do?" he appealed. "With no powder I had to improvise and use a catapult. And besides, what are a few oranges next to the pursuits of science? You would never let an

orangery come between you and your passions would you, Lord Devlin?"

Dev touched his lips. "Ah, to taste an orange again... You pose quite a conundrum, sir, choosing between the green cheese of the moon, or an orange here on earth. A difficult decision. Savory or sweet..."

Miss Winton froze when his gaze rested on her. Her hand found her keys again, but she managed to hold steady. She took a deep breath and then swallowed. He could not help but smile, but his grin did her in and her gaze dropped.

"Oh, but the moon's cheese is like manna from heaven, Lord Devlin," Mr. Beauchamp said, attempting to regain his attention. "When the little men seized me, I cringed at the bulbous green mold. However, when forced to eat it, I could not get enough. I would have remained there with the creatures, but they wanted my brain, you see. I could not oblige them, though it meant forgoing their heavenly ambrosia."

In the months Dev had been at Ballencrieff, he had listened ad nauseam to Mr. Beauchamp's accounts of pale little men with their egg-shaped heads and huge almond eyes.

"You are wise, Mr. Beauchamp," he said. "Better to keep your brain within your own skull than have it bobbing in a jar to be prodded by—"

"Lord Devlin."

He had wondered when Lady Tippit would take over. She had been fussing and fluffing while Mr. Beauchamp held forth, but apparently at last satisfied with her appearance, she now commanded his, as well as the entire company's, attention.

"Why have you not come to tea before now? It has

been ages. One never knows what to expect in this place." She turned to Miss Winton. "Winton, why wasn't I informed his lordship would be in attendance? I would have worn my puce with the bobbin lace." She shook her head and turned back to him. "But perhaps you thought to surprise me? You put me in mind of Lord Rivkin."

"I don't believe I know the gentleman, Lady Tippit."

"Poor man was excessively fond of me. Poppa never liked him. Rivkin would try to stay away—to excise my visage from his heart—but it could not be. I would finally relent and send for him to give him another sustaining glimpse. But it was never enough. He finally married that troll, Miranda Harper. What a grasping chit she was. Never mind. You may kiss me now." Her ladyship tipped her head back and pursed her lips.

He did not mind. The old woman was officious but harmless. He bent to buss her cheek. A screech and a missile smacked him on the side of the head.

"Stay away from her, you ravenous fiend!" Mrs. Nester had risen, another pillow at the ready.

"Ah, Mrs. Nester." He should have been more prepared. Phoebe Nester had taken a violent dislike to him from the very beginning of their acquaintance. Miss Winton rose as well. It was unclear if she were ready to defend him, or Mrs. Nester.

"I did not see you there, madam, you blend in with the furniture so."

The woman seemed torn between defending Lady Tippit and protecting her own person. But when she looked up into his smile—*touché*—she retreated, sinking back into the plum damask.

"I beg your pardon, madame." He made a slight bow. "You need not have any fear of my gobbling up her ladyship this afternoon, delectable as she is." He risked a wink at Lady Tippit who squirmed in her seat. "Lucky for all I have been fed my porridge recently." He handed Miss Winton the pillow, hoping to catch her gaze again. Mrs. Nester snatched it, hugging it tightly against her as she sat, and once again, completely disappeared into the furnishings.

He turned back to Miss Winton, smile still in place. "Indeed, I am so sated I do not think I could even stomach Mr. Beauchamp's celestial cheese if it were handed to me on a silver platter by the moon goddess herself. But a sweet orange…well, that is a whole other matter." Ah, now he got a full-fledged blush.

The time for levity was over. Hives had him in this room for a reason. Better to face these memories before a headache obliterated them. He crossed to the far corner of the room where the small chess table stood.

The board was still set up just as it was the last time they had played.

Dear God, why? Why had Cummings done it? The major was getting better.

Cummings would have won. Only a few more moves.

Mr. Beauchamp's yammering receded farther and farther away until finally he returned to the window where he continued to hold a furtive conversation with the drapes.

Dev reached out and took up the white knight. The ivory was cold and hard in his hand. He held it in his fist, wanting to give it some warmth. *Why? Why did you do it?*

The sharp edges bit into his palm. Still so cold.

He laid it on its side in the middle of the board. The

other pieces stood as mourners. Had anyone outside this castle mourned the major?

"Lord Austin," Lady Tippit's voice pierced the quiet. "I understand the marquess is painting your portrait?"

"Yes, your ladyship, that is the plan, though I must take the early train for London tomorrow."

Austin was leaving again? But they had just started the portrait. And worse, his brother's departure would likely mean he would not see Miss Winton. His head throbbed like a soundly struck bell.

"Ah, how does your dear father?" Lady Tippit purred. "Malvern wanted me too, you know. At my come out ball, the gentlemen were like bees to honey." Her ladyship's hand dipped into her décolletage. Miss Winton rose hastily and handed Lady Tippit her cup and saucer, laying a napkin discreetly over her breast.

"Oh, Winton. Yes, tea."

"He is somewhat better. I thank you, Lady Tippit." Austin sipped his own tea. "However, I must attend my lady wife."

"Oh, is she ill? I hope not," her voice rose. "It is such a bother to lose a spouse. It is one of the reasons I decided never to marry. Well, that and Poppa did not—"

Tea had begun to slosh over her ladyship's cup. Anne Winton, ever vigilant, mopped at the wet mess. The subject of marriage was apparently an emotional one for Maddy Tippit. Austin had filled him in on her ladyship's history. Jilted at the altar at the age of thirty-six. Then, rumor had it, only a few weeks later she was intercepted on her way to Gretna Green with a plain Mr. Banks. This last had sent her ladyship into a decline and then to Ballencrieff, where she had been for the last several years.

Oblivious to any of the drama surrounding him, Austin answered, "No, Lady Tippit, she is well. She is merely increasing."

The words rang in Dev's ears amid Phoebe Nester's cries of caution, and Lady Tippit's gasp as tea soaked her skirts.

Austin's gaze locked with his.

A child. Austin's child. Red pain flared in his head but a black desperate feeling shrouded his heart.

"Felicitations, Austin. I did not know," he managed to say with even a modicum of good will.

"Sorry, old chap. It slipped out. I should not have said anything."

"Is it so early?"

"The doctor said the beginning of next year. But this science is never certain."

Hives' eyes narrowed infinitesimally, and he cleared his throat. "The duke must be pleased. We will have to make sure you are well enough to attend the christening, Lord Devlin."

First facing Cumming's death, and now his brother would have a child. Life and death went on around him, yet he remained frozen in this hell.

"Poor lady," Phoebe Nester sobbed, "she will likely lose it. The first loaf never rises, they say. Tell her she must drink only pepper-water and burn the husks of acorns into a powder to put under her pillow at night. It did not work for me, but she may be luckier. Though God will do what he will—"

"Miss Winton." Doctor Hives gestured to the door. "Would you please see Mrs. Nester to her room and administer the broth I prescribed?"

"Come, Mrs. Nester. You must not excite yourself." Miss Winton's gaze found his as if her words were meant for him instead of her charge. Somehow she knew of his anguish and took a slow calming breath, which encouraged him to do the same. Almost as if she was breathing for him, he drew in the air she expelled. Slow in, slower out.

The flaring in his head turned to cooler green. She nodded almost imperceptibly even as she ushered the agitated Nester out of the room.

Something brushed his sleeve. Austin stood before him pity in his eyes. *Sod him.*

Doctor Hives was no doubt mentally scribbling in his bloody notebook. *Patient obviously startled at news of Lady Austin increasing. Must probe further.*

The old duke would not necessarily be salivating at this news. Austin bore a striking resemblance to Lord Desmond, who had been unceremoniously dumped by Beatrice Fletcher when the newly widowed Duke of Malvern had come courting. Austin had been born to the new duchess seven months later. But even a cuckoo in the nest was preferable to the taint of madness.

Ballencrieff's walls pressed more firmly in on him. If he didn't get out soon, they would crush him into oblivion.

Chapter Nine

Nearly three weeks Dev had cooled his heels waiting for Austin to return to Ballencrieff, only to have him return and some wench in the village catch his eye. With Margaret now increasing, clearly Austin felt freer to indulge elsewhere. So today his "angelic" brother had chosen a tumble rather than sit for his portrait. And who could blame him. The painting was shite anyway.

All this damned stopping and starting. And when Austin did present himself, he'd find some reason to pop up every five seconds, or have poor Miss Winton fetching this or that for him. Austin simply didn't understand the artistic process, not possessing a creative bone in his body—except the one between his legs. Again, who could blame him.

In truth, he missed his Owl more than his brother. He had come to rely on her calm spirit. It was as if a silken line bound them together, a connection in which Austin had no part. Only their shared secret. He could not explain it. It must be her magic. He'd asked Austin once if he felt her peace, but his brother had only laughed and called him a *Poor Tom*.

The *snick* of the lock turning snapped his gaze to the door. What had Ivo forgotten?

Not Ivo. The shock of the cold floor against his bare feet as he stood was nothing to the surprise of seeing Anne Winton entering his cell.

She stood by the door as if, now that she had entered the room, she'd forgotten why she'd come.

He waited.

Finally she spoke. "I went to the North Tower, but there was no one there. Are you ill?"

"No, Lord Austin had some urgent—business in the village. But I expect his absence has more to do with the Midsummer fair than business. I am sorry you weren't informed."

"Ah." She seemed to hang like a drop of water. Would she stay, or would she go. "We missed our reading." She held up her Bible. "Doctor Hives likes to adhere to a routine whenever possible."

So she had volunteered to mind the madman for this afternoon. What was she about? Was this some new test?

If only he could see her face more clearly, but the light was behind her, and the remnants of a fire gave little more than a glow. Midsummer Eve, the longest day of the year but his room, with its eastern view and still boarded windows, would soon fade from gloom to dark.

Miss Winton set a branch of candles on the small table which stood in the corner next to a chair. Her shadow cast a long path across the floor, reaching toward him in the far corner of the room where Ivo had left him shackled.

"And where is Ivo?" His keeper was the last thing he wanted, but he had to ask. He kicked the chain under his cot.

She flinched at the sound and then smoothed her skirts. "He begged to go to the fair." As if that fact could possibly explain her presence here alone.

After some dithering, she dragged the table, chair, and candelabra not five feet from his bed. Well within the length of his chain. The gallant part of him wished he could help her, but then he'd miss the show—her juggling handfuls of skirts with furniture and dripping tapers.

"Apparently the scullery maid had been to the village and filled his head with tales of a Persian llama. He was desperate to see and touch the beast." Miss Winton winced as a trail of wax caught her finger. "Mrs. Coates left me in charge." She put the finger to her lips.

Oh, to be that finger…

His eyes must have looked as licentious as his thoughts, for she hid her hand behind her back and firmed her lips.

"I suppose I have a soft spot somewhere," she said as her lashes dipped to fan her cheeks.

"I daresay you do." He bit back a smile though he needn't have, she was suddenly busy squaring her Bible precisely with the corner edge of the table. "You did not wish to see the festivities? I would have thought you might be Lady of the Flowers."

She froze, her lips pulling even tighter.

Ah, too much flattery for his poor Owl.

She spent an inordinate amount of time adjusting the candles. Finally pleased with their arrangement, she stood still, her Bible now in hand.

No Austin.

And no Ivo.

The rules had changed. She knew it. No doubt that was why she was prattling on about llamas and scullery maids. And soft spots. It was the most he had heard her say, ever. What had turned her into such a chatterbox?

She caught her lip with her teeth as her gaze dipped to his bare feet and the chain he'd tried to hide.

Five feet between her and a madman. Would she fly? She gripped her Bible like a shield, definitely unsure of her next move. Perhaps it was a bit of Midsummer Madness but she sat.

"So, the Good Book again for our entertainment," he said sitting as well. She seemed to have given up on her knitting.

She cleared her throat. "It is what Doctor Hives prescribes." No glance to the spy hole this time. No voyeuristic observer lurking behind the wall?

"Then by all means, we must follow the doctor's orders," he said to the hole, just for good measure. Miss Owl took no notice. A good sign.

What if he suddenly charged at her and took her in his arms? Surely that would flush any rat from his hole. Hell, it might be worth the punishment to embrace another human being, if only for a moment. And if no one came charging to her rescue…well that might mean something quite different.

"We had just finished Exodus." She paged through the book, head bent, her tongue peeping between her lips.

No, he would not assault her. He did not want to risk her leaving him. Not just yet.

"Thank God we have finally exited Exodus." He meant it facetiously, but if she got his jest, she made no sign. "Austin will be ecstatic. What is next?"

"Leviticus."

"Oh, no, out of the smoke and into the fire. Must we have more stoning and slashing and chopping off bits?"

She frowned and pursed her lips. "You do not fancy, 'I will release wild animals that will kill your children and destroy your cattle, so your numbers will dwindle and your roads will be deserted'?"

Was she actually making a small joke? "Oh, is that the best you can do? Too tame. Can't we have a good beheading and some pestilence, or perhaps a plague of vipers?"

She started to thumb through pages.

Dear heavens, she was a literal little thing. "Bloody hell. Please, I beg you, Anne, skip it."

Her hand stilled mid-way through a turn.

Anne. He had used her Christian name. Well, he would not apologize for it, or cursing for that matter. Rattling her was worth flouting decorum. He liked her off balance.

The page still hovered in limbo.

"In fact." He sat forward, his elbows on his knees. "Let us skip the whole blasted book," he whispered. Suddenly it seemed vital she let go of that page. Let go of Hives' orders. Let go of herself.

She closed her mouth and dipped her head, and then turned unerringly to the middle of the book.

No, too much to hope for. He settled back for another sermon.

What was beneath her hideous, shapeless frock? Half her body would glow like ivory bathed in candlelight, the other half, would be cast in velvet shadows.

Her hair looked to be stick straight and as glossy as an oriental princess'. If she let it down, would it tease her bum? A few tendrils always managed to slip free, no matter how severely she twisted it up into that neat, uncompromising bun.

He would trace her soft feathery brows first, and then thread his fingers through the wings of her hair. Pins would slip out of the lush black silk. Long braids would loosen with just the brush of a hand. She would try to stop him, but he would catch her hands, full of heat and vibration, and together they would skim over his chest, down his belly, to rest at the root of his cock. She would bend to take him in her—

She cleared her throat, and his fantasy unraveled. Smoothing her hand over the page, she sat up straighter pulling her shoulders back.

"'The Song of Songs, which is Solomon's. Let him kiss me with the kisses of his mouth: for thy love is better than wine.'"

What the—? He blinked, trying to fit this primly sitting maiden to the liquid honey voice that dripped a naïve sort of seduction.

She plowed on paying no mind to the clinking of his chains and him half rising from his cot. "'Because of the savor of thy good ointments thy mane is as ointment poured forth, Therefore do the virgins love thee.'"

Her voice had sped up and dropped in volume for this last line. If he were in a teasing mood, he would have tortured her, making her repeat it, but he no longer felt like teasing.

"'Draw me, we will run after thee: the King hath brought me into his chambers:'" She cleared her throat again. "'We will be glad and rejoice in thee, we will remember thy love more than wine: the upright love thee.'"

One thing was surely upright. He shifted, his chain shushing along the floor.

Miss Anne Winton seemed to have lost her place.

Spy or no spy, he couldn't give a rat's ass. He took up the poetry. "'Behold, thou art fair, my love; behold thou art fair; thou hast doves' eyes.'"

Her dove's eyes were looking straight into his, her lips softly parted.

The moment hung with promise. She shook her head minutely and frowned. "You have skipped." Logic reared its oh-so-practical head.

He leaned closer. "I make no apology. I remember the parts I like and toss the rest."

"Hmmm." She nodded like some wise sage.

"No doubt you are putting me down as one of those naughty children who sampled a bite of every sweet and then only took the ones he liked, leaving the rest to his siblings. Well, you would be correct. Though in my case it is sibling. Singular. And only a half one at that. And possibly even not a sibling at all if the rumors are true." Banal words flowed from him, poor substitutes for what churned underneath.

She caught her lip between her teeth.

Yes, she felt it too.

Insistent as a drum, the throbbing of his cock had him hugging himself to make sure the rest of him was still there. He had not had a woman since being shut up in this place.

The poison did odd things to his desires, sometimes snuffing them to nothing, and sometimes making them rise and rage. A mere brush to his skin could send him over the edge—or just some words from the bloody Bible. He could not trust his body just as he could not trust his mind. But he no longer craved that feeling of loose dissipation where his mind and body disappeared into the walls and floor, into the sheets where he slept and gruel he ate.

He didn't want it. He wanted to be whole.

As he faced this girl, this woman, with her earnest

eyes, he so wanted to trust her. And to have her trust him. *Please don't let her be simply Hives' puppet.*

Her unflinching gaze flayed him open surer than any surgeon's knife, but instead of guts and pulsing organs, she went right for his soul. He shifted again, feeling like a table with three legs.

Could Anne Winton fill the vast emptiness within him? By God, this little brown owl might have that much power over him. More than any drug.

He shook his head. *Stop.* He was too damaged, too jaded for this girl-woman. He was not capable of love.

"I envy you, Anne." It was the first real thing he had said to her all evening.

She blinked. "Why?"

"You are good and true. You are a clean open book and must be eager to add to your pages. Your story is not written yet, it is still full of promise."

She did not reply. But finally shut the book.

"You do not agree?" He pressed. "Surely you would not want to trade places with me?"

She hesitated. "No," she said softly, yet firmly. "I would not want to be you."

"You are wise beyond your years," he said, trying to lighten the mood. "And fortunate."

She looked up sharply as if he had suddenly grown two heads.

"What? Have I offended you?

She shook her head, but he was not sure it was in answer to his question.

He waited—something he was not used to doing.

Finally the weight of this heavy pause tipped the scale in his favor.

"I live because someone—your father, I suppose—

gives me shelter. I am not low-born, but I am as friendless as if I'd been born to a chimney sweep." She touched the edge of her Bible, tracing the worn leather. "Women are prized for their ability to bear children yet I will likely never even marry. What lies before me is a long road of service."

She sat up straighter. "I had hoped to be allowed to participate in the therapies here at Ballencrieff, but I was naïve. Thus far Doctor Hives is not convinced of the value of my opinions or talents."

Yes, her hands. He wished she might tell him of her gift.

She closed her eyes and shook her head, her hands gripping the book. "On second thought, perhaps I would change places with you."

"We are a pair." He smiled to cover his disappointment, but she had turned away.

He leaned toward her, wanting to bring her back to him. "Where did you find The Song of Solomon? That book is cut out of every Bible I have seen in this place."

She smoothed her hand over the cover. "Lady Tippit."

"Ah, I must remember to thank her." He smiled again, but she only looked down. "And why did you choose to read it to me today?"

She glanced sideways at him as if she were peeping through the crack in a doorway, not knowing what lay beyond. "It is beautiful," said with such sweet simplicity.

"And that is the only reason?"

She was going to shut this particular door, he was sure of it. Still, he waited.

"No."

He should let it lie. She would be in over her head

with him. Or maybe he was really the one in trouble? "Could you elaborate?"

She stared out into space as if the answer might be somewhere in the air. "It is like music. And as an artist, I thought you might like it as well."

Oh, to be free to walk to her and gather her in his arms. He could, his chain would stretch that far, but he wouldn't. No, she would have to come to him or not at all.

She set her book on the table, and then smoothed her skirts and stood.

He rose right along with her, as if they were already one.

Then she turned away, reaching for the candelabra.

His heart dropped into his belly. She was leaving him. He squeezed his eyelids tightly. The little owl was wise after all.

The faint light behind his lids plunged into total darkness. Confused, he opened his eyes.

The space between them had disappeared along with the light.

She stood directly in front of him.

****

Anne stood still as stone.

He did not move either. Though she would swear he surrounded her, rushing over her, to swirl into every crevice. The pulsing hum of him buzzed the tips of her breasts, her eyelids, cheeks, and lips. Even her back. She had not been so near him since that first day. The day he had cut himself. If she reached down, would she feel that heavy ridge of his manhood?

She was playing with fire. She had told herself she would read to him, fulfilling her duty, and then go.

Still time to step away and stop this madness. Still time to take up her Bible and return to the safety of her dull life.

But even as her head lambasted her heart with its cold, hard facts she stepped closer still. She could touch his fire, if she were brave enough. Here in the dark of his cell, the world seemed so very far away, as if God had cupped His hands around them, and nothing could touch them.

The Almighty had not given her the gift of beauty. He had made her to heal. That ability gave her peace when she had seen other girls go off into the world beyond Ardsmoore where they might marry and hold their child.

She had wrapped herself in her gift of healing. It had to be enough. But now, with this man filling her senses, she dearly wished for beauty.

"Anne." He breathed against her temple. "Anne." His lips hovered over her brows. She blinked as the air hit her lashes. "Anne." Breath skated over her cheek, hovering on the edge of her mouth. Her name, a deep refrain, so beautiful on his lips.

Please, yes. Not knowing quite what she wanted.

She swallowed and her toes curled in her boots, her hands fisted by her sides.

A fan of warm breath escaped his parted lips. No name now. Just breath. And a faint smell of cloves... She opened her mouth to draw in that breath—to take him inside her.

Please, yes. The humming within her grew. She trembled with it.

"Please, James," his name escaped on a whisper. And like a key opening a door, his lips touched hers.

The light brush of his mouth against her own shocked, almost hurting her with its reverence. Her naïve imaginings evaporated in the face of this visceral reality. So different from the press of her own fingers against her lips in the hushed darkness of the dormitory at Ardsmoore. Or even last night in her bed here at Ballencrieff.

His arms came about her making it real. Him real, after so many dreams. She opened her eyes, wanting to remember everything.

His kisses were a sunset of colors. First pale blue, then a whisper of pink, then bright yellow as he pressed harder, then deepest purple as his teeth caught her lip, then—

His tongue flicked out. Red and hot. She gasped as it ran over her teeth, and then plunged inside her.

Is this what lovers did? How to answer? But thought evaporated with the sudden tangle of their tongues.

Legs trembling, she reached up for his strength. His hair curled around her fingers as they found the back of his neck, so springy—so different from hers.

He cradled her head, angling it to fit her mouth more tightly against his. His tongue danced with hers; a waltz in their mouths, the humming between them providing the music.

More. Closer. "Yes," was all she managed.

The ridge of him pressed long and hard against her belly, but she wanted it lower, deeper, in the place where the music lived. She plunged her tongue into his mouth, wanting to fill and be filled. *More, I want more.*

She reached down for him.

The humming music stopped. She stumbled forward with the loss of it. His chain rasped along the floor.

"Go." The word came like a blow. He stood at the far end of the cot, his chain strained. As far from her as he could get.

Cold lanced through her body without him next to her.

She stepped toward his heat.

"I said, go!"

She spun away, instinctively shielding her face. Her skirts tangled around her, and her hip bone cracked into the table, sending the candelabra crashing. She nearly tripped and fell to her knees as an animal—a cat—streaked past her as she flung open the door. She did not stop running until she reached the safety of her room.

What had she done?

Shame flooded her cheeks and squeezed her pounding heart. She touched her lips. They were swollen and throbbing, her breasts as well. And down below where she felt so empty.

Tears slipped over her cheeks and ran into her open mouth. She flung herself on her bed burying her face in the pillow.

He did not want her.

She pulled her legs up to her chest, but it was no good. It only made the place below more open. She clamped her hand between her legs. Still it throbbed.

Please—

She pushed a finger inside. Oh God. So wet.

Yes. Yes, better.

She arched into the fullness. Her other hand brushed her breast. She squeezed, hard.

"Yes." Shocked at hearing her voice she stilled. But her finger was moving again as if it had a mind of its own. "Please, please, please—"

"Ahhhhh!"

It took a long moment to realize the cry was Phoebe Nester's and not her own. Horrified, she jerked her hand from between her legs and sat up.

"Winton!"

She ran to the wash basin, shoved her hand into the frigid water, and then grabbed a towel as she headed for the door connecting her room to Mrs. Nester's.

A reprieve this call to duty.

But as she soothed Phoebe Nester from her latest nightmare, Anne could not let go of the feelings Lord Devlin had stirred within her. Surely such an awakening could not be wicked? It seemed to hold the potential for another kind of healing. One that promised—

She did not know. But something awesome lay beyond this pulsing fullness, and she had only touched its surface. Could she let this feeling die? One complaint about her to Doctor Hives and she would be gone with no money and no reference.

No. She must quash these beautiful feelings before they ruined her. They were an indulgence she could not afford. Thank God, he had not wanted her in the end.

Tears dropped next to Phoebe Nester's now sleeping head.

Yes, thank God.

Chapter Ten

"Ah, Lord Devlin, please be seated," Doctor Hives said, lowering a handkerchief from his mouth and gesturing to the chair opposite his desk. Macready stood by the door, holding a brown burlap sack. Dev had not had the pleasure of seeing the keeper's ugly face in weeks. His smirk told him to be ready for a surprise.

Something stank, and it wasn't Macready's distinctive odor of cabbage and farts. Dev adjusted the chair so that the door was not entirely to his back, and then sat.

Both he and Anne had been summoned from the North Tower. Austin had not seen fit to show up. Again.

After mauling her yesterday, he had expected her not to appear either, but she had come armed with more knitting and a frown fixed on her face. A stickler for routine, his Owl. Other than a nod to him and a "good afternoon" to Ivo, she'd made a bee line for her corner and hadn't moved or looked up until Hobbs had come saying Hives wanted to see them both.

The keeper had ushered him into the office, leaving Anne outside to await her interview. Had she come to Hives with tales of seduction? Is that why they were both here now?

"Now then, Lord Devlin, the portrait is progressing?" Hives had the habit of making a simple question sound like an indictment.

Damned sure he hadn't been summoned to wax on about the bloody portrait, he said nothing. But the possibility Hives had been spying as he and Anne kissed had him shifting in his chair.

"I am told the light in the North Tower is more suitable?" The doctor tapped the pads of his fingers together.

Such pleasantries. "It will do."

"Painting was supposed to be beneficial. I had hoped we had begun to make some progress at last."

"We?" *What was that smell?*

"Did you paint yesterday?"

"Why do you bother asking?" He glanced at Macready. "You know I did not."

"How did you fill your time?"

He slid back in the chair. "I meditated on several Bible verses."

"Bible verses? Really?"

He flexed his hands imagining them squeezing Hives nonexistent neck.

"Then how do you explain this?" The doctor gestured to Macready who eagerly stepped forward, ever ready to play his part. He jerked open the mouth of the sack and thrust it under Dev's nose.

He recognized the smell now. It was the putrid smell of death.

A large cat lay in the bottom of the bag. Its belly had been cut open to expose the internal organs and a number of small matted balls. Her kittens.

Bile rose in his throat, and he squeezed his eyes shut. A white featureless face filled his brain. *No, not now. You must not come now. I promise I will deal with you later. When I am alone.*

He made himself look. He was stronger now.

Penny. Ivo had named the cat Penny. He had been trying to tame her for weeks. A feral scrap of hissing, matted fur that had nearly devoured his beloved mouse, Pocket. But rather than see the cat as evil, he had tried to make it a friend. The cat often hid in Dev's room where Ivo tried to tempt her with bits of food.

Penny's frozen, dull eyes stared up at him. Dear God. Only a monster would do such a thing.

The doctor held his handkerchief in front of his mouth and nose, his watery eyes stared directly into Dev's. "Do you have anything you wish to tell me, your lordship?"

He made himself breathe. "Poison, I would say." Macready, his twisted lip glistening, never flinched under Dev's accusing glare. "A few weeks back I might have supposed she'd gotten into my dinner." At least Hives had the decency to look away, if not precisely guilty. "I should not like to be so much as shaved by this butcher. Whoever did this did not know a hawk from a handsaw."

The doctor pursed his lips in utter disapproval. Apparently quoting the mad prince, Hamlet did not sit well with the good doctor. After what seemed an infinite amount of time, Hives waved the henchman away. "All right, you can bury the thing. And Macready, I will speak with you later."

The servant made a show of tying up the bag and then giving Dev a smirk before closing the door with a heavy click.

When first coming under Hives' care, Dev had tried to rile the doctor just to see if he could make a dent in the man's implacable façade. Over the months he learned the punishment was not worth the little discomfort he produced. He'd counted a total of four expressions—well, once he had seen a fifth, but that was only because his hands had been wrapped around the doctor's neck at the time.

Number two was in place now: his eyebrows drawn up in a sort of startled surprise, as if he could not quite believe he had to endure whatever was going on. Hives took up a pen and began to write in a notebook. Another similar journal lay on the corner of his desk. A red flare of panic speared his gut. Anne Winton had a book much the same. Did this notebook contain a neatly penned tale of seduction? The *skritching* of the doctor's pen against the paper made his teeth grind.

At last Hives closed the book.

"The cat seemed to be looking for a spot to have her kittens."

The white face rose again, floating in the middle of the black hole of his memory. He swallowed. *I will get through this. I must. I am better now.*

"Penny, her name was Penny," he ground the words out.

"Yes, well, someone said." Hives' hand strayed to the second notebook. "The cat was last seen near your room."

"Who? Who said?" The words came out too forcefully.

The doctor's eyes narrowed—expression four—as he looked down his negligible nose.

"Not my brother," he made his voice light, almost casual and not a question. "And never Ivo. He wouldn't—"

The answer was clear even before his ridiculous

95

process of elimination, but he did not want to see it. She had been by his room—in his bloody room yesterday. Was his ego so inflated by this smitten girl that he was blinded by her calf-love of him? He felt supremely stupid. The girl was only doing what she had been asked to do: her duty. One fumbled kiss did not shift alliances. Anne Winton was not his.

Perhaps their kiss been only mere curiosity on her part. A dare. Another test. Could something he had thought so beautiful be so ugly?

He did not know anymore. Like any caged animal he had only his instincts to guide him. It had been so very long since anyone had touched him out of kindness much less with passion… She had called him James. He had tossed in his bed remembering her 'doves eyes' and his name on her lips. He'd spent himself over and over thinking of her mouth on his—

"The cat was discovered in your room, by the niche near the window. Along with this." The doctor held up a sliver of broken glass. He turned the shard to show a bit of blood and yellow fur.

He made himself say the words. "And who flew to you with this juicy tidbit? Did this person suggest this butchery was my work?"

Again, the doctor said nothing, only sat forward in his chair.

Dev felt as if they were about to play a game of chess where the checkmate may decide his freedom or doom. If it was Miss Winton, why could she not lie about seeing the cat? About the glass? Apparently Miss Anne Winton did not lie.

"Contrary to popular opinion, I am not convinced you were the cause of this poor creature's demise. At any rate, I need to believe you did not perform such a heinous deed. We are running out of time, Lord Devlin. We both stand to benefit from your recovery. However, your year is almost up."

Yes, his year to reform himself. To recover his lost memories and deal with them. To become heir material.

"We all have our dreams, Lord Devlin. One cannot simply bide one's time and wait for providence to grant them. One must use one's wits and available resources to achieve one's dreams."

Nothing to say. At the moment his dreams seemed as dead as poor Penny.

"We are prepared to put this episode aside and allow you to complete the painting. But it is time you gave us something as well."

A standard opening. "Tit for tat? Or should I say, cat?" Hives remained stoic. "Very well, I would expect nothing less," he answered with a similar move. "I will be on my best behavior, and you will get your masterpiece. Are we finished here?" The sweet stench of death lingered filling him with a nearly poisoning panic.

"Not quite, Lord Devlin." Hives pushed a sheet of foolscap across the table.

"What is this?" He recognized his father's secretary Tally's neat script.

His head jerked to meet Hives' cold gaze. The doctor's upper lip protruded as his chin receded farther into the folds of his cravat. Dev grabbed the papers.

Miss Phyllis Thornton? Daughter of Mr. Gavin Thornton. The name meant nothing. He read further. *As soon as the marquess is found compos mentis by the duke's experts, the betrothal will be fixed and Lord Devlin and Miss Thornton will marry by special license that very day.* He flipped to the next page. There it was, the marriage settlement contract.

Checkmate.

The pain in his head flared as he stood, flinging the papers away and the chair sideways. Hives reached for the bell. Dev fisted his hands, his nails digging into the flesh. He found himself at the window and jerked open the draperies, inhaling deeply despite the window being firmly shut. There were no bars here. The glass would break in an instant he could be running across that palette of verdigris and violet that colored the Scottish moors.

But to what end? Beautiful as they were, they were death traps. He'd found that out the hard way in his first week. The Hall, perched on a crag, was surrounded by sucking bogs. Besides, Hives' thugs would be on him within a few moments. Even now, he could see the doctor reflected in the glass, bell in hand, poised to summon help.

His forehead met the chill of the glass. Dear Christ, he was so tired of terrifying people. Tired of being manhandled with no say in his life. Tired of being denied such simple pleasures as choosing his own clothes, what he ate, walking in the sun. Being touched with love… Kissed…

And now, he could not even choose his own wife. Forced to tie himself to a stranger who would, in all likelihood, be terrified of him, simply to secure the bloody succession.

The phantom of Phyllis Thornton was soon replaced by Anne Winton's face.

His Owl. He would much rather Anne Winton as his bride.

Like a piece of a missing puzzle, always there but

never tried, a plan formed. Why not? Why not use her schoolgirl infatuation to tie her to him? As his wife she would have the authority to remove him from Ballencrieff. She might hate him for it, but she would never leave him to languish in this hellish place, of that he was sure.

Anne as his bride… He would not delude himself he could love her as she ought to be loved, he had long ago resigned himself to an empty marriage, but his body certainly wanted her with a desperation he had never known.

Outside a wind blew, ruffling the heather into silver sheets.

Of course, it wouldn't come to marriage. He was going to pass his father's test and be free of Ballencrieff without ruining Miss Anne Winton. But plans were never sure. How did Hives put it, *available resources*? Right.

Hot guilt crept along his neck. He shook it off. After all, if it came to it, she would benefit from his plan as well. Being a marchioness was nothing to sneeze at.

So, for now he would play their game, but he would have an ace up his sleeve. And by all the fires of hell, he would not be shackled to Miss Phyllis Thornton.

He still had some power. Spy or not he would make sure when the chips fell, Anne Winton would end up on his side. She was half in love with him already. It wouldn't take much more to tip the scales. And by God, he would enjoy tipping them.

"I will sign this farce of a betrothal, but you must give me something as well." He laid out his stipulations, and Hives slipped into expression number two but then nodded.

What was Mr. Herbert Spencer's assertion? Survival of the fittest?

Dev took up the pen and scrawled his name on the contract.

****

Anne dug her fingernail into the flesh of her palm. Macready had left Hives' office with a sick smile on his face and a sack that stunk. Shortly after, she heard a crash from within. Hobbs jumped to open the door but was never summoned.

Moments slid by. Had Lord Devlin told the doctor of her brazen behavior? A crescent of blood marred her hand, and she swiped it away. Finally the door opened and Hobbs jerked forward to escort Lord Devlin. She caught his gaze but could tell nothing from his guarded eyes.

"Miss Winton?" Hives was waiting. "Come."

She entered the office, shutting the door behind her.

"Well? What have you to tell me?"

What a fool she was to think no one had seen her running from the marquess' room. What utter folly to risk her place here at Ballencrieff for a mere schoolgirl fantasy.

"I—" A notebook lay on Hives' desk. Her heart jumped. Her private diary and patient notebooks looked much the same.

"Miss Winton, you will answer me."

She reached for the book. "Lady Tippit continues to—"

He intercepted her, placing his hand over the journal. "Not Lady Tippit, Miss Winton. I have more pressing problems than her ladyship's penchant for lewd displays. What of Lord Devlin?"

"Lord Devlin?" Her mind raced over the words she had written last night when she could not sleep. *Try as I might, I cannot let go of this new awakening. He invades my dreams, my very being. I must put this attraction behind me.*

"You disappoint, Miss Winton. I thought I could trust you to report everything to me."

She took a breath. "Doctor Hives, I assure you whatever Lord Devlin told you, it was my fault—"

"Shocking is the word that comes to mind."

"Again, sir, you must not blame—"

"Weeks, weeks have passed and this is the result? There has been no progress."

"Progress…?"

"Am I surrounded by incompetents? The Marquess'—the famed James Drake's new masterpiece."

James…his Christian name. The name she had whispered last evening in her desperation.

"Miss Winton, what of the painting?"

The painting? A bubble of laughter rose in her throat. She turned it into a cough. He did not know. She was safe. For now.

The doctor thrust her notebook at her in disgust. "What has he been doing? Answer me!"

Not her diary. Only her patient notebook. She pressed the groove where her nail had cut into her palm.

"Lord Austin has been gone a great deal of the time. I have tried to provide a routine despite—"

"It has been nearly four weeks, Miss Winton. Over three since he has gotten his precious light."

What was there to say? She knew naught about making a portrait.

"I went up to the North Tower yesterday when everyone was at the fair. I could not believe the lack of progress. And now I have been informed that Lord Austin is leaving. Again. He does not know when he may return."

Good. Then she would not have to see the marquess. At least not until Lord Austin returned. Perhaps by then she would have recovered some sanity.

Doctor Hives gripped the arms of his chair. "I did not like this painting idea in the first place. And now it seems it will sink me. Miss Winton, are you aware that the duke expects his son to be "fixed" in a little over two months?"

"Fixed?"

"Yes, his father will listen to testimony and hear his son's plea for release in exactly eight and a half weeks. The painting must be finished by then. And it must be brilliant. Lord Austin has been assuring his father this portrait will be ocular proof that the marquess has recovered his wits and his morals. If I am not successful, the duke will retract his bonus. I have risked—worked too hard and too long to have that be a possibility, Miss Winton."

"I will do anything in my power to help, Doctor."

"Well, it seems you must. I like this proposition even less, but Lord Devlin says he cannot paint if he is not inspired. His exact words were, 'I am an artist, not a trained monkey'."

She firmed her lips quashing the smile that threatened to overtake them.

"He even went so far as to say, he could not paint a man. It seems absurd, but there it is. However, I do know he cannot paint a subject who is never here to sit for him." He snorted and shook his head. "Worse it appears he cannot paint at all." He wheeled on her. "Your duties with Lady Tippit and Mrs. Nester will be further curtailed. You will report to the North Tower each day just after prayers."

"Doctor Hives?" She did not understand.

"You will be Lord Devlin's new subject."

Chapter Eleven

Dev persuaded Ivo to take his growing menagerie to the far corner of the tower. The giant had wept bitterly over the death of Penny, but Cook had given him a white kitten of his very own. This newest recruit had a spot on his nose very like the boot-shape of Italy. Dev suggested *Gattino* for a name, but Ivo had looked at him like he was barmy, and said his name could only be Blackie. Apparently, when first discovered, the animal had been covered in soot.

Hunkering down in his corner, Ivo was at the delicate ask of introducing his mouse, Pocket, to this new kitten. The keeper was proving to be very conscientious in the care of his pets. Dev included. He must remember to thank Austin when he next deigned to pay a visit.

What time was it? The light was perfect, clear and diffused. She wouldn't be late, would she? God, he felt like a popped champagne cork, one he was trying to shove back in its bottle.

He heard nothing, but somehow Miss Winton had slipped in silent as a cat in the midst of his frenetic fussing. The most celebrated Paris Opera dancers moved like clods compared to this woman.

She hovered just inside the door, her hand grasping the knob as if it were a lifeline. When Austin sat for his portrait, Anne had gone directly to the small chair by the fire—her spot. This new situation had her flummoxed.

Had she noted Ivo's new out-of-the-way position? If so, she said nothing.

This girl-woman would enter a wild animal's cage if she thought she might help the beast. Didn't she know he could devour her? Tear her to pieces and leave her in ruins? What she knew of the ways of the world would fill a nut shell with space left over for Ivo's mouse to take a nap.

Still, he had to be careful. One of his stipulations for signing that sham of a betrothal was no interference from Hives, no coming up to check on his progress, and no probing questions. Of course, Miss Owl was supposed to be Hives' eyes and ears, but he would take care of that. Soon she would have some secrets of her own. And if exposed—well, he hoped it would not come to that.

He gestured for her to come into the light where he had painstakingly set up a rather ornate chair upholstered in cream velvet. A scarlet paisley, draped over its back, would be the perfect foil to her coloring. Earlier he'd had Ivo sit in it so he could get the position just right. Likely a wasted effort. Miss Winton was no more than a quarter of the giant's size and as pale as his keeper was beechnut brown.

"Good morning." He could not quite bring himself to call her Miss Winton. Not after whispering Anne in her ear and against her neck and lips. "Or is it afternoon? Never can see the sun in this God forsaken land, and I'm allowed no time-piece. Might use it to harm myself. Or others."

She stared at him as if he were—well a lunatic.

And what did he expect after assaulting her with his kisses? And then there was poor Penny. Did she believe him capable of performing such a grisly act on a preg—

Dev shook his head hard. *No, not now.*

"Sit," he barked. "Please."

She smoothed the skirts of her gown, a habit, he was learning, when she was nervous.

Good, that made two of them.

His fingers itched to begin. Ideas crowded his mind with shapes and light. With possibilities. This new portrait would kill two birds with one stone, fulfilling his desire to capture this extraordinary woman, even as he made her a staunch ally. His savior both physically and mentally.

But he had to play this just right or risk her flying the nest, straight back to Hives.

As if she could hear his thoughts, she glanced toward Ivo, now on his belly arranging a tower of small boxes, his tongue out and working as hard as his hands.

She turned back and stared straight ahead of her.

Damn it. Was she so frightened of him? "Must you look as if you are in the tooth drawer's chair?"

She half popped up off her seat, and then sat and smoothed her bloody skirts again.

"It was a joke about the watch. You must know that."

"The watch?"

"Yes, harming someone with a blasted watch. A joke."

"Oh. I'm sorry. I did not see it as a joke. My mind is—occupied elsewhere."

"Anne, I had nothing to do with butchering that unfortunate cat—"

"No." She cut him off. "I cannot believe someone… No, you could not have." She made this pronouncement as if the possibility had never entered her mind.

"Then tell me, what has your mind in such a tangle?"

Ah, a blush, smoothing skirts and even a dip of her chin.

"Come now, it can't be so bad. Did you break old Lady Tippit's mirror? Has Cook forgotten your birthday? Don't tell me Macready is bothering you? By God I'll—"

"I have heard you are used to painting the most beautiful women in England."

His frazzled nerves collapsed in a limp heap where he did a mental jig on them. "Don't forget the Continent as well." She was not afraid of him. She was afraid she was not enough.

True, Anne Winton was no rounded, blonde, blued-eyed miss, the current fashion. She would never fall so neatly into a category. A diamond of the first water? No. She was far too unusual for that title.

This woman was a study in contrasts. The strong line of her often-furrowed brow fighting to claim dominion over her luminous, sable-colored eyes. Her lips, too red and too full, her nose too long, its tip turning down just the barest fraction, and finally, her chin, too sharp. All these features cast within a canvas too pale for such stark abundance. Most people would look at her embarrassment of riches and dismiss her as plain. If pressed, those same cretins would say her eyes were her best feature. But they did not know how to look at this woman, how to appreciate her rare beauty.

She was a subject worthy of a masterpiece. He saw it within her. But how to make the rest of the world see what he saw? How to capture all facets of her? Her pain, her stillness, her wisdom. Her sensuality.

Only a fool would underestimate this woman. And

by the look of her, the world was full of fools. She trod so carefully, as if conscious of the perils of stepping outside some unseen boundary. The way she ducked her head, held her hands in her lap, deferring to those around her. It mesmerized him and made him angry, all at the same time. Yet she displayed no arts, or guile, no manipulation. What kind of life had she endured that kept her so watchful, so inside herself, so contained?

Well, not always contained...

Seduction knocked her off her plate well enough. He bit back a smile. That blush, so transparent on her white skin, would flood her neck and cheeks and her eyes would blink in astonished confusion.

Oh, yes, he enjoyed Anne Winton off balance.

Holding his pencil out in front of his face, he closed one eye and sighted her figure. Now able to ogle her to his heart's content. She would assume he was working and not simply looking his fill. He made sure his little frown was fixed in place—his disguise.

"Could you turn more to your left—toward the light? Your whole body. Yes! There. Now move your hand to the back of the chair and lean into the corner. I want you to use the whole chair."

She took direction well. Lithe as a panther, this one. He would swear her tiny frame lengthened to drape itself over this lump of furniture. She managed to make the lavish Rococo chair look cheap and gaudy. He would have to change it. Or perhaps the contrast would work?

"Yes, just there." His breath came fast, like the huffing of some green boy dallying in his first haystack.

A small scar marred the underside of her chin. Must have split it open one fine day chasing chickens, or keeling over from boredom while at prayers. Or any number of provincial scenarios. He wanted to trace it with his lips.

Jesus. His hands were shaking. He was getting ahead of himself. Too high on possibilities, when she could fly back to Hives with tales.

An owl. Only a useful owl.

She would learn she could not cow him with those soul-searching eyes. He was immune to such tricks. Yet another lie. His bloody cock stiff as a harrier sensing a fox. Would that his brain was half as responsive. He tore off a sheet of paper and then wadded it up, throwing it across the room. He might have saved his theatrics for all the attention she paid him. Devilish minx.

Charcoal lines flew across the page, capturing the shape of her head, long neck and shoulders, then the curve of her back against the cream cushion, the sweep of her skirts over her legs and down to her crossed ankles. He whipped off the page to unearth a new one.

This next part required a bit of self-control. In the past he would have simply put down his crayon and had a go at the lass. They'd always been more than willing.

But Anne Winton was no flirtatious doxy looking for a tumble. Even a fool could see the girl had *chaste* written all over her.

Hands off. Well, at least until he needed her. If the other day was any indication, poor lass would drop like a blown rose. Hell, he would still have to call a halt just as he had yesterday.

Wouldn't he?

"Did you paint at Ardsmoore?" Anything to get his mind off lush lips and a silken neck.

Her gaze darted to him and then back. His question must have startled her.

She shook her head.

"Miss Winton, you may speak. And breathe," he added.

Her eyes flicked to his again. "We were never allowed drawing materials." She barely moved her mouth.

"Yes, there! Look at me just like that." She had thought to hide from him, looking out the west window, but he wanted her eyes directly on the viewer. "Good God, what kind of education is my father providing where a young lady does not draw?"

He could see her hesitate, unsure if the question was rhetorical.

"Paper was too dear, much less paints or even crayons." She frowned at his growing pile of discarded sketches. "Students' chalks and slates were collected each evening and locked in a drawer. Any drawings or writings would be erased at day's end."

"That is a shame."

"Not if you saw my drawings."

Finally, a small jest! "And your writing? What did you write?" He tossed another sheet next to the other four.

"Stories mostly."

"Ah, ah, keep looking at me and forget about the paper. If you must, you can save it to squirrel away." Her gaze, once again, met his. "Stories about?"

She wanted to look away, but was too obedient not to follow directions. "Otherworldly creatures."

"Like Mr. Beauchamp's tales?"

She bit her lip. Not a smile yet, but perhaps the prelude to one. "No. No egg-shaped heads and dissected brains floating in aspic."

"What then?" He would not let her off the hook.

She fidgeted and then resumed the exact pose. "I wrote of a fairy world where the folk had magical powers."

"So your stories were autobiographical."

Her lips firmed to a straight line. "You are teasing me."

"No. No, I am not." How could he, when he had felt her magic, her fey, healing hands. But Miss Anne Winton was used to making herself small. An insignificant, bit of gray to fill out a shadow. Did she ever ask herself if she liked this role? Did she ever yearn for something more?

Despite her drab feathers, this woman was color, all color. He wanted to show her what he saw. To see herself in glorious color.

He ripped another sheet off, but this time he did not crumple it up.

"Since we will have no Bible readings, to pass the time you will entertain me with your stories."

****

Why would he want to paint her?

The question had persisted for three days now. Three days of him seemingly fascinated with her. Always frustrated when their time was up. *Why?*

And how could she continue to squelch her feelings when every time he looked at her—and he constantly looked at her—this heavy throbbing inside pulled her toward him. What was worse, she would swear he felt it too.

It was time to take a look for herself.

She had stolen a few glances at herself in Lady Tippit's mirror over these last few weeks, but never studied her face. Truth be told, she was frightened of what she might see.

She approached the mirror now as if it was something to vanquish and sat before she turned coward.

Not so bad.

An ordinary woman stared back from the mirror. Certainly no one worthy of paint, to be immortalized for centuries to come. Would some young girl, far into the future, gaze upon Anne's portrait and see her secrets? What would be revealed within James Drake's brush strokes and choice of colors?

Tilting her head one way and then the other, she explored all angles. Common brown eyes—well, maybe they had a bit of green in them—yes, a ring of green at the edge and flecks of yellow. More golden than yellow. Not the slightest curl to her hair. Or lashes, for that matter. The black fringe only making her eyes look bigger. *An owl.*

She shouldn't frown so much. She must remember that.

Her fingers brushed over her cheeks and across her jaw…pale skin. The girls at Ardsmoore had envied her skin. Yes, smooth.

She tried out a smile, but her lips were stiff and it looked more like a grimace than an expression of mirth. She hated her smile.

Should she take down her hair? Was there time? No, that would have to wait.

Her hand had drifted to the high neck of her gown.

You must not frown.

She slipped one button free, then two and three buttons, enough to expose her throat. More pale skin and bones. A few more buttons and the tops of her breasts appeared. Then another few, until the nipples showed under her worn chemise. The old ribbon had a knot in it, no tantalizing bow to tempt traveling hands. Perhaps she would ask Lady Tippit for a replacement. Her ladyship had scads of ribbons squirreled away here and there.

She pulled at the neck until her left breast popped out.

The skin was very white here and her breast, though not overly large, was high and round. She supposed it was pretty. Her finger brushed the peaked nipple. A hiss escaped her mouth as the flesh drew into an even tighter bud. The woman in the mirror flushed, her mouth parted, her eyes half-closed. Heavens, this wanton could not be the same frowning owl of only moments before.

Would he see her this way? See her as beautiful?

The humming within her had not dissipated. At night her hands traveled over her body despite her brain's admonishments. Something vital was missing. She had a terrible feeling the elusive release she craved was something only he could provide. Hours in his company, three sleepless nights and mounting frustration had eroded her will to resist him.

He had not repeated their kiss. He teased and shouted orders, paced before his easel, and demanded more stories, but he never came near her.

She quickly buttoned herself up.

****

Lord Devlin was waiting, hands on his hips, paint brush clenched in a fist.

"You're late," he barked. "And flushed. Are you ill?"

Anne touched the line of buttons on her bodice; no, all done up. Could he tell what she had been doing? She had made sure her hair was tidy and thought her color had subsided before coming to him. Just one of his moods.

"Mrs. Nester had a difficult night. She is nearing her time. And she has had a letter from her husband."

"*Humph*, that would explain her frayed nerves. Archibald Nester, from the little I know, is an ambitious cur. No doubt having a wife who is mad is not helping his political aspirations. She pays for that, I'll warrant."

He had adjusted the screen. It now completely hid Ivo and his animals. She heard a snuffled snore.

"Ivo had a long night as well." His lordship smiled his pirate grin.

Unsure what to do, she crossed to her chair.

He whipped the cover off the painting. Thus far he had not let her see. And she was not a cheater. An artist should have his say in these matters. Besides, it was almost better not to look. To be faced with her image— how he saw her—would be perilous. Better to have a fantasy. At least for now.

"Is it progressing?" she said, just to fill the silence.

He snapped his brush against his thigh. "So eager to end our sessions?"

Lud, he was peevish today. She would not favor him with an answer. Instead she settled herself into position.

He worked in silence for a good long while. The only sound an occasional snore from behind the screen.

Expressions rolled over his beautiful face like passing weather. Always something new to see. Another fantasy wove its way into her thoughts as she imagined him catching her eye, flinging his brush away, and then rushing to pull a beautiful, new, robin's-egg-blue ribbon from her suddenly pristine silken chemise...

"This isn't working." He flung his brush but did not rush to her. Instead he began pacing.

Now used to his artistic tantrums, she took advantage of the break and rolled her neck imagining his lips there.

"Take your hair down."

Jerked out of her fantasy, she snapped to attention. "I will never get it back up properly."

"Good. Perhaps it will cover some of that sack of a dress you insist on wearing."

He knew very well she only owned two dresses and this was her best.

He paced like Mr. Harlow whilst in the throes of a passionate sermon. But instead of edifying words, the only sound came from his chain punctuating each step as it clanked against the stone floor.

Very well, she would let her hair down. Really, men could be children at times. She pulled the first pin and slid it into her pocket. By the second, he had stopped dead and stood watching her as if something crucial might be lost if he moved. It finally dawned on her thick brain in the middle of removing the third that she had his entire attention. Of course that knowledge made her fumble the fourth. As she scrambled to pick it up, her hair fell in a rush, the ends brushing the rug.

"I have been aching to see that since I knocked your bonnet off in the great hall the first day you came."

He was so close, nearly face to face with her. Taking the pin from her shaking fingers, his hands framed her face and then brushed over her head, searching for more pins. When he found them all, he released her hair. It fell heavy and swinging down her back and over her breasts.

Wishing to hide or to savor this moment, she closed

her eyes. He smelled of linseed oil and cloves. And something else that was deep and earthy, as if he had just sprung from the ground.

His hand brushed her skirt. She blinked. He dipped into her pocket and then dropped the pins. The bone of his knuckle hovered next to her thigh. Only one thinnish petticoat between them.

She would slip her hand in with his and then lift her mouth—

He jerked the delicious heat away and then yanked her to her feet.

"Stop looking at me that way, for God's sake. How am I to concentrate on anything?"

Stupid tears pricked at her eyes. So foolish, persisting in the belief that his smallest gesture might be one of seduction. Steeling herself she met his gaze.

His breath came fast, and the hand he had just withdrawn from her now clenched white with tension. Not just in anger, but something else as well.

She would find out what the something was. Insolent and stubborn, Mrs. Abbot had called her. Her knees still bore the scars from being made to kneel on sharp stones from morning prayers until tea. Lord Devlin would find out his Owl, as he called her, could be tenacious as a hawk when she truly wanted something.

"Sit down. Quickly."

She did so. But *not* quickly.

"Lie back in the chair. Yes… No! Don't touch your hair. Now drape yourself over the chair's arms. Yes, exactly, your head back like that. Now, lick your lips and look at me."

She loved these orders. He exuded power in giving them, but she had learnt a valuable lesson today.

She had a bit of power as well.

Waiting until his full attention was back on her, only then did she lick her lips and arch her back ever so slightly.

"Yes. All right." His Adams Apple bobbed in his neck. "Now you may resume your story. I think we left off yesterday just when the Troll-Lord was about to remove Cristabelle's wings. And don't skimp on the details. You know how I like seeing everything."

"My stories are no longer free." His gaze snapped to meet hers. "But I am prepared to trade you for the next installment." Flirting with disaster she was. Not only her position here at Ballencrieff, but something more dire, her heart. So be it. She would suffer the consequences of both.

His eyes were entirely fixed on her lips. His chain clanked against the bare floor. "A trade?" He flicked his paintbrush against his open palm. "It would appear, Miss Owl, you are learning the ways of the world. Very well, I am open to a fair trade. What would you have of me?"

She sat up straighter, struggling to maintain her new-found power. "A kiss."

His brush dropped to the floor.

Chapter Twelve

Hell and damnation, wasn't he supposed to be the one seducing her?

Little Miss Prim sat placid as a potted plant after firing her cannon shot directly at his guts.

Step up to the wicket, man, and take her.

But Anne Winton was not his usual model. If she was unchaste, he was the Pope. A virgin from her endearingly furrowed brows to her ugly cracked boots.

"Perhaps you are no longer desirous of a story?" Her low whisper sent another round at him. But this time the volley hit his heart.

"Oh, I am desirous, never you fear. But let a man get his feet under him first before you completely fell him with your feminine wiles." He bent to pick up his paintbrush, but really the action only served to give him a moment to gather himself. When he rose, she had also risen.

He stepped toward her. She answered with her own step forward.

Three feet separated him from those lips.

He licked his. She bit hers.

Ludicrous to be so nervous. In a last rush, he filled the space between them. Devil be damned, he could never play the saint.

****

She is just a little brown owl, he told himself again

and again. But each day he looked forward to her unraveling her hair along with her tale of the fairy-woman, Christobelle and her hapless Prince Gallant. Each day he could not wait to pick up his brushes attempting to capture just a shred of her magic. Each day he rewarded himself with a kiss—a benediction on their time together.

His eager Owl wanted more. More than his rather chaste kisses. Hell, he wanted more, but somehow he could not compromise her further as if his ardor would somehow blight her. His bloody chivalry did him no good—certainly gave his plan no help. But still he continued to push her away at the end of their sessions. She would frown and bite her lip. Then resigned, she'd take up her diary and furiously scribble pages of notes.

Scoundrel that he was, he tried to read them once but could not decipher her crammed writing.

He would go back to cleaning his brushes, or sketch, or sometimes play cards with Ivo. Anything to prolong their time together.

****

June, 30th (after 6th painting session.)

Anne paused over her private journal, the one she hid away. Not trusting the servants. Here she recorded her most secret thoughts, ideas and observations.

D is fractious today. He has finally stopped pacing and settled down to playing games of solitaire.

Painting seemed to go well enough, (though he asked again if I had another gown to wear.) His kiss was hurried today (still nothing beyond.) And he pushed me away as if I were some tormentor. Even my story did not please him. He took issue with Cristabelle. He did not like her new dilemma, to betray the king of the fairies.

Perhaps it brings up bad—

Her pen jumped and ink spattered as his fist banged the table they shared. She waited until all was again calm.

—memories for him. (Apparently he is not winning at solitaire.)

Ivo sits in his corner still trying to teach Blackie that Pocket is a friend and not dinner. I wish D had just a bit of Ivo's patience.

She closed her eyes and stretched her cramped fingers, then took up her pen again.

D continues to be plagued by blinding headaches. Perhaps they are his memories that press at his brain. I cannot—

"You asked me why I painted devils." A tower of cards stood before him, his eyes loomed just above the tallest tier.

Afraid if she so much as breathed, his structure would topple, she froze. How had he accomplished this so quickly? The man was either still and concentrated as a monk at prayers, or as aimless as a squirrel with a lost nut.

He flicked over the next card on the pile. The Knave of Hearts.

Doctor Hives' assertion that silence encouraged talk had proven true, so she lay her pen down and waited.

"The truth is I don't know why. I can't remember. One day I was fine—well, not precisely fine, but well enough—and the next…it was as if my brain had broken. Whole memories gone." He stared at the face card as if it might speak. "I woke up tied to a bed in my father's house."

The night the young girl died. Supposedly murdered

by Lord Devlin.

"They filled me full of drugs, bled me, purged me— all manner of things, trying to adjust my humors. It didn't help. Finally, I was too much of an embarrassment— Austin's marriage to negotiate and all that folderol. Evidently I needed a place to—rusticate, and my father kindly provided one. The duke is rife with good will for all his little charities and projects. Now, I am one of them. Here I have been for ten months, six days and." He looked out the window. "I know not how many hours."

He seemed to have lost his thread of thought.

"You have no recollection of what happened?" she nudged.

He blinked and then shook his head. "Austin has told me—apparently he was there that day—but I block it out every time. Hives says I am the one who must remember. But my memory is like this house of cards. Images stack up one on top of each other, building toward…something." He carefully set the Jack to form the roof on his growing tower. "And suddenly a devil slips in between the crevices and—" He connected his thumb with his middle finger and flicked. His tower came tumbling down.

"I cannot put a face to these demons." He swept the cards into a ragged stack. "And if I try to push back, to lock the door on their creeping poison, they only rush in faster."

Laying his palms open, she placed hers on top of his willing her calm to flow into him. "Lor—James, I would like to help you see your devils. I believe it is the only way through. The drugs only mask them, twisting them so you cannot recognize and conquer them. You are strong enough now. You will not break. I will not let

121

you."

His gaze searched hers. "What did you say?"

"I will not let you break."

"No, before."

"James?"

He nodded. "No one calls me that. Except that you did."

Yes, when he had kissed her. "Is it so wrong? You call me Anne."

"That is true." He gave her a half-smile.

"Then I will call you James."

"Yes, Anne. You will call me James." He smiled and squeezed her hands.

She nearly smiled back before remembering she did not like her smile. "If you cannot speak of these devils, then you must draw them. Like you drew on the walls of your room when I first came. You must draw your dreams."

He shook his head. "Anne, I am better now. I don't want to go back there. I don't want to go back to—before you."

A lovely and unexpected gift. She hugged his words to her. Tonight, when lying in her bed, they would warm her, but now she must push him to open—to not be safe.

"I have begun writing down Phoebe Nester's dreams. They are quite…shocking, but within them there is truth and healing. I believe she is better now, calmer and more ready to face her fears. She has allowed some light into those dark places. I have made headway with Lady Tippit as well, though to a lesser degree. She is more guarded."

"Do you know she is at Ballencrieff of her own free will?"

She nodded.

"She is truly barmy." He shook his head.

"A little, but she needs to feel safe. The world has damaged her."

"And what of your dreams, Anne Winton?" White teeth, lips hitched to one side as if he had a delicious secret. A smile he must know set her heart hammering. "Do I ever make an appearance?"

Her dreams. No one had ever asked her such a question. Ah, if he only knew the nights spent in her tiny room, on her tiny bed, with her huge fantasies.

"You are evading me." He looked at her as if he could see straight into her.

She had no defense against this jaded man.

His patience eroded her fortress of privacy; the moat she used to surround her draining away under his steady gaze. Silence was not so much a defense as habit; no need to speak when no one ever asked what she thought.

She brushed her fingertips against the feather of her pen and then, feeling self conscious, put her hands in her lap. "I dream of my parents. I only remember bits and pieces. And even those I am not sure if they are true facts or what I have made up over the years. When one is an orphan, one has the luxury of making one's parents into whatever one wishes them to be."

"*Hmmm.* Yes, I suppose that could be called an advantage. My early memories are all too real and not very pleasant." He picked up the deck of cards and executed a complicated shuffle. She imagined he must have done this hundreds of times in the outside world of his past. He would be breathtaking in his element, flashing his grin, holding court among a glittering crowd of admirers.

"But you still have not answered my question." There, that smile again. A rogue's smile.

Was she so transparent to him? "Yes, I dream of you. You are in a category all your own."

"A category? Remind me I should never look to you for flattery."

"Do you wish to hear, or do you wish to be flattered?" Perhaps if she talked of herself, he might open as well.

"No, Anne, I wish to hear. I could listen to you spouting Fordyce's Sermons and be happy. Hell, I've listened to half the bloody—and I do mean bloody—Old Testament just to hear your honey voice. But to find out your dreams, that I would love above all things. Well, most all things."

Outwardly she ignored his innuendo, but inside could not contain the hitch in her heart. "I believe I have begun to know more of my parents through my dreams."

And the nightmares, but she would not think of those now. Those memories would not serve him.

"They told you nothing of them at Ardsmoore?" He had picked up his crayon and began to sketch her.

"Only that they died. That they were sick. I could not save them."

Despite her will, old memories rose. A shovel unable to pierce the frozen ground. Her father, so heavy in death, his skin yellow and waxy. Covering his face with an old tattered quilt.

"Non, ma petite," Let him sleep. *"Mon ange,"* her *maman* had said, through a haze of delirium.

Her child's hands burned in sympathy, as she laid them upon her mother's breast, willing her to breathe, trying to take on some of the fever. *"Mon, ange."* My angel. *"Tu dois etre courageux."* You must be brave. "DeVere. You are a DeVere. You must take care of your father when I am gone."

In the end she'd curled around her *maman*, still desperate to give her some life even as her body turned as cold as stone.

Like jumbled pages in a book, beautiful pictures mixed with images of terrible suffering. With each page she turned, she never knew which picture would appear. Passing time made the pages easier to turn, but the story always ended the same. Always in death.

"I was lucky to be placed at a school instead of in the workhouse. The vicar, Mr. Harlow, intervened. I owe him a great deal." His hands had stilled over the half-finished drawing, his eyes full of questions. Ones she did not want to answer.

He traced the shape of the lips he had drawn. "You believe the answer to my demons lies in my dreams?"

"I do. Perhaps not all the answers, but dreams are a window into greater clarity." She waited. "Let us leave the devils at bay for the moment. Perhaps you can tell me why you paint?"

"Why I paint?"

She nodded. Obviously he had never asked himself this question.

"Why…" He made a few scribbles on his paper. "If I did not paint… I would dissolve. I would melt into these floorboards. My worth is in this crayon and paper. With it, I can be king of the world. Without it, I am nothing." He put his sketchbook down and carefully set the chalk on top. "I suppose that sounds like drivel coming from a marquess."

"No, not at all. You are privileged, but you are also

human. Wealth does not mean one is happy. Indeed, I believe my parents, poor as they were, were very happy. But perhaps that is my fantasy."

Time to reveal more of herself, to show him it was safe. "I suppose you have felt the heat in my hands."

He sat forward. "Yes. I have never experienced anything like it."

"I have always been this way for as long as I can remember. When I first came to Ardsmoore, I did not speak for a time. They nearly sent me away thinking me possessed. Perhaps I would have ended up here as a patient." A stray breeze ruffled the edge of his drawing. "Mr. Harlow stopped them. But no one would come near me, touch me. They called me The Witch."

The memory made her shift in her chair. "For nearly four years, I believed there was something horribly wrong with me. I often slept with the youngest girls who were more tolerant of me. But when the school's cow, Daffy got sick, it was winter and there was no milk. The children cried with hunger. I could not stand by and do nothing. So I snuck out one night. As I got closer to the barn, I could hear Daffy's piteous bellow, and my hands got very hot despite the bitter cold.

"I laid my palms on her. Her eyes opened, and she looked at me as if I were some angel." She would never forget Daffy's beautiful face, a patina of sheered brown velvet, worn thinner at her nose and softly blowing nostrils. "Her cries eased and then stopped. I seemed to be one with her for that time—one vibration."

He nodded. They had made that same vibration.

"I could not save my mother, but I believe I saved Daffy. It was then I knew this oddity of mine was not evil, but a gift. Eventually, I gained control over it and was no longer afraid."

"What of those horrible girls who had called you a witch?"

"Oh, they were not really so horrible, only easily led."

"What do you mean?"

Heavens, she did not want to delve into this, not now. But if she were asking him to face his terrible memories, she should reveal some of her own.

"Anne, are you well?"

She jerked her head up. "I did not tell you the full truth when you asked why I came to Ballencrieff. There was an incident that—caused me to lose my place."

"An incident?"

"A girl, Madge Barrow was her name. She came to Ardsmoore last autumn. Her family, though well-off, despaired of her and thought a strict school would be beneficial. In no time she had most of the older girls following her, believing her terrible lies. Only no one believed her tales of me. Madge could not stand this betrayal, for that was how she saw their devotion to me. She resurrected 'Witch Winton' and turned many of the students against me."

His fingers gripped the crayon until she thought it might snap.

Still, once begun, she must finish. "One afternoon Madge approached me. She smiled and said she wanted to show me a book. She had it under her mattress and insisted I come with her to see it. I was hesitant but thought perhaps if we could speak alone, I might begin to understand her.

"But once we got to the dormitory she began to scream. She tore a scarf from her neck, red marks ringed her throat. I rushed to her, thinking she was having some sort of seizure, but her smile made me freeze. The girl was almost laughing as she screamed. Then she put something into her mouth.

"When Mrs. Abbot and some of the other girls rushed in, white spittle foamed from between Madge's lips. Her smile had turned to sheer terror as she pointed at me, clutching her throat.

"The watch was called. Even the book she was to show me condemned me; it was a book on witchcraft. She insisted I gave it to her. Mr. Harlow somehow talked them out of taking me away. But I could no longer remain at Ardsmoore."

"But you would never—"

"No, I would never. But Madge Barrow was my devil, and just like your tower of cards, my world collapsed. So, Mr. Harlow sent me here to Ballencrieff."

Confession must be good for the soul. Hers felt lighter, as if she had shed a heavy cloak.

He reached for her hands touching them with a kind of reverence. Then he looked up into her eyes. "I am sorry. But I am certainly the luckier for your being placed here. With me."

She squeezed his hands. "Your devils are not within you either. You are merely a sensitive soul. An artist. Your creative passion has been squelched. Your freedom taken from you. You have been drugged and misused. These devils are only your poor mind trying to make sense of this terrible abuse."

She brushed her fingers down his long ones and then set the crayon in his hand. She opened his book to a blank page.

He pushed back from the table, his arms

outstretched, his head ducked between them. Slowly his fingers slipped off the table's edge until his body fell onto his thighs.

Still too soon. Too much for him. She drew the pad away, but his arm snaked up, his fingers biting into her wrist. He sat up, his face like a death mask.

They sat in silence connected not just by flesh but by something more, as if the very air between them pulsed with a tangible web tying them to each other. Finally he released her arm and gripped the crayon in his fist like a child. He hunched over the paper, his body heaving as if retching. She ached to comfort him but knew she should leave him be.

Heavy dark lines filled the page as if his hand was guided by some unseen force. He pushed the paper toward her and turned away as if he could not bear to look.

Angling the book to face her, a huge moon-like face crowded the entire page. Wedged into the corners were devils and serpents whose black tongues licked at the white, reaching for the deep empty pits which must be the eyes.

"It is a face," she suggested.

He nodded. But then shook his head.

"James, can you tell me more?"

He fumbled for a crayon—red—and, without even looking, drew a ragged line down the middle of the face. The crayon snapped. He looked up, pain and guilt filling his eyes.

In that one stroke, the face had become a pregnant belly. The murdered girl's white, bloated belly.

No, not murdered. He had been trying to save this child and her babe.

Just as he would never harm the cat, Penny, he had never meant to harm this girl.

If only she could tell him, give him back this memory. But she could not. He would have to find his salvation through his art.

Mere praise would be paltry in the face of his bravery. No words could suffice. She rose and walked to him. Taking his head between her hands, she touched his temples. Her fingers threaded into his hair. And then she pressed his forehead to her breast.

Chapter Thirteen

Over the next few days, layers of grime sloughed off with each new dream-drawing. Maybe one day he would understand them. But for now the drawing was enough.

The pages were tucked safely beneath the loose floorboard in the niche where Austin stashed his laudanum. Now the space was empty save for the drawings. Normally this fact would have had him twitching, but perhaps these drawings were another way to bring peace—a different kind of peace. Maybe one that might be lasting.

Now, back in the North Tower, Dev adjusted his stance and shut his mouth, suddenly aware he stood poised like an eager puppy. Hell, if he had a tail, it would be wagging furiously.

Today he and Anne would be entirely alone. Ivo had just left for the barn. The new piglets would occupy him for hours.

Anne's portrait was finished. It was his secret. Less than two weeks to complete, and his best yet. He was sure of it. Anne Winton glowed within the canvas, innocence mixed with hidden sensuality. A myriad of colors against pure white. This second painting would be quite different. Again, his secret. But he needed to do some research before beginning.

She arrived breathless, with apologies on her lips.

He wanted to stop them with his own, but his chain

would not reach that far. God, he hated the sound of that clank against the floor, the constant chafe around his ankle as he strained against the leather cuff. He pushed the anger down. He had no time for it. Not today.

"I have been thinking. I do not believe Cristabelle would treat Prince Gallant so shabbily." He spoke of her story rather than tell her how he had longed for her. "Gallant will be her lover, yes? Even though she has been walking in the human world she would not be tainted by the trolls. She does not have guile in her character."

She held her hands together in front of her, very like his old nanny, Mrs. Baxley. "I passed Ivo on my way here. He seemed very excited and could not spare me a moment." She raised her eyebrows. "Is this wise?"

"You are the owl. You must tell me." She could turn and leave. He would not stop her. Or blame her.

Her answer, the soft click of the door closing. She turned to face him.

Releasing his pent breath, he met her as far as his chain would go. Her mussed hair tickled his lips. To remedy the situation, he reached up and pulled out the pins. It had become a bit of a ritual. One by one they fell to the floor like petals from a daisy—she loves me, she loves me not...

She tried to catch them, but he was too quick. They would find them all. Later. He was getting fairly adept at getting the lush mass back up into some semblance of prim.

Like heavy silken ropes, her hair parted and flowed between his fingers. He grabbed a fist full, wrapping it around his hand, and tipped her head back.

He had to be careful of this magical owl with her

hidden colors, her golden touch and her wise, soulful eyes. She could snare him in a heartbeat without even batting her ridiculously long eyelashes. He had to keep his feet firmly on the ground.

"Unlock me."

Her eyes widened along with her mouth. "Will we be safe?"

Sweet Jesu, she was worried about them being safe from the staff, not that he might do her harm.

"I believe they are all preoccupied with Mr. Beauchamp's latest launch. Come now, I want to show you something, and I don't want to rush."

"Is it the portrait?"

"No, that you cannot see. This is something entirely different. A gift of sorts."

She looked around the room and then took a small chair and wedged it under the doorknob. Clever girl.

She flew back to him and arched up, so ready, bless her. "I don't remember ever receiving a gift before. Shall I close my eyes and hold out my hands?"

He brushed his lips over hers and to her ear. "Unlock me. Now."

She tried to capture his mouth.

"Ah, no, my lady, not so fast. First…" He jangled the keys at her waist. He could take them from her in a heartbeat, but he wanted her to do it. To set him free, if only for an hour or so.

She fumbled for the keys at her waist, unhooked the ring, and then dropped to his feet. He waited, eyes closed. The leather collar slid around his ankle, her fingers fluttered as she worked, and finally the *snick* of the lock as it opened.

Free.

Her skirts pooled around her like thick mud, her face upturned, a white lotus.

He hauled her right up against him. The music of her hit him full in the chest, and he spun her round and round. It turned into a waltz of sorts. Technically it was more of a gallop and she his rider, as he lifted her right off her feet. She melded into him as if they were one. And then he heard real music.

He stopped mid lurch. By the goddess Athena, his Owl was laughing.

Head thrown back, a waterfall of hair cascading down her back. She had a tiny gap between her two front teeth—he'd never really seen it before—and dimples.

His hands bracketed her face. "You are so beautiful, Miss Owl. But when you smile, you are the rarest of birds."

She ducked her head, to hide her glory, but he would not allow it. He whisked her up to cradle her in his arms. She felt like air and curled into him like a wing. Could she hear the thumping of his heart? Certainly she heard his hiss when her bottom brushed his cock.

He laid her gently on the small fainting couch and sat back on his heels.

Flushed cheeks and parted vermillion lips. Deep sable eyes with a ring of black plum and emerald flecked with gold. Indigo hair spilled exactly as he had pictured it over the chintz upholstery. The palest cream where her pulse jumped in her throat. So much color.

What other treasures lay beyond this shapeless sack she wore? The color changed from a washed out grayish charcoal to the dun brown of this gown, but the shape remained the same, always too large everywhere. What would she look like in perfectly tailored silks, her hair softened, a smile on her solemn face? He realized none of that really mattered. Well, except her smile. That would become her more than any fripperies.

Would her nipples be shell-pink or dusky-mauve? Large or small? Her maiden hair would be dark—no doubts there—but would she be smooth petaled or frilled? Salty or sweet?

Eventually he would uncover all her glorious secrets, but there would be no rushing.

Her ribs were like a harp. He could count them through the thin fabric of her woolen gown and her stays. He strummed over them and was rewarded with a musical sigh.

"Now, off with these boots." She sat up to help him. "No, you lie back or you will spoil it."

"Boots? But…you said… Your gift?"

"Mercenary little thing. I am afraid it is not that kind of gift. In fact, if I am totally honest, which I'm not often, it is really a gift for me as well. Do you still want it?"

She nodded, her eyes grave.

"Good. I am egotistical enough to want you to remember that I am the one to give you this. I am the first. Now, your part is to stop thinking and lie down."

She settled back, but only to her elbows. Very well. He would allow it. For now.

The boots came off to expose not so carefully mended stockings. Once again, she tried to rise, but his look stopped her. "Not much of a seamstress, are you? Good, I am happy to know you are not perfect. Perfection is highly overrated." His hands skated up her ankle, over her knee, and then on to the place where the cotton met her skin. "Easy, remember you must relax."

She lay back down.

Her skin was the softest peach. He found her garter and pulled. Her stocking sagged. He hooked his forefingers under and pulled downward, catching the garter along the way.

The stockings joined her boots.

He kissed the inside of her ankle just under the bone where the hollow fit his tongue so perfectly. He ignored her gasp. Really, he could spend several hours just on her feet. So tiny, yet so well-made. The smallest toe curling under the others, begging to be found.

"Oh!"

If he had not had a firm hold, he might have gotten kicked. He smiled and dipped his tongue into all four crevices, just to be fair.

Now up over the arch to her ankle, lips brushing the soft down on her calf to rest just below her knee. He pushed her leg up along with her drawers. Her skirts pooled higher, bunching in a heap onto her thighs.

She was back up on her elbows.

He pressed his mouth to the inside of her knee— another hollow for his tongue.

Her hands fisted in her skirts and a small c*hirp* escaped her.

"Are you well?" he teased.

Another faint *chirp*.

"I will take that as a yes."

He could smell her now. Salty and sweet. Apricots and sea.

His hands folded over hers, and he pushed her skirts up farther. She tried to sit up again, but it was easy to push her back. Limp as a wet feather.

He captured her other foot, splaying her open. He licked and nipped up her thighs, hopping from one to the other, keeping her off balance.

Another *chirp*, followed by a soft crooning. Her feet pushed against his palms and her bottom lifted just a fraction. Not so limp now. He gave her a reprieve until she settled again.

He could see her now all glistening pink with darker, frilled edges. An exotic flower dripping sweet nectar.

A bee. He was a bee. He went right for the honey.

"Ahhhh! Oh… I… Oh!"

****

Moments slid by while she recovered. He longed for his sketch pad to catch her utter languor, but that would mean moving. Finally she fluttered and then sat up, dragging her drab skirts back down over her glory. Now gathering her stockings and easing her feet into her boots.

He sat back on his heels, hoping to catch her gaze. Hoping to hear her gush and fall at his feet.

Damn it. He couldn't stand it.

"So? I do have my manly pride. How was it?" *How was I?*

She took what seemed forever to lace up her boots.

"Not as bad as all that, I hope?" He teased. But he could not help but begin to doubt his prowess her answer was so long in coming.

She straightened from her task. "It was a bit like an over-due sneeze," she said matter-of-factly.

He gawped. "A sneeze?"

"A very large sneeze," she amended and then added, "a sneeze of the entire body."

When he said nothing, she continued. "You are very—adept."

"Adept? Better and better. Your praise is

overwhelming."

She frowned. "Yes, that is the word. Overwhelming. I am overwhelmed," she said quietly, ducking her head.

He could only stare. She could not know the gift she had just given him by her simple words.

"I will recover though," she said, smoothing her skirts as if she were making a bed.

He laughed. "Yes, I daresay you will. We wouldn't want you to—catch cold now, would we?"

She rose, and then started for the door, slightly wobbly he noted with some satisfaction.

"I am known for my strong constitution. I never take sick." She paused, and then added, "Though I do keep a handkerchief in my pocket at all times."

And she left the room.

Ah, well, no sitting for a portrait this day.

****

Anne carefully closed the door. She'd told him she would recover, but she wouldn't. Her body would no doubt stop this beautiful humming soon. Her breasts would loosen and her nipples would not ache to be touched. The heavy, swollen feeling between her legs would subside, and she'd be able to walk without blushing. But the damage to her heart would not dissipate. Of that, she was sure.

He had laughed and teased her. She was so transparent to this jaded, knowing man; a dumb fly caught in his brilliantly constructed web of silvery seduction. Mrs. Abbot had constantly warned of these men, dredging up poor Florence Burbage who had succumbed to the temptation of the handsome blacksmith's boy and ended in ruin. But wasn't it worse to live without ever knowing such bliss?

Stripped to the bone—no, not bone—bones were cold and anonymous; he'd exposed her naked flesh, her folds and most secret places. Exposed her passion. Her love for him.

Yes, this physical love was definitely a weapon. She could see that now. And so she had fled. If he knew, he could slay her in a moment.

Chapter Fourteen

"The prodigal returns," Austin announced from the doorway. He made an elegant bow, then walked into the tower room as if he'd never left. Never been gone nearly five weeks.

"Don't you have that wrong, brother?" Dev spared him another glance. "I believe that role has always been mine." Never did he think he would be disappointed to see his brother, but Anne had only arrived and he had just persuaded Ivo to try a game of blind man's bluff.

Anne gathered together her notebooks. "I will leave you to visit with your brother, Lord Devlin. Good afternoon, Lord Austin." She made a curtsey.

Amazing how quickly his rare bird turned herself back into the owl, her head ducking, her wings folding in around her, becoming smaller.

Austin stepped aside to let her pass.

"We will see you at tea, Miss Winton?" Austin's question snared her at the door.

"I—yes, I believe so, your lordship." And she slipped out.

"An odd little thing, your Miss Winton."

"She is not mine."

"No? I got the impression she is quite smitten with you."

He did not want to discuss Anne with his brother.

Austin smiled and then turned to Ivo. "I see you

have acquired more friends."

Blackie was draped round the giant's neck, her tail flicked and she yawned. Ivo pulled the blindfold up, exposing one eye. His huge paw rose to stroke the cat. "Friend. Blackie."

"An excellent name for an excellent cat."

Ivo grinned. Never a pretty sight.

His brother settled into the chair Anne had just left. "How is the portrait coming?"

He shrugged. He did not want to discuss that, either.

"I must say I was surprised when Hives wrote to say you insisted on painting Anne Winton."

Austin was fishing. When would he figure out Dev was not in a biting mood?

"Well, she seems to have done you good. You are looking well, better than I have seen you in months."

"Clean and wholesome living."

"Stubble it, Dev. It's not fair to punish me with your frosty airs. While you have been languishing here with Miss Winton and your beloved paints, I have had to deal with Father, not to mention Margaret, who is still casting up her accounts every bloody morning. The doctor assured her it would ease after the first three months, the liar. Meanwhile, Macey—you remember the old steward at Malvern Grange—"

He didn't.

"—is warring with the new man I've hired. With all the clamor about taking the waters in Malvern village, they want to put a railroad through—never mind. Suffice to say, I have been run off my feet. Someone has to hold down the fort."

"How is Father?" Why did he continue to care?

Austin raised an eyebrow. "His heart is still a

problem."

"He has one?"

His brother ignored the jibe. "The doctor says he must not become too agitated. I have tried to keep the scandal sheets from him, but Tally, ever faithful, gets them despite my wishes."

The room felt suddenly stuffy. He yanked at his cravat. It was as if he should know some illusive set of rules but hadn't the foggiest notion of the game. He shifted in his chair.

"I had thought to keep them from you as well, but then rationalized, the devil you know, and all that."

Dev swiped his brow. What the devil was Austin yammering about?

The answer came soon enough when his brother pulled a sheaf of broadsheets from within his coat and laid them on the table.

Why would these papers make him want to throw up? He swallowed. He would not close his eyes. He would not let the face come. Not in front of his brother. Instead he made himself reach across the table and take the topmost sheet.

Lord Devil to Reveal his Angel?

It is rumored the M of D, who has been "rusticating" for several months due to an unfortunate episode, is producing a new masterpiece. His whereabouts and his subject are being kept very hush-hush, but apparently she is not his typical beauty, but a woman of scrupulous morals. There are even rumblings of a betrothal. A plain Miss for our illustrious marquess? We wait, agog with anticipation, to meet this

Puritanical Angel.

He reached for the next. And the next. These rags

had no imagination. He pushed them back across the table.

"Well, I must say, you took that better than I expected."

Fucking leeches.

"Don't ask me how it got out. I must own I did not keep Hives' latest report under lock and key, and I suppose anyone could have snooped about. Servants these days are not what they used to be. But I assure you, it will not happen again." Austin leaned back in his chair. "Though the leak may have come from your end, here at Ballencrieff." He neatened the corners of the broadsheets. "How well do you know your Miss Winton?"

Anne? The thought bit into him. He pushed it aside. Preposterous. He parried back. "Who is Phyllis Thornton?"

"Ah yes, that little wrinkle."

"I signed the betrothal contract, but I won't go through with it."

"We will cross that bridge when we come to it. In the meantime, continue to indulge Father in this. I have a plan. You must trust me." Austin stood. "By the by, do you know why Miss Winton is here?" His brother sounded almost taunting. "Consigned to a madhouse instead of teaching at Ardsmoore or some grand house?"

Dev's hackles rose.

"Seems there was an incident where a student nearly died. Poison. Apparently they found arsenic in Miss Winton's pocket." Austin seemed to look for some dramatic reaction. He was disappointed. "Anyway, the vicar, a Mr. Harlow, smoothed it all over, but Miss Winton was removed from her position post haste."

"Sorry, old boy, your gossip is old news. Miss Winton told me the whole sordid tale."

"Did she?"

He did not offer a reply.

"Right, I must meet with Hives. I can only stay a few days, but I will see you again at tea?" Austin fished into his pocket. He held up a vial. The glass caught the bit of sun that leaked in from the window. "Do you need this?"

His mouth suddenly felt huge and hollow. He ground his teeth and pressed his tongue against them and then turned away.

"Very well, if you don't—"

"Leave it."

Austin laid the vial on top of the papers and left the room.

Reaching out, his fingers closed over the familiar shape. A balm for his reading enjoyment. A friend.

No, not his friend. His enemy. The darkness and devils were fading. He was stronger now, able to look deeper into the black hole of his memory. But once exposed, would he be able to fill it?

Huge dark eyes flooded his mind, washing away his doubt. Anne…his balm?

But the image of her cramming her notebook with reports to Hives—no, no she would never. At least she would never willingly betray him. She could not. Besides, she knew nothing of this betrothal. Or did she? Would Hives betray him?

The thought kept niggling, making his head suddenly throb. Wasn't he willing to betray Anne if it came down to it? Ruin her to gain his freedom. Would she betray him for hers? He did not know any more. If only this hole in his memory would fill, he would not need to rely on anyone.

The floorboard came up easily. He shoved the vial into the hole, but the corner of one of his dream drawings caught his attention. He pulled it out. A snake writhed, its body covered in jewels.

Only a piece of jewelry. No, a piece of memory. He had given it to…

Nora stood, hands on her hips, her magnificent bosom thrust out.

Something flashed and slithered over her chest. He blinked, trying to make it stay still. Emeralds, amethysts, with ruby eyes—a snake. Ah, only her brooch. He smiled and stepped closer, his fingers opened, ready to cradle her breasts.

"She is increasing."

"What?" Dev's gaze moved from her tempting bosom to her face. Not good. He started backing toward the door.

"Lily, she's pregnant."

"Lily?"

"Lily, the girl you rescued from Cuddle Lane. Did you know? No, obviously not. You do not even know the child's name."

"Of course I know her bloody name—" God, his head felt like it had been struck by a cleaver.

"You, being a man, can only see what might give you ease and pleasure."

Since he'd brought the girl to Nora, she'd become more wet mother hen than delectable mistress.

"It had better not be yours, or I will shoot you where you stand."

He waved his hand dismissively. Nora Havermere knew better than to accuse him of tupping a girl of two and ten.

"Never mind me, I am distraught." She paced the floor. The snake at her breast seemed to come alive. Sodding Satan, he had to sit down before he passed out from watching her perambulations.

"Well, there is nothing for it," Nora stopped—thank God—and turned to face him. "As soon as Havermere dies, I shall simply adopt them both."

The girl—Lily—appeared at the top of the stairs, her green eyes accusing. A white diaphanous gown covered the slight swelling of her belly. The snake whipped his head toward the movement. Seeing the girl, it hissed, leaping off Nora's breast to strike at Lily. But she took no notice of the glittering reptile as it slithered, wrapping itself round and round her body as if it had no end.

Nora shouted at him to do something.

But he could not move. Lily's condemning eyes froze him where he stood. Despite the snake strangling her body, her belly grew and grew—

The drawing was a crumpled ball in his fist. But why?

Swiping the sweat from his brow, he spread the paper open on the floor. A coiled snake? Floating breasts? An endless stairway?

"Bah!" He pounded his fists against the floor. Gone. Not a shred of memory remained, only the ruined paper and his throbbing hands.

Useless. He was still a broken man.

Chapter Fifteen

"The moon is full, you know." Mr. Beauchamp hovered by the window of the drawing room. "And Mercury in retrograde. A perilous combination."

"Mr. Beauchamp, come and have your tea." The man's only response was to duck behind the curtain. With a long-held sigh, Anne put the cup of now tepid tea back on the table. Doctor Hives was in Edinburgh, presenting a paper on the efficacy of mesmerism. He would return on the morrow. And then, in a few short weeks, James would be leaving; going down to London to meet with his father, his year of recovery over. She would never see him again. Hoped to never see him again. That he would be free of Ballencrieff forever.

"Winton." Lady Tippit eyed herself in her small hand mirror. "I am thinking I will return to London and society after Phoebe delivers the babe. I have decided to take you with me, as my companion. Poppa is ill. He can't last much longer. I believe with you by my side I shall be well able to navigate the capricious waters of the *ton*. I will speak to Hives when he returns."

A fresh cup of hot tea nearly spilled onto the carpet. "Lady Tippit, I am sorry to hear your father is not well, and while I am flattered by your proposition, you know I cannot accept. I thank you though." She refilled the cup and added a splash of milk.

"What do you mean you cannot accept?" Her

ladyship slapped the mirror down. "Of course you will accept. Who would choose Ballencrieff over the delights of London?"

A smile tugged at her lips. "Well, you, for one, your ladyship," she said, placing the cup in Lady Tippit's waiting hand.

"Do not be impertinent, Winton. I am a mature woman who is firmly on the shelf. I know that now. I can no longer be hurt by fortune hunters and others… It is time to reemerge."

"Oh, Lady Tippit." Phoebe Nester had roused herself from the couch where she lay. "I would like that above all things. I cannot bear to think of you here at Ballencrieff when I am far away in Town. Miss Winton, you must come."

"No, she cannot be spared." Mr. Beauchamp had emerged from his cocoon of curtains, flapping his arms and shifting his feet. "Miss Winton has begun to record my visitations. It seems my star friends communicate with me through my dreams. But they are very clever and use symbols. Did I mention, Miss Winton, in my dream last night they spoke to me through the bed-pan?"

"Nonsense." Lady Tippit dismissed him, turning to Anne. "A woman does not dabble in the affairs of men, much less creatures from beyond. It is not seemly. You will be much better in Town with me. Heaven knows there are enough foreigners there to keep you occupied if you crave the bizarre. I shall tell Hives myself."

"Lady Tippit, I am very honored by your invitation, but I must decline. No doubt you will find a far more elegant companion in London, one who knows fashion, how to dress hair properly, and all the latest gossip." Assuredly, James—no, she must begin to think of him as

Lord Devlin again—would move in a very different circle of society than her ladyship, but Anne would not risk the possibility of him looking through her to smile at another woman. Much better to bury herself in the frigid Scottish Highlands where she might one day be of some use.

"Stubborn female. I want you, Winton. No one can soothe me as you do. I shall see—"

"Ohhhh!" Phoebe Nester sat up, clutching her belly. "No! Not now. You must not come now." She rocked back and forth, crooning to her swollen belly. "Please stay safe inside. Please stay."

Anne leapt to her feet and was by the lady's side in a moment.

"Mrs. Nester, you must breathe. Look at me, Mrs. Nester. Phoebe! Look at me." The woman did seem pale, her features pinched with pain. "Tell me what you are feeling." But the woman only shook her head.

"Lie back. Let me massage your shoulders. It is likely just a momentary pain and will pass soon."

"No." She pushed Anne's hands away. "It is the baby, I know. Oh, but it is too soon. They have been coming since last evening."

"Since last evening? Why did you not say, you silly woman?" Lady Tippit marched across the room to get a closer look at her friend.

"You see!" Mr. Beauchamp clapped his hands while hopping about. "I knew the stars were not agreeable. Oh, great Jupiter, she has leaked." He pointed to a darkened spot below Phoebe's waist. "Is that supposed to happen?"

Phoebe moaned.

"Do be quiet, Beauchamp. Do you imagine you are

helping matters?" Lady Tippit sat beside Phoebe. "Now there, my dear, Winton says all will be well. You know she never tells a falsehood."

"Mrs. Nester, it is likely your waters have broken" She laid her hand over Phoebe's heart. Fast, but not racing. "It is time. Your child is ready to come and meet its mother. This is as it should be."

Except it wasn't. Doctor Hives was away. Again. Most of the staff was at a memorial for Major Cummings who was finally to be laid to rest with a proper stone just outside the churchyard. There was no one.

A pillow served to mop up some of the wet.

Blood? This did not seem right. She hid the pillow beneath the couch and crossed to the bell pull. Esther was sure to be in the kitchen. Please God.

"But what of the Doctor? Hives is away." Beauchamp danced and flapped. "Doomed, she is. The stars are never wrong."

"Please, sir." She took his hands. He settled. "You must help us, Mr. Beauchamp. Do you know where the kitchens are?"

He nodded.

"You must go and get Mr. Macready or Esther." He nodded again. "You must tell them to get the midwife in the village and to bring Mrs. Coates back from the funeral and anyone else that might be of assistance to Mrs. Nester. Make haste, sir." The man nodded again but did not move. "Mr. Beauchamp, sometimes we must go against fate."

"Lord Devlin…" The man frowned.

Phoebe moaned again.

"No," Anne spoke slowly. "Not his lordship. You must go to the kitchen. It is below the conservatory.

Now."

Still he did not move.

Taking him by the hand, she towed him to the door and then opened it. "Go now. The servant's staircase is at the end of the hall in the niche. Do you see?" Another nod, with the addition of a flap. "Good. Then simply go down. If Macready is not about, Esther will know where to find him."

"Winton!" Lady Tippit shouted. "Something is wrong."

She shoved Beauchamp toward the stairway. "Go!"

Phoebe was curled into a ball, her face so pale.

"Lord Devlin—"

Good God, Beauchamp still lingered by the door.

"Lady Tippit." She took the older woman by the shoulders. "You must stay with Mrs. Nester while I fetch help."

Her ladyship looked her square in the eyes and nodded.

"Very good. I will only be a moment." She touched Phoebe's belly. "Mrs. Nester, I am going to get help. You must hold on and not push. Can you do that?"

Phoebe only rolled her eyes in pain. Anne ran to the door.

"Miss Winton!"

"Not now, Mr. Beauchamp, please release me. I must get help."

"But that is just it. I know who can help."

"Please—" He was stronger than he looked. She tried to wrench herself away.

"Lord Devlin. We must get his lordship. He will help."

What?

"His lordship. The marquess studied under the great Sir Barton Wainwright. Granted, Lord Devlin was chiefly interested in the human musculature, for his painting, but Wainwright thought of Devlin as a protégé." Beauchamp wrung his hands. "Oh, if only Sir Barton could see my creatures, how he would love to study—"

"Mr. Beauchamp. Please, is this true? You believe Lord Devlin can deliver Mrs. Nester's babe?"

"Why certainly. After all, it is only one small human child."

James? Could it be? But the girl had died.

Phoebe screamed.

It would have to be his lordship, there was no time.

With no light she had to feel her way along some of the narrow halls. On the last staircase, her boot heel snagged on her petticoat and she fell. Pain lanced her knee, and she felt blood run down her calf but she could not stop.

Finally, his door. Too many keys. Her hands shook so. She could not make the key fit. There!

"Jam—Lord Devlin—I"

Ivo was shaving him. His hands were chained to his chair. The reality of his day to day life always a shock.

"Anne."

She wanted to kiss him, to touch him, have him touch her as he had when he caused her to shatter and lose herself. If only they could go back in time.

But there was no time.

"Lord Devlin, you must come. You must come this instant. Mrs. Nester is having her baby."

"What?"

"Please, there is no one else. Ivo, unlock the

marquess. Now. Do you understand? You must"—she pointed to the keys at his waist—"Never mind, I will do it."

Blast! Which one? Devlin shook his head. "Anne, I cannot—"

"You must. Mr. Beauchamp said—he said you could do it." *Where was the bloody key?* "You must do this. You must." Tears blinded her. Meanwhile Ivo had found his key and opened the locks.

"Anne, please. You do not know… You cannot know…" He had turned white beneath his half-shaved face.

"There is no one else. You must save this baby. Phoebe Nester cannot lose another child." Dear God, what was she asking of him? What if in trying to save this child he regressed?

He swiped his face with a towel, revealing a hardened mask. "Beauchamp is wrong. I cannot do it." He flung the towel away.

"But what of your studies with Sir Barton Wainwright? Mr. Beauchamp said you had worked with him."

"Wainwright?" The mask cracked as he frowned and shook his head.

"Sir Barton. He is an anatomist? A surgeon, perhaps?"

Like clouds moving swiftly to reveal the sun, his face cleared. "Barton…my God, Bart. I had forgotten…"

"You see, you can do this. Come, we must hurry." She pulled him from the chair.

"No." He spun away. "No, I haven't—I don't know—"

"There is no one. I need you." She approached him

153

as if he were a wild animal ready to take flight. "Please, if you care for me at all, you will try. Please, James, please try. For me." His hands shook as she clasped them in hers. They were ice cold. She held them against her beating heart. "You are strong enough. You are strong now."

"I am strong…" he repeated.

She smiled and nodded. "Yes, I will be with you. We will do this together."

"Together?" He seemed so far away. She squeezed his hands against her breast. His eyes focused and he squeezed back. "I will come with you to see…the situation, but I…"

She had lost him again. "James—"

His gaze snapped back to her. Time hung like a droplet of water, gathering itself, pooling to drop…or not. He turned to Ivo. "Bring the razor."

She released her held breath.

"And find a sewing kit, Anne. We may need it. Have her waters broken?"

"No. I don't believe so." Should she mention the blood? "But she is bleeding."

He stopped mid stride. "Dear God. Is there no one else?"

His gaze was so vulnerable. Was she doing the right thing? Would he break under this terrible pressure? Please God, let them succeed. "No, there is no one."

****

Dev pried the floorboard open and closed his fingers around the vials Austin had left for him. The red wax seal would crack off so easily, the stopper ease out. He could tip the liquid into his mouth and slip into oblivion. So easy…

He shoved the vials into his waistband. "Very well, let us go before I regain my sanity."

As they made their way through the halls, he remembered what he would need—if he did this thing. "Lots of linen towels and boiling water. And salt. And whiskey. Find me whiskey and plenty of it."

Anne took his hands. "I must leave you for a moment to gather the things you need. Will you be well? Ivo is right here with you, and I will return in a few minutes."

Could he trust her? Would she set him up to fail? Someone screamed. That would be Nester. He found himself nodding as he sucked in air. Anne peeled off, disappearing into the dark hallway.

The screams got closer and closer until only a door separated him from his greatest fear.

He pushed it open.

What an ironic joke. Phoebe Nester sat in a pool of blood. The dark wet matched the couch's burgundy upholstery perfectly. The very same couch she had disappeared into weeks ago at tea. She was disappearing yet again, poor woman.

"No! Get him away!" Nester pushed back into the cushions. "Do not let him touch me. He will steal my baby and give it to his master."

Well, some things never change.

"Don't be delusional, Mrs. Nester," said Beauchamp. "The Devil doesn't snatch infants. He eats them."

The woman wailed.

Lady Tippit smacked her, hard. "Settle, Phoebe," her voice surprisingly calm. "Are you going to give any credence to Horace Beauchamp? A man who listens to bedpans? Lord Devlin has done this before. He knows what he is about. You must trust him, my dear."

Trust, indeed. The last time I ended up killing the poor girl.

The thought spread over his mind easy as butter on hot bread. He had not been able to remember for almost a year, and now it was right there before him…

Lily. Her name had been Lily.

Memories flooded in. He shook his head trying to focus them. Old images mixing with the here and now.

The door opened.

Nora? The face warped. *Was he back at Greene Street?*

This woman was surprisingly calm. "I have brought the brandy and plenty of linens. The tea water should still be hot."

Tea water? "I can't do it, Nora. I need Wainwright."

"Wainwright is not here. You can do this."

"No. It's too risky. I'm not capable."

But Nora wasn't listening to him. She was a blur of movement. He shook his head to focus, but it only made matters worse.

"Don't you see, I will kill her. I will kill Lily!"

A terrible moan came from somewhere nearby. He covered his ears and backed away.

Nora was beside him, pulling his hands away.

Hot? Why were her hands so hot? Her dark hair hung like straggling vines—no, that was wrong, Nora had red, curly hair… He shook his head. He had to make her understand.

"But it's too early," he reasoned. "I checked her only yesterday. She has at least seven or eight more weeks."

"It is time." Fiery hands squeezed his. "There are the

towels, hot water, and whiskey. What more do you need?"

Whiskey. Yes, he needed something to drink. His hand shaking, he grasped the bottle and took a long pull. Earth and sun and rich fruit filled his mouth. The taste of his past.

Nora tried to take the bottle from him. Must he do this? Could they not just leave Lily and retire to their room to make love? Or better yet sleep? Yes, he would dearly love to sleep.

Devils pulled and feinted, trying to distract him. He pushed them away. But they made him look.

Lilly lay writhing on a couch. An immature body, swollen with child. A girlish face with such old eyes—eyes full of pain and resignation. That face branded into his brain. Her twelve-year-old tits now the size of small tea cups. Bigger since he had last seen them. When he'd found her crouched in a doorway on Cuddle Lane. He'd given her his jacket then to cover herself. He must cover her again.

"No. You must save her and the child."

The devils howled in his throbbing brain.

"Nora, I can't. I can't do it."

"James."

He shook his head. Devils rattled. He shook harder, but they would not leave him.

"James. Look at me."

Hot touched his arms, his hands, and then his cheeks.

"I am Anne.

A face came into view.

"I am not Nora. I am Anne."

Anne? Not Nora. Liquid, soulful eyes, Anne. His

Owl. His beautiful Owl. Thank God. It had been a dream, a terrible waking dream. "Anne…" He tried to pull her to him, but a moan tore open the space between them. He could not look down.

She touched his hand. He held a bottle of whiskey. He could taste it on his tongue. She pried the neck from his fingers. "Nora is in the past. Lily is in the past. You can do this now. I am Anne, and this is Mrs. Phoebe Nester who needs you."

Another moan, the sound so piteous.

Not Nora.

He looked down. The memory still hung there. Lily pregnant. Nora pleading with him. The nightmare merged with reality. Anne. Now Anne. She needed him.

"James, you must help Phoebe Nester deliver her child."

He looked into Anne's beautiful eyes and then down at the body.

It was the same. The situation was exactly the same as it had been with Lily. Dear God, he couldn't do it again.

To jeopardize his freedom. If Phoebe Nester died, he would never get out of this hellhole. Never.

He pulled the vial of laudanum from the waist of his breeches. The red-brown liquid winked in the candle flame, teasing him. Sweet oblivion only a moment away.

His year was almost up. He was stronger. His memories were returning bit by bit. It would be madness to attempt this surgery.

But all his reasoning faded in the face of Anne Winton. Still so many questions between them, but she needed him. He must save this woman for Anne. And he must save Phoebe Nester and her babe for himself. He looked down again.

Not Lily.

This body was nothing like Lily.

He was not at Greene Street.

He was at Ballencrieff.

And Anne stood next to him, waiting for him to act.

Lily was dead. Her baby dead. He had a second chance.

"Ivo, Mr. Beauchamp, move her onto the table by the windows and open the curtains. Miss Winton, gather all the candles and get me that hot water.

"Mrs. Nester," he said as her pain-glazed eyes focused on his, "we both are loathe to do this, but it must be done. Do you understand?"

The woman whimpered but did not shake her head.

"I am going to touch you now. You must be still. Can you be still, Mrs. Nester?"

She nodded and then turned her head into Lady Tippit's bosom.

He pulled her skirts and petticoat up to her chest. She wore no stays. Her chemise ripped easily. Not Lily. Older, with a silver net of scars over the belly—her other pregnancies, and heavy, pear-shaped breasts.

Moving his hands over Nester's stomach, he pushed and prodded. About thirty-two to thirty-three weeks. Bloody Hell. As much as he wanted this child's bottom to be its head, he was sure the babe had not turned. Or dropped. "You say her waters have not broken?"

Anne looked to Lady Tippit.

"No. At least I don't believe so," her ladyship said her hand covering Nester's ear.

"She did not complain of any pain until just now?"

"Phoebe always complains of this and that, Devlin."

Lady Tippit stroked Nester's hair. "But apparently, she has been having pain since last evening."

He laid his ear against her belly. The room hushed. Yes, a faint beat. "Your baby is well, Mrs. Nester."

A collective sigh released within the room as if a near to bursting dam had opened a sluice.

Lily's face threatened to creep in and cover the older woman's.

He passed the vial of laudanum to Lady Tippit. "Here, get this down her and cover her face. If she is foolish enough to wake up, it will not be a pretty sight."

"Phoebe, drink up." Lady Tippit would have made a very fine general. Nester whimpered but took the drug.

He swallowed along with her. "Where is that whiskey?"

Anne thrust the bottle into his hand. He took a swig. Endless months since he'd felt that familiar fire in the back of his throat. Before he was tempted to take more, he poured the liquor over Nester's belly and then handed the whiskey to Ivo.

Shoving his hands into a small bowl of the hot water, he welcomed the burn. Anne ripped linen sheets and wound them into tidy bundles. She had carefully set all the sewing supplies on the tea tray, neat as any surgeon.

He settled between Nester's legs.

Shite. Nothing. Maybe a few centimeters, if that. He had to get the child out. It would be useless to try for a normal delivery. Only exhaust the mother for nothing. He stood and faced the mound of white belly.

"Lady Tippit, give her a bit more of the stuff."

The company looked at each other sensing the dire shift in circumstances.

The world wound down, hushed murmurs stuttered

and then stopped all together. Razor in hand, sweat rolled into his eyes. A cloth swiped his brow. Nora…

No, Anne. This was Anne.

"If any of you have any faith or sway with the Almighty, best to employ it now. Ivo, Beauchamp, hold her tightly. How do her eyes look, Lady Tippit?"

"The pupils are small as the head of a pin. I should say she is feeling no pain."

Right. No more prevaricating.

"Miss Winton, be ready with clean towels and the scissors and then tweezers when I call for them." Anne's earnest face was enough to spur him on. He would go through fire for this woman.

Holding the razor over the lamp flame, he then felt for the pubic bone, measured three fingers up, set the knife, and pressed.

A hiss, and the smell of burning flesh.

Someone went down with a *thunk*. Beauchamp. Good, the man was useless and had been standing in his light.

He glanced at Anne. She swallowed, clearly fascinated yet trying not to cast up her accounts. The body beneath his hands jerked.

"Keep her still, I say." His words rang in his head, a jarring melody to the bass of his heart.

Anne mopped his brow again.

"Press a clean cloth here." Her hand appeared. "That's it."

The drawing room became Barton Wainwright's operating theater. His hands steadied. He'd done this before, at least twice. Of course, those women had been cadavers. No blood to deal with. No life to lose. No loss of freedom in the balance.

"Now gently help me pull aside this fatty tissue. And now this bit—this is called the parietal peritoneum. Excellent. Here is the womb. Damn it, I need more light." Someone moved a lamp closer. "Now, when it's punctured, you must have a large cloth at the ready to mop up the fluids. Are you ready?"

"Yes."

He spared a glance up at her. She looked a bit green, but by God, she stood transfixed.

"Here we go." Fluid gushed, and Anne mopped. She tossed the sodden rag aside and pressed another to the opening.

"Now, let us see which end is up." He flexed his hand and then plunged it into the uterine cavity. He pushed farther, his wrist and forearm disappearing. "Can't turn the babe. Too much of a risk. Come on, you slippery fish…come on… There!" He felt an impossibly tiny foot. "I have it." Gently twisting, he eased the baby out by its feet.

No need to smack its bottom. Arms flailing, the tiny red-wrinkled face screwed itself up and wailed, clearly unhappy at the loss of her soft cocooned world. And who could blame her.

One refrain rang out over his pounding heart and the child's caterwauling, *Not Lily.* This woman was not Lily.

He laid the baby between Nester's legs. "Now, Miss Winton, cut a thread and tie it here." He pointed to a spot on the cord. She did so while he tied another bit a few inches beyond hers and then, using Nester's golden embroidery snips, he cut the cord. "I need a pot—anything."

Lady Tippit emptied a vase of flowers onto the poor rug and handed it to him. The placenta looked to be intact. He dumped it into the vase. The old carpet was soaked and covered with bloody footprints. It would finally have to be replaced. He laughed. Odd what comes to mind in times like this. He lifted the baby. "Take her and wrap her up tightly."

Anne reached out her arms.

"No, Anne, I need you."

Huge hands took the babe. In only a moment, Ivo began to croon, trying to sooth this newest soul.

"Ivo, rub her and make sure she is breathing. I want to know if she stops. Do you hear me?" *Not like Lily.*

"I hear…" The huge man breathed, never taking his awestruck gaze off the child.

"She is bleeding!" Anne reached for a new towel.

A gush of fresh blood. Too much blood.

It spurted between his fingers as he scrambled to find the source. Had he nicked an artery? "More light, damn it!"

But had he ten lanterns trained on Phoebe Nester's gaping stomach, he knew he could not see anything. Too much blood. His fingers slipped as he felt inside her womb. Even if he found the bleeder, he would never be able to tie a ligature without the proper tools. It could not end this way. More blood gushed. His fingers slipped again.

The baby mewled as if sensing her mother's peril.

"Devlin," Lady Tippit barked, "she is very pale. Do something!"

Dear God, Phoebe Nester was going to die.

He backed away.

His hands dripped with blood. He stumbled back. What a fool he was to attempt this. His life now over as surely as poor Phoebe Nester's.

"Lord Devlin—James, please. Use me. I can help."

Someone smacked him. He turned. Lady Tippit faced him. "Devlin, stop this nonsense and listen to Winton!"

Anne stood with her hands over Nester's gaping belly. Her gaze radiated calm in the face of this tragedy.

Yes, Anne. In his panic, he had forgotten Anne.

He stepped closer to her warmth.

"Tell me what to do," she said in her beautifully calm voice. "Together we will save Mistress Phoebe."

Yes, her powers of healing. Her heat.

"We must hurry."

Still he stood marveling at her calm.

"I need you to guide my hands. Will you do that for me?" Her gaze so earnest, so forgiving.

He could almost taste the iron of blood in his mouth. Before he lost nerve, he stepped up to the body and took Anne's hands in his. So hot. She believed in him. So he must believe in himself.

Together they delved back into the gaping wound. "Can you feel a rush of blood?" Her fingers fluttered against his, seeking. "Yes, just there. Do you have it?"

But her hands became like fire. He had to let them go.

She closed her eyes as if in prayer, her hands deep within Nester's womb. Her brow furrowed with an intensity he had never seen. Her breath came out in a hiss, as if she were burning inside.

"Anne?"

She shook her head.

Now her assistant, he mopped up the blood. He set the razor to the candle's flame. The metal sizzled as blood met fire.

But when he turned back the bleeding had stopped. Miraculously, cauterization was not needed.

"She is looking better," Lady Tippit said in hushed awe.

Anne's face relaxed into such serene beauty. She swayed.

He flung the razor aside and reached for her.

"No." Her eyes opened. "I am well. What is next?"

"Are you sure?" She nodded. He took her wrists and gently placed them in a bowl of water. Pink. Dark pink now. He took a needle from the tea tray and handed to her. "Can you manage to thread this?"

She nodded.

"It is silk, correct?"

"Yes, from Mrs. Nester's own embroidery kit." And she gave him the threaded needle.

"Very fitting. Now will you take these tweezers and pinch this tissue together? Yes, exactly. Very good."

Her hands brushed his. Still so hot. Again her brow furrowed, and she seemed to be concentrating all her will into her hands. He could imagine her willing the skin and organs to knit together. Willing his hands to be steady.

"There." He finished the last stitch. "It is lucky you are not the seamstress here, is it not Miss Winton?" He gave her a smile, thinking of her poorly mended stockings. "Mrs. Nester should be thankful as well, though I am sure I will never hear any praise from her lips."

Not Lily. Lily was gone, but this woman and her babe lived. He had done it. No, not him. They had saved them, him and Anne together.

"Now, a new cloth. Press this very firmly against the incision."

He lifted Phoebe Nester's eyelid. She moaned and twisted her head away. "Lady Tippit, you are a brick."

"I am no feather-headed ninny, Devlin. I know a tinker from a tailor when it comes down to it."

He moved to the babe swaddled in Ivo's hands. How tiny it looked. Pulling the cloth away, he examined her briefly. Small, yes, but a healthy pink and most unhappy to be uncovered. Finally, he knelt beside Mr. Beauchamp, who was just coming to. "Beauchamp, you have missed a celestial visitation. I believe the Almighty has come down to our poor realm to grant us a bit of grace.

"Grace." Phoebe Nester murmured. "Yes, she will be called Grace."

Lamp flames quivered as the door swung open. Macready and Esther stood in the doorway.

"What the bloody blazes—"

"By crikey, it's a baby." Esther gawped and looked at Dev as if she were not sure if he was God or the Devil.

"Mr. Macready." Lady Tippit's voice dripped every bit of her ten generations of breeding. "The marquess has safely delivered Mrs. Nester's babe. If you value your position, you will take yourself and this inferior gel off and do something useful. I for one could use some tea and a biscuit or two."

Grace added her outrage by wailing. Ivo wrapped his smallest finger in a bit of the swaddling cloth and stuck it in her mouth.

"I knew you was going to get up to something eventually." Macready looked slightly green. "Flaying open that cat was only the beginning. I just had to bide my time, didn't I?" The two stepped farther into the room.

Esther, her face screwed up, tried not to step in the blood. She was unsuccessful and screeched.

"Let's go, Lord Devil. You've done quite enough here this day." Macready strutted forward like a rooster through a brood of hens.

"No need for brutality, Macready." He raised his hands in surrender. "I am very happy to go into the cold pool. I could certainly do with a bath."

"Oh, you'll get more than a bath, your lordship, don't you worry."

Anne stepped between him and Macready.

"No, An—Miss Winton. You must remain with Mrs. Nester and Grace. I will be well enough, and my job is done. Besides, Macready and I are old friends."

Ivo looked mutinous.

"No, you must stay as well, Ivo. Make sure the babe stays pink and breathing." The giant seemed torn between his new charge and his old one. But when Grace mewled, he instantly fixed on her, weeks of bonding with Dev supplanted in a heartbeat. Well, he could not blame the man.

"Miss Winton, when Mrs. Nester is up to it, you must see if Grace will nurse. Give willow bark tea and the laudanum for pain when she needs it. And, she will. Also, you might apply honey to the incision for the first few days then let it open to the air."

Anne held her hands over Phoebe Nester's belly like a benediction, but her gaze never left his. Hundreds of words flowed between them. Not one of them spoken aloud. Yet he knew of her pride in him, her wonder, and her love…he thought he heard her love.

"Come now, none of your theatrics, your lordship."

Dev walked calmly up to Macready. By God he felt invincible. "I am yours, Mr. Macready. Do your worst."

Chapter Sixteen

"Sit down, Miss Winton."

How many times she had stood before Doctor Hives in this very room and not once he had offered her a seat. She sat.

"I have examined Mrs. Nester and baby Grace and they appear to be thriving. I believe you had a large role in saving Mrs. Nester's life. Indeed, I am told she would have perished without your assistance."

"Lord Devlin is the hero, sir. I acted as a nurse, as you say, assisting his lordship." She sat up straighter. "I hope you have removed him from Mr. Macready's— care. The marquess deserves praise, not punishment." Emboldened, she continued. "And I trust his actions will go a long way toward securing his release."

"Do you? Well, you have always been forthright with your opinions, but in this case, I agree, Miss Winton. Now everyone can move on."

"Pardon, sir?"

"What I mean to say is, I am confident his lordship will be leaving us in a few short weeks."

She only nodded, her throat too constricted to speak. This was what she had prayed for, but the death of her foolish dream of love left her feeling hollow and empty.

The doctor narrowed his eyes as if trying to determine if she were friend or foe. "Lady Tippit vowed that your hands literally stopped Phoebe Nester's hemorrhaging." He held up a staying hand when Anne would speak. "This was corroborated by Lord Devlin. I have been skeptical of your talents, but I believe it is time I felt this "gift" of yours for myself."

This was the opening she had been waiting for, a chance to demonstrate her worth.

"Now, Miss Winton." He touched the pads of his womanish fingers together, forming a steeple. "When you observe me, what do you see—or feel?'

"May I come closer?"

"Yes, of course." The doctor slid his chair back to afford her more space.

She rose and approached Hives. She closed her eyes and lifted her hands, palms facing him. Intense red light flared at the area around his brow and down to his ears. A greenish-gray color wrapped around the doctor's neck. Her hands became hot and the tingling started. After a few deep breaths, she opened her eyes.

Hives mouth hung open, his palms only a hairsbreadth from hers. "I can feel the heat without even touching your palms."

She brought her hands to his forehead and then his temples. Red ebbed away as a tide of cool green took over. She opened her eyes and stepped away.

Hives' face had relaxed to such a degree that his mouth was nearly swallowed by his cravat.

"Your headache is gone?"

The doctor only nodded.

"There is something wrong with your neck. A growth. Perhaps Derbyshire Neck."

Doctor Hives touched a fold in his cravat. "Yes. A large goiter."

"I believe you needn't worry. With proper care, it

should shrink. I would have seen if it was cancerous."

"Well, we must take the proper care then." The doctor rose. As they stood eye to eye, she sensed a palpable shift in their relationship. Perhaps even a glimmer of respect on his part.

"Miss Winton, Lady Tippit made some mention of leaving Ballencrieff soon and bringing you with her as a companion."

A painful lump in her throat rose. "I—excuse me." She swallowed. "I have told her that is not possible. I am committed to you and Ballencrieff."

"Good." Hives touched his neck again. "Well, I will leave you to your duties, Miss Winton."

She turned to leave, but the elation she ought to experience lay heavy in her gut.

****

Dev felt raw—newly cleansed. And the feeling had nothing to do with Macready nearly drowning him in a freezing pool or burning his body with purging cups and stinging lashes.

Only a scant few hours before, Hives had arrived putting a stop to ol' Mac's ministrations, still, the keeper had used his time very creatively. The man would be duly punished, Hives assured, but Dev would believe that when Mr. Beauchamp flew to the heavens.

Memories now spun out unfettered, filling the empty spaces in his brain, as if the recollection of Lily and her death had punctured a wall of his prison and now a surge of memories razed the remaining barriers to rubble.

Days lost to drink and too many indulgences. The thrill of winning Lord Harvey's matched pair and then racing them all the way to Richmond. Combing the

Spitalfields with Wainwright and persuading a young, grieving mother she had much better take their coin for her dead son's body than trusting Josh Hogan of the watch to bury the lad. Their blunt had put food on her table for her five surviving children, and saved him and Bart the trouble of having to fish the corpse out of the Thames where Hogan would have dumped it.

The rush of euphoria while sparing at the Clapton Boxing Club and felling a bruiser who'd been two stone heavier and had a left hook that came out of nowhere. Hell, he hadn't been able to hold a paintbrush for a week. But the pain had been nothing compared to bragging rights and seeing the utter surprise on the huge Irishman's mug.

Who had he been painting at that time? By God, he could remember in minute detail a three minute boxing bout, but could not put a face to the woman he'd been tupping. He did have a vague recollection of dodging a vase when he'd put her off while he healed, but beyond that—nothing.

There had been so many women. Still, it was no excuse. His paintings emerged clearly, but the names attached to the models remained a blur. All except Nora.

How was she faring? Last he saw her she was in shock and covered in Lily's blood. Austin had hauled her out of the house before the watch descended. Thank God.

The first time he'd seen her was at the Haymarket— he couldn't recall the play—so smitten he was by her astounding beauty. Havermere, the cruel bastard, delighted in displaying his young wife like some trophy for all to admire but never touch. Dev vowed he wouldn't touch, but he must paint her and had pursued her with a fiendish drive. Only later, when she revealed her utter despair and his words of comfort had not been enough, did they become lovers.

Poor Nora. He'd been too caught up in living to stop and see he was really dying. And he had nearly taken her down with him. If Nora had been found amongst the carnage…

Nora and Lily. They had been locked inside his mind all this time, revealing themselves in his nightmares. And now in his dream-drawings. All his lost memories were there, buried within those scribbled lines.

He had never truly loved Nora Havermere. He knew that now. And she deserved love. Was the old earl still alive? Sodding Satan, he hoped not.

Anne Winton… She deserved love as well. And so he must let her go. Let go of this remarkable woman who had faith in him. Who challenged him to be his best. Who believed in him when he couldn't. Who made him stronger and gave him hope. Well, he would survive without her. His sweet Owl now truly safe from his schemes.

Ivo, trudged silently behind, as they made their way back up to his cell. Once again, he faced the oaken door with its barred hatch, but it did not fill him with dread as it had in the past. This place would not be his end.

"You may go back to Grace, Ivo. I will not need you this evening."

The giant tentatively touched Dev's forehead as if he knew the change that had gone on inside, then he grinned, his eyes nearly disappearing as his heavy cheeks rose and bunched to almost meet an overhanging brow.

Not wanting to spoil the moment with words, he simply clasped Ivo's hand. They stood for a long while simply grinning at each other. Finally he squeezed the man's huge paw and then stepped inside.

An orange lay square in the middle of his throne chair, the only bright spot in his lifeless chamber.

Anne...she had remembered he'd longed for the taste of an orange.

"Goodnight, Lor-Dev."

"Oh, yes. Goodnight, Ivo," he murmured, never taking his eyes off the gift.

He barely registered the click of the lock's tumblers as they slid home.

Drawn to the fruit's simple beauty, he crossed the room. Raising it to his mouth, he brushed the cool, pebbled skin over his lips. The press of his fingernail into the flesh released a *spritz* of zest, tickling his nose. His mouth watered. Not so much for the orange, as for the giver.

Never one to savor a treat, he always gobbled it down in a trice, leaving him wanting more.

But this night, he would have control. He would fill the time with her gift. He would spin his own fairy story, each section of orange adding a new element. And when he finished, she would appear. Very like her fairy-heroine, Cristabelle.

Carefully separating each section, he lined them up along the arm of his chair.

Juice ran down his fingers. He lapped it up. Now the last piece, a pale crescent of sunset-orange glowing translucent in the fading light. He had made the fruit last far longer than he imagined, but alas, it was only a story. She had not appeared.

The last bite exploded in his mouth. He swallowed it down whole. The rind, a spiral of flesh he'd removed in one careful piece, would go next to him in his bed.

He stood. Time for sleep.

His body froze at the fumble of a key sounding in the lock. *Steady, old boy.* Probably just Ivo returning to perform some forgotten task. He turned.

His heart pounded and the rind dropped from his fingers.

"Anne—" He stepped toward her.

She did not meet his gaze, but took the chair Ivo sometimes used and wedged it underneath the doorknob. Testing its strength, she seemed satisfied, but still did not turn to him. Instead she laid her forehead against the door.

"Anne?" He took another step toward her.

Her candle's flame shuddered and nearly went out as she spun and rushed to him. He had the impression if he had not called her name when he did, she might have fled.

Her small body curled into him, her hair silk against his chin. She reached up, her fingers skating along his lips, as if she might taste with them. So shy, yet so brazen. Her breath fanned hot against his thumping heart.

He smiled and her fingers spanned his lips as they pulled wide. "I have eaten it all, but would you like a taste?" He nipped at her fingers. Capturing one, he touched the pad with his tongue. The light quivered with her soft gasp. He rescued the taper before she dropped it, and then brought his other hand to her cheek. She turned her face into it. She would smell and taste orange all over him—his fingers, lips, tongue.

"Yes," she whispered. Her tongue flicked out to lave the very center of his palm.

His breath hissed over his teeth as he sucked in air. Now he was the one who nearly let the light go out. He set the taper on the nearest surface, the arm of his chair, and then lifted her chin, dipping his tongue into her mouth. Like sliding home.

He tasted her, claiming his gift in a whole new way. His free hand threaded around her neck and into her hair. It came down as if a dam had broken. He would never get used to that heavy silk rushing down her back if he lived to be ninety.

For once she did not seem to care how many pins were lost. He wound her hair around his sticky fingers and looped it over his wrist as if he might bind her to him.

She pushed his shirt apart and pressed her lips to his heart.

Yes, eat it, eat it up and carry it inside you. Keep it safe for me.

Such a glutton he was. *Settle.* He could so easily scare her with his desperate need.

"And what of my gift?" she whispered against his chest. "What do you have for me?" she repeated, now meeting his gaze.

God, she was luminous.

"Ah, was the fruit just a first course?" he said smiling. My, his Owl learned fast. "You have a second in mind? Something I might provide?"

She nodded solemnly. Thick, perfectly straight eyelashes cast long shadows over her cheeks as they dipped. "I would like that." The shadows lifted as her gaze again found his. "I am very hungry."

Sweet Jesu, save him from sultry virgins.

His mouth opened wide over hers and she answered gamely. Teeth clashed, as their tongues jousted seeking to claim territory. Her hands left his neck and fluttered at her throat. She pulled back for air but he dove after her to capture her mouth once more.

So much for holding back. At this rate, he would have her on her back in about five seconds. Not what he wanted—well, not what should happen. He did not need to use Anne Winton. He was strong now. He would pass his father's test.

She fussed with the buttons that snaked up to just beneath the scar under her chin. He'd forgot, he wanted to ask her about that. A new story from his fairy owl.

When the hideous dun brown of the gown parted, only then did it dawn on him she was undressing.

"What are you doing?"

The lump in her pale long neck bobbed as she swallowed, but her hands never stilled, and her gaze remained steady, almost calm.

"Anne. Stop," he admonished, when he wanted nothing more than to push her hands away and do the job himself. "You must stop," an edge of panic now coloring his directive. "You do not know what you are doing."

"No, I admit I don't. But I am hoping you will teach me."

The thread-bare cotton of her chemise begged to be ripped open.

"My dear little Owl." He stepped away, hoping some distance and sarcasm would make her see her folly, but more importantly, give him respite. "Do not tempt me with your naïve wiles. You have no idea how hungry I am. I may just pounce on you."

"Yes, that is precisely what I wish."

Well, that pulled his ballocks a notch tighter.

"I would like for you to…pounce on me."

Sweet Jesu.

"You do not know what you are saying." He meant for his words to come out more forcefully, but they sounded hollow and breathless to his ears. "You are a maid."

"And that fact makes me unsuitable? Unattractive?"

"Unattractive?" He shook his head trying desperately to rein in the situation. "I do not make a practice of debauching virgins, Miss Winton." He blamed himself. He had set this in motion—her in motion. Needing her to be his. But they were going too far. He would not ruin her this way.

Besides, he'd never had a virgin. Always thought it likely not worth the effort. Dead wrong, that notion.

"Anne, if Hives could hear you, he would surely lock you up along with Tippit and Nester. You are not thinking." Please let these sobering words douse the fire building between them.

"No, you are right. I am not. But I do not want to think. Not tonight. I only want to feel. To feel you within me."

Oh, dear God, this virgin just heaped burning coals on the pyre. His blasted reason fizzled and writhed under her sultry gaze.

She had not stopped with the buttons while he scrambled to save them from the inferno. Her deft fingers had got down nearly to her waistline.

In a last ditch effort, he prayed to the Almighty for logical reason to swoop down and take her from him. If God was just, He would spare her.

Flick. Anne stared brazenly into his eyes. Apparently, the tiny buttons came free quite easily. *Flick, flick.*

He caught her hands.

"Don't stop me. I want you to—to do it all. I know what happens now. I want this."

Her hands escaped his and found the ridge of his penis.

"This, I want this."

For the love of—This green-girl would un-man him yet.

He took her hands firmly. "No. Anne. That, you cannot have." Apparently, God had it in for poor Anne Winton. "I will do the other. What I did before."

Her gown gaped open, all the secrets within, still hidden in shadows, but only a whisper away. He turned so his body no longer blocked the light. A bulky roll of petticoat obscured her waist. Never the seamstress, she must have to hike the fabric up so as not to trip. He'd always supposed her waist thickish, like a young girl's. Likely this dress was a castoff from a larger girl and never altered.

Either God had abandoned him, or somehow, in a moment of profound mercy, granted him this respite of joy. He would not squander such providence. Dipping his hands into the opening, he pushed aside the fabric until they spanned her true waistline. His fingers met easily and then splayed over the surprising roundness of her bum, also buried under the massive petticoat.

What other treasures did she have hidden beneath these dull feathers?

Her breasts, his wicked mind answered. He licked his lips. Just up over her ribs and he could test their fullness and weight.

Devilish girl, she knew the temptation and moved his hands upward, pushing herself forward to fill his open palms.

"Oh, Anne…you do not know…"

But the humming, which until now had been a low rumble in his core, now took over his entire body

She pressed into him harder and the miraculous vibration buzzed between them.

"But I do know. I do," she whispered. "You will leave me soon. Your father will see you are recovered and you will be free of Ballencrieff. Free of me."

"Anne, I will never—"

"Let me finish. You must go. I want you to go. You are meant to be in the limelight, among your own people. Among the beauty and color of the world. Beauty should be with beauty. Of this I am certain." She dipped her head to kiss his hands. "But I have grown selfish. You have made me selfish." Her gaze met his again. "I cannot allow you to leave without granting me this one wish. This gift."

Once he had her, could he ever let her go? Would his Owl survive in the often vicious world of the *haute ton?* A world of pretense where preserving rank was paramount. Bloody hell, why did he even want to go back? How could he ever think of subjecting her to such trite cruelty?

"James, will you give me this?"

Her liquid gaze poured into him, washing out the dregs of his resolve. "You must promise to tell me when to stop. And I will. It may kill me, but you must trust that I will stop. We will go slowly, Anne."

And if she did not speak up, he would have to have the ballocks to stop himself.

In answer she pulled her gown fully open and then dropped it to the floor.

****

Anne would have smiled at the look on his face if she weren't so nervous.

The petticoat was not as easy as her gown. A stubborn knot thoroughly spoiled the drama of the moment, giving him time to get his wits together to come to her. She pushed his hands away, but after a tenuous moment he took the knotted string between his long fingers and snapped it in two. The petticoat joined her dress.

"Anne…" He stepped away now, his gaze raking over her. "You are Venus emerging from your shell. A pocket Venus, but a goddess none the less."

She resisted the urge to cover herself. "Not your Owl?"

"Always. But you forget, a goddess can transform herself. You goddesses are very tricky for us mere mortals. You lure us into perilous waters. You make us do things we ought never do." He shook his head and backed away.

She did feel rather powerful just now. "Now you. I want to see you."

Again, he hesitated, but once more his decision fell her way. Shadows jumped on the walls as he kicked off his shoes. He opened his fall and pushed the waistband down. Hooking his thumbs in the fabric, he slid them down and then stepped out of his breeches and hose, and finally, his smalls.

His legs were long and beautiful, so different from hers. Muscled and dusted with dark curling hair. His shirt tented at his crotch.

"The shirt," her voice rasped. "I want the shirt off as well."

He hesitated and turned to the candle.

"No! I want the light. I want to see."

"Anne…"

"Very well, I will go first." She prayed her fingers would be steady enough to pull the new silken ribbon that wove through her old chemise. She had replaced it only this morning when she planned her seduction. The bow released with no effort, silk sliding against silk. The neckline gaped and hung from one shoulder.

Would he want her? Would she be beautiful enough?

James Drake, the Marquess of Devlin, would be the first to see her naked.

She gave a tiny shrug and the cotton slipped down her body.

Now utterly exposed, the urge to look down, to see what he saw felt enormous. She resisted. His mouth parted, his lungs laboring beneath the fine linen of his shirt. He stepped toward her.

"Wait. Not yet." She gestured for him to remove the last barrier.

"You may regret this. I am not so beautiful as yourself."

Silly man. He would be perfection. "I will be the judge of that."

He closed his eyes, crossed his arms over his body and grabbed handfuls of linen. Then in one quick movement, he wrenched it over his head.

Oh, my.

Indeed a weapon. A sword. A mighty broadsword polished and glistening, primed for battle. The place between her legs throbbed in answer to the unspoken battle cry. Her gaze rose to meet his eyes to tell him she was ready but she never got past his chest.

"I warned you." His voice was raw. He shifted the shirt, still in his hand, and began to put it back on.

"No!" Her feet tangled in her skirts. She stepped from them, kicking them away. Still several paces from him, she stopped. He would hate her tears. He flinched, seeing her grit her teeth. "No," she said again, meeting his wary eyes, desperate to make him understand it was not his scarred body that had made her grimace.

She crossed the last few steps separating them, took the shirt from him, and tossed it aside.

She touched the welt nearest his heart. He hissed and pulled back.

"Shhh. Please, James. Let me." She traced the red blotch. "You are my gift. My beautiful gift. So beautiful. You cannot take it away from me now." She bent her head to kiss the wound. Fine, soft hairs tickled her nose. The beat of his heart pulsed heavily against her kiss-swollen lips. She reached around his chest, her fingers skating over ridges of ruined flesh. She squeezed her eyelids shut willing the tears to stay locked away until she was alone back in the safety of her room. She would have plenty of time for grief. But later. Much later.

Now she only cared that she loved. She could not make him love her. One could not control love. It would be like trying to hold an ocean within your hands. This evening would be enough—would have to be enough. She would hold this memory to her breast, and her heart, like a bellows, would keep the flame alive over the long years ahead.

His arms wound around her and he nudged the top of her head with his chin. She raised her face to him.

Their tongues mingled desperately. A conversation of need and hot insistence calling to each other, filling the empty space, mocking his earlier resolve of going slow. There was no possibility of stopping. He must see that now.

Arms locking about his neck, her feet left the ground as she wove her legs around his hips. Her breasts crushed against his beating chest, her belly against his throbbing member. She dug her fingers into his hair, her tongue thrusting deep, wanting to be connected everywhere.

They were moving. Moving to his cot.

He lay her down. Dimly she registered the creak of the ropes as he covered her with his body.

"Tell me to stop, Anne." His words ground out next to her ear.

"No."

He bit her ear. "Say it. Say, stop."

She bit his neck in response, sucking the flesh between her teeth. She tasted salt.

"No," she repeated as she kissed where she had sucked, reining little soothing kisses along his collar bone to distract him. "No." The word felt deep and sultry in her mouth. He arched his neck giving her more room to explore. "No," she said again because is felt so good. Her hand slipped from his and dove between them to find his hot cock. "Yes."

In an instant, she found herself flipped, now on top of him, her hands firmly caught in his. Heavens, he was strong. And fast. She would remember that for next time. No, not next time. Only now. She only had now.

"I know we can do it this way as well." She had found Lady Tippit's naughty books with all the tantalizing possibilities. "You will not stop me. I am quite determined."

He smiled then. His wicked smile. The one she

could imagine him unleashing on so many women. How they must have clamored for this man. But they did not have him. He was hers now. At least for this night.

"Now." She squirmed against his hot velvet. "I want this inside me now."

"Ah, ah." He sucked in air, as if she hurt him. "You are an eager little thing. Better not to rush these things. We will go slow, Anne. You must trust me on this." His thumbs circled her nipples, light as breath.

"Hmm…ah!" She bit her lip trying to keep those sounds inside her, but his torture continued as he pinched her peaks and then pulled.

"Where have you been hiding these? They seem to be made to fit perfectly into my hands."

Her teeth ground. *Pinch them again.*

But of course he could not hear her.

"James, please, I like—I would like—"

His lips closed over her nipple and he…sucked.

"Oh. My. G—don't stop. Please don't stop."

Crash! The terrible sound penetrated their intimate nest.

"Stop!"

The voice was not hers. Could not be his either, his lips still fixed around her breast. The shout came from the door which stood open, the small chair now on its side. The candle flickered as a figure stepped into the light.

"Bloody blazes Dev, what have you done?"

Chapter Seventeen

"For Christ's sake, get off her!" Austin scooped up Anne's dress and petticoat, threw them at her, and then turned his back. "Get dressed."

Anne sat frozen on the bed, her clothes scattered around her.

Fucking Austin. Dev handed her the gown and held the petticoat up to cover her. She fumbled, trying to make her limbs work to find sleeves, her fingers to find tiny buttonholes. "Let me—" He reached to help her, but she pulled away. She ended up gathering the neckline of her gown and then holding her petticoat in front of her as she stumbled to the door.

"Anne." He took her arm, but she shook her head and would not meet his gaze.

His mouth throbbed with life from her kisses, his insides yawned open, bereft with the loss of her.

She yanked her hair, caught under the neck of her gown, and he winced as it snagged on buttons. His fingernails dug into his palms. She would not welcome his assistance.

"Anne. This is not the end."

"Miss Winton, now." Austin stood at the door. "You will leave now."

Bless her, she raised her chin, and like the goddess she was, she walked to the door and went through without a backward glance.

He shoved his feet into his breeches, yanked them up over his shrinking cock, and then buttoned his fall.

"Bloody fucking hell, Dev."

He winced at his brother's disgust.

"What the bloody—"

"Stubble it, Austin." He grabbed his shirt and threw it over his head. His skin, still too sensitive, chaffed against the homespun linen.

"Unfortunately, I can't. I am the vanguard. Father arrives tomorrow."

He froze mid button. "The duke is coming to Ballencrieff?"

"As you say." Austin shoved his fingers through his hair and gestured to the now closed door. "What of this woman?"

He shook his head and went to the door as if Anne might magically appear.

"Settle, Devlin. Settle." Austin took his arm. "It will be all right."

He yanked out of his brother's grasp.

"Here, take this." Austin pulled a vial out of his pocket.

Ah, the promise of blessed oblivion. His teeth ground, but he shook his head.

"Come, you are pale and shaking. You need to take the edge off. Don't worry. I'll make sure it's all right. She won't say anything. I'll make sure of it."

"Leave her be, Austin. She is nothing to worry about."

"But what are you—"

He wheeled on his brother. "What would you do if you were shut up like a bloody monk for months on end with only your hand as comfort? Leave it, I say. She was just a means to an end."

"Are you sure? Because—"

"She is nothing! Do not speak of her again."

Austin raised both hands in defeat and stepped away. "That is well, because Father is bringing the girl."

"What?" But he knew very well what, and who.

"Phyllis Thornton. Your betrothed. If you pass muster, the duke will see you married."

****

Anne had ducked into the first door she had come to, the small room next to his cell, where she might gather herself and restore her clothing and person to some reasonable state of decorum. As if she could ever return to the woman she had been before this night. Her dream, gone. All gone in the blink of an eye.

A faint arrow of light spilled through a small hole at eye level. Hives' spy hole. She turned, pressing her back to the wall.

"…just a means to an end." His voice. His words.

"She is nothing! Do not speak of her again."

The words lisped into the room like a snake, coiling around her, strangling her breath, but she could not move away. She had dallied with the devil, and she must take her poison.

Phyllis Thornton? She stuck her fist in her mouth to stop her cry. *Betrothed?* All this time he was betrothed?

Her sob lay wedged in her aching throat. She could not breathe.

Decorum be damned. She thrust herself from the wall, wadded her petticoat over her gaping bodice, and then pushed open the door. Tears blinded her as she ran down the dark hall, thinking only of the safety of her tiny room.

Nothing. She was nothing. Only a means to an end.

Chapter Eighteen

The hearing was to be held in what used to be the castle's library, though from what Dev remembered, the shelves held no books. Row after row of emptiness. A fitting image for this pile of stones.

Austin bobbed and weaved, fussing with the fall of Dev's cravat and some imagined lint on his coat.

"Are you sure you can trust Anne Winton to keep your—dalliance to herself? I never thought *she* would be a temptation. But I should have known, with your history—and what if Phoebe Nester had died? Or her child? It was a stupid risk, Dev. Why would you ever go back down that terrible road?"

Bucking, he threw off his brother's hands. His old clothes chaffed his skin. Austin had brought them from London. The cobalt blue coat made by Poole himself, with its lining of charcoal gray silk, tailored to the barest millimeter—it had once fit his body like a second skin. Now it hung from his shoulders, making him look like a tricked out scarecrow.

"Here, look at me." Austin took hold of his arms and forcibly turned him. "You must try to stop shaking your head. You need to get through this, and then we will stop the drugs. I'll get you all the help you need."

"Sod off, little brother." His tongue still felt thick in his mouth.

"By God, Devlin, you may curse me to Hell, but you

190

need me."

This morning the good doctor had suggested a dose of laudanum "to quiet the marquess' humors." Dev had thrown the first vial against the wall, but then the suggestion became a mandate. Finally, when Ivo had refused to participate, dear Ned Macready was brought in. Resistance no longer an option. It seemed everyone was bent on having him dulled down to nothing.

They had shoved him into his strait-waistcoat, propped him up in his throne chair, and employed all nine shackles to keep him fixed in place. Then the laudanum.

And something else. Macready, or someone, had slipped in another drug. A new taste on his tongue, something he couldn't identify. And the devils, which had been gone for weeks, came back with a vengeance. The leather band at forehead and temples bound him to the back of the chair where the fiends ripped into his brain, trying to obscure his thoughts.

The powers that be had left him there all morning. Then, about an hour ago Austin had come back with Ivo who'd shaved him, trimmed his hair, and then they both helped him into his suit.

Still slightly fuzzy, but the devils were, for the moment, blessedly banished. Well, all except Austin who paced and tore at his hair like some Greek tragedian going on about "for your own good" and "having no more sense than a flea."

How was Anne faring? He would right that ship later when he could breathe free. Hopefully she would listen.

Thank heavens he would not have to use her—tying her to him in a sham marriage. Good thing because other than her scuttled seduction of two evenings ago, they had only indulged in a few kisses. Well, and he had made her come, but she was so bloody tempting, and he was only human. If Austin had not burst in to interrupt them—well, he hoped he would have stayed true to his resolve not to take her virginity. He was a selfish bastard, but not without some scruples.

Once he passed this test, he would get out of this ridiculous betrothal. The portrait of Anne was his best work ever, his memories had returned, and he had saved Phoebe Nester and her child. He would be free without dragging his Owl into his coil.

He shook his head again, just for good measure and nodded to Austin. He could do this.

The huge library doors swung open. "Lord Devlin and Lord Austin," a footman, dressed in the Malvern livery, intoned.

The rest of his father's retinue dotted the room, standing guard in their old-fashioned frock coats and powdered wigs. Always one for pomp and propriety, his sire.

Tally, his father's ever-faithful secretary, stood next to an old man in a bath chair. By God, his father…

He bowed briefly. "Sir."

The gray, lined face flinched. His sire obviously shocked by his son's appearance, but Dev could say the same of the duke. Much diminished. Certainly a contrast to the ranting, beet-red-faced man who'd had his son carted out of Malvern House nearly a year ago.

A runnel of sweat coursed down Dev's temple to be swallowed by his cravat.

The old man gestured to Tally, who solicitously pushed the wheeled chair up a few feet. The bulldog of a secretary now reduced to more of a nursemaid than a shrewd man of business.

Doctor Hives sat stiffly on a very uncomfortable looking bench, expression number one fixed in place. Ivo, dressed in some footman's castoffs, which were much too small, shifted from foot to foot. His huge hands, encased in gloves, hung from his body as if they were foreign objects. Poor man, a footman's livery provided no pockets where a beloved mouse might be stowed.

A man Dev did not recognize sat with a young woman next to the windows. No doubt this poor girl was Miss Phyllis Thornton, who would be shackled to him for the rest of her natural days if all went according to the duke's plan. She ducked her head after gawping at him like some bovine. He had the urge to moo at her.

What a cast of characters.

"Good morning, Lord Devlin, Lord Austin." A be-wigged man rose from his seat behind a large desk in the center of the room. "I am Mr. Lowery." He made a bow. "I am from the Lunacy Commission, but His Grace has asked that I be here in an unofficial capacity. I will be asking you a few questions, Lord Devlin. Your father wishes to ascertain if you are ready to take up the reins of the duchy should the need arise. Do you understand?" Lowery chirped as if they were all gathered for a picnic instead of determining his fate.

He considered a rude gesture, but only nodded.

"Will you take a seat, your lordship?"

The bookshelves seemed to move in closer. Austin glanced at him with a tight smile. He pulled the chair Lowery indicated back a few inches and sat.

"Very good. There are several tests which the Lunacy Commission uses to determine a sound mind.

Your sire, the duke, will hear your answers to these questions. We have already heard and read much of the testimony of various people who have surrounded you these past months. I am glad to say we are generally heartened by their accounts." The man spoke to him as if he were a babe in leading strings.

The quill-driver seated next to Mr. Lowery *skritched* on a paper.

"Can you state your full name?"

"Yes."

They waited.

Mr. Lowery coughed and looked to the duke who only raised an eyebrow. "Pardon. *Will* you state your full name?"

"Certainly. James Henry Nathanial Drake, Marquess of Devlin."

Lowery nodded and smiled as if Dev had divined some here-to-fore unknown proof. The underling made a note in his book. Lowery pushed a stack of coins toward Dev. "Will you count this? Please? Take your time, there is no rush."

Stacks of silver and gold. "Twenty-one pounds, seven shillings and three pence."

Lowery sat up straighter. The clerk took the money and tallied it up, just to be sure and then nodded to Lowery.

"Enough for a good poke at Madame Floras and dinner, if you've a mind to splurge." He grinned. "Well, perhaps you may have to leave off the good champagne. What do you think, Austin? I have been rusticating so long, I can't be sure if inflation has driven up the price of a good whore."

Someone let out a small gasp. Miss Thornton. Her

father hushed her.

The duke frowned. Dev had forgotten, the man had absolutely no sense of humor.

Lowery cleared his throat. "Make a note Lord Devlin computed correctly." The poor man seemed a bit less jubilant now. Thank God. "Do you recognize your father in this room?"

Dev nodded.

"Will you point him out?"

He indicated his sire.

"Excellent." Lowery nodded his head fiercely and the scribbler made a note. The commissioner seemed as proud of Dev's small triumph as if he'd hung the moon. "Now, will you take the candle from Mr. Turner?" The man next to Lowery set down his pen and rose. "And will you now light it?"

Like some sort of trained monkey, he obliged, and then blew out the twist of paper.

Mr. Lowery smiled and bobbed his head, pleased as punch. Dev had the absurd urge to turn a cartwheel.

"There has been no instance of madness in the Malvern line since the creation of the title in 1639. Nor in the Hammel line, either." Lowery shifted papers, stacking them into a neat square.

His freedom drew nearer and nearer. His devils could go to Hell. He swallowed and made himself breathe.

"Your Grace, would you care to question the marquess?"

"Austin said something about a painting?" It was the first thing his father had said. Memories of admonishments and shame rushed Dev's head sinking like cold fog to surround his heart.

Mr. Turner whispered in Lowery's ear. "Oh, yes, the picture."

Austin stepped forward. "Sir, I do not think we need bother with the painting. Let it suffice that my brother has fulfilled all the requirements you deem necessary."

"Nonsense, Austin," their father said. "I have heard you nattering about this painting for months now. Even the papers have made a to-do over Devlin's bit of artistry. We will see what has been occupying my son's time."

Something was off. Why would Austin not want the painting shown? It was his best work yet.

"I have no objection, Father," he said with more bravado than he felt.

"Excellent, then let us see this masterpiece."

Two bagwigs left through a side door and returned bearing an easel and the painting shrouded under a linen cover. They set up the stand and placed the picture upon it.

Lowery himself rose and, in a flourish, whipped the cover from the painting.

"What the—" Dev jerked his gaze from the painting to his brother. "You bastard!"

****

The knock on her door startled Anne out of a fitful sleep. Up much of the night with baby Grace and Phoebe, she had just closed her eyes to rest.

"Miss Anne Winton?" A footman stood at attention outside her door. "You are summoned before the duke."

The Duke? Dear God, had Lord Austin betrayed them? He couldn't. It would do irreparable harm to his brother to have their tryst brought to the fore.

One of the duke's minions had already interviewed

her. Everything written neatly in a ledger. Full name, age, education, duties, perceptions of the patient, etc. etc.

What more could she possibly have to say?

As they progressed through the halls and various rooms, Anne thought of only the most mundane of things: the man's heavy footsteps with their distinctive click of his heels, while hers were more of a whisper against the stone floor. A pin slipping from her hair. She did not move to fix it, only noted its progress with each step she took. Would it fall in another three steps, or would it take perhaps seven?

Two. Only two steps. She felt her hair against her collarbone just as she heard the ping on the floor. The urge to rip every pin out and tear at the wanton hair that refused to bend to her will made her grip her hands into fists. They stopped at a large set of doors. The castle's library.

The man paused, knocked, and then he opened one of the doors, gesturing for her to go through. "Miss Anne Winton, Your Grace."

Lord Devlin—she would not think of him as James—stood across the room, directly in front of her. No, stood was not the right word, he was being held up by two burly men, one wigless, the other's ridiculously askew. She wanted to laugh, but shockingly a sob broke through instead. Mortified, she quickly turned away and covered her mouth.

A plain girl, who could only be Phyllis Thornton, sat with a man who must be her father. Again, Anne had to stifle a laugh-sob. This woman was nothing like the bride she had imagined for Jam—for his lordship. Though the girl was seated, she seemed very tall and rather plump, yet she cowered next to her father, sniffing into a well-used handkerchief. She looked terrified.

"Miss Anne Winton?"

Her gaze snapped toward the voice calling her name.

"You are Anne Winton?" The man behind a large desk spoke. She nodded. He introduced himself as Mr. Lowery.

An old man, the duke, sat in a bath chair, his face so like his eldest son's. Lord Austin stood at his side. Blood dotted a handkerchief he held to his nose and one eye was swollen shut. She looked back to Lord Devlin.

He shook his head as if he were trying to dislodge something.

Her hands tingled. Had these men hurt him?

"Anne—I—" He shook his head again. "Miss Winton, you must tell them—this is wrong!"

Confused she followed his gaze.

How had she missed it? The painting stood in the center of the room.

She stepped back, nearly tripping on her petticoat. No, it couldn't be. Every face focused on her as if she might provide an answer.

"For God's sake, get her a chair before she swoons," someone said.

Another someone pressed her into a hard chair. The edges cut into her fingers as she gripped the seat. She embraced the pain, hoping it might root her to reality.

"Miss Winton, I gather you are shocked by what you see?" Mr. Lowery rose.

She could not make any answer.

"Miss Winton." The man now stood directly in front of her and gestured to the painting. "Is this the— portrait—Lord Devlin made of you?"

She shook her head not knowing where to look.

"Are you saying this is not Lord Devlin's work?"

Again, she shook her head. "I—"

"Surely this is a simple answer, Miss Winton."

Devlin jerked forward. "Tell them! You must tell them, Anne!"

Oh, dear God, what to say?

He strained against his keepers, his face so imploring.

"He—that is, the marquess…" She squeezed her eyes shut. *How could this be?* "I never saw it," she whispered.

She heard a collective gasp.

"What?" Someone rapped for order. "Will you repeat yourself?"

"I—I have never seen the portrait."

"Miss Winton, am I to believe in all the days you were a subject for the marquess you never once saw the painting?" Mr. Lowery's voice was incredulous.

She could only shake her head. No breath left to speak.

"Never? Not once?"

Again, she shook her head.

He charged back to the desk and found a paper. "In the forty-three days you never once peeked out of curiosity?"

"He told me—not to look." If only she had more breath she could make her words strong and true, but there was no air. Gathering her courage, she made herself look at James. Dear God, once again his house of cards had just collapsed. Only this time she was the devil that had razed his fragile world.

Oh, what had she done?

"I see. You there." Mr. Lowery gestured to a young

footman who stood behind the painting. "Take it away. I think we have seen enough."

The boy shot forward, no doubt eager to see what had everyone so up in arms. He stopped dead, utterly confused, and looked at the assembled company.

"But there's nothing here."

Chapter Nineteen

Horrified by his outburst, the boy jerked the painting off the easel and scuttled out of the room.

Something was terribly wrong. Anne had seen the drawings he'd made. He had worked so diligently. So intensely. But all this canvas showed was a wall, a wall with some color, but ostensibly a blank canvas with not even the shadow of a figure. Very like his earlier attempt to paint Lord Austin.

"I will be heard!" Mr. Macready burst into the room shaking off two large footmen. "Pardon, Your Grace, but I have something I think you should see."

"Who is this man?" The duke attempted to rise.

The keeper could only be here to stir the pot of trouble.

"Mr. Macready, you are interrupting. This can be dealt with later." Doctor Hives moved faster than she had ever seen. He gestured to a footman and Ivo.

"Oh, I think the duke will want to see these, Doctor." Macready once again jerked out of the footmen's arms and strode forward.

"A maid found these in the marquess' room under a floorboard and gave them to me. I think they may be very telling." He held out a roll of drawings and a packet of what looked to be letters.

Doctor Hives stepped forward, clearly unsettled. "Mr. Macready—"

He ignored the doctor. "Your worship, I can hold my tongue no longer. Evil will out in the end."

"Once again, I ask, who is this man?" The old duke made his way with the help of his servant to stand before Macready.

"Your Grace, he is a keeper here." Doctor Hives bowed his head solicitously.

"Do you believe these may be pertinent, Hives?" the duke said.

The doctor's lower lip worried the edge of his cravat. "Mr. Macready is no longer—"

"Got too close to the truth, I did, so he got rid of me."

The duke gestured to lay the drawings on the table. "I will see them."

Mr. Lowery's assistant cleared a space while the inquisitor untied the ribbon securing the scroll. The duke and others gathered around.

Anne squeezed her eyes shut. She could not look.

But for the *shush* of paper, silence descended on the room.

His dreams. He had trusted her with his dreams. The terrible pictures that came out of his head. She had seen dozens of them. And now they were on display for all. Once again, she had betrayed him.

No longer able to stand the silence, she opened her eyes only to find all their gazes fixed on her. She rose and approached the table.

Not his nightmares.

A woman. A nude woman. And beautiful.

"Doctor Hives?" The old duke leaned heavily on the desk, his manservant now supporting him. "What is this?" he said to the doctor, though his piercing gaze never left her face.

Did they think this woman was she? Anyone could see this lady, so languidly laid out upon the couch, so sure of her beauty, so confident in her power to command love, could not be plain Anne Winton. She looked to James, sure he would refute their assumption. But he didn't. His gaze only held an apology.

Was this how he saw her?

A tiny tingle of delight crept over her skin, but was quickly doused in the face of everyone's condemnation. Their disgust cracked over her, soaking her with contempt. They did not see the beauty. These people only saw something shameful. She hugged herself, feeling as if she were truly naked.

"Doctor, you will answer me." The duke flicked at the drawings as if they were too rank to touch.

"Your Grace. I am as shocked as you. She will be dismissed at once." Doctor Hives, who had drawn near, tried to gather up the rest of the drawings.

Dismissed? Of course she would be. But she was too numb to think of her future.

The duke stayed Doctor Hives' hand. "We will see them all." The second set of drawings was unrolled.

The nightmares. She shuddered, not from the gruesome images but from the terrible exposure of his mind purging itself of its poisons. Private drawings she had encouraged him to make. Crudely drawn, madmen and devils filled page after page. Blood dripped and insides festered, riddled with worms. Demon-faced rats feasted on hearts and coiled bowels. Angels plunged into the fires of Hell where they became grotesque creatures. A baby torn from its mother's womb. This time she had no courage to meet James's eyes.

The duke gestured for his bath chair. He sat with the help of his servant. The old man gazed down at his hands lying open in his lap. No one spoke.

Finally his hands fisted. "Is he mad?" The old man stared up at his son like he was some unknown creature. "Could a sane man produce this filth?"

She made herself look. James stood utterly still, as if he had a noose around his neck.

"We—" Hives' gaze seared into her and then he turned back to the duke. "I have been doing some new work with Lord Devlin, Your Grace. Ah—it is largely experimental, but much like my theories on mesmerism, I believe these drawings help release your son's demons."

"You are experimenting on a Drake, and the heir to the Malvern Duchy?"

"In the most benign way, Your Grace."

The old man worked his mouth as if he wished to spit. "These do not look benign to me, Hives."

"They are only his nightmares, Your Grace." She stepped toward him unable to remain silent. "Do you never awaken with your heart pounding and fear lodged in your throat? Haven't we all experienced terrors in the dead of the night? Lord Devlin's are just—very vivid. And he, unlike the rest of us, is able to draw them."

The duke frowned.

Macready whispered to Lowery.

"Your Grace, Mr. Macready has more to say, if you will hear him."

The duke rubbed his eyes but then waved his hand to proceed.

"He says," Mr. Lowery coughed, "he says he has proof Lord Devlin committed a murder. A Major

Cummings?"

Anne gasped along with the rest of the company. Then the room went silent as if suddenly entombed.

Macready stepped forward, taking the floor like an actor who had a brilliantly rehearsed soliloquy to impart. "The blood that he painted them walls with was not just his juice; it were the major's as well."

Phyllis Thornton gasped and stood. "I won't do it! You can't make me—" Once again, her father *shushed* her and jerked her back in her seat.

Macready rushed on, not to be upstaged by a vaporish girl. "After Esther—I mean the maid—found the loose floorboard, she called me up to have a look see. I found these letters, along with the major's medals and a ring. It's why the marquess went all daft the very day the major died. It were because he killed him, you see. A one-armed man hanging himself? Naw, he had to have help, seems to me."

"Why did you not bring this up before?" The duke looked to Doctor Hives, and then back to Macready.

"I had a notion, but no evidence, as it were. I only just found his little cache just before you all was summoned to come here."

"Let us read these letters," the duke said.

"No!" James shouted.

Everyone looked to him. But he only shook his head, his face a mask of terrible confusion.

"I am sorry, Lord Devlin, but I must." Mr. Lowery pulled the string on the packet and spread out the first letter. After reading, he set it aside and wiped his brow and then went on to the next and then a third and fourth. With each letter the tension in the room hitched higher. Anne thought she might be sick soon. Finally Lowery stopped and pushed the rest of the pile aside.

"Well, what is it, man? What is the gist of these letters?" The old duke sat forward, gripping the arms of his chair.

"They are love letters, Your Grace."

"Love letters? I don't understand? How could this mawkish pap be evidence?"

"You are correct, Your Grace. This is not evidence. Mr. Macready, you have it wrong. These letters do not incriminate Lord Devlin. They are merely a sad epistle to a degenerate life."

"Aye, degenerate, no doubt. But why did his lordship have the letters? And why were they tucked away along with the major's ring here? The marquess didn't want it known and had something to hide himself. Or mayhap he was as sickened by this unnatural creature and decided to rid the world of such a one. That, I can't blame him for."

"Lord Devlin, did you know of the major's...tendencies?"

"Oh God..." James closed his eyes.

"So which was it, Lord Devil?" Macready grinned. "Did you kill him because you hated him, or did you kill him because you loved him?"

"Merciful God!" Mr. Thornton had sidled up to the table, his daughter lurking over his shoulder. He picked up a letter and began to read. "What is this obscenity?" He looked at James, utter disgust on his face. "I have seen enough. I withdraw my daughter. No amount of money or stature would convince me to ally my offspring with a man who is capable of—this!" Spittle flew from his mouth as he threw the letter down. "He may not be insane, but he is surely still the reprobate he has always been. Come, Phyllis."

Thornton all but yanked his still gaping daughter out of the room.

James dropped his head in his hands and pulled at his hair. "I did not know. Dear God, I didn't even know—"

When he straightened, he was gone. The blank, fixed stare she knew so well sliding into place. That dead hopeless look. The one that protected him. The one she could not reach.

The old duke rose with the help of Mr. Tally. "I have seen and heard enough. Even if his portrait of this woman is found, it matters not. My son must remain at Ballencrieff. Take him away."

No. This scenario was all wrong. Someone had played a terrible trick. And she had unwittingly been part of it. James would not survive in this place. He may not want her. He may have used her, but she would not leave him to die in his tiny room with no light and no beauty.

"No!" She stood, her chair clattering backward.

All eyes went to her.

"You cannot take him away. I will not allow it."

"Am I surrounded by lunatics?" The duke sputtered. "How dare you presume to give orders."

"I dare because I am going to have his child."

Chapter Twenty

The puppet-like people jerked into pictures, much like a Punch and Judy show. But he remained outside their frenetic world. They could not touch him. A word or two broke through the pounding in his head, but they no longer mattered.

"…must remain…take him away." His father's mouth moved as he gestured toward Dev.

A devil slipped from his brain to whisper in his ear, *Now you will never be free!*

He shook his head but the devil held on. *Pay attention! They are going to leave you here!*

He tried to cover his ears, but the footmen held him fast.

Say it! Say you and the Owl are married! Save yourself!

The room spun. He opened his mouth praying his words would be heard. *We are married! She is my wife, and only she can keep me here!* But the words lay trapped in his throat. It was all too late.

She wasn't his. He had never made her his. Stupid blighter. So confident he would escape this hell on his own merits. Even if the devils released his tongue so he could make this grand declaration, would she only call him liar?

Just as well he could not speak. Anne Winton would not lie. Not even to keep him safe. Hadn't she already demonstrated that when she only had to tell these vipers she had seen his portrait of her? But she could not. And who could blame her.

"No!" The sound of her voice startled him, and his devils scattered in fear. His Owl stood like Joan of Arc against the fire. Such a brave girl, his Owl.

Heated words flew around him, but he could not decipher their meaning against the roaring in his head.

His father barked at Anne, and Dev jerked forward. *No!* But no one paid him any mind. *Leave her be!* But again, no one listened.

The air vibrated with tension. Everyone in the room strained toward his Owl. She was speaking. He needed to hear.

Desperate he shook his head. Hard.

Her voice came ringing through. "—going to have his child." Her gaze found his through the thick air. She touched her belly.

The pounding in his head stopped. *His child?*

"She lies!" Macready pointed at Anne as if she were the devil. "Don't you see, she's part of this? Under his spell, she is. She will do and say anything to spare him. She is his whore!"

Austin stood to hush him. Macready pulled away.

His father shuffled forward with the help of Tally and stared at Anne as if his eyes might flay her open. "Who is this woman?" he hissed.

"She is from Ardsmoore…brought in as a nurse-companion…female patients." The doctor alternately poked his head up, and then down into the folds of his cravat. His words kept fading in and out. "I assure you I had no idea—"

Waving Hives away, the duke started toward Anne

again, shaking his fist. "Do you imagine…" Dev strained to hear. "…my son to marry a common slut?"

Slut? Damn it. He could not make his brain follow, if only he could speak to Anne. *His child?* But they had not—

"What is your name, girl?"

Leave her be, I say. But though his mouth moved, the words stayed locked within him.

"Anne Winton, Your Grace."

"Well, Miss Winton, you are undoubtedly a grasping chit who saw the opportunity to cozen a madman and took it. Never mind, you are easily dispensed with."

Tally moved to the duke and whispered something in his ear.

"What? Nonsense, Hives says the girl is a charity case, from Ardsmoore."

Tally bent again and held out a paper pointing to a place on the page.

Anne took a step forward, her brows furrowed in that earnest frown he so loved.

Lying. His Owl was lying for him. There was no child. Could be no child.

His sire slowly lowered the paper and looked at her as if she might be one of Mr. Beauchamp's otherworldly creatures. "What was your mother's name?"

"No! Leave her alone. She is innocent!" The footmen on either side of him clamped down on his arms. Faces turned to him. By God, he would not let his father tear her apart. "It was me. I took advantage of her. I preyed on her, trying to use her to aid me. She is blameless!"

"Silence, Devlin!" his father cried, showing a flicker

of the powerful man he used to be. He turned back to Anne. "Your mother's full name, girl."

"Eleanor DeVere Winton, Your Grace. Despite being an orphan, I am a lady." She raised her pointed little chin.

The old man's face dropped as if all the earlier fire had suddenly burned from it. "Eleanor DeVere?"

Anne nodded. He motioned for her to come nearer and then looked deeply into her eyes.

"Devlin, is this true? Is this girl carrying your child?" His father's voice sounded warped and far away.

He shook his head. If only he could see her clearly. *Why? Why would you do this for me?* Should he deny her words? Set her free? She looked away from him. He could not blame her.

His gaze tracked over the room to settle on Austin. Too many questions crowded his mind. How had that empty atrocity replaced his portrait of Anne? How had Macready found his drawings? And Major Cumming's things? Only Austin knew of the hiding place. Eyes stared at him, waiting. His jaw line twitched, and he willed the muscles in his face to turn to brick; an impregnable fortress to shut out the prying eyes and the painful questions.

"Devlin, you will answer me. Now. I will not have this subterfuge."

He shook his head. As if his brain were the clapper of a bell, scarlet pain rang against his skull, into his teeth and jaw. He could save himself. Use her and take her offering.

Could he possibly make her happy?

He didn't know. But what difference did it make? When it came down to it, he was a selfish bastard.

"Yes." His voice sounded raw and painful in his ears. "Yes." He looked at her. "My child."

"A lie! It is a fiendish lie!" Macready shook Austin off. "Another deception. Another plot to cozen you, Your Grace."

The man spun to take in all the onlookers. "You cannot actually believe him? Have you forgotten his evil butcheries? Or Major Cummings? He's a murderer! He and his kind are nothing but filthy murderers!"

"Remove that man. Now," his father ordered.

Ivo and a footman crossed to Macready.

"Hives, you will not get away with this betrayal. I will see to it!" Macready ran out of the room.

The rest of the company stood about like chess pieces locked in a stalemate. At last the duke spoke. "Austin, come to me."

His brother looked contrite as he came to stand before their father.

"You have kept the estates together. You have stood by my side through all my infirmities. Margaret is finally increasing. But it is not enough. You are not my heir." He sighed heavily. "I wish you were. Dear God, sometimes, I wish you were. But, your mother, she was already—" The duke shook his head sadly. Then he flung off Tally's hands and stood straighter.

"I want Ballencrieff searched from dungeon to towers. I doubt we will find the portrait, but we must try. Austin, I will speak with you privately and," he signaled to the two footmen nearest the door, "find that Macready fellow." The men bowed and then left the room.

"This family has aired its dirty secrets far too often. It is enough. It is time to begin anew." The duke's eyes, so like his own, found his.

Dev saw despair, disappointment, but he also saw a glimmer of something so foreign to this family. Hope.

Chapter Twenty-One

London

The Scottish crags and moors turned into verdant hills, which then ran to flatlands dotted with more and more villages. After nearly ten hours of travel, they must be nearing London.

Anne turned from the window to study the sleeping Lord Devlin. Her husband.

Surely she must be the one dreaming. Soon she would awaken to find herself back in her tiny room, her life restored to normal. To the life that should be her fate.

But the Flying Scotsman's opulent, private compartment and the extreme ache in her bottom, no matter how plush the velvet cushion beneath, told her all this was impossibly real.

And the man next to her, his hand so casually lying not three inches from her hip, was no dream. But he was no longer her *James*. In reality he never had been.

He must have been given something to sleep, or simply be too exhausted from the last few days. Try as she might, she had not a prayer of sleeping.

Could she touch him? Would doing so make this stranger real? She dared not. After all theirs was not a mutually-agreed upon union. She had thrust herself upon him out of desperation. Saved him, and he was likely grateful, but he did not want her. Would never have chosen her. That was the difference. Just a means to an end. She mustn't forget that.

Poor besotted wretch, she would choose him in a heartbeat. She had. Stepping up in front of everyone and declaring herself with child. How utterly brazen of her.

How could she possibly wear the mantle of Marchioness? To navigate this strange, new world? If the old duke's behavior were any indication of how society would treat her, she was in for a rough ride.

Shifting her aching bum, careful not to brush his hand, she smoothed her gray skirts over her crinoline. Her wedding dress.

Mrs. Nester had offered a gown for the nuptials, but when Anne tried it on, she looked like a child playing at dress-up. The hem would have had to have been hacked off nearly a foot before hemming it another five or so inches. And that would only solve the length issue.

Lady Tippit had dragged out her old court dress from the dusty trunks that stood packed against the walls in a tiny room. She'd insisted Anne wear it. The jewel encrusted gown must have weighed as much as Anne herself. But again, she could not condone it being butchered for the cause.

So, in the end, she had worn the gray, the best of the two gowns she possessed. The one Mrs. Harlow had given her when she had healed young Earnest Harlow of the croup.

Phoebe Nester had trimmed it out with some silver-gray velvet ribbon and a bit of ivory lace. Like making a silk purse out of a sow's ear. Another bit of lace had been unearthed for a veil, and Mrs. Coates had sacrificed some of her precious orange blossoms for a nosegay.

She had not looked in the mirror—not really. Only

giving it a cursory glance to please the ladies, but in truth, she had been too afraid what the reflection would show. Certainly not marchioness material and never would be.

Just before the ceremony, Mr. Beauchamp had conspiratorially pulled her aside and pressed a crystal into her hand, whispering it was very ancient and powerful, and she must treat it with the deference it deserved. The stone fit perfectly in her palm, and she had clutched it during the brief ceremony, praying that its solid, smooth planes would give her strength.

The stone now lay within the pocket of the newly trimmed gray gown, next to her hip, next to her husband's open palm. She dipped her hand inside the pocket and squeezed. The crystal pressed against the heavy ring that encircled her finger, biting into her flesh.

What's done is done. She must move on through the charade and hope—for what—well, she did not know. She would cross that bridge when she must.

The train's whistle hooted low and long. Lord Devlin stirred. A spew of steam and fog surrounded the narrow window. She fumbled with the latch.

The stench hit her head-on like a solid mass with weight and substance. She put her hands to the window as if she might push the thing away.

"London Town!"

****

Dev's dream of feathered wings brushing his cheeks and the gentle sway of tree branches high above the earth corroded as fetid air hit his nostrils.

He snorted, but the intrusions persisted along with shouts and now screeching brakes.

He knew this smell. He knew these sounds.

Home. He was home.

The two great Doric Arches of Kings Cross Station soared above, enduring and timeless. The arches, smells, and sounds might be the same, but the fact that Anne Winton sat next to him made everything new. Brand new.

He rolled his neck. His mouth as dry as toast, his head muzzy from sleep and whatever Hives had given him for the journey. He should not have taken it, but once again, he had not been given an option. Hives wanted him gone, that much was clear.

"Anne," he said as if saying her name might make her real. She turned from the open window, her face now wreathed in shadows. "Welcome to London."

The Malvern town coach stood, like some great black winged raven, defying all traffic rules by swooping in to whisk them away from the riffraff and squalor that inevitably surrounded a terminus.

His father's footmen, Dev counted six, made a phalanx around Anne and him. Never had his father's old-fashioned carriage looked so inviting.

"Please, m' Lord, 'ave ya got a copper?" One cheeky bugger breeched the small army.

"Away, you." The footman nearest poked the boy's chest with the end of his whip.

Anne frowned. Dev took her arm more firmly and shook his head when she began to protest.

"Best to do it from the carriage."

He fixed his gaze on the open door and held his breath. What a pair they made. The Mad Marquess and his Benighted Bride.

Once inside, the footman latched the door closed.

"Drive on!" He rapped on the roof. The command

came like second nature, and the carriage, mercifully, moved forward. He filled his hands with coins, not knowing if he tossed sovereigns or pence, only that the hoard fell back to scrabble in the dirt. Lemon oil and lavender mixed with the dank must of an unused carriage filled his lungs as he took his first deep breath since arriving.

His bride faced the shuttered window. She would want it open to see out, while he only wished for a dark cocoon. Wanting to do something for her, he reached over to roll up the shade. No, he did it to gain her attention. Perhaps even win a tiny smile?

Nothing.

If only he could touch her hand, but she had wedged herself into the far corner. One hand held a handkerchief over her nose, and the other lay deep within the pocket of her cloak.

"Anne, are you well?"

She only nodded, now nearly pressing her nose to the window.

A clam. His wife was a damned mollusk where not the thinnest pallet knife could hope to slip between her shells. Certainly not his ineptly chivalrous overtures.

Stupid, jealous fool. Leave her be. Are you so starved for attention that you must deny her the first glimpses of the city?

He pressed back into the velvet squabs. The buildings, the parks, the opulence of Mayfair he could draw from memory, just as he could the squalor of Seven Dials or the docks at Wapping. But he could not roll back time to make it all new. As he watched Anne, her neat bottom perched at the very edge of the bench, he was struck by the difference between them, she so eager to see everything, while he wanted to blot it all out, to ride on and on and never have to stop.

Less than a year in exile, but it felt like a lifetime. And this woman, plastered to the wall of the carriage like some limpet, was now his wife.

He closed his eyes.

The woman who had sacrificed her own freedom to set him free.

Scottish law was very convenient for a hugger-mugger wedding. Hell, they could have stood in the blacksmith shop over an anvil and become man and wife. That easy. No anvil for the marquess, but certainly no St. Georges church either. A few mumbled words and some signed papers and the deed was done.

The wedding breakfast, hastily scrounged from the village, had been more than his poor stomach could handle. The smells had tantalized him, yet when he tried to eat a simple beef pie, he'd nearly cast up his accounts and had to excuse himself. Who would have thought he could ever long for Ballencrieff's over-boiled mutton.

She had not looked at him once during the hurried ceremony, and they had not kissed. Her ring was not even of his choosing, just some old family relic his father had brought for Miss Thornton. After he had slipped it over her trembling finger, she had kept her hand in a fist against her belly. He wanted to think she did so to keep the thing from falling off instead of out of extreme agitation.

Tally had taken care of smoothing Thornton's ruffled feathers. A wad of blunt in his pocket, and his daughter to receive highly-sought-after vouchers for Almack's and, with any luck, a reasonable husband.

The old duke had blown hard, insisting Anne be

checked by Hives before the marriage took place. Not bloody likely. He had told his father to shove his examinations. He could either trust his son or not.

The ruse had been a gamble, but one he was willing to take. He could not countenance Anne being subjected to that degradation on top of everything else. Playing on the uncertainty of Austin's parentage, his sire relented.

Still, the falsehood of the child lay like a wriggling snake between them. There was no babe. Anne DeVere Winton, now Marchioness of Devlin, was as chaste as his maiden aunt, Hortense.

If only he could find the words to tell her how sorry he was.

Except he wasn't sorry. Selfish bastard. Oh, he was sorry for her, but for himself...no. Guilty, but not sorry.

No painting had been found. Not the portrait or the nude. One look in Macready's eyes and Dev knew they would not be discovered. Someone had taken or destroyed them. Someone who wanted to keep him at Ballencrieff. Wanted to see him fail.

Hives? No, it didn't make sense. Wasn't he to be rewarded by the duke for seeing Devlin recovered? Macready was involved for sure. But on his own? The man had vanished.

And then there was Austin.

The vials of drugs. Secrets being leaked. The newspapers getting involved. Could his brother hate him so much?

He pushed the terrible thoughts away. But what other explanation could there be? Austin had been given charge of the painting.

There had been no time to question him, what with the haste of the wedding and then departing for London.

Did he owe Austin an apology? Certainly his brother's blackened and swollen eye suggested as much.

But, again, there had been no time. Austin had gone ahead with their father and Tally. And Dev was just as happy to let the truth lie, for now. Just another hidden snake, this one to writhe between him and the brother he loved.

The carriage turned on to Seamore Place where Malvern House had stood for over a hundred years.

The house's yellow granite had darkened over time to the color of rich butter cream. With its smoothly uniform walls and whimsical pediments, every doorway and window festooned with fanciful garlands and swags, the manse looked as if it had been manufactured by some renowned pastry chef. Even the hedges surrounding the house added to the illusion of an elaborate confection. A myriad of textured greens made for a parquetry-like table where the house proudly stood.

Passersby often made a special side trip down to the end of the street to gawk at perfection. The old dragon, Mr. Hiro, must still be in charge of the gardens.

A footman opened the carriage door and held out his hand to Anne.

Dev leapt ahead of her and waved the man away—by God, he would help his own bloody wife out of the carriage.

He tried a smile. But her frozen hand was a perfect complement to the frigid mask of her face.

"Welcome home, Lord Devlin." Greely bowed then sniffed. "Lady Devlin."

Ah, the old butler still at the helm. Implacable as ever. Anne would have her hands full with Greely.

Taking her elbow, he led her into the great hall.

The two potted palms, imported from Italy, still stood as sentinels just inside the entryway. He'd climbed the one on the left when he was five or so.

A half dozen of his father's flawlessly turned out servants had scrambled below, plotting how to extricate one boy who scarcely came up to their perfectly tied garters.

The adventure had been worth the whipping. As had the ride on the chandelier pull, which is how they'd finally got him down. Silly blighters. If they'd just ignored him, he would have come down on his own in time for his tea. He'd always loved Cook's apricot jam.

He'd carved his name up at the very top. Was it still there?

"Devlin?"

Austin. Impeccably turned out, as usual, however a frown marred his beautiful face. Dev shoved his fingers through his newly-shorn hair. He must look a scrub next to his golden brother.

Austin made a bow to Anne. "Lady Devlin. I am sure you are tired from your journey. This is Mrs. Norton, our housekeeper." He gestured to a woman Dev did not recognize. "If you would like, she will take you to your rooms."

"Yes, I thank you." Anne stood tall, steady as a bark on a choppy sea, though she must be ready to drop with exhaustion.

"I have prepared a cold supper in your room, my lady, and a bath," Norton said.

"A bath?"

"Yes, your ladyship, unless you would prefer to wash in a basin?"

"No, no, a bath—yes. Thank you, Mrs. Norton."

Poor Owl, she'd likely only had a proper bath once in a blue moon. Yes, by God, a hot bath did sound like heaven. No more icy cold plunges. He followed like some drooling puppy.

"Dev, are you well? Do you need something?" His brother reached into his coat.

He bit the side of his cheek as Anne disappeared at the bend in the stairway. Reaching out, he touched the smooth bark of the old palm tree. What a fearless boy he had been to scamper up thirty feet into the air. He stood straighter, imitating his wife. "No." He looked Austin straight in the eyes. "No. I am done with that, little brother."

Chapter Twenty-Two

Steaming water surrounded him. He leaned back against a pillow of toweling. A bath. Dear, Sodding Satan, how he had missed this pleasure.

Was Anne in hers? Her hair floating around her breasts, catching on pebbled nipples, her hands drifting to touch between her legs…

"Ahh!"

Ivo stood next to him grinning, empty bucket in hand.

"That is enough hot water, man. I must get out before I shrivel into a prune."

There had been some consternation about Ivo parting from baby Grace. But the fact that Pocket and Blackie were to travel to London with him in a private train car adjacent to the bride and groom, had placated the keeper, at least for the time being.

It only seemed fitting that the lad continue to care for Dev as his valet. And he was proving a quick study, though he had come up empty when Dev had sent him off in search of brandy.

"Thank you, Ivo, you have done well." His cheek now sleek as Corinthian leather. "You may go see Blackie in the kitchen now."

The giant made a rather solemn and dignified bow. By God, what a sight. Soon he would be demanding fine clothes and hair pomade. But in answer to Dev's grin,

Ivo's face split wide, his huge head bobbing with glee.

Alone now.

A stranger stared back from the mirror. No longer the dashing marquess of old. And certainly not the happy and expectant bridegroom.

He opened his banyan robe. The welts were fading and the blisters healing, but he would never return to the man he was.

Thank God. For all his polish and *savoir-faire*, that man had been more gruesome than the gaunt, sunken-eyed man in the mirror. Good riddance.

But who was he now? What did he have to give?

He felt very like that terrible empty canvas whose stark whiteness still haunted him. Nothing there. Yet he knew it had been filled—filled with Anne's light and grace. Filled with new ideas and possibilities. If only he could look upon it again, surely he would see reflected back the brilliance he remembered?

The anxious-looking man in the mirror faded, as Anne's image filled his mind's eye. And who was she now, his sweet Owl, who had only wanted to heal—to be of use? He had taken that dream from her. Oh, she had voluntarily stepped in and rescued him, but he had really left her no choice, as desperate and pitiful as he had been. As he was. Had he consigned her to an empty life as well?

He swiped his hands over his face and then cinched the belt of his banyan closed. Enough mawkish drivel. Time to make a child.

He'd been put in a different set of apartments to the room he had used on the rare occasions when he had stayed at Malvern House. This suite was configured for a married couple, a withdrawing room separating the two bed chambers and dressing rooms.

His hand trembled slightly as he lifted it to knock. He was about to rap again when the door swung open.

His wife stood before him. Her stance put him in mind of a prisoner in front of a firing squad.

Sweet Satan, had he downed an entire bottle of brandy it would not be enough for this assignation. Oh, to feel a ball of waxy opium on his tongue… Anything to dull some of the nervous anticipation rolling through him.

Someone, had seen fit to give her a gown and a wrapper. Likely Margaret, judging by the style of this ensemble. Altogether too many bows and ruffles on his petite bride.

In contrast, her hair, tied with a simple white ribbon, hung in a maidenly braid over her shoulder, while her pink toes peeped beneath the gown's flounced hem. He had to stop himself from dropping to his knees and kissing them. She would surely question his sanity.

No, his Owl was gone. Wisely, that girl had flown away. This new woman, dressed so richly, he did not know.

Not yet.

"Was your bath pleasant? Did you eat? Is the room to your liking?" *Idiot.* Hardly questions framed for lovemaking.

She looked at the floor and then the ceiling and finally at her hands. "Yes. I thank you."

He did not want her thanks, by God. He was the one that owed her. All he'd had to do was stand there, mutter a few words, and sign a few papers.

She twisted the ring on her finger as if it chaffed her. She must have wound a bit of ribbon around the band to keep the damned thing from falling off.

Monstrous ring. He wanted to pull it off and heave it out the window. It cheapened her.

On the morrow he would go to the jeweler first thing. She would have something new, something of his choosing. The Drakes had troves of gaudy rubbish he could give her, but she required something simple, unblemished, and all her own.

She dropped her hands, hiding them behind her back.

"Anne. We do not have to do this tonight."

"What?"

"You do not have to lie with me."

"Lie with you?" She frowned. "But—I lied." She lifted her chin. "I lied about…about the child."

"Do you imagine you are the first to do so?"

"But your father, the duke, said he will send you back if we—if there is no child."

"Yes, that is true."

He could have said more. He could have given her another chance at a reprieve. But he didn't. He was a selfish bastard. He wanted this new woman. This wife.

His look must have told his thoughts. She glanced at the bed and then turned her back to him.

Silly Owl. Did she imagine turning her back would preserve her modesty?

She bent her head, exposing the white column of neck feathered with down just at the nape.

He licked his dry lips.

She fumbled with the tie at her waist and shrugged out of the wrapper. The silk ran down her arms. *Sweet Jesu,* the sight of her profile, her surprised mouth parted, as she caught the robe before it dropped to the floor, had him nearly leaping on her.

Her fingers smoothed the silk. She frowned as she carefully laid it over a nearby chair.

Before he could drink in her shape minus one delicious layer, she snuffed the lamp and then quickly slid beneath the sheets. Timid as a fledgling.

His Owl of old, the one back in his cell at Ballencrieff, would have slain him with her schoolgirl seduction.

However, the Marchioness of Devlin was a whole other kettle of *poisson*.

His cock bobbed against his belly, so eager to dive into her pot.

At least in the full darkness, he could slip out of his robe without exposing himself to her gaze. Though he needn't have worried. His audience was tucked up to her chin, her gaze fixed on the bed's golden canopy.

He dropped the robe to the floor and joined her.

She lay stiffly next to him and he, who had satisfied dozens of women, had not the first idea of how to approach a wife.

She even smelled different. Some perfumed scent, not unpleasant, but not his Anne. The rose aroma mixed with her heat, adding another subtle layer. What would her neck taste like now? Her breasts? Her belly? Her...

The gold and cream room with its cherubs clustered around a central frieze—it looked to be Zeus as a swan, pursuing his Leda—so unlike his old environs, did nothing to ease his bridegroom nerves. Nor did the plush feather mattress, or the fine linen sheets. Somehow, being fettered in chains, tucked up snug in his cell, he had been freer than in this opulent bedchamber in the heart of Mayfair.

He couldn't touch her. His wife. His Owl.

He jerked the covers off his stiff cock and bolted out of the room.

****

The door clicked shut, a period to their brief encounter.

Foolish tears stung Anne's eyes. What had she expected when their marriage was a sham? Apparently, the need for a child was not enough to override his not wanting her. Now out in the world, her meager charms were not enough to tempt him.

She flung the bedclothes aside. Ignoring the chill, she jerked the curtains open, wanting to somehow change the room. She unlatched and pushed open the casement. Cold pricked her skin. She welcomed it, wanting to flush the smell of him from her nose. This new, clean smell that had her aching to press herself against his body, to taste his flesh.

Light. She wanted light. The sulfur of a dozen matches took care of any lingering smell he might have left in the room. A waste of lamp oil, but what did it matter? She was a marchioness. She must learn to waste.

An enormous full-length mirror stood along the wall balanced between two golden birds. Cranes? She thought they were cranes. She had avoided the looking glass thus far, but now it drew her. What would it be like to see her entire body without one stitch of clothing?

Already she could see the shadow of her maiden-hair beneath her silken gown—the gown Lady Austin had insisted she wear for her "Bridal Night."

Silk filled her hands as she gathered more and more of the fabric, exposing her ankles, her calves, her knees, thighs, the dark triangle at her center, and then her belly and breasts. She dragged it over her head and let it drop to the floor.

Next, she pulled the end of the ribbon that held her hair, and in a mere breath it unraveled itself to spill over her body. One nipple poked through the dark curtain as if playing peek-a-boo. Her mouth parted in a gasp as her fingers grazed the pink nub. Yes, she liked that. James had pinched—

"Ahh!"

She turned her back on this wanton woman. But unable to resist, she looked over her shoulder. Fascinated, and not a little shocked, she pulled her hair aside and looped it around her wrist as he had done at Ballencrieff.

Her bottom was very round…and firm. Her hand slid up, dipping to settle at her waist. It felt so nice. She did it again. Would he like it too? Would he delight in this curve of round bottom to dimpled waist? Would he see it as beautiful? Was her body beautiful?

He had not even stayed to see. He had risen from her bed as if he could not even bear lying next to her. The hair at her nape stung as she yanked her hand from the tangled mass. Tears blinding her, she ran around the room snuffing every lamp, as if they had eyes to see her shame. Without even donning her gown, she threw herself into the bed, its feather mattress a cocoon for her shaking body. But she couldn't stand it—the sheets against her bare body too much. She ended wearing her old gray gown to bed.

If only something could be the same. If only she had some handhold in this strange new world. Was Malvern House to be yet another Ardsmoore, but this time a gilded cage instead of a cold, dank, schoolhouse? When would she finally belong somewhere? Be wanted and needed. Be loved.

Her hand settled on her belly. So flat and empty. A child would need her, love her. A child who would not have to be alone, who would be cherished.

A beautiful dark boy with gray eyes and a crooked smile.

But what if the child were a girl? What if she had the gift? Could it be passed on? Had one of her parents had it? She couldn't remember.

Well, no matter. She would make sure she was there to explain the sensations and the rolling vibrations. Her child would not have to wonder if she were possessed by the devil or endure being called a witch. She would not have to sit alone, far from the other girls who made sport of her. Her child would be protected, taught to know a blessing lay within her, not a curse.

Her new husband may not want her, but she was his wife and they needed to make a child. She needed to make her lie a reality. She would see it done. And she would at least have the beginnings of a family.

Tomorrow she would be ready.

Chapter Twenty-Three

"Devlin." Austin stood in the doorway.

Dev clamped his teeth and turned away.

"We must talk. You cannot shut me out forever. I am your only brother. We must hash this out."

After leaving Anne he'd spent the entire night pacing this library searching through every nook and cranny for a bottle. Nothing. Now Austin. He did not want this conversation. Not now. Austin scanned the chaos. "What happened here? You look like the devil."

He snorted.

"Sorry, not the best comparison. Did you lose something?" His brother hovered just inside the door as if unsure it was safe to enter.

"Couldn't sleep." As if that was a reasonable explanation for the room being in a toss.

"It is early. You have only just returned. You must give—yourself—some time."

"Anne, you mean. I must give my bride time to adjust to being shackled to me." His laugh sounded demonic even to his own ears.

"Dev, I hate to see you this way."

God, he knew the flask had to be somewhere in this bloody room.

"Will you hear me out?"

He must have made some sign of acquiescence, because Austin entered, righting this and that as he gravitated farther into the room.

His brother's tidying set Dev's teeth on edge. He retreated to the windows. The back garden still boasted its perfectly-clipped topiaries—a new one looked to be in the shape of a Japanese pagoda. Mr. Hiro must be four score and then some, but obviously still wielded his shears with fierce precision. It occurred to him that his brother would make a very fine topiary—not a leaf out of place, all perfect angles and curves. A mix of symmetry and artful whimsy.

"I should never have let the painting out of my sight. Father needed me, and of course I went. Like always." Austin placed several books back on a shelf, and then lined them up according to size. "I should never have trusted Macready. I checked the floorboard under your cot. Of course there was nothing. How was I to know you were stashing private drawings there?"

Was Anne awake now? Had she slept at all?

"Dev?"

"Yes, I heard, Macready." He dragged his gaze from the ceiling to the now perfectly ordered books and then to his brother. Was Austin lying? Best to play it close to the vest. For now. "I suppose you cannot be blamed for Macready being the shite he is. Ever since he lost his prime spot as my keeper, he had to find ever more creative ways to get to me."

"I was supposed to be the strong one at Ballencrieff. I was supposed to take care of you."

"So why didn't you?" So much for keeping his cards hidden. "Hives, or somebody, was clearly poisoning me those first months at Ballencrieff, yet when I tried to tell you, you would not believe me."

"Dev, you were sick. Hives was the doctor. Was I

supposed to second guess his therapies?"

"Yet you provided me with extra laudanum."

"You begged me to help you sleep, complaining Hives would not give you enough."

He had been grateful and began relying on Austin for his peace. Perhaps, he should not have done so.

"I guess I let it go to my head a bit." His brother scuffed at the edge of the carpet. "You finally needing me. Being your life-line."

"Austin, stop. You give yourself too much credit, or rather power. We neither of us have much of that when it comes to our sire. Father was never going to renege on his one year plan for me."

Austin leaned his forehead against the shelf. "You don't understand."

"Then let's turn this page. What's done is done."

Austin shook his head. His laughter held a bitter edge. "Remember how I used to dog you? But you never minded a little half-brother who, if the rumors are true, is no brother at all." Austin shut the door of a glass-fronted cabinet.

Where was that damned flask? He'd been dead sure he'd tucked behind a hideous Staffordshire dog when he'd been escaping from his father over ten years ago.

"But as you got older things changed. You were the 'heir.' Suddenly all the attention was on you."

All the negative attention. God, he could not so much as fart without his tutors or his father reprimanding him, reminding him of his duty.

"You changed. I was no longer a comrade, but a nagging brat. I tried so hard to find a way back to you, but it was useless. I was useless. I was only the 'spare' and not a reliable one at that." He stood in front of the fire box and kicked at a dead coal which had spilled out onto the tiled hearth.

"When Father would not let you go away to school, I was ecstatic. My big brother was not leaving me. But I was wrong. You had left, just not physically. I think that was the hardest for me—you being there, yet not being there."

He remembered that time. Vaguely. It had been torture. No friends, being isolated except for a stable of tutors. His only happiness came from concocting elaborate mathematical equations or painting. Then one day he came upon two poachers. Terrified, they ran leaving their disemboweled prey.

The organs lay like jewels within a casket of skin and bone. Muscles knitting the body together... So beautiful. Never a religious man, yet looking into that slain deer, one could not doubt the presence of God.

"Dev, are you listening?"

He opened his eyes. Austin now stood before him.

"Do you remember when I smashed this very window?"

The huge mullioned bow window winked in the light. He shook his head.

"Don't you recall it used to be filled with hundreds of stained-glass roses?"

By God, yes. As a boy the colored glass had fascinated him. He'd spent hours tracing the twining patterns of leaves and blooms. Now, plain diamond panes replaced the once glorious window. Showed how much he'd paid attention.

"On my twelfth birthday I stood, rocks still in hand, right in the midst of the broken glass, and nobody even blinked. They simply scurried around me with their brooms whispering about what 'the marquess has done.' Some new stunt you had pulled. It was then I knew I really didn't matter. I became jealous as hell. It was in that moment I decided I would matter. I would be the good son; the son Father loved and relied upon."

He must have been sixteen or seventeen. What had he done to have the household so up in arms? Hell, he couldn't recall. "Then, when you were flitting around the Continent with Wainwright, I thought this is my chance."

Ha, like a bull out of a chute he'd been. Independent and so hungry. God, he'd wanted to try everything. And he had.

"I pushed myself to excel at school, married Margaret because Father wanted the match, and I immersed myself in the workings of the estates. But it was no good. I was no good because my mother was a whore and I'm, for all intents and purposes, a bastard."

"Austin—"

"Let me finish. So when Father sent you to Ballencrieff, I decided I would be your champion. If you had to depend on me, only me, we could go back to being best friends. And with you out of the picture, Father would finally see I was the son he'd always hoped for. A sap-sculled idiot, that's what I am. Trying to play both sides." He shook his head. "I should have gone into the army as I'd wanted. That was my role as second son. Why did I not take it?" His brother touched one of the diamond panes in the window.

"You are too strong for me." Austin ran his finger over the bevel in the glass. "And you do not need me. I have lost everything. Father is still fixated on you, I am saddled with a wife I do not love, and now I have likely lost the only family I care about." Austin turned to him.

"You."

And he had always envied Austin being the second son. What a joke the pair of them were.

Sweet Satan, all this confession called for a drink. Or ten. He pushed away from the windowsill to troll the room once again. Heedless of disturbing the odds and ends Austin had so carefully set to rights. Why the hell was his bloody father a teetotaler?

Eureka! A tarnished silver flask stood wedged between the books. *Ha.* That's right, he had switched the hiding place, shelving the liquor next to Shakespeare's sonnets, where he was sure no one would bother to look.

His hands shook as he twisted the stopper and then tipped it up. Nothing.

Harsh laughter spilled from his lips as he collapsed to the floor. Every blasted drop dried up.

"Excuse me. I did not mean my apology to be a joke."

Shite. "My apologies, Austin. When one lives in one's head for too long with little company, one tends to act inappropriately."

"Have you heard anything I've said?"

"Yes, dear brother. It seems we would have done well to have switched places." Far better to be a bastard and be free of all this constraint and enormous pressure. Though he would not want to be saddled with Margaret. Saddled was just the word—a great horse of a woman. He bit his lip to stop the laughter.

"Dev, might we begin anew?"

"Yes, anew. We should toast with some good French brandy."

Austin frowned.

"Oh, come now. You would deny me a snort or two?

I can't stop everything, brother mine. I have to have some vices, or I'll really go mad in this mausoleum." He had certainly not taken the edge off his lust. What must Anne think of him? Would he have the courage to go to her tonight? To bed her?

He pushed the image aside, far more useful to talk of practical matters. "Listen, Austin, if you want to show your good faith, you could see that Margaret is kind to Anne and takes her under her wing."

"Of course, but won't you be here to see to her yourself?"

Biting his cheek he tucked the empty flask into his coat pocket. "I can't really say at this point."

As it stood, he just might do her more harm than good. Who was he now? A husband? A painter? A man who eschewed drugs? Someone worthy to be a father?

No, he was none of these. What he was, was a man who had not the slightest idea of how to gain footing in this old yet new world. Lord Devil was dead, he prayed. The Marquess and Worthy Husband must rise out of those ashes.

And his brother…? Had Austin turned into someone unrecognizable as well? Keeping him imprisoned at Ballencrieff simply because he craved attention and power? Or was he a jealous, spiteful man who, perhaps, was now an enemy? One who would use drugs, or perhaps even poison, as a way to manage his elder brother and keep him weak?

My God, Austin could have been plotting against him for years. Had the arrival of the police at the townhouse on Greene Street been Austin's doing? Yet another ploy to play the hero, arriving just in time to get Nora Havermere to safety, but leaving Dev to suffer the terrible scandal as the police stormed into the house.

Looking at the picture of his angelic, contrite brother, he honestly did not know what to believe. Austin was not the doting, benign little boy with the angelic curls, but surely he could not be so evil either. One thing was certain Dev could never think of his brother quite the same.

"You must believe I had nothing to do with the disappearance of the painting. Well, other than trusting Ned Macready."

Suddenly cold, Dev turned toward the fire. If only he could disappear. If only he could retreat into a warm cocoon where worries were far, far in the distance.

But he could not. He must deal with life as a marquess. He must take an interest in finances and the estates. He must eventually face a blank canvas and try to paint again. And he must put a babe in the woman who lay in the room just above his head.

The door clicked shut. He had been so far away he had not even heard Austin leave.

Self-absorbed is what he was. Always had been.

His suit jacket suddenly felt like another strait-waistcoat, though it still gaped on his body. He ripped it off and flung it to the floor.

A pea-sized ball of bluish-ebony rolled out. The opium lay like a bullet on the parquet floor.

His tongue rolled in his mouth, almost able to feel the smoothness of that perfect round ball. A bit of his past come back to tease him. To make sure he had some options. To make his life infinitely harder.

Chapter Twenty-Four

"The tea is Darjeeling, your ladyship."

Anne glanced around before remembering she was her ladyship. The use of the title unnerved her. Inside she was plain Anne Winton and did not even feel like a lady, much less the Marchioness of Devlin. Though certainly it would help if Greely looked her in the eye when he spoke instead of addressing the air above her head.

"The Drakes have always enjoyed the finest of teas," he finished with a sniff.

Only used to watered-down tea made with re-used leaves, this brew's sweet and musky aroma perfumed the stuffy room. She smiled and nodded. "It is lovely—its fragrance puts me in mind of how I might imagine a bazaar in India."

Greely's rejoinder was only to raise his eyebrows which, when lifted, pulled his lips even tighter. Perhaps he was really a wooden marionette puppet disguised as a butler?

She took a sip of tea to stifle her urge to laugh. "And Lady Austin, will she be joining me today?"

"I'm sure I do not know, your ladyship. I could have her maid summoned if knowing is paramount to your ease." Greely rubbed his pristine glove over a satinwood table already polished to within an inch of its life. "However, if I were to presume," his eyebrows rose— "and hazard a guess,"—his lips pursed, "I would not expect Lady Austin. She does not usually bestir herself to come down for tea—or indeed for anything—these days."

She shifted. She would have to use the necessary soon. How ladies ate or drank anything being laced so tightly was beyond her.

Where was her husband? Likely holed up in the library again with Lord Austin and a bevy of stewards and financial advisors led by Mr. Tally.

She desperately wanted to ask Greely if his lordship might be joining her for tea, but shouldn't a wife know? The butler already looked at her as if she were something to be scraped off the bottom of his perfectly buffed shoe.

"Thank you, Greely." She nodded as she had seen Lord Austin do, but the butler remained. "That will be all. You may go now."

He sniffed, clicked his heels, and then quit the room, closing the massive door behind him.

An ornate long-case clock ticked loudly—her only companion of yesterday and the day before and the day before that. She reached for a biscuit. Anything to soak up the tea. A log in the fireplace popped. "Oh!" Hot tea sloshed over as her cup rattled in the saucer, and her nose pricked with threatening tears. She thrust the cup and saucer down on the table, heedless of the ring it would undoubtedly make.

Where did her husband go after seeing to business affairs? Why did he not come to her? She swiped at a small wet spot on her skirt. Tea or tears?

Was she so odious now he had his freedom? Was this to be her new life? Swilling tea while holding conversations with frosty butlers and relentless clocks?

Rain spattered at the windows, yet another reminder

that she had nowhere to go, no one to see.

The same imperious stares from the venerable Drake family censured her as she ascended the grand stairway, just as they had an hour or so ago when she'd descended for tea.

As she passed his bed chamber door she hesitated. No sound. He was not within. One easy turn of the knob and she might enter. A few steps and she could be at his bedside where she might lay in the impression his body made in the feather mattress, bury her face into the pillow he slept upon and breathe in his scent.

Fool. She let go of the knob and fled to her own room.

Yet another day as a lady in waiting. Well she would lose herself in the mysteries of Africa. Again.

But as she approached the bedside table with its stack of books her gaze snagged on a small square.

A box, deep blue velvet, sat squarely on the white pillow. No note, just the box.

Her hand trembled as she reached for it. The velvet felt plush and slightly cool against her fingertips. Her heart thumped with anticipation. A gift.

She did not recall ever receiving an actual physical gift, excepting Lady Tippit's silver brush and comb and Phoebe's dressmaking skills. Her parents must have indulged her as a little girl. A well-worn fabric doll with two golden braids? Yes, she had named her Myrtle. But never a gift from a man. No, not true. She had forgotten Mr. Beauchamp's crystal, which she kept under her pillow—

Now a marchioness, she must get used to presents. Perhaps this was what husbands did when they needed to appease their wives.

She took a breath and snapped open the lid.

Nestled inside was a ring that held one perfect, smooth, milky-white stone. Its beauty was in its simplicity. But as she took it from its satin nest the stone came to life, flashing a rainbow of colors—brilliant blues and green, pinks and yellows, lilac and even orange and red. His choice of jewel so simple, yet within its polished dome lay a whole world.

For the second time today, tears burned her eyes. He had called white the queen of color.

Her old ring dropped with a clunk onto the table next to her books. Already she felt lighter. This ring of white fire slipped on her finger like it belonged there. Perfect. Gullible or not, she believed he had chosen it specifically for her.

"Your ladyship." Yvette, her lady's maid, had entered.

She hid her hand behind her back as if she had been caught out. Honestly the girl always seemed to turn up at the worst moments.

Lady Austin had looked at Anne as if she'd had feathers between her ears when she'd balked at wanting a lady's maid. But she soon found out this was a battle she would never win so "Yvette" had remained. The girl's French accent was as false as her simpering smiles. Anne had the urge to actually converse in French just to confirm the fact, but she could not be so cruel. Besides, when one is desperate for a friend, why risk making an enemy?

"Will you be wanting za bath now, your ladyship?"

Anne touched the ring on her finger. Immersing herself fully in the huge copper bath was such decadent pleasure. But much as she would like nothing better than to ease her tense body into a hot foaming bath, she could not.

She was bleeding, just near the end of her cycle, which never lasted more than a few days. Thank heaven with all the stress her courses had been slightly late. If not, the duke, had he persisted, insisting on an examination, would have known in a moment she was not with child.

"Shall I ring for za water to be brought up, your ladyship?"

Unused to having a maid, she did not trust Yvette's dogged fussing. Knowing all too well how an ember of gossip could become a full-fledged inferno.

"No, just a bowl of hot water, please. I will attend myself."

Yvette looked utterly offended, *humphed*, and swung her generous hips out of the room.

Now refreshed, Anne was just donning a wrapper when someone knocked.

James? Perhaps he had come to see if she approved of his ring. As she passed by, the mirror showed flushed cheeks and parted lips.

"Oh, Lady Austin."

Margaret Drake stood at the door.

She had made an overture of friendship with her gift of the nightrail and wrapper on Anne's first evening. "My lovely bridal night clothes were utterly ruined—but you—well, at least that nasty bit is over for you." She had shuddered. "Still a horrid business, if you ask me. But one we wives must endure."

Endure? Anne had pretended to understand. Her little experience with love making had felt miraculous and not in the least bit horrid.

"I am sorry to disturb you, Lady Devlin, but I could not contain myself. I nearly came down to tea, but the thought of getting dressed overwhelmed me." In her condition, Anne had yet to see Margaret in anything other than a dressing gown, and not once beyond the upper floors.

"Please, come in, Lady Austin." She would never get used to these silly titles but did not feel as if she should be the one to suggest they dispense with protocol. "Thank you."

Margaret Drake fairly danced into the room.

"Shall I order tea?" The thought of more tea set her teeth on edge, but this woman was company and it was important to do things correctly. "Please sit down, Lady Austin."

"Sit? Oh, heavens no, I am entirely too excited to sit. So many plans to make. So much to do. I wonder if Cook is up to the task. Perhaps we should hire a French chef for the occasion? Oh, but they are so hard to come by and the duke can be stingy at times."

"I am sorry, I am not following you."

"The ball, Lady Devlin. The ball!"

What ball?

"Surely the marquess has told you?"

Anne shook her head, a sick feeling of dread inching around her belly.

"Oh, these men. The duke is throwing a ball in your honor! Your introduction to society."

Oh, please no. Her stomach heaved in sympathy.

"We have never entertained properly at Malvern House. What with the scandal—" Her ladyship covered her mouth with her hand. "What I mean is the duke has not been well. But, no matter, now we will finally have a *grande fête*, and I will be able to dance before I am forced to retire. Oh, do not look so shocked, Lady Devlin, I am not as far along as you would think. I have gained a stone or two, but who could blame me with nothing to occupy myself with all these endless months."

Lady Austin finally sat, and Anne happily followed suit, but her ladyship popped up again a bare moment later. "Lord Austin only told me of the plan this morning. Apparently, the duke is anxious to get you seen and accepted before… Well, before you retire for your confinement."

"Confinement?"

"Yes, the babe. Believe me, once you become too large, everyone wants to shuffle you out of sight as if you had some dreadful disease. I will be allowed to make an appearance at the ball and then I shall retire. I warn you, this baby business is tedious. But it must be done. I own, I am relieved you have come to take the burden from me. With any luck it will be a boy."

Anne looked away.

"Then I suppose you must try for the spare just in case…" Lady Austin touched her rounded belly distractedly as she gazed out at the rain. But in the next moment she set to pacing the room again her momentary melancholy seemingly forgotten. "I hope the duke will not change his mind. He suffered another bout of palpations last evening. The doctor was with him this morning."

Anne rose. "Is there anything I can do?"

Again Lady Austin looked at her as if she had two heads. "Do? What would you do?"

Deflated, she sat.

"Here is the best part. I thought to bring in my

modiste for the ball gown. We can have some other things made for you as well, but the gown must be one-of-a-kind."

"Is all this necessary?" One look at her sister-in-law's face told her it was most definitely necessary. "Very well. I am at your disposal."

"Trust me, you can do no better than Madame Bathilde. She is *de rigueur* these days, but I know she will come posthaste for me. I am one of her most loyal clients."

"I thank you for your help, Lady Austin. As you see, I know nothing of fashion."

"Yes, I can see that all too plainly. Plainly, being the key word. But, no matter, we will have you looking *a la mode* in no time."

Anne tried to smile despite the sick feeling in her stomach.

"I adore designing gowns. I vow if I were not high born, I would have made my fortune as a dressmaker. I am sure if I write immediately, we can get Madame Bathilde to come within the hour."

"Today?"

"But of course. You must remember you are the Marchioness of Devlin not to mention the Duke of Malvern's daughter-in-law. Soon you will be the duchess!"

Anne tried another smile. "Not too soon, I hope." Perhaps Margaret Drake would be a friend.

True to her word, a scant hour later, Anne stood in her shift being prodded and measured by Madame herself.

"She ez *tres petite*." The woman had circled her three times already, *tisking* and poking a limb here and

247

there. Finally she stopped her perambulations. "But I can work wiz it." she pronounced, as if Anne had managed to pass some arduous test.

By the time they were finished, Anne had been nearly smothered in swaths of silks and satins, stabbed at least seven times. "Do not bleed on zee fabrics!" Madame had screeched. Her head and feet ached and she had been roundly admonished when she had the temerity to ask to use the necessary. Madame was to return on the morrow where Anne could expect the real work to begin.

At least she had not been alone today. Margaret, as Anne had been given leave to call her, had found her pet project. And Anne was happy enough to acquiesce if it meant some company.

The next afternoon, having been subjected to another round of pokings and proddings and hearing of her various deficiencies, Margaret had offered to give a tour of the mansion.

"What is this room?" Anne stopped by a door at the end of a long, narrow hall. She and Margaret were now at the very top of the house.

"I don't know. It is likely locked."

Anne turned the knob. Yes, locked. After giving one last twist, she was about to turn away when the tumblers gave way and the door swung open with a groan.

Shadowed faces stared out from the walls.

"Oh my, I had forgotten." Margaret must have followed her into the room. "I suppose this is where they got stashed."

Not only were the walls filled with portraits, they were also leaning against them, stacked one behind another.

"The duke insisted all Devlin's paintings be

248

collected from his studio and townhouse after he—went away."

Anne looped back the heavy and dusty drapes, but it made little difference in the lighting.

Woman after woman looked out at her from the shadows. Blonde, brunette, ginger, smiling, pouting, in various states of undress, sitting, standing, lying— mostly lying.

Margaret flopped down in one of the chairs after it was clear they were not leaving any time soon.

One woman stood out. She had been painted many times. Anne could see why. Dark red hair, white flawless skin, eyes the color of violets in the spring. But it was not her extreme beauty that drew Anne as much as her expression. Wistful, poignant…full. Yes, full seemed the best word.

This woman had known her husband better than she. What had she meant to James? Perhaps, still meant to him?

Do not torture yourself. She moved on to the next beauty, one who had also likely shared her husband's bed, but the red-haired woman would not let her go, and she found herself once again staring into those hooded and sultry eyes.

The first impression of languid, and poignant grace still held true, but deeper within the layers of paint, James had captured some terrible sadness. She wanted to hate this woman who had so clearly captivated her husband, but could not.

"Oh, I see you have found the famous beauty, Nora Havermere."

Nora. "Of course, his Nora," she said out loud before she could catch herself.

The Nora he had called out to while delivering baby Grace.

Dozens of violet-blue eyes stared back at her from around the room. *Paint what is in your heart,* the eyes seemed to say.

She had never asked him about the countess. Indeed, she had barely spoken ten sentences to her husband since their marriage, and five of those had been her marriage lines

"I have never seen the countess in person. She is quite reclusive, I believe." Margaret had risen and now stood at her side. "Surely Devlin has exaggerated her beauty. I imagine one does when one is in lov—" Margaret laughed uncomfortably. "I mean, no one can have eyes of that color. She is only a fantasy."

Looking into those violet depths, Anne had a terrible feeling Margaret was dead wrong.

Chapter Twenty-Five

His father's hunched figure appeared in the pier glass above the sideboard. What was he doing up at this hour of the morning, let alone out of bed? The doctors had swarmed over the house since Dev's return.

He was not ready to face the old tyrant.

Unfortunately, the mirror caught him backing out of the dining room, and his father looked up.

Damn.

"Ah, here you are, Devlin. Tally said if I arose early enough I would catch you before you disappeared into the library, and then to—where ever you go for much of the day. And night."

He toyed with the idea of turning tail, but he would have to face the man sometime. He dumped himself into the nearest chair.

His father sat before a bowl of grayish porridge, very like the stuff Dev had been given ad nauseam at Ballencrieff. It was all he could do to keep his seat and hold down the little food he had in his stomach.

A footman came by with coffee, but he waved him off. "Ale. I would like some ale." What he wanted was a brandy. He had gotten one of his father's lackeys to bring in a case, but the hour was still too early, even for him.

"How is the girl faring?"

And too early for an interrogation. He shoved his chair back.

"Don't pull up stakes, boy. You know what must be. You must see to her."

The ale arrived just in time. He took a long pull. Yes, better. "And why the devil should I? You of all people should not be counseling me on how to attend my wife, sir."

His father *humphed* and dug back to his porridge.

He stuck his nose in his ale. Over a week with no sleep and too much drink had him nearly shaking. He flexed his shoulders. His bones felt sharp beneath his skin, as if they might break through.

That horrible, empty painting haunted him day and night. Each time he approached a freshly primed canvas, he panicked. His brushes felt foreign in his hands, the light was wrong, the model wrong. Even the smells were wrong. If only Macready were here, Dev would wring answers out of him.

"You look like hell."

He raised his glass in salute. "As do you, sir."

His father *humphed* again.

"What do the doctors say?" The question popped out before he could stop it.

His father waved the question away like an insistent fly. "Those quacks will poke and prod and feed their leeches with my ducal blood. All I need is an heir, and I will be right as rain."

Mouth still parched, he took another long pull.

"I told them they had much better see to the marchioness upstairs."

Ale sloshed over the rim of his mug as he lurched to his feet. "You bloody well will not. I will choose Lady Devlin's doctor. I will not have you interfering."

"As you say." He blotted his lips and carefully

folded the napkin. "I just want to be clear, if she is not with child, she had better be increasing. And soon."

Enough. He shoved his chair under the table startling the footman who normally jumped to assist him. "If you will excuse me, sir, I find I have no appetite."

The rattle of dishes stopped him. His father stood clinging to the edge of the table, the cloth pulled askew, his reed-thin arms visibly shaking beneath his coat. The footmen rushed to his side, but the duke waved him off.

"What would you have me do, Devlin? I ask you, what would you have done if you thought your son and heir had truly lost his wits?"

Christ. His fingers bit into the edge of the doorframe.

A bout of hacking coughs sent the old man collapsing back into his chair. The footman jerked forward but again his father stayed the man.

"Leave us. I will see to him." The servant hesitated but then bowed and left.

He handed his father a fresh napkin and then poured him a glass of water.

Ignoring both, his father sat back in his bath chair, eyes fixed on the plate in front of him, but it was clear he was not seeing the pasty gruel. "You are like your mother. A sensitive soul." His thin lips twitched. "We were not—well suited—the duchess and I." He fingered the unused knife in the line of cutlery at his place setting. "But I did my duty. The match went forward." He took a long wheezing breath. "I gave up trying to make her happy. Until you. You made her happy. For a time…"

His sire waxing on about old disappointments and regrets? He pulled out the chair next to his father and sat, then dragged the pitcher of ale to him and tipped another healthy dose into his mug. God, they were a pair.

"Then she died." The old man thumped his fist on the table, and the silver jumped.

His mother had produced him in their fourth year of marriage and then, after more than three years of barrenness, she had the temerity to expire from what seemed a trifling cold.

His poor mother was barely cold when his father replaced her with Lady Beatrice. Austin had arrived a scant seven months later.

"You are my heir, damn it." His father's bloodshot gaze bore into his. "And by God, I know my duty. I had to get you away." This last tirade seemed to have exhausted him. He shook his head. "Austin's marriage looming, the Queen nearly getting involved, my heart unsteady."

Now this was more like the father he knew and despised. "God forbid there should be a whiff of scandal around the Malvern name."

"A whiff? The stench from your—debacle—would have leveled the Queen's guard." He sighed heavily. "Austin was supposed to see that you were well enough." He leaned forward. "Do you imagine sending you away was easy for me? The last I saw of you, you were thrashing about, held down by no less than five footmen, and could not stop talking about all the blood. You could not 'stop the blood'."

The picture assembled itself in vivid color. Another memory restored as ale roiled in his empty stomach.

"Believe me, I would be happy enough to shuffle off this mortal coil, but I will see you well established, and by God, I will see my grandson first."

The foam on the rim of his mug ran creating a

pattern of dark and light. "It may be a girl."

The duke frowned as if the possibility of a female child had never occurred to him. "Nonsense. The Drakes always have boys," as if his saying so decided the matter.

"If you'll excuse me—"

"Why?" His father wheeled his chair into Dev's path. "Why this girl? Was using her your only option?"

"You think she is lucky to have me?"

"You are a marquess and my heir. Any woman would want you." He sagged a fraction in his chair. "Well, not any woman. You certainly burned your share of bridges. Got to be I couldn't get anyone of quality to take you and, by God, I wouldn't settle for the dregs. You got near dregs, boy. A half-French penniless aristocrat without an ounce of polish."

Leaning down over the chair he gripped its arms. "You don't see it, do you? She is—never mind." He heaved himself away. "You could not begin to understand."

"What I wish to see is her belly swell. That will be enough for me."

"Right, the succession must go on no matter how cruel we become. You say I am like my mother, but you are wrong. There is more of you in me than you know." He turned and rang the bell. The footman appeared a mere second later. No doubt he had been lurking by the doorway should his grace call out. One never knew what his depraved son might get up to.

"I wish you a good day, sir." He took one more look at the congealed mush of gruel and left the room.

****

Anne should not have been in the garden. It was too early and too wet. The window should not have been opened, but it was. She should have moved away when she'd heard the old man and his son talking, but she had not.

The thought of lying in that bed and having to, once again, face her maid's inquiring eyes, had her hastily dressing and descending the back stairway like the servant she felt like, and still should be if fate had not intervened.

But fate had intervened. She had been useful to these people for a brief moment, and now they had to live with the result. Her lie the catalyst for it all.

The old duke was right. She did not belong. She was a fool to think otherwise. To think her husband could really care for her.

Yet, what's done was done. The marquess was free, and she must live with her part in it because if she hadn't tried to save him, she could not live with herself.

Mrs. Abbot had always said, "You make your bed, and you lie in it."

Well, she would. She would lie in it with this stranger, and they would make a child.

Chapter Twenty-Six

One…two… The fire was almost ashes now. And three.

Anne counted the mantel clock's chimes just as she had over the previous hours. Just as she had over the last eight days.

What did he do in the evenings and into the small hours of the morning? The image of the beautiful Nora Havermere took shape next to her, managing to crowd her in this huge bed.

The door lock clicked. Her eyes snapped open as her breath froze in her throat. Deprived of air, her heart fluttered in her breast like a hungry hatchling.

A shadow drifted by the window and stumbled. The same breeze that ruffled the curtain brought the scent of him to her. Sweet tobacco and smoke, what she thought must be some strong liquor, and a spicy perfume.

She willed herself to lie still.

He came right up to the bed. She closed her eyes, pretending sleep. His breath came fast and heavy, as if he had been at some vigorous exercise.

Would he stay? Would he pull back the coverlet and lie beside her? Would his hands find her?

Still, she waited. The shadow of his body blotting out the faint light beneath her eyelids shifted. He was moving away. Leaving her yet again.

No.

The time was right. Time to make a baby. And she wanted him. He was her husband. She wanted to know this man as so many other women had known him.

"James," she whispered.

The shuffling stopped.

"Stay, I want you to stay."

He stood poised like an acrobat on a wire, halfway between her bed and the door.

"James?" she repeated, hoping to infuse the atmosphere with some of the ease of their past.

His feet shifted. "I'm sorry. I did not mean to wake you." He glanced longingly at the door obviously thinking that way the safer route.

"You didn't. I was not asleep." She propped herself on her elbows.

"You must get your rest, Owl." His words were soft and slushy, but not like when he had been dosed. Drink. He must have been drinking.

"Why?"

He shook his head. "What?'

"Why must I get my sleep?" She sat up fully, her fingers finding the smooth shape of his ring. "I have done nothing all day but drink tea and read."

"Then you have accomplished far more than I." He started to leave.

"I want a child."

That stopped him mid stride.

"It is the right time, now. The moon is full," she pressed.

A bark of laughter. "You sound like Beauchamp."

"Stay. I want you—to stay."

Every sinew canted toward him, every nerve, every hair on her body primed for his touch. Every bit of her ready to claim every bit of him. Mine. This is mine to have—to take.

"Anne, not this way. I am half-foxed." But his words had lost their round, laxness. His Adam's apple bobbed in his throat.

"Stay. I am used to you being—out of sorts."

"Once done, there is no going back. You understand?" Her demands seemed to have sobered him right enough.

Did he want the option of nullifying their marriage? Before she could back down she lifted the corner of the coverlet.

"Sweet Athena, I can deny you nothing when you look like that."

He fumbled with his loosely tied neckcloth, finally wrenching it off. His other clothes soon followed.

The moon being their only light, it rimmed the furniture, the bed, and his body in an otherworldly glow.

She moved over, the cooler sheets a relief against her hot skin.

So what if he came to her out of duty? She would get something from it. She must or she would go crazy with her love for this man. This want would fill her up and choke her. He must at least give her an outlet—a child.

The air was thick with vibrations, that delicious, expectant humming so uniquely theirs. Did he feel it, too? Yes, she thought so. Their miracle.

The bed dipped as he lay down, and she rolled toward him. He hissed as if she burned him and took her mouth immediately, pressing his tongue deeply into her. She tasted spirits. His hand cupped the back of her head, fingers working to unravel her braid. His other hand found her buttock.

"Oh." The word came unbidden then was lost in a tangle of tongues.

He yanked the silk of her nightgown up and up until it caught under her arms. She sat up to accommodate him, but in his impatience the fragile fabric tore. At the sound he threw himself back on the bed away from her. "I am sorry. Don't be frightened, Anne. I will leave you. I am—"

"No." His arm was lean, hard, muscle against her fingers. "No, you will not leave me. You will be my husband this night."

The muscle rose and bulged as he raised his hand and raked his fingers through his hair and down over his face. "Your husband," he sounded almost reverent.

She did not trust herself to say more. He seemed more frightened than she. Did he think a ripped piece of silk could send her scurrying for cover? He had much to learn of her. She would teach him a bit now.

Sitting up, she pulled her arms though the ruined gown, and then tossed it aside. After all, she reminded herself, the sight of her naked was nothing new. He had seen it all before. Still, her skin felt tight as if she might burst like a chrysalis and fly. Before she lost her nerve, she threw a leg over him and climbed on up.

The brush of her woman's hair on his belly made her buck. How could she be so wet down there? Mortified, she eased off of him, but he pulled her back with a deep groan, pressing her to his flesh, indeed, arching to fill any space between them.

"Anne…you are so lovely."

It wasn't true, but it didn't matter. No mirror could convince her she was not Helen of Troy at this moment.

His words slid by, one by one, like pearls on a string. She would take them out later and run her memory over the pure, roundness of them… But for now she must savor each moment of this joining. This miracle.

Deep depressions and too-prominent bones still etched his face, made deeper by the dim light.

She touched the circles under his eyes. He was not sleeping either. His day filled with estate business and then out all night—

Stop, do not think of that now.

His body had changed. His muscles harder and fuller than when she had touched him back at Ballencrieff.

She ran her fingers over his ribs, mellowed into rough hills as opposed to the sharp crags she remembered. His belly was ridged as well, but more subtly, like ripples in a pond.

A dark arrow of hair led down and met her darker triangle. She traced it with her finger.

He hissed again and grabbed her hand. Her ring bit into her. He eased his grip and took her fingers between his. Her hand small and white, like pages in a book against his leathery cover. He turned her hand this way and that, and then traced the opal. His gaze found hers and he opened his mouth to speak. But instead, he pulled her hand to his lips and kissed her finger. A sort of benediction. An acceptance?

Then, his hands where everywhere. She rose, lifting her arms and closing her eyes, feeling him feel her.

"Oh!"

He'd flipped her on her back. His gaze bore into hers that rogue smile on his lips. He dipped into her neck and bit. She stretched long, opening to him.

He was speaking to her. More of a song. Whispering

in her ear and to her breasts. Murmuring endearments to her belly and—lower. But she honestly could not attend. She felt only the vibration of his breath and the rumble in his chest and her own answering quiver.

So very skillful—the way his fingers oh-so-lightly brushed her curls, and then his cheeks against her thighs, his hot breath there, and finally the flick of his tongue finding that spot. So sure of himself. So experienced. All those beautiful women…

"Easy, love. Relax. Open yourself. Such a beautiful bud. Let it open to me."

Love. Air, long pent up, rushed between her lips. She imagined a tightly furled rose opening itself to the sun and rain. To capture life within its petals.

"Yes," he crooned.

"Yes," she echoed back. He sucked. Hard. Her hips bucked yet he held on. "Oh, yes!"

His hands found her bottom, cupping and squeezing the full roundness. But his hot mouth was gone.

Her eyes and mouth snapped open, her hands reaching to push him back down there. *Please don't stop, not now. Not when I'm so close.* But one look at his face told her to trust him, that he knew her better than she knew herself.

The hot tip of him nudged her opening. Her body a sheath for his sword.

"Anne, I can't stop. Don't ask me to stop."

As answer she pressed toward that hotness. "Ahh!" Stinging pain gripped her.

"Easy," he soothed. "There, love," he whispered. "No need to rush. Take little sips. That's it."

His breathy words brushed her cheeks and fanned her lashes. *Her smell on him.* She turned her head to capture his mouth. Not unpleasant. The taste. Like the earth and salt. He pressed harder as if he sensed her attention straying.

"Ah!"

"That's the worst of it. All downhill from here, sweeting."

He bent to her with such focus. His eyes dark and liquid as he pressed in deeper then retreated. Back and forth, back and forth, deeper and deeper. She pushed up to meet him.

He smiled the most beautiful smile. She swallowed, wanting to keep up, but it was all so—full—so—overwhelming. He picked up the pace, steadily building his delicious assault on her body, a dance that urged her to join in his vigor. She pushed as he thrust, learning the steps instinctively. Seeking to match him.

"Yes, my love." His eyes still held hers, their breaths as one. Their motion as one. Something big was building. An enormous wave that must surely drown her.

Yes, yes, let it come. Let it take me.

"Now, Anne, now." He dipped his hand to where they joined finding her bud.

"Ahhhhh!" The wave crashed over her shaking her to her core. Lost in its tumbling tide, she did not care if she ever emerged.

Slowly the waters fell away leaving her drenched and limp on the white linen sheet.

She drifted, she knew not how long, so wrung out that only the shift in his energy pulled her out of her bliss.

It was clearly his time now, his careful finesse gone. He tucked his chin to his chest as he drove into her. Thrusting, retreating. Thrusting, retreating. She reverently touched his arms, his chest, amazed at the machine of his body which gathered and stiffened as if he were on some precipice. He threw his head back, neck stretching, his mouth open in a silent roar. Oh heavens, he was magnificent. Then she burst apart again.

Her body had deserted her long ago. She lay open and slightly bewildered at the enormity of what they had just done together. This morning she would rise out of these sheets and put on her clothes once again, but she knew she would never feel quite the same, ever again. He had given her that gift. And perhaps, that sorrow.

His hands drifted over her. As if they could possibly have a hope of shoring her up. She relished this loose-limbed feeling where her body seemed to have no boundaries. This must be what it might feel like to move through water. To swim. Oh, to never come back to shore and drift forever in this bliss of love.

But reality intruded and worries surfaced. Nothing was fixed. She would be a naïve fool to think this one night of magical love might cure all the problems that lay between them. But it was a beginning.

She cradled his seed within her. Please let it take root, please.

And please, when could they do it again?

****

The bong of the clock jerked her awake. Sunlight spilled into the room. She blinked at the light.

James.

She reached for him, but he was gone. The whole encounter could have been a dream except for the sweet ache between her legs and his musk on the still warm sheets.

And her shredded night rail.

And the smears of blood between her legs.

And the giddiness that bubbled within her.
Not a dream. Not a dream at all.
Perhaps even a beginning.

Chapter Twenty-Seven

"To freedom."

Dev toasted the image reflected in the darkened window.

His shadowed twin saluted back.

Free. The concept rang around him like a clanging bell. A vibration so penetrating—at times euphoric with its promise, but mostly the notion had him pulling in around himself. This brave new world all too much.

One twitch and the curtain extinguished his ghostly companion. Brandy swirled in his glass, its amber legs running down the sides thick and even.

What time was it? Three minutes after he'd last checked.

Once again the elaborately scrolled medallion on the ceiling drew his gaze. If only it could penetrate the horse hair and plaster to divine the scene in the room above. Was Anne waiting up there for him tonight? Would she want him again?

When he'd slipped into her room in the early hours of the morning, he promised himself, as he had every night before, that he would only look—to watch as she slept. But she had been awake. And she had called him James.

His beautiful Owl had taken charge, putting a halt to his delinquent neglect. She wanted a child. Likely she only acted because she could not stand a lie, needing to

266

make the babe a reality, but still…

Sinking into her softness had been like nothing he'd ever experienced. Driving into her center, filling himself even as he filled her. And the aftermath, a different sort of drug, one of focus and clarity. She made him clean. She made him whole and full of promise. He craved that feeling again. But did she?

Still too early to go up and see. God damn these endless nights. The burn of brandy filled his mouth. He set the glass aside before he took another.

Ten days he'd tossed and turned in that monstrous bed, his bride only a withdrawing room away. He always ended up on the bloody floor, huddled beneath one thin sheet. Yet the hour or so he had slept next to her, had been the soundest he could remember.

He shifted a ledger filled with his ideas for shoring up the Malvern coffers. Over the years they had been severely stretched. Apparently farming was not as profitable as it had once been. He flipped to the last pages. A four thousand pound bonus recently paid out to Doctor Hives. No wonder the man was so keen to have the Mad Marquess "cured."

Old Tally was proving a good tutor and seemed to value Dev's ideas. He'd always been excellent with numbers. Austin also attended the meetings. He smiled and bobbed his head like a good yes man. Though it was patently clear he resented Dev's suggestions. *One may smile and smile and be a villain…*

The line from Hamlet tugged at him.

He'd searched Austin's rooms but found nothing—no paintings, no incriminating letters. His brother went to his clubs, saw his mistress, bet a goodly amount he was fairly sure Austin could ill afford. Nothing nefarious. Hell, things he had done himself before being shut away at Ballencrieff.

What a sapscull he had been back then. And now, apparently an even bigger fool to be goaded into trying out his old life. Gilbert Nightly, hearing Dev was back among the living, had corralled him into coming out. It only took one visit to his old haunt to bring painful enlightenment.

The reliable rakes and wastrels at Coggan's Raid had cheered and clapped him on the back with shouts of, "The prodigal returns!"

Nightly had ushered him to a faro table. Within moments he'd been handed a bumper of brandy, a whore had draped herself over his lap and her heavy, cheap perfume had filled his nose. She looked slightly familiar. Hell, most likely he'd bedded her, but her name eluded him. He was sure he had smiled, making all the appropriate sounds, and he must have drunk the brandy because the glass was immediately filled by another nameless whore who hung expectantly over his shoulder. The panic inside him would have started an avalanche had he let one part of it out.

He'd stayed to play several hands. They would have chewed him up and spit him out had he not done so. Dressed up rabid dogs they were, all poised to tear him to shreds should he let down his guard one fraction. His friends. And he had been just like them not so long ago.

He'd left them in the small hours of the morning with a raging headache and his suit reeking. He'd never gone back.

His glass was empty. Should he have another? No, no fuzziness when he went to Anne tonight.

He pulled open the desk drawer. A sheaf of

architect's drawings lay bound in a red ribbon. Anne's home. Their new home.

He had engaged Mr. Elton Menlo, an architect whose modern ideas he admired. The land had been purchased and the footings were about to be poured. A surprise for his bride. He planned a huge library and a medicinal garden. And a multitude of windows.

The conservatory needed something more. He had an idea for a window much like the one that had once graced this library—maybe an orange grove instead of climbing roses? But as he drew the folder out, a heavy vellum card embossed with the Queen's crest fell out. Just where he'd thrust it eight days ago.

Damn it all.

Might as well face it. He ran his finger over the blue wax seal, cracking it in half. He flipped the page over. Formal letters, all in tidy rows, invited him to exhibit at Her Majesty's National Art Exhibition. Signed, Sir Charles Brocket. The same twit who at last year's event had had the temerity to "sky" his portrait of Nell Whittley. Nell's lovely face hung just under the bloody rafters making the perspective all skewed. All tits and no head.

Brocket was a jealous ass. Always had been. Well, it hadn't helped that his wife had come to Dev's studio seeking to have her "portrait" painted by a "master."

Of course he had buttoned her back up and sent her packing without so much as a peck on the cheek, but her husband could not let such a betrayal slide.

So he had paid. Paid doubly, as Miss Whittley had withdrawn her favors after being dubbed "Mounds with Tiara" by the rags.

He reached for the bottle of Camus Frères, but

instead, pulled the latest broadsheet toward him. He'd committed most of it to memory, having read the thing five or more times.

Speculation runs rife about whether the Marquess of D will submit an entry to her majesty's charity exhibition. And if he antes in, who will be his subject? Will he paint one of his famous angels, a devil, or perhaps another ghostly, blank phantom? White's betting book is chock full of possibilities. But others would say the M of D's talent has dried up now he is newly married.

No doubt Brocket was stirring the pot with the papers, licking his chops for more revenge.

Dare we speculate a certain red-haired beauty might consent to be hung? One thing is certain, Miss N W will steer clear of the M of D's brushes. She is now a favorite of Manet. As for the new marchioness, perhaps that blank canvas was in fact her portrait? No one has seen this phantom bride.

He slapped the paper against the table. That arsehole, Brocket, needed a good shove up his own rafter.

By God, his next painting would not be hidden and snubbed. It must be irrefutably magnificent. Lauded. And the *ton* would eat their crow right alongside Sir Charles. They would not dare to call James Drake anything but a genius.

Except that masterpiece was, as yet, a blank.

A terrible new devil had taken up residence in his brain. Time and again he'd push it away, but the fiend slipped in, its blackness polluting the images waiting to come out through his hands and his brushes. It whispered even now.

Perhaps you cannot paint without your drugs.

He felt for the hard knot of opium against his breast. Still there. His eyes burned from so little sleep, his cheeks were raw with biting them, but so far, he'd resisted

A rush of wind blew down the chimney feeding the flames in the firebox and causing the ceiling medallion's golden flourishes to cavort with their neighboring shadows in a jolly country dance.

Would Anne have mended her night rail with her awkward childish stitches, embarrassed to have her maid repair it? Or, would she have shed it, leaving it in a pool on the floor as she hastily kicked it off? More likely she'd methodically lay it over the chair by her bedside table, neat and proper. Would she tentatively touch herself, pretending her fingertips were his? Wanting to feel him inside her.

Had they made a child? Their child.

They were both like characters in a farcical play— thrust into the roles not knowing any of the lines, enacting a plot not of their choosing. She must produce a child, and he must paint again. The audience sat salivating, waiting for them to fail.

But at least she was his now, giving herself to him bodily as well as contractually. No going back. No dissolving the marriage.

Typical glutton that he was, always wanting more.

Right. Enough torture. Enough brandy. Time to go up there and see if he was welcome.

The door to her bedchamber opened with nary a sound but she immediately turned toward him. Awake.

Moonlight cast a luminous path along the floor and onto her bed. Waiting for him? No way to tell from her solemn eyes, but he so wanted—needed to believe she had been. She did not speak only lifted her arm, a ribbon of white through the pale beam. His ring shot fire, a dragon's breath in the cold room. Seeing the opal on her finger made his heart pound and his skin flush.

"James…"

****

Now, hours later, he lay on his side his body deliciously wrung out. He'd worried she would be sore, but he was learning his wife was good at getting what she wanted. And she'd wanted him, three times, in fact.

She stirred and burrowed her mouth into the pillow.

Soon she would wake. Time to leave her before she could look in his eyes and see he was a sham and not the confident man who came to her in the darkness. The one who had no scars. The one who made her writhe with pleasure.

She frowned in her sleep, as if she could divine his falseness. As if, with the coming light, she could see he was not her dark prince, just a broken man who stumbled in the light.

Shadowed lids fluttered and lifted. "James."

His name on her lips still felt new and unreal. A gift in itself.

He stopped his hand from touching her brow. "I must go. The scullery maid will be in soon to poke up the fire."

"I was hoping you would stay"—her lashes dropped—"to poke up my fire."

His bloody cock jumped like a circus animal. "You must never be let loose among a group of young blades, Lady Devlin. You will surely slay them."

"Hmm." Her mouth firmed up, the lushness of her

272

lips pulling tight.

Still slightly embarrassed at what her body did, and said, in the dark of night, his sweet Owl. Those tiny pent-up whimpers, released after so much effort to keep them inside. Each one a reward for him.

She rolled on her back, exposing one exquisite breast. It puckered up, a delectable raspberry just ripe for plundering. "I only want to slay you," she said in her matter-of-fact voice, the one he loved, so incongruous with the siren splayed before him.

"Well, then consider me dead and buried, my wife." The chit reached for his bobbing cock as if they were both conspiring against him. "Now, none of that. I must go."

"Why?" She half-sat up. The other breast said 'good morning.' Twin cups of cream topped with a single bit of red fruit. "Why must you go?" She certainly could look mulish when the occasion called for it.

He did not have an answer, at least not one he wished to share with his beautiful bride. *I am afraid you will see the wreck you are saddled with for the rest of your days. I cannot stand the truth you demand of me.*

No, he could say none of these things. He was selfish and would not risk losing these dark hours. "I see you got my ring." Unearthed after hours of trolling through practically every jeweler's shop in Piccadilly until he found perfection. He had touched the jewel just last night, but still, he wanted to hear her acknowledge the gift.

"Yes."

Did she like it? More importantly did she like him. "I thought it suited you," he nudged, since she was being a clam.

She ducked her head.

Really, his Owl could be bloody inscrutable when she wanted.

"It is an opal." Another prod.

"Yes."

Of course she bloody knew. She hadn't been born under a rock, for God's sake.

Her finger traced the curve of the stone. His mind immediately imagined that finger touching the curved tip of something else that changed color as well.

"—understand the colors are determined by the spacing between the planes and their orientation with respect to the incident light," she said, as if reciting for her governess.

His cock bobbed like a good student. The sheet had slipped again. "Bragg's law of diffraction," he answered, and then cleared his throat. "Though I must say I was not thinking of Mr. Bragg or his theories when I selected it for you."

"Oh…"

His smile seemed to shut her down. He waited to see if she would recover her footing. He knew the power of his smile and used it with lethal precision.

"I found a book on gemstones in the library." Her hand drifted to the bedside table to touch one of her many books that were stacked neatly there. "You could not know, but it is my birthstone."

Bloody Hell. What a sapscull he was. He did not even know his wife's birth date. He could map nearly every mole on her body but did not know when she had come into this world. An opal—October, if he recalled rightly. Still time. "When?" His voice sounded harsh in his ears, so anxious to right his terrible gaff.

"October the third." She shook her head, biting her upper lip. "Birthdays were never celebrated at Ardsmoore. Though some years I was fêted on All Hallows Eve, when the girls believed me a witch."

The third. Over a month. "Remind me to hunt down those hoydens and give them the punishment they deserve." What should he do for her? "A Libra. Loyal, diplomatic, gracious, fair-minded—I dare say Mr. Beauchamp would approve, if he ever paid any attention to anyone other than himself." But his words applied to him, just as easily as Horace Beauchamp.

"And passionate. Do not forget passionate." She drew a large looping circle over the sheet at her breast. "I do not know your birthday, either."

The circles became smaller and smaller. He licked his dry lips. "April. April tenth."

"Ah, that explains a lot." She took his hand and placed it to her breast. "You are fire."

"Anne…" He swallowed. "I must—"

"You must…what? Go?" She cocked her head. "Why? Because you must paint?" She sat up more. "I read the papers. And, in this, I agree with them. What you must do is paint." She folded her hands primly in her lap. "Have you found a model yet?"

"I—no, not yet."

She looked up at him as if she had all the answers within her and was patiently waiting for him to catch up.

"Anne, I must go now."

She sighed. "Will the maid be so offended to see my husband sleeps with me?" She took his hand while shaking her head. "I do not understand these rules. I do not like them."

He pulled his hand away, and settled the sheet and

coverlet up over her. He had only so much resolve. "You will catch cold."

She placed her fingertips against her eyelids and sighed.

Light knifed its way between the pulled curtains. He could not stay. He would be groveling at her feet in two shakes of a lamb's tail.

Like some kind of vampire, he escaped into the hall before he turned to ash.

Chapter Twenty-Eight

The leaning tower of Pisa.

Anne stared in horror at the pale woman in the mirror.

Baedeker's Guide to Italy lay at the top of her growing stack of books. The tower fascinated her. How had it managed to stand all these years? How could hair—

"*Non,* do not touch, it is perfect, madame." But Yvette's expression did not seem to match her compliment.

Her maid re-adjusted a huge tiara that must weigh nearly half a stone. It crowned the mass of loops and frizzed curls that had once been her straight-as-a-pin hair, and continued to list no matter how many pins the girl jammed into Anne's head.

The acrid tang of burned hair, mixed with a heavy floral perfume, made her already nervous stomach heave.

Oblivious, Yvette wielded her various curling irons with such ferocity Anne shuddered to think of encountering the maid on a field of battle. She had ended up closing her eyes for sanity, whilst her scalp had been scraped raw and her hair wrenched into its present tower. She took it as a tolerably good omen that only one of her ears had been branded. "*Oof!*" A pair of jeweled combs joined the tiara in a trilogy of pain.

"There." Yvette stepped back, her hands held out in front of her prepared to catch whatever might fall from her masterpiece. "Stop!"

Anne froze.

"Don't move yer 'ead!" The French maid suddenly turned a cockney. "Only the eyes. Think of yerself as a queen this night. You are regal." The maid rolled her wrists, punctuating the exaggerated rolled "r," her accent now firmly back in place along with her confidence.

The headache ran up the back of her neck, circled the crown of her head, and pushed out toward her ears.

"It ez time, your ladyship. Lord Austin ez waiting."

Tentatively she fingered the heavy matching gems circling her throat. Lord Austin had brought them earlier in the day.

Where was her *husband*? For nearly four weeks he had only seen fit to steal into her bed every night and then leave with the dawn without so much as a word. Well, that was not strictly true; he did murmur some words, but she was usually incapable of deciphering them as she was otherwise occupied.

Resigned, she hefted herself out of the slipper chair—no easy feat. The new corset bit into her, squeezing her breath to somewhere just under her collarbones. She gazed longingly at her bed, but teetered to the door on her new high-heeled shoes.

"Remember, madame, regal," Yvette admonished.

Lord Austin and Margaret awaited her by the stairway.

Dear heavens. She stopped cold upon seeing her ladyship in her finery. Anne looked down—ah! She caught the tilting tiara just in time—righted the thing, and then cautiously cast her eyes at her own gown which seemed a smaller version of the one in front of her.

"Ravishing, simply ravishing." His lordship bowed deeply. The bow, she suspected, was partly executed to cover the grimace on his face.

"Did I not tell you, husband? She will be the belle of the ball." Margaret's horsey grin showed all her teeth. And gums. "I hope you do not mind, Lady Devlin, your gown proved to be so stunning I had Bathilde make mine to a similar pattern."

Yes, she was afraid that had been the case. "Not at all, Lady Austin." She could not go so far as to offer a reciprocal compliment.

"Oh, and I see Yvette was able to achieve the hairstyle I had in mind. Unfortunately, I am too tall for such a creation, but you—well, mark my words, no other lady will touch such perfection."

"I trust no one will touch it. I fear if they do, it will fall around my ears."

Margaret did not seem to comprehend her little joke.

"Let us descend, ladies. I believe my brother is already waiting with the duke."

Austin took her left arm and Margaret's right. What a trio they must make—Lord Austin's elegant and understated splendor book ended by absurdity.

Once again, she resisted the urge to roll her neck. *Regal. You must think of yourself as a queen this night.* Then she saw him.

He stood utterly magnificent in his black cut-a-way tails and pristine white linen. An utter stranger, and utterly—

Aghast.

Oh, why had she not trusted her instincts? One look at his face confirmed the horrible, irrefutable truth. The hours in Madame Bathilde's and Margaret's company had been tedious at the time, but it was nothing to seeing the frozen surprise on her husband's face.

Copious amounts of French floss now tickled her neck and bosom. And feathers. Her nose twitched. Please, you must not sneeze. Certainly no Owl this evening, more like an overblown peacock. If only she could be an ostrich instead. She would have turned around to escape back to her rooms, regal be damned, but for Austin's firm arm keeping her fixed to his side.

How she made it to the bottom of the staircase she never knew, but the gorgeous stranger who was her husband now stood beside her. Being two feet from him was rather dizzying. Never seeing him so formally dressed, she could have gazed at him for hours, but her humiliation, and the fact that much of her concentration was employed in keeping her head erect, prevented her from doing much of anything.

"Lady Devlin."

She cut a glance to her husband.

His mouth had closed. Thank God. His jawline jumped, and she thought she saw one side of his lips twitch. Did he imagine her plight was amusing?

She could not tell because he chose that moment to bend over her hand and kiss her glove. When he straightened, his face was as blank as one of his primed canvases. "I see my dear sister-in-law has been busy."

"Let me see the chit," the old duke said from his bath chair as he motioned a footman to wheel him forward. "I hear the dress cost an absolute fortune. Near as much as the new water closet Austin insisted I put in." His old rheumy eyes shifted over her body. "*Hmm,* Devlin, if you paid by the yard I'd say you got your money's worth. A gel this small might have gotten two or three frocks for that amount of fabric. Never understood women's fashion." He glanced at Lady Austin, *humphed*, and then returned his gaze back to Anne. "Gave her the Hatten Rubies, did you, boy?"

"No. I did not." James looked pointedly at his brother.

"No? Well, they are a bit overwhelming on the marchioness, but then just about everything is, what? Still, it is well they are getting some air. Been in the vault since my great grandfather gave them to his duchess."

"Shall we go meet our guests?" Her husband offered his arm.

Anne began to nod but felt an infinitesimal shift in her tiara and said, "Yes, my lord."

Faces and names ran into one another as the crush of over-perfumed humanity streamed by narrowly disguising their disdain. Her dark pool of a headache burst into a raging storm of pain which crashed over her teeth to eddy into the place below her brow, where it settled into a pounding throb.

And this was only the receiving line.

A bewigged footman offered her a flute of champagne. Parched, she gratefully reached for it before realizing she would have to tip her head in order to actually drink.

"Come, we must open the ball." James deposited the glass into a miraculously waiting hand, took her firmly by the arm, and towed her out into the middle of the room.

"My Lord—" Despite not having drunk a drop, she'd somehow acquired the hiccoughs.

But the music began and his arms surrounded her.

She had no time to even get her bearings when the hum of their bodies overtook even the music.

He stepped backward, bringing her with him into what must be a waltz.

At least her fright had caused her hiccoughs to stop. However, her body now hesitated and stuttered as the pressure of his hands signaled her to move. But where and how?

She stumbled, and he caught her. "I see you do not dance."

"No."

His jaw flexed again. "Relax. And try to breathe. We'll get through this."

She dare not look down at his feet. Oh, how would she manage? She opened her mouth to beg a reprieve. But his steady gaze held her as surely as his arms, telling her she was no coward.

Subtle pressures on her back and gentle squeezes of his hand in hers gave her the cues she needed. But mostly this newfound confidence came from his eyes, locked onto hers. "Down, up, up. There you go," he murmured as he took her into a turn.

A kaleidoscope of faces and glittering gems whirled by as she found her rhythm, her feet miraculously mirroring his steps. He was an exquisite dancer else she would have been lost.

Bless Bess, she was dancing.

She breathed with the music. Much like lovemaking, every bit of her matched every bit of him, their bodies singing their own unique music. His eyes smiled into hers and everything else disappeared.

"Another turn now." He need not have spoken; she was ready. His mouth smiled now to match his eyes. She must have smiled back because his lips hitched into his roguish grin. He pulled her slightly tighter to him, her French floss now brushing his waistcoat and cravat, her enormous skirts belling out from the press of his legs.

If only they could waltz right out the open doors, never to return.

But the music had slowed, signaling the denouement. He bowed over her hand. A smattering of applause was soon swallowed in a collective gasp from the surrounding company.

"Lord Devlin," A dour looking lady dressed in black stood before them. "You look quite recovered. I am glad to see it."

Every guest seemed to be bent in supplication. James made a deep bow and Anne managed a reasonable curtsy given the encumbrance of her tiara.

"The papers have made a great show over you of late. It is regrettable how they take such an interest in the *ton* these days. I do not approve. However, they would have nothing to report did people behave as they ought. I had hoped your bride would have a better influence on you"—she gave Anne a stern look—"but, if the rags are to be believed, it appears you continue in your rakish ways?"

"Your Majesty, we are most humbled by your attending our affair." James turned to Anne. "May I present my bride, Lady Devlin."

Dear Heavens, was this tiny woman the Queen? All the calm she had achieved during their waltz vanished. Her highness held out her hand, and Anne mimicked her husband. "Your Majesty."

"*Hmm*, I like your face, Marchioness. However I do not approve of your gown. One must try to remember less is more. I was entirely too fussy in my youth. Death always brings perspective." She turned back to James. "While your body appears recovered, I trust your morals have as well."

The old duke, with Tally guiding his chair, appeared from behind the Queen. Margaret trailed after, followed by Austin.

"I did not dare to hope you would attend, ma'am," the duke actually smiled. Anne had never seen him do so and was struck by how much James favored his father. "I know you prefer to keep quiet these days."

"Yes, as quiet as one can with a gaggle of children to tend." She turned to Anne. "I understand we have hope of a blessed event?"

Did one answer the Queen? Dear God, what was the punishment for lying to your sovereign? She smiled and played shy.

"I can always tell when a lady is increasing." The Queen looked pointedly at her. "Always." Margaret coughed and turned away. "Ah, Lady Austin. You'll be ready to retire soon?" Margaret gawped and nodded. "*Hmmm…* They say a female child steals its mother's beauty."

She turned back to James. "I am most anxious to see what you will produce for the art exhibit."

"I had not thought to enter anything this year, ma'am, being newly married."

"Nonsense. You must get back on the horse, as I am doing by attending this evening. Show them the Malvern fortitude. My charity for waifs and strays will thank you for your contribution." She looked down her nose at James, no small thing as her highness stood at eye level with Anne.

"And when the time comes, you will attend the House of Lords." It was not a request. "I must depart now." She turned to the duke. "Malvern, I trust Doctor Gull has done you some good? He worked wonders with the prince."

"You are all kindness, ma'am. The doctor is most attentive." The old duke bowed his head.

"I am glad to hear it. One must always be vigilant in supporting good health. It is shoddy to neglect one's person and squander God's favors."

"I am devoted to that end, ma'am. I must see my grandson born."

"Yes." The Queen's gaze found Anne's. "Yes, I look forward to that as well, Malvern. And to the Marquess' painting. Until then, I bid you all a good evening."

The Queen turned and then walked through the throng of lords and ladies who, like falling skittles, curtsied and bowed as she moved past their ranks.

Now that Queen Victoria had departed, the old duke seemed to collapse within his starched cravat. "I never thought she would actually attend." The duke speared a look at his eldest son. "We will not disappoint Her Majesty. Not after such condescension." His gaze shifted to Anne, his eyes narrowing. "I count on the both of you." Her hands burned to ease the duke's suffering. "I am for bed now I've done the pretty."

"Shall I take you up, Father?" Austin stepped forward.

The duke barely raised a hand to wave his son off. "All right, Tally, shuffle me off now, I am all in. Still, a good day's work here tonight."

Austin drew back, a tight smile plastered on his

beautiful face, as his father and manservant moved off. "If you will excuse me?" Lord Austin bowed to the company and disappeared into the crowd.

"Devlin, so refreshing to have you back among us." A middle-aged gentleman with a hawkish face and thinning hair presented himself. "The *ton* has been quite tame of late, but it seems your reemergence is worthy enough to bring our Queen out of hiding. What a coup."

"Sir Charles." James stepped slightly in front of Anne.

"Missed the receiving line. But couldn't help overhearing you'll be exhibiting after all. I must say I am relieved. All this tittle-tattle about your talents drying up—well, the world will be able to judge for themselves now, won't they? The exhibition would not be the same without a James Drake portrait." He leaned in conspiratorially. "Wouldn't do to go against our sovereign's wishes, now would it? Disappointing all those poor waifs and strays."

James said nothing.

"Don't tell me you're still peeved about our little misunderstanding? I wondered, when you did not reply to the Academy's invitation."

Sir Charles, she now remembered, was connected with the famous art exhibit she had read about in the papers, and apparently, no friend of her husband.

"Aren't you going to present me to your bride?" The man smirked. "I came expressly to entreat you to join the exhibition, but I did want to meet the new marchioness."

Her husband clearly did not want to make the introduction, but good manners won out. "Lady Devlin, may I present Sir Charles Brocket. Sir Charles, this is my wife, Lady Devlin."

She curtsied, and the man bowed.

"I must say, I never expected you to go so easily, Devlin." The man reeked of some overwhelming toilet water, likely used to mitigate the stench of his rotten breath. "What a shock to hear of your hasty marriage, especially after being away from Town for so long. But I can see that the marchioness is quite irresistible." The man looked pointedly at Anne's belly swathed in ruffles.

She resisted the urge to smooth her hand over them. Not that she need worry. A small family could hide under her skirts and have no fear of detection, let alone a several-month-old fetus.

James stepped forward and caught Brocket by his upper arm. He turned to her and Margaret. "If you will excuse us, I believe Sir Charles is in need of some air." Her husband and the older man headed toward the French doors leading to the balcony.

"Your pardon, Lady Devlin, I hope you will not think me too forward approaching you without an introduction, but I am in raptures over your gown." A woman with an astonishing amount of facial hair and dressed entirely in black curtsied. A girl followed in her wake.

Margaret beamed and stood taller, if that were possible. "Lady Markham, may I present Lady Devlin, Marchioness of Devlin. Lady Devlin, Lady Markham."

Again curtsies were performed. Apparently, the girl peeping out from behind did not warrant an introduction.

"What an astonishing gown, Lady Devlin. Is chartreuse the newest fashion? I had no idea. Joanna,"— the girl took a small step around her ladyship's skirts— "we shall have to take Madame Broussard, our *modiste*, to task for keeping us in the dark. But then, that shade of green is such a difficult color on most complexions. I vow my dear Joanna could not hope to pull it off."

The poor girl looked at her slippers and sniffed. As plain as the girl was, her gown was stunningly beautiful, a simple ivory satin with tiny pleats as its only adornment.

"Now I remember," her ladyship continued. "I did see the color of late on Lady Harper's eldest gel. She looked an absolute fright. Positively pea green. But, of course," she continued, her eyes narrowing as she raised a quizzing glass and turned to Lady Austin, "the girl has not much in the way of beauty to begin with. Such a trial for her dear mama," she *tsked*. "However,"—she smiled at Anne—"you, Lady Devlin, are very brave." Her gaze swept over the dress once again. "Very brave indeed." And she curtseyed and trundled off, tittering to her slack-faced daughter.

Tears burned Anne's eyes. She blinked them away.

"Bertha Markham is an absolute troll." Margaret slapped her fan against her gloved hand. "At my own come out, she said something very similar about my gown. I believe she is jealous. She had her cap set for Lord Austin as a son-in-law. As if Joanna Henry had near the portion to tempt even a second son."

She fluffed one of the thousands of ruffles on Anne's gown. "Though Madame Broussard is touted by some as being one of the most elegant seamstresses in England, I have never seen it. Everything she designs is too plain. If one is to pay thirty guineas for a gown, wouldn't one want a few embellishments?"

Where was James?

"And that affectation of only wearing black. Old Markham has been in the ground since before the flood, yet her ladyship insists on rigorous black." Margaret jerked harder on one of the ruffles. "Such a toady, aping The Queen. Who does she think she is? I vow, if Lord Austin died, I should be so grieved to don widow's weeds. Black does nothing for my complexion. I believe we are alike in that way. We need color."

Margaret shifted from foot to foot, her enormous skirts tolling like a bell. "Lady Devlin, you must excuse me. I have need of the—I must go to the ladies' retiring room."

No! Her brain screamed. *You cannot leave me.* Instead she murmured something about being well enough on her own.

She could not be more conspicuous if she had been center stage in full limelight. Or felt so utterly alone, a wallflower of the worst kind. Even the old duke, leaching his considerable derision, would have been preferable.

Behind each fluttering fan and pristinely gloved hand, she swore her name was being whispered. The "belle of the ball" relegated to an object of scorn.

For the hundredth time, she resisted the urge to adjust her enormous tiara. If only she could have another glass of champagne, just to take the edge off this interminable evening.

But, no. She'd not had even one glass of champagne. Indeed, she'd never even tasted wine excepting the thimbleful she had taken at Ardsmoore every Sunday at Communion. And that had been so watered down it had barely retained a blush of its former color.

She signaled to a passing footman. He immediately stopped with his tray.

"Thank you," she said, evoking her watchword of 'Regal.'

She put a hand to her tiara, took a gulp and almost choked, unprepared for the fizzing bubbles that tickled her nose and rushed her cheeks.

So this was champagne. She liked it. The glass was soon empty, and she signaled the footman—now her friend—to bring another.

Fortified, she looked about her. She suspected she made a rather haughty picture in her ridiculous confection of a gown with her nose up in the air. Heavens, she bit her lip to stop the laughter gathering behind her teeth.

Not so frightening, this group of over-indulged folk. They probably had their lot of troubles just as Lady Tippit and Mr. Beauchamp.

As she turned to survey the other side of the room, she saw that dreadful man again, the one James had chased off. He approached her now.

Drat, where was Margaret? Or her husband, for that matter?

"Lady Devlin, my humble apologies for any discourtesy I may have shown. Will you prove your good will and stand up with me?" He extended his hand to her.

Perhaps it was the champagne talking, or her new-found regality, or the fact that her husband seemed to have deserted her, but she found herself saying, "Yes." She held out the empty glass to her footman friend and then took Sir Charles's arm.

At least it was another waltz. She thought she had the gist of it now after spending a half hour or so dancing the steps with James.

But as Sir Charles took her in his arms, she knew she'd made a dreadful mistake.

This man did not feel remotely like her husband.

Cloying cologne swamped her senses. Anne focused on his cravat, which looked like it had recently been put through a cider press and then yanked back into place. Only slightly taller than she, she was in the direct path of his breath. A gag rose in her throat. The stench put her in mind of a chicken yard.

He lurched into the first steps—his stride too long for her to keep pace. She managed to recover her footing when he took her into a turn. Not the wonderfully effortless gliding her husband had demonstrated, where she seemed to float rather than dance, this man's turn was more of a hard corner.

Faces jerked by. So hard to maintain her regal demeanor when one felt like a sack of potatoes. And one's stomach heaved. She was about to excuse herself when a face stood out among the tittering crowd.

A face she would know anywhere.

A face that stopped her dead.

The inevitable happened. She finally lost her battle with the Hatten tiara.

Still, she rose onto her tip toes in an effort to see beyond her husband who was charging toward them.

"By God, you have gone too far, Brocket," James ground out. Sir Charles' smug smile froze as James's fist smashed into it.

Chapter Twenty-Nine

Dev fled the ball and hied away to his refuge.

The garret was proving a good investment. Not so much for painting, but as a haven.

From this vantage point, so high above, he felt removed, almost god-like. Each time he climbed these stairs, the world fell away. The sounds of the city still punctuated the air, but they were far below and somehow manageable.

He tapped his pencil against his empty sketchbook and looked out over the Thames. The "mud larks" had come and gone, trolling for bits of treasure revealed as the high tide ebbed away.

Now sailors and stevedores scurried like dung-beetles, slaves to the water and winds. Ships groaned like arthritic old dowagers, their sails snapping in answer as bells clanged over the din.

Already noon time? He felt like a blown dandelion. Time to sleep.

Gingerly he unfolded himself from his perch and tentatively stretched his aching jaw. Charles Brocket had got one good blow in before Dev had laid waste to him.

Humph. In the past he would have counted this as a victory. Something to brag about with the younger blades. But now the whole thing left him sick.

And Anne, in that ridiculous atrocity Margaret had concocted, everything else around her in a riot, including her magnificent hair which had thankfully burst its cage of contrived twists and crimps to fall heavy about her shoulders, stood as tall as you please—all five feet of her—a quiet look of composure on her face.

God, she had been magnificent; a perfect foil to his complete bestiality.

Austin and several other fellows had yanked him off the cur, Brocket, who then extricated himself from the enormous floral arrangement which had toppled during their scuffle. He spit a tooth at the mangled greenery and crushed roses now littering his feet.

Anne had calmly looked them both over, nodded and said, "I believe I shall retire now, my lord. It seems the principal entertainment has concluded, and I fear anything else we might provide will pale in comparison." And she had sailed across the floor like Cleopatra upon her barge—her enormous ruffled skirts seeming to bear her up as she disappeared into a sea of shifting humanity.

He could not go to her bed. The shame of his behavior had him skulking off to lick his wounds here in his garret. He did not deserve his lovely and wise Owl.

The cot against the wall beckoned him.

The bed had been installed when he'd taken the place. Along with a shower bath, a water tower to catch the rain, and a heater. Admittedly a luxury, but after Ballencrieff and those freezing pools, he never wanted to endure a cold bath again.

His landlord, Cheswell, had the cheek to actually waggle his eyebrows and mutter something about a love nest, but Dev paid no mind. The cot was proving as good an investment as the shower. Thus far, other than a few hours in his wife's bed—and he usually endeavored to use that time more wisely than for mere sleeping—it was the only place he could manage a bit of rest.

The cot groaned its familiar groan. His feet hung off the end. He told himself this bed was nothing like his old cot at Ballencrieff, but of course it was a lie. He reminded himself he could leave this room at any time and be fine down there in the real world. Another falsehood.

He raised his arms toward the iron headboard, waiting for the snap of—

No. He squeezed his eyes shut and curled into himself, pressing his still sensitive wrists together between his thighs.

Rest. He must rest, and then he would paint. Or better still, go home and face his wife. He only needed sleep.

The soft slap of boots on the stair brought him bolt upright.

Not a new model. He had not engaged one for this day. And not Cheswell. The landlord knew which side of the bread was buttered. Dev paid him well for tight lips and no questions. Enough money and no one gave a shite what devilment you might be up to. Besides, the footfalls were too light to be his obsequious landlord.

He swiped his hand beneath the straw mattress and pulled out his knife. Situating himself slightly behind the door, he waited.

A key scrabbled in the lock. *Fucking Cheswell.* He would let the man have it when next he saw him. Poised and ready to attack, the voice behind the door stopped him cold.

"You would have to take yourself up to the top of the blasted city."

The locked *snicked* and the door swung open.
Nora.

If possible she had grown more beautiful.

He started toward her. Then stopped. He'd gone to her out of habit, he supposed.

She waved him off with one hand, the other on her belly. "Ninety-three."

"What?"

"The number of steps one must climb to get to you. Do you fancy yourself as some sort of Rapunzel?" She straightened and took a deep breath. "Well, it is not entirely your fault. I did have Struthers lace me particularly tightly today. Somehow the notion of encountering you made me think I needed the extra fortification."

Her little speech over, they stood as if ready to duel but had no weapons or desire. The last time he had seen her she was covered in Lily's blood and Austin was hauling her out of Greene Street.

"Rather Spartan for you, Dev. Oh, but I see you have not skimped on the things that count." She picked up his half-empty bottle of Camus Frères.

"How did you get the key?" It was not polite, but his manners had fled when she had pushed in and denigrated his lair. Now she was at his brandy. His mouth watered in agreement.

"Is that how you treat me after I came all this way?"

Guilt flooded him. He had hardly thought of Nora since—well, since Anne…

She tossed her veiled bonnet onto the bed, revealing burnished copper curls. "Really, need you ask? I found your dear landlord, Mr. Cheswell, at the Rose and Thistle next door. Took one look at me and I had the key in a nonce."

Touché. Nora Havermere was a veritable juggernaut

when it came to the male sex. She could lay siege to an army of salivating mortals with just a bat of her lashes. God help the man upon whom she turned her full arsenal. He had been one of those poor sots.

He swiped his hands over a rasp of beard. He needed a drink. "And…you are well?"

This new relationship was vexing. Time was when he would have not given her a moment before taking her into his arms, hiking her skirts, and pressing his cock into her.

What now? What were they now?

She waved his question away. "Shouldn't you be home facing your wife?"

The thought of Anne sent him to rescue his bottle. "You must have seen the papers. I'm sure they had a field day with my antics of last evening." He took the bottle and poured out a measure.

"Didn't need to. I passed Lady Brinley in the street. She gave me an earful. And then, on the way over here, we had to stop for an impromptu street show near Pall Mall. Some swells were acting the whole thing out. They certainly did you and Brocket justice, but the blade playing your lady wife did not have nearly her *savoir faire*. One must give the proper credit to a lady who survives losing her crown just as her husband is losing his head. Though I'm not sure the papers will frame it that way. Quite a trio you were. However, to my mind she came out the distinct winner of all the combatants." Nora looked out the window and sniffed.

"And I suppose you would have simply stood there and let that cretin Brocket make a fool of her?"

Nora raised a beautifully arched eyebrow. "And do you imagine you did her any good by adding to the spectacle? If you'd restrained yourself, Brocket would have looked the fool and the Hatten tiara could have been retrieved without half the *ton* scampering about beneath ladies crinolines hoping to find a missing ruby."

He dumped himself on his cot, nearly crushing her bonnet, his glass cradled against his pitiful heart.

She made an unladylike *humphing* noise which he chose to ignore.

"Charles Brocket has always been an ass. Why did you expect he should suddenly change his spots?"

Blast her, she was right. Just played right into the arsehole's hands by clocking him.

"Wouldn't surprise me if Havermere didn't put Brocket up to it. My husband and Sir Charles are very thick, you know." She rescued her hat and took his glass from him, inhaled the liquor's perfume, and took a healthy swig. "The bit I am curious about is if the papers had the gumption to call you mad."

That neck. So lovely. The old Dev would have either tupped her right then and there, or taken up his brushes and painted her. But now, he only thought of Anne in her poorly mended night rail, one shoulder slipping to expose a creamy white shoulder—

Wait. "What?"

"The papers. I wonder if they've linked your name with madness again." She crossed to the window and looked out.

"They wouldn't dare." The cot echoed his indignation with its own protest. But his words rang hollow.

Those rags would like nothing better than to resurrect The Mad Marquess. It would be near impossible to live that moniker down a second time. Had such a ring to it. The appellation would likely be on his gravestone. *Here lies the famous Mad Marquess and his Overwhelmed Owl.* He winced.

"Until some other fool makes a bigger scene, you and your bride will be the unfortunate darlings of the press for the foreseeable future. Ever since Lord Randle gave up wearing dresses, society is hungry for fresh meat. I fear you are the *tartare* of the moment." She shrugged and twitched at her gown, a sure sign she was hiding something.

He retrieved his glass. "All right, out with it. Give me the worst."

She attempted to hold onto the brandy, but lost the fight.

He crossed to the table to refill their glass.

"You are not the only idiot in this room," she said plucking at the lace on her sleeve.

"Ah, I am relieved to hear it. What have you done to merit the title?"

"I could not stay away."

His hand froze in the middle of pouring. "No." This was awkward. He was not the same man who had sheltered her in his arms over a year ago. She deserved someone who loved her. He was not that man. "Nora I— that is we—"

Her derisive snort brought him to a halt as she wheeled away from him. "No, I don't mean now. Today. I am a fool, not a sadist." She gripped the sill of the window, her profile now beautifully framed. "I mean last night. I know I should have stayed away, but I couldn't. I had to see her. I escaped my husband for a few hours to see who had supplanted me in your heart."

"Nora—"

"Let me finish, if you please. Confession is not easy for me, Devlin." Nora turned to face him. "She saw me, you see."

"What?"

"Your Anne, she saw me as she was dancing with that troll, Brocket. Honestly, I did not think she would know me, but she clearly did. She jerked with the recognition, and I don't know if I can claim all the credit. Perhaps Brocket took the opportunity to miss-step or possibly you charging in to save the day... At any rate, that was when she stumbled and her tiara went flying."

He sank to the bed. "My poor Owl."

A ship's bell sounded in the distance and a fishmonger called out, "Three for a pence."

"Owl? Really, Dev? Is that your pet name for her?" Nora seemed to have shored herself up, taking refuge in sarcasm. "I cannot think such an appellation sweeps her off her feet."

"Would that were the least of my problems."

She raised an eyebrow. "Don't tell me you have failed to have her eating out of your hand. Your Owl."

Maybe Nora had changed more than he thought. "Bitterness does not become you, Nor."

"Bitter? *Ha!* You imagine I am bitter?" She flicked at a bit of non-existent dust on her bodice front. "No, not bitter. Perhaps finished? Dead? This last year, since the—well, you know—the earl keeps me on a very tight leash. Has his toadies watching his—investment. Yes, I am a commodity that has no value except as something that others may look at, covet, but never touch. Except that you did. God help us if he ever finds out."

She laughed once. A hard sound. "You are correct. You have always been able to see through me. Perhaps I am bitter." She fingered the bottle of brandy and licked her lips. "Good God, and maudlin too." She laughed truly now.

Something of the old Nora.

"He can't live much longer. He must be four score and more," he offered.

"Eighty-five. Six in December. But who is counting?" She picked at a bit of flaking paint on the window casement. "He put a stop to all my little pet projects. 'Dabbling in the underbelly of society is beneath the Countess of Havermere.' Especially sullying myself with prostitutes who were stupid enough to get themselves with child."

"Nora." He rose. "I am so sorry about Lily—"

"Don't. Please, don't speak of—and don't be sorry. You must never be sorry." She sniffed and looked away.

Suddenly his head throbbed. He couldn't get his breath.

"Devlin? Are you well?" She rose from her seat at the window. "Do you wish me to leave?"

"No, I am sorry. I sometimes go back…" That terrible white face would always have a name now. He could face it now. He could.

She nodded as if she knew all too well. "You are not taking any opium now?"

"No." The ball still rested next to his heart. A constant reminder he had a choice. "Drinking. Too much." He held up the half-empty glass. "But no drugs."

He set the glass away from him. "They are clamoring for a portrait. Those insatiable clods who determine who will rise to the top and who will drown. And now The Queen has added her edict so there is no hope of retreating. I do not want to drown. Not again. I want to show those sanctimonious bastards I still have the goods. It's ridiculous, I know. Why should I care? But I do. I want us accepted."

"Us?"

"Anne. Anne and me."

"Ah, yes, of course." She ran a long, beautifully tapered finger around the brandy bottle. "Has she never mentioned me?"

He could see what it cost this beauty to ask. Still, he could not spare her. "No."

"*Hmm.* I do not know quite what to make of that. Perhaps she is frightened of me? Should I be flattered, or perhaps it is because she thinks me so inconsequential?"

He said nothing. Nora looked as if she'd eaten a bad oyster.

"Devlin, if you need me, I will sit for you. I know you have gone through at least ten girls already. I assume you paid them well, but soon you will not be able to keep them from going to the papers."

How had she known? Cheswell again?

It was true. Twelve women, to be exact, had come to be looked over. He had even tried to paint two, but they were wrong. All wrong. Would Nora be right? "What of Havermere?"

"Oh, sod him. I hope the picture will cause him to have an apoplexy."

A smile tugged at his lips. "No, though I thank you. Not worth the risk. I will find someone."

She cocked her head and narrowed her eyes. "*Hmm,* I would like to think you are worried for me, but you are not."

"Nora, I—"

She held up her hand. "You are thinking of your

Owl. That she will be jealous. Silly man. You needn't be. From the little I observed of your marchioness last evening, she is well able to handle the likes of me or any other jade who has the temerity to poach her man."

"I am sure you are right, Nor. But for now I will not test that assertion. I will find someone."

Chapter Thirty

"Well, do not stand in the doorway like some servant. Come in." The duke waved, dismissing the footman next to him. The man hesitated and then bowed and left.

If only Anne could simply perform a curtsy and scuttle away, following the servant out, to a long list of duties. Instead she was a marchioness whose only task had been to keep her tiara on her head and not disgrace the family. She had failed miserably last evening. Better pay the piper. She entered the breakfast room.

Taking a roll and an egg, more for something to occupy her than out of want, she also filled a teacup and then sat half-way down the huge table.

She had hoped to catch James before he disappeared, but had slept too late. One of the consequences of waiting up for your husband until the wee hours of the morning.

Tick, tick, tick. Her knife against the shell of the egg, then the crunch and snap as she decapitated its head. Yoke spilled onto her fingers in a rush of deep yellow. Not daring to look up, she lay her knife aside and wiped the goo on a pristine damask napkin.

"I cannot make you out, Anne DeVere Winton Drake. You are nothing like your mother."

The bite of egg, half-way to her mouth, returned to her plate. Her mother? What of last evening and her terrible gaff?

"Though you have her eyes. Nothing more."

"How—"

"Being a duke does not have much to recommend, but it does afford me a pack of 'yes' men who are only too happy to dig into mysteries."

A gardener's head bobbed outside the bowed window, his clippers making a *shushing* noise as tiny bits of hedge flew here and there.

"You were certainly a tough nut to crack, I'll give you that. My toadies ran in circles for a good long while before they unearthed a couple with a young daughter living in Little Burne in '45. That would put it about right, wouldn't you say?"

Little Burne? An age-blackened sign, long-forgotten, came into focus in her mind's eye. It had hung upside down suspended on a pitchfork. She had just finished learning her alphabet and had stood flummoxed by these foreign letters.

"*Ha.* I see I have struck a nerve." The old duke nodded. "Pack of groveling peahens, my retainers, but they know how to find a needle in a haystack when called upon."

"Excuse me, Your Grace, but how—"

"Back at Ballencrieff, my man Tally put the name DeVere with the old French family of that surname. Couldn't believe it. Frankly, I didn't want to. But there is no denying your eyes are Eleanor's."

Eleanor's? This man had known her *maman*?

"No doubt my son would have relished the thought of marrying a commoner. The boy has always delighted in thwarting me at every turn."

More hedge bits flew, and a bird shrieked and darted

away.

"I get reports on all the charity cases that go to Ardsmoore and Ackermoore. Tally finally unearthed your file, which had been mislaid. Not much there." The old man blotted his thin lips. "A cobbler, whose horse had thrown a shoe, found you half-starved and nearly frozen curled up against your mother. He had quite a time getting you to let go. You did not speak for some months after. By the time you did, your file was tucked away. Just another poor orphan with no past."

"Do I—is any of my family still alive?"

"No, all dead now." The finality stung. "Your father had no family, and your mother's people moved back to France after your mother's elopement. They had come to London seeking a match for their only daughter. That is when I met your mother." The duke sniffed. "Would have taken her in a heartbeat, but Winton, a penniless inventor, had already wormed his way into her heart."

This man and her mother?

"I married Devlin's mother the next season." His grace looked down into his teacup as if it might provide a foretelling of the future. He shook his head and took a swig.

"I blame her for the boy's scribblings. Why could she not leave well enough alone?" His mouth pulled tight. "Too indulgent by half. A veritable bluestocking, always putting some nonsense in front of the boy. He got a thirst for it. Devlin had a thirst for everything. Always 'why.' Could never accept a thing just as it was, had to always delve into it. Wanted to know how it worked."

The old man's hands trembled so he nearly dropped his cup. It clattered into the saucer. "Should never have allowed him to go to Edinburgh. Falling in with that heathen butcher, Wainwright. From then on the boy was lost to me. Plundering graveyards in the name of 'science,' experimenting with God's creatures. Repulsive. I blame Barton Wainwright. If I could find the fiend I would not hesitate to have him brought up on charges of indecency."

The duke, lost in his memories, looked up as if he'd caught her eavesdropping.

He cleared his throat. "Claymore's girl was to be Devlin's bride. But she was skittish, like her mother, so in the end it didn't take. And then there was Prince Albert's niece—what was the chit's name? No matter. That went by the wayside as well. Once that story of butchery got leaked to the papers...well, that was it. What family would tie its fortunes and lineage to a madman? Not even a dukedom could persuade those overprotective mother hens to throw their daughters to such a man. But even if they had, I could not in good conscience foist him off on some unsuspecting innocent. Only God almighty is privy to how Devlin's mind works. I have had no luck divining its mysteries. Why He sent me this son to tax my heart and brain, I will never hope to know."

The old man looked at her as if he might gut her like a fish—a smelly fish at that. "So, you have no conversation. Am I to be left to prattle on interminably? Are you such a timid thing to be so afraid of an old man?"

"I did not think you were looking for a rejoinder, Your Grace. You seemed to be happy enough venting your frustrations."

"*Ha!* I suppose I was." The duke's eyes narrowed. "And do not 'Your Grace' me. You are no longer an inferior." He nodded once as if by doing so he had settled her into a slot in his mind. "So, Lady Devlin, how do you propose to be a good helpmate to my son?"

"He must paint." The words came out decisively before she could even think.

"What? Oh, yes, the Queen's Exhibit. Damned inconvenient—I wish he could leave off painting altogether, but I suppose we must make a show for the old girl."

"I believe he is having a difficult time beginning again."

"Painting?" The duke sniffed. "Yes, if that travesty at Ballencrieff was any example, I would say he has a large problem. Odd, as a boy he defaced anything and everything with his scribbles. Couldn't get him to stop. So, what do you collect is the problem?"

"I am not sure." But she could guess. *Paint what is in your heart.* Perhaps his heart was bereft. Perhaps, now that he was free, being shackled to her was stifling him.

Still, she could not discount what happened between them in the dark, decadence of night.

She told herself during the long days of pallid monotony, she would resist him tonight—turn him away. But as the shadows deepened, and the lamps were lit and then extinguished, her resolve faded as the hands of the clock swept the hours away accompanied by its soft chime.

Just before dawn, he would come to her smelling of the outside world and she was there waiting, wanting any piece of him. She'd raise her arms so impatient for his touch.

He'd slip into her bed and touch her so gently, as if she were something he worshiped. But soon, he would claim her body in ways that made her blush to remember.

After he had gone, when she rolled into the impression he had left, and pressed her lips to his pillow, when the day slipped in between the curtains, then the insidious doubts came.

She was not his beauty.

Not his love.

She was merely a vessel for the heir he must produce.

Nothing more.

For the first time he had not come to her last night after the ball. Had she been such an embarrassment for him? Or was he already tired of her? And had the beautiful Countess of Havermere taken her place?

"You are his wife." The duke's voice intruded. "You must find out what the trouble is and fix it. Soon. I believe the exhibition is only a few weeks away."

Her hands trembled and her heart sped up as she sensed the duke's agitation.

"The blasted ball was too much too soon. Put the cart before the horse. I own that now. But there is no time." The old man pressed his hand against his heart.

Concerned, she sat forward.

"The Queen seemed taken enough with you. But, Devlin…Devlin must do his part. If we could find that painting of you, I would feel surer he is up for this task. You are positive you never looked at the portrait?"

"I am positive. Your Grace—sir, perhaps you should lie down—"

"Do not imagine you can languish here at home. The *ton* demands you be seen! One failure does not signify defeat. You must ante up, or you will lose, Lady Devlin."

"Sir, I believe you must—"

"The Malvern name cannot survive another scandal,

Lady Devlin. I cannot—"

A hacking cough wracked the duke's frail body.

She rose, but he waved her back in her seat.

"Those infernal quacks, always muttering about my heart. Most people will tell you I don't have one. Oh, don't bother to refute me, I know what I am, what I've become. A dukedom requires discipline and sacrifice, Lady Devlin. I must have the succession secure. And soon. I cannot leave—"

The duke's face turned bright red then white again as he clutched his chest.

Hesitating only a moment, she rushed to his side.

He waved her off again, or tried to, but he had no strength.

She tossed aside the thick shawl covering his shoulders and chest. Next came his cravat, the seemingly endless yards of cloth reminding her of Hives. She dropped the linen to the floor and unbuttoned his shirt at the neck.

His eyes grew wide as her fingers brushed his chest. She paid no mind, took a long slow breath, pushing her calmness into her hands and into his lungs and heart.

Her hands grew very hot, nearly as hot as when they were deep within Phoebe Nester's womb. Afraid she might burn him, she eased up. But he clasped her hands more tightly to him, his rheumy eyes never leaving hers.

How long they remained locked together, she could not say. Time always seemed to freeze when she was in the midst of healing. Finally, his heart slowed until it beat at a steady pace, matching her own. Satisfied, she stepped away. He would wish to collect himself.

Her tea had long gone cold, but she sat and sipped the heavy brew. Darjeeling.

"We will say nothing of this little—episode." The duke sat up straighter, his color restored.

She inclined her head, in accordance with his wishes.

His gaze, once again, bored into her, but now with a difference. No longer an unsavory fish, more like one of Mr. Beauchamp's other-worldly creatures. Thank heavens he had not called her a witch. Not yet. She had experienced both reactions to her gift—awe and horror.

He rang the bell. The footman appeared. "Take me to my room."

As the duke was being wheeled out it was still unclear where she fell in her father-in-law's mind.

Chapter Thirty-One

Two nights penance tucked up in his garret was enough. Dev could not stay away another. Time to see if he was welcome back in his wife's bed.

The door clicked closed behind him. His cock hardened, so ready to be inside her.

"Go away."

Her voice, a raw rasp, penetrated his lust filled brain.

"Anne, I—"

"Leave me! Please." She curled herself into a tight ball.

"My sweet Owl, I am sorry. I can be an ass—pardon, I lost my head seeing you with…" She was not listening. He thought he heard a soft groan. "What has happened?" He clenched his fingers wanting to touch her. "Anne, won't you look at me? Are you unwell?"

She was wearing clothes, her night rail. She turned her face into the pillow, her hands fisted in the sheets.

"If you are ill—"

"I am not ill."

"Thank God. It is just that I have a temper when it comes to—"

"You were brilliant. I wish I had struck him myself."

She forgave him. She even thought him valiant. He lifted the cover.

"I said get out!" She jerked it away.

"But, I—you said—"

"I am indisposed!"

Indis—? Oh, thank God. "Bloody hell, you gave me a scare." He lifted the sheet to get in.

She wrenched the sheet from him and scuttled to the far side of the bed. "Go. Now."

"But Anne, it is only a little blood, we can do other—"

"Get out!" She threw a pillow at him.

Bloody Christ. He'd known plenty of women who became witches during their time, but he never thought his Owl would be one of them. "Very well, I will only hold—"

The other pillow hit him square in the nose.

"All right. I will take myself off. If that is what you truly wish."

Her answer was to put the covers over her head.

Right. He picked up both pillows from the floor and deposited them at the foot of the bed, lingering, hoping she would think better and turn to him.

She did not.

****

The click of the door closing released a dam of tears long held in check. No pillow left to muffle her sobs. She wadded the bedclothes to her mouth. *Stupid, stupid man.*

He came and went. He had his estate duties and his—his other distractions—she would not say the name. But as his wife she had this one thing to do. This one thing to be. And she had not done it.

No. Not stupid him. Stupid her. Ridiculous her. To pin all her happiness on making a child.

The fullness in her breasts she'd ignored. The slight cramping was just sleeping wrong, or the rich food she was still not used to, or even her tightly laced corset. But this morning there could be no more denial.

Yvette had come in wanting to remove the chamber pot as Anne lay curled up on the floor behind the screen trying to make her words not sound like they were thick with messy tears.

"Yvette, je voudrais une tasse du the."

Asking for a simple cup of tea had this "French" girl turning tail and scurrying away in a trice. Of course the tea never came.

****

Anne scrubbed her swollen eyes. Pillows littered the floor along with most of the covers. Her night gown was twisted around her body. A faint light leaked through the curtains. Another day.

That's it. Enough. She flung the thin sheet aside. Quite enough of playing a rabbit in its hole. If Margaret did not want to go out, if her husband was too busy with the duchy and his secret plans, and not painting, if the great Malverns did not dare let her entertain, then she would simply take Yvette or a footman and see the town. She would not lose herself to this man.

After taking care of her needs and dumping the soiled water in a vase of faded flowers, she rang the bell.

Yvette finally arrived, sleep creases and shock on her face.

"Did you ring for me, madame?" Anne never rang for anything, much less at six in the morning.

"Yes, I did. Several times, as a matter of fact."

"I am des-oh-lay, madame. Shall I—"

"Yvette, you are no more French than I am an Amazon. Could we please dispense with this charade and try to be honest with each other?"

"But, I told Lord Austin—"

"You are not working for Lord Austin. You are working for me. Are you not?"

The girl looked rather confused.

"I will tell him I prefer that you are a plain English maid—"

"Oh!" The girl clutched her chest.

"What is it?" She rushed forward.

"You think me plain, madame?"

Bless Bess. She squeezed her eyes shut and bit her lip. Heaven save her from vain and silly maids.

"Bring me my best dress. We are going out."

"Out, madame?" Yvette perked up like a flower in the sun.

"Yes, out. I think we'll start with the British Museum. I have longed to see the Elgin Marbles. And then on to Hatchards book shop. And music. I think I shall study the piano forte."

The maid wilted just as quickly.

Enough reading about this new world. It was high time she experienced it.

Chapter Thirty-Two

"Ah, here you are." Dev had left Anne alone for five torturous days. And nights. He closed the door to the music room giving them privacy. He did not remember the walls being papered in puce flocked wallpaper. Margaret's talents must not be confined to apparel.

"I am easily found if one has ears. I don't believe there is anyone else in the household who plays the piano." His wife sat poker straight on the bench as if she were ready to do battle with the instrument.

The Aubusson carpet might as well have been made of eggshells, he treaded so carefully toward her. "Well, I would counter by saying I don't believe anyone in this house actually *plays* the piano." He raised an eyebrow just to punctuate his silly joke.

Her response was a painfully faltering set of arpeggio scales. He had been summarily dismissed.

"Don't tell me Greely has sent you in to do his dirty work?" she said over the din.

"How do you mean?" He winced at a particularly resounding chord.

Thankfully she stopped her torture and looked at him as if trying to see if he were part of some joke. Evidently he passed muster. "Greely finds any excuse he can to take me away from my practice. I have found the door locked on a number of occasions and the key mysteriously gone missing." She held up a shiny key from her chatelaine. "That is no longer a worry. However, I believe the small fire set last week in order to disturb my play was the outside of enough."

Ha! Didn't think old Greely had it in him for such subterfuge.

"Is a fire, or the blatant disloyalty of a servant, reason for mirth, my lord?"

Oh dear, had he been smiling? "I trust you are feeling better?"

She nodded once.

"Greely tells me you are exploring the library. Improving your mind?"

"I believe, next to music, books are my passion." She frowned and gave her head a little shake, likely embarrassed at the word she chose. "I have found a few that must have belonged to you."

"Really?"

"Their pages are filled with scribblings. In ink." She pursed her lips.

"Yes, well, I was a boy full of ideas. But that was long ago." Another tentative step toward her. "And you enjoy the garden as well?"

"It is peaceful," she said in a slightly defensive tone.

"As long as you are not attempting to improve Mr. Hiro's bushes." She raised an eyebrow. "About the same time as I was defacing tomes, I had a notion that the topiary in the shape of an elephant would look infinitely better without its trunk. I believe I had hopes of turning him into a rhinoceros." He took another step. "Did you happen to see any purple rhinoceroses in my books?"

She shook her head.

He was yammering. He knew it. She knew it. But he could not seem to stop. If he did, she might take up her scales once more, or worse, he might take her in his arms. He could think of many ways that shiny expanse of piano could be put to better use. What music they would make together.

Sweet Jesu, get a hold of yourself, Devlin. You are here to woo your wife, not maul her.

"I spent the next month being Mr. Hiro's slave," he continued. "We used to have some Pyracantha bushes—also known as Firethorn—in the far corner of the garden. I recall having to remove every dead branch and damaged leaf—twenty or so bushes in all. And that was just the beginning."

"I would not dare to interfere. Mr. Hiro is an artist like yourself." Her hands drifted over the piano's keys. He steeled himself, waiting for another onslaught, but she must have thought better of it and settled her hands in her lap. "He has given me a small bush-like tree called a Bonsai. I will likely kill it, but Mr. Hiro accounted it could be sacrificed to facilitate my education. I believe he could be a surgeon if he chose to change professions."

"Hiro gave you one of his precious shrubs?"

"Yes." She did not seem to consider this the minor miracle he knew it to be. "And Ivo has been given one as well. Though I should not have said. I think he means to surprise you this Christmas."

Unable to keep away, he sat next to her on the bench, his thigh a hairs-breadth from hers.

She took this gesture as a sign to commence her scales.

Signore Brunelli must be hard of hearing. Or Dev paid the music teacher far too much. He shut his mouth—would that he could his ears as well—and waited. He was learning—albeit slowly—if he waited long enough, she would open to him.

Sure enough, she paused in her banging. "The duke thinks we should go out."

"Does he? The tyrant." When had she spoken with his sire? "Don't let his agenda force you into anything you don't want, Anne."

"No, what I meant to say is, I want to go out. I want to go out with you." She turned on the bench to face him squarely on. "You are my husband, and I am your wife in truth now. As you yourself said, there is no going back."

He stood, unable to remain next to her and not take her in his arms. As added protection, he clasped his hands behind his back and paced to the window. "No, there is no going back." Did she wish for that option? God, he felt like such a callow youth in the face of this calm woman.

"I have been to the British Museum five times now. And though I could go another five hundred if only to gaze at the Rosetta Stone, or marvel at Lord Elgin's marbles, I would like to do something new. I enjoy playing music—I mean to say that when Signore Brunelli plays, I am…transported."

"But not to the moon," he quipped thinking of Beauchamp and his cheese.

She ignored his stupid joke. "I would like to go to the opera. Signore says *La Traviata* is playing at Covent Garden Theatre."

"Signore says?" Drat the man. Dev had taken care to hire the rabbitiest-looking music teacher he could find. Norbert Brunelli would have no problem wedging a large olive between his upper front and bottom teeth and still have room for a bit of Beauchamp's cheese. And if that weren't enough, Brunelli blinked so, that much of the time he addressed a person with his eyes half-closed. It was unclear if he did so to spare himself or the person who had to watch his incessant flutterings. Still, jealousy stabbed at Dev's gut.

"Well, it seems he has anticipated me. I spoke at length with the Signore just last week after your lesson, and he assured me you would be thrilled by the prospect of hearing Miss Lind. I thought to surprise you for your birthday."

"Oh. But my birthday is tomorrow."

"I am aware of that fact. Ivo has badgered me with suggestions ever since I foolishly asked him what I might give you. You will be happy to know I did not purchase a zebra, or a ferret—his other suggestion. Though do not be surprised if he comes up with the ferret on his own. He was quite insistent it would be the perfect gift."

She smiled her funny half-smile. He smiled back and immediately her brow furrowed into that sweetly earnest frown. When would she give up attempting to cover the tiny gap in her front teeth? Didn't she know her smile was the best gift he could ever receive?

She looked up under her lashes. "The papers say it is sold out."

"I think we will manage. My family has a box."

"Oh, of course."

"Being a Marchioness has it burdens, Owl, but it also has its perks."

She nodded sagely.

"Right. So, will you do me the great honor of attending the opera with me tomorrow evening? It is likely to be a crush." A snare of panic looped deep in his belly. Could he handle the crowds and the gawking they were sure to endure? Excepting that disastrous ball, and his one foray to Coggin's Raid, he had managed to steer clear of the throngs.

"Tomorrow will suit me just fine, my lord." His wife looked like a well-satisfied feline who had just dispatched a nice fat mouse. "I thank you."

Good. That went rather well. Now perhaps he might try bedding his wife in the light of day. "Where are you going?" he called after her.

"To find my maid. We will need to spend much of what remains of the day and most of tomorrow removing yards of ruffles, bows, and lace."

****

The comforting weight of a flask against his chest, and the promise of the brandy's warm rush only a moment away, kept his teeth from grinding—that and the ball of opium wrapped in a twist of paper, as yet untouched, but a reminder. It lay nestled next to the rope of perfectly-matched pearls.

He had stopped taking so much of the drink, but the idea of the *ton* pressing in on him and possibly having to shield his wife from their talons made him rethink his resolve and carry some fortification.

This time when his wife appeared at the top of the staircase, he could at least focus on her. Gone were the rows of ruffles, all the bows, and that hideous flossy stuff that had overtaken her bosom.

He smiled. By God, let her wear a sack to the opera for all he cared. This was his wife. After the debacle of the ball, he didn't give a rat's ass what the toplofty thought. He only wanted Anne to be happy. If wearing ruffles and bows made her so, then he was well enough.

"I have something to augment your beauty, sweet

Owl. I believe they will go well with this gown." *Or no gown at all. Perhaps we can try that later in the evening?*

She frowned at him. "You have done too much already. I have never had such a day in my life."

He pulled the pearls out, just catching the ball of opium which must have snagged on the strand. He almost tossed it away but dropped it back in his pocket. Not yet.

"You received my books?" It took quite a lot of resolve not to nuzzle her neck as he fastened the string around her throat. A large crate had arrived several days ago. He had ordered every book imaginable on healing and herbal properties as well as texts on anatomy, mesmerism, and several volumes on the art of Bonsai. Another smaller box contained fine fountain pens and various-sized bound journals in which she could write her stories.

"Oh!" She touched the pearls and then brought them to her lips. Like a child caught out at some decadent pleasure, she dropped them. "You are too extravagant, my lord."

"Ah, but on this day, I am allowed to be extravagant. And what's more, you cannot stop me from indulging myself."

"Yourself?"

"Yes. By indulging you, I indulge myself, three-fold."

She pursed her lips and smoothed her blessedly unruffled skirts.

****

The Malvern box hung in the first dress circle—her husband, splendidly turned-out in his black evening clothes and blinding white linen, was certainly an eyeful, a glimpse of the marquess of old, and a sparkling beacon in a firmament of lesser stars that sat in rings around him and Anne.

He regaled her with the history of the theater as well as that of their nearest neighbors, pointing out this lord and that lady. The grizzled man with enormous side whiskers, Lord Suttan, who dozed from the opening of the massive velvet curtain to its closing. And in the next box, Lady Kendle and her ancient mother, the dowager Countess of Whittenborne, poised with ear horn in one hand and opera glasses in the other lest she miss one morsel of the entertainment.

James was flirting with her. At first she had not been sure. He did like to tease and she was getting used to that, but this had a subtle undertone of…heat.

She liked it.

Yet there was a brittleness about him as well. He was too bright, too polished, as if balanced on a wire high above this glittering rabble and if he let down his guard one jot, he would fall and be consumed by them. His behavior so different from the man who came to her in the dark morning hours. Once stripped of his clothes, only then did he become totally open and free.

When would these two men meld into one? Would they ever? And would she continue playing Madonna to his Courtier during the day, while at night they became Jezebel and Casanova?

Half the theatre sat gaping at them—mostly women, she noted with not a little ire. Several even went so far as to peer at them through their opera glasses. Apparently these rings of boxes supplied as much entertainment as the stage performance.

She sat up straighter in her chair, raised her

beautiful, mother-of-pearl glasses to her eyes—yet another gift from her husband—and stared right back.

"Ha! Brava, Anne. Give them as good as they get."

There was no reason why her husband's compliment should please her so, but it did.

If only she had Lizzy Gruber's pea shooter. The one Mrs. Abbot had snapped in half when Lizzy had been caught pelting Hattie Fenton's head at prayers. She would dearly love to hit that silly miss with the wreath of roses in her hair right between her prying eyes.

Her husband settled and then wove his arm along the back of her chair. Her eyes might be engaged in a staring duel with an over-stuffed matron dripping in diamonds, but her body was wholly focused on the man next to her. The matron dropped her glasses and looked away. One down, fifty or more to go.

A finger brushed the skin just above the fabric of her gown and then painted a small circle there. Her glasses wilted on their handle as her bottom inched its way closer toward those wandering fingers. Jealous standoffs evaporated as one finger dipped under the fabric to trace the ridges of her spine. Somehow James secretly touching her while on display for all to see excited her as much as if they were fully naked in her bedchamber.

A hush fell over the theatre and she could well believe the company held their breath right along with her in anticipation of what James might do next. However, when the magnificent curtain rose to reveal a wonderland of magic, even her husband's attentions were forgotten.

****

"Anne, I will be happy to haul you out to the theater every night and brave this gawping rabble if only to

323

watch your enjoyment."

He stood to stretch his legs for yet another intermission, while Anne sat, still riveted to the stage.

"I cannot imagine why you would wish to squander your attention on me when you might be experiencing—words fail me." She gestured toward the now closed curtain. "How can one small body produce such a sound? This must be God at work."

"Sweet Owl, I think we need to adjust your glasses. Miss Lind is hardly small." But I suppose, when one compares the voice to the body, her voice must claim the greater size."

"I am constantly overwhelmed—by Mr. Verdi's opera, by this theater, by the White Tower, the dome at St. Paul's…" She rifled in her reticule. "My heart is so full it has overflowed and leaked out my eyes."

He bent to whisper in her ear. "I can think of another thing that overwhelms you, little Owl." Of course he had to insert himself and his blasted ever-thirsty ego into her musings. "I believe you likened it to a sneeze that first time, if I recall rightly?"

She pursed her lips in that prudish way he loved. "Yes, you are quite right, my lord. Indeed, I believe if I were to compile a list, that particular—sneeze—would be very nearly at the top of things that are overwhelming."

"Very nearly? I shall take that as a challenge, my lady. I am all too happy to take you home this minute and commence work."

"Yes, I suppose you could. But I find I am becoming a glutton, sir. I would like both, Mr. Verdi and then my sneeze, if you please." She sat back folding her handkerchief into a neat square.

His cock twitched and then sat up like a good dog when it smells a juicy bone. He straightened again to make a bit of room for said bone while his wife sat as unruffled as a cat lazing in the sun. Drat her. He'd like nothing better than to bend her over the rail and—

Havermere? What the devil was he doing out?

He nearly reached for Anne's opera glasses just to make sure his eyes were not deceiving him, but the glasses were unnecessary. Even if he had not known the earl, he knew with infinite detail the woman entering the box just behind Havermere. That's what comes of drooling over one's wife instead of paying attention to one's surroundings.

The old sot now stared daggers at the Malvern box, which happened to be directly opposite. Nora leaned into her husband when he spoke to her. Her gaze flicked over to him and Anne, she stiffened, and then abruptly left the box. A burly footman exited right behind her. Just as well. Anne did not need to be subjected to this drama.

"Who is that man?" Sure enough, her glasses were trained on Havermere's box.

Drat. But had she seen Nora? Should he assure her the countess meant naught to him? *Stupid.* He had nothing to hide. Still, he had the urge to protect his bride. He took the glasses from her. "No one. Do not regard him, Owl. The earl is an old reprobate."

The lights dimmed as the curtain rose for the second act, and though his wife sat on the edge of her seat, handkerchief at the ready, he sensed some of her joy had gone.

He sat down. However his focus was pulled once again to the earl's box as someone new entered. He snapped the glasses up.

Brocket? Now what? Was Sir Charles working for Havermere?

By God, he would skewer the man if he had the temerity to consign this year's entry to the rafters.

Except there was no new entry. No masterpiece.

Anne turned to him. He had risen in his anger. He sat back down and tried to concentrate on his wife's creamy back, which stood out in the darkness. The ball of opium felt heavy as lead next to his hammering heart. *Damn Charles Brocket.*

He removed the flask of brandy and took a pull. If only he knew he still had a great painting within him. But thus far he faced a dozen half-finished portraits. Every one a different woman. Every one flat and empty.

Lind was beginning Sempre Libera. Determined to put his attention back on his beautiful wife, he took final look across the theater.

The flask nearly slipped from his fingers when he spied his brother Austin entering Havermere's box.

****

"Damnit, Austin." Dev intercepted his brother in the passageway, heading for the stairs. "I've tried to give you the benefit of the doubt, but you continue to push me. What the hell have you to do with Sir Charles Brocket?"

Austin shoved his hands through his hair.

"Were you the one who invited him to the duke's ball?"

"Not entirely. I did not oversee Margaret. Sir Charles is connected to a crony of Father's and I suppose she just went down the usual list."

"I do not want him near Anne again. Ever."

Austin shifted his feet.

"What?"

"I am in a spot of trouble." His brother took out his own flask and took a furtive sip.

"Trouble? In what way?"

"I seem to have overextended myself this quarter."

This was not news. He knew his brother was in deep. "How much?"

"Under a thousand." He raised the flask again, but Dev stayed his hand.

A conservative lie. "How much under a thousand?"

"Nine hundred and eighty-nine." Austin at least had the scruples to look sheepish.

"And how is Havermere involved?"

"Firstly, I did not know I was meeting the earl. Sir Charles only told me he had a friend who might be able to help me with funds. I never thought to see you here."

Lord Percy Unger toddled by with his newest doxy. The brothers nodded.

"You are to have nothing to do with Havermere."

"What has he done to you?"

"Nothing outright, but he is Nora's husband, and while we were discreet, he was always suspicious, hounding Nora until she ended up in my arms and eventually my bed. The cruel things he did to her—I would have called the bastard out if it wouldn't have looked like murder."

"He wanted you to paint the countess, didn't he?"

"Yes, when they were newly married, he had me in to admire his prized possession. I vowed then and there I would paint her, but not for that heartless brute to hang above his mantel. When I wouldn't do it, he hired Brocket to bully me. I didn't know Brocket was still pimping for the man."

Austin fidgeted with the fob on his watch.

"You only met the earl this evening?"

"Yes."

"And what did he offer you to square your debt?"

Austin shoved his hands in his pocket and looked at the floor. "Nothing. The man is in a foul mood. The meeting proved a total waste."

"All right." He touched his brother's shoulder and waited for him to meet his gaze. "I am not one to cast stones, but I caution you to rein yourself in while you still can. Take a page from my history. You don't want to fall into debt."

"No, I see that now. I just had a few bad days at the tables. My luck is going to change."

"Luck? Listen, Austin, stay away from the hells for a time."

"Right, of course you are right. Thank you, Dev. I will pay you back as soon as I'm flush."

"Very well. I assume that will be at the beginning of next quarter."

"Next quarter."

"You are not involved in that ridiculous bet at White's, are you?"

His little brother looked at the floor and then at the ceiling. "No. No, though I have been quizzed numerous times about who might be your model." He laughed ruefully, finally meeting his gaze. "You don't want to give me a hint as to your paramour?"

A bevy of would-be detectives, eager to uncover any shred of news, dogged Dev. He'd seen one man in a series of ridiculous disguises several times. "No. No hints. And she is only a model, not my paramour. If you'll remember, I am lately married."

"Yes, of course." Austin almost smirked. "Is it not Nora Havermere then? I know she is the obvious choice, but sometimes the simplest guess is spot on. Hiding in plain sight and all."

"Leave off, brother. Isn't it enough I have half of London on my heels? Must I add my own brother to that rabble?"

"You are right, forgive me. Besides, you'd be barmy to use her. Havermere would have your head."

"Fuck Havermere. Nora may do as she pleases."

"*Hmm*, I wonder." Austin looked as if he wanted to say more but wisely shut his mouth.

Ushers began to fan out to take up positions at the various doors. The act would be over soon.

"I will give you a draft for those funds. I must get back to Anne."

"Yes, of course."

"Stay away from Brocket."

The roar of applause sounded.

Chapter Thirty-Three

They stayed until the end of *La Traviata*, but the magic of the evening had disappeared.

He stood like a skittish rabbit in the hallway next to the door to her bedchamber. The pearls glistened silver in the lamp's light. They grazed her breasts, dipping slightly into her cleavage, leading to the perfect silvery globes of her bosom. *Touch me* they winked. But his wife remained mute. "Well, happy birthday, my sweet Owl. I trust I will be welcome later?"

After a whisker of hesitation, her answer was to pull him inside. She slammed the door shut and pressed him up against it.

In thirty seconds, at most, he'd flipped her, lifted her skirts, and pushed inside his sweet, generous wife.

On trembling legs, hers still wrapped about his waist, he carried her to the down filled mattress where she'd get a proper bedding. After laying her down, he yanked at his cravat and coat, then jerked his breeches, already skimming his hips, dragging them down along with his hose. Damn shoes. Hopping around, he nearly took out her bedside table before managing to shuffle them off. Then shucked off the wad of hose and breeches. He was just lifting his shirt over his head when he heard a soft snuffle.

His hedonistic bride was asleep.

Lips, bruised with his kisses, the dark fan of her

lashes against her cheek, white fingers threaded in the strand of pearls. So utterly beautiful.

He watched her through several bongs of the clock. Now, time his patience was rewarded. Sliding his hand under her pillow, he pulled her closer and blew in her ear. She stirred.

"What is this?" Something cool and smooth filled his palm. He drew it out. A finger length of stone caught the light. A crystal.

"It is nothing." Anne tried to snatch it, but he was too quick. Her hand fell back to the pillow.

Jealously reared its head. "It is clearly something, sweet Owl." *A birthday gift?* "Is it a charm you must keep under your pillow?" He should not tease her. She rarely got his jokes anyway. And when she did she usually put his poor efforts to shame with her infinitely more subtle wit. His humor was a great swath of color globed on the canvas with a pallet knife, while hers was laid on with the finest miniature brush.

"It was a bridal gift."

"From whom? Ah, let me guess, Beauchamp?" She frowned. "Ah, so it is a charm. Perhaps for fertility?" He stroked his finger over a long sheer facet. "I have a much more potent one, madam, if you would care to see." He guided her hand down to his already bobbing cock.

"Give it to me. You are making fun." Swifter now, she evaded his grasp and reached for the crystal.

"No, I will take good care." He avoided her fingers easily. "After all, we need every ounce of help we can get."

She looked away then.

Blast!

He'd ruined the mood with his teasing and then

bringing up the lie of the child that was supposed to be already growing within her body. He slid the rock back under her pillow.

"Come, let us make our own magic, my Owlet." He pulled her to him. She buried her face into his neck. Her silk hair flooded his fingers, running in rivulets over his wrists and forearms, catching in the bend of his elbow. He brought it to his lips. So soft, yet so strong. He bit a piece, feeling it against his teeth. He brushed the ends over his lips. Back and forth and then took it into his mouth his tongue jousting with the pointed tip of hair.

Gently he pushed her onto her back, wanting to see the moonlight on her face. She turned away. He took the wet tip of her hair and painted her eyelids, the corner of her eye, down her cheek to circle her ear. She shuddered and licked her lips. He'd removed the pearls and loosened her gown and stays an hour or so earlier. Now, pushing the bodice down, he continued on to her breasts, carefully wetting the tip of his brush again, to flick it over her nipple which drew into a tight peak.

A small moan escaped, reward for his work.

She tried to keep these little sounds inside, still slightly embarrassed, but he could not let her off so easily. Whenever one pushed its way over her lips, he smiled.

Eventually she would be freer with her noises. He would like that too. But for now these mewling kitten sounds sent him.

He abandoned his improvised paintbrush, deciding to use his tongue instead. He found the tiny space between her front teeth. She closed her mouth. She did not like the space. He opened her again and flicked his tongue over the gap once more. *I love this,* his tongue said. He wanted his body to tell her what his words could not. Could she hear him?

****

Anne felt utterly spent. Her gown and beautiful pearls lay in a heap on the floor along with her stays and stockings.

Oh, if she could only let things lie. But she could not. "I would like one more gift."

"Anything." Her husband burrowed into her neck.

Good, he was well and sated. "I would like a promise."

"A promise? Of course, I promise." His lips traveled lower.

High time to see things for what they were, one way or another. This not knowing was worse than losing him. "You cannot promise. You have not yet heard what I want."

"I don't need to. Your wish is my command." His lips teased her breast.

"*Hmmmm.* That is not wise."

"I am not wise when it comes to you, my sweet Owl."

"Well, you must be. You must not be rash. You must not always let your passions rule you."

"How can they not when I am with you?"

She sat up and pulled the cover over her breasts.

"Very well." He flopped on his back and looped his arms above his head, "I will be most attentive."

"You have not found a model yet, have you?"

"Anne, I beg you, let us not talk of painting." He tugged the sheet down and kissed her breast.

"James, stop. You promised me. Anything."

"Very well. I am all ears." He propped himself up

on an elbow and scrubbed his fingers through his hair.

"The exhibition is in three weeks. And the Queen expects a masterpiece. Correct?"

"Yes, but I cannot—"

"You must paint the countess." There it was out. Not so hard.

He sat up. "What?"

"The countess—" She took a breath. "You must paint Nora Havermere."

"Nora?" he echoed.

"Yes." *Please don't make me say the name again.* "There is no time to shilly-shally with trying to find a proper model. You must paint what you know."

What is in your heart.

She wanted it done. Either she would win, or Nora Havermere would. But at last this uncertainty would end. She could go on when she knew what the rules of her life were going to be. She would know that the lover who came to her in the night was only that, a consummate lover, not a real husband. Or she would finally know that James was truly hers—all of him.

He took her hand in his. "Anne, I will find someone."

She stared at her hand within his. "Tell me, are you so afraid to be in her presence? Is she such a temptation?"

"No, of course not. It is only—"

She looked up into his worried eyes.

He shook his head. "Are you sure you want this?"

"Yes, I am sure." They would move forward together or apart, but at least she would finally know. Thrusting Nora Havermere under her husband's nose would tip the balance. And in the end the countess would claim him as hers, or, just maybe, Anne would finally have the husband she longed for.

She made herself get up and cross to the window. Dawn was just breaking. "Now go and make a masterpiece."

Chapter Thirty-Four

Nora sat perched on the windowsill, looking wistfully out at the Thames.

Dev shifted the round brush in his hand for the flat-angled brush he held between his teeth. After spending so much time in his garret, he had a new appreciation for seascapes. How Mr. Turner could never grow tired of painting the same bit of water again and again.

He stood back. "Blasted, sod-sucking hell!" *Wrong. All fucking wrong.*

Already moving, a pained look on her face, Nora rubbed her bottom and cast her eyes longingly at the bread and cheese on the table.

"We'll try the couch again." The windowsill was a mistake. He was no Turner. Besides, the setting competed with the subject. He wanted the focus completely on her.

She flopped onto the couch. He shifted his easel to face her.

No. No. No! Having the fainting couch hauled in had been a colossal waste of effort and blunt. It was wrong. All wrong. Too fussy. Too…too utterly wrong. Too much like his paintings of old. He wanted something fresh. Something new.

"Move to this chair."

"You might try a little civility, commander." But she moved quickly enough.

He did not mean to bark, but his last shred of patience had fallen away two hours ago. "Can you not look quite so…"

"Quite so what?"

"As if you have just come from a lover's bed."

"If only," she groused, but sat up straighter.

"Your hair is wrong. Can you make it more—managed somehow?"

She only raised an eyebrow.

"Never mind. Here, hold this. No, not that way. More simply." He stood back, his hands out before him making a frame, his vision narrowed. "No, no damn it." He yanked the thing from her hands and heaved it out the window. When he turned back, Nora had moved and was pouring a drink. He charged up to her, took the glass, and then tossed the liquor out the window as well. He pointed with the empty glass to the chair.

"We have not a moment to waste. I need you alert. You do realize the exhibition is in less than two weeks' time?"

"My dearest Devlin, I could not forget if I tried." She sighed wearily, but dutifully sat and folded her hands in her lap. "Perhaps I could wear some color? You know I look atrocious in gray."

"This portrait is not about your beauty. That speaks for itself. It is about something more. Something—"

"Something I don't possess."

"Nonsense. You are one of the most generous, self-assured people I have the pleasure of inflicting myself on. And you put up with me. That alone sets you above the rest of the population."

"Ah, such high praise indeed." She cocked her head as if she were about to impart something to a child.

"Perhaps I am the wrong subject for this masterpiece."

He scraped off part of her nose.

"Perhaps you have moved beyond me, and now need someone quite different."

"Rubbish. You are my muse. You always have been. You are like Mr. Turner's harbor for me. I could paint you a hundred times and still see something new."

"Hmmm," was all she said. Or didn't say.

"Blast it! Now you've moved again. Is there no stillness within you?"

She settled and he slapped some cadmium red onto the canvas, a highlight in her hair. Then scraped it off. Why in the blazes was it so difficult to stay still?

"Dev, I thought I saw Lily."

Vermillion glopped out of the tube. A bloody waste of pigment. "What?"

"You heard me." Nora twirled her finger round and round a curl that should not have even been there. Why must she have such a bloody riot of hair?

"I know the girl was not Lily. I am not daft. Our Lily is dead. But this girl-child had the same halo of white-blonde hair. And you recall the slope of her nose and her cheek?"

He didn't want to recall, he just wanted her to be still.

"She had that pert little nose and such high cheek bones. So very like—like our Lily. Even to her coltish lope." A small stifled sob erupted from between her lightly pressed lips.

Oh, blast it all! "Here, take this." He shoved an old rag at her as he knelt down beside her. She laid her head on his shoulder and wept in earnest. Her tears soon soaked through his shirt, the rag lay useless in her hand.

"All right, Devlin. I am done being a watering pot." She sniffed. "You may paint my nose now. All that red on your pallet will not go to waste."

"Are you sure you are well enough to go on?" Honestly, she looked like hell.

Waving away his concern she flung his rag back at him. He scraped off her left eye and part of her chin. Wrong, all bloody wrong. He had to get the shape right.

"Havermere is apoplectic." She squirmed in the chair. "Might I have a cushion?"

"Hold still—please."

"The bit in the Tattler about your model having ginger-colored hair got him so red in the face. I almost waved the paper in front of him like a cape in front of a bull. Perhaps then he might keel over and leave me in peace." She shifted. Again. "Lady Bentley has been an absolute brick. You will paint her, won't you, Dev? I promised her you would, as she has been my savior. That house is a warren of old tunnels. I enter the front door and voila! I come out behind the mews. Someone was doing some very nefarious things when they built that monstrosity."

Why. Could. She. Not. Be. Still! And quiet!

"What? Now what have I done? You needn't frown so, my Mad Marquess, or I shall take myself off."

"Sorry, Nor. I do beg your pardon. It is just…" His brushes hung limply from his hands.

"I am not your wife." She put her hands on her hips, in her best fishwife mode. "You are in but thick, my lord. Go home and see to her, Devlin." She stretched one leg and then the other. "And if this painting goes on—which I hope you will realize it must not—you will get me a bloody cushion. A girl must have some comforts."

Chapter Thirty-Five

Ballencrieff Castle
October, 8ᵗʰ
Winton,

A change is in the air. Mr. Beauchamp has declared that the planets are back in alignment and harmony restored. I cannot agree more. Poppa finally had the good sense to die, so I have decided it is high time to come home and re-join the world. One can only rusticate so long before one begins to rust.

Mrs. Coates continues to hold down the fort since Hives' defection. Rumor has it he got a windfall and hied off to India! Well, good riddance, I say. Those heathens may have him as far as I'm concerned.

Phoebe and Grace will continue at Ballencrieff for the present, but since receiving your last letter, I have decided you need me far more than Phoebe. I shall be a buffer to the capricious ton which you face. By the way, you must not heed the papers. They are odious—always have been. Lady Markham, in particular, is a veritable vampire when it comes to sucking the life out of any young matron who attempts to wade into the rivers of society. You must not regard her or her like.

I will arrive in town on Friday next. You will meet my train.

Matilda Tippit
"Winton."

Anne saw the hair first. Her ladyship would have made an excellent masthead as she parted the crowds at Kings Cross, her umbrella raised like some avenging angel come to vanquish all the lowly demons who dared thwart her.

Anne did not correct her ladyship's address. It was refreshing to simply be Winton once again.

"Where is Barkley?" Her ladyship juggled her quizzing glass whilst jabbing her umbrella at an unsuspecting and innocent footman.

An ancient man in an even more ancient livery tottered forward.

"Here is a man," Anne said dubiously. "Is this Barkley?"

"Barkley, *lud* you have grown old. Where have you been? And where is the carriage? I cannot imagine how you could manage to hide a coach, but you have. Never mind, we shall depart now for Poppa's house. No." She jammed the tip of her umbrella into the ground. "I must remember it is my house now."

They settled into the ancient carriage while her ladyship's luggage was being stowed.

"I am seriously out of patience with you, Winton. Your last letter was not very forthcoming. You are holding out on me ,and I will not stand for it. Now I have come, you will give me all the particulars."

Her ladyship narrowed her gaze, taking Anne in from hat to boots. "*Hmm,* you have filled out some. That is well. Still too pale. Not increasing yet, are you?" Before she could answer, Lady Tippit barreled on. "No, I didn't think so. He has bedded you though, hasn't he? Yes, I can see that he has. Good lad. I'm sure he knows the right end of the stick. Yes," she said again, "I can see he does." She sat back satisfied. "Only a matter of time before he plants a babe. Never you fear."

"How is Mistress Phoebe, and Grace? Has she grown—"

"Phoebe continues to be a ninny. I told her to come on to town with me, but she insists her despicable husband will either attempt to bed her or kill her. Likely she is correct, but she does not understand my considerable power. Of course I will have to reestablish myself, but now that Poppa is gone, I feel ready to take on Victoria herself."

The old carriage shook and then heaved as a particularly large trunk must have been loaded on.

"Have a care, Barkley! Mama's Boscher jewel casket is in there." She patted her wig. "Now, Winton, when we arrive at Luscombe Hall, we will have some much needed tea, and then you shall rub my shoulders."

The house lay situated on a corner in Belgrave Square, one of the huge manses among the smaller terrace homes.

"Here we are." Her ladyship stood before the house. The coach rattled past them on its way to unload in the mews around back.

"Lady Tippit? Are you well?"

"What?" Her ladyship seemed to have forgotten Anne was there.

"Shall we go in, your ladyship?" She gestured to the house.

"Oh, yes. Yes, I suppose we must." Lady Tippit shivered but still did not move.

A man, who could only be the butler, stood by the open doorway.

"You are chilled, and you promised tea, madam,"

she prodded.

"Oh, yes. Yes, I did. Tea solves a good deal, doesn't it, Winton?"

"Yes, decidedly, your ladyship."

Using her umbrella as a sort of cane, Lady Tippit ascended the stairs.

"And who are you?" She gave the poor butler a freezing look. "And why are you letting all the heat out of the house? Stand aside and then shut the door. It is cold—what is your name?"

"Perkins, my lady."

"Well, Perkins. We shall see. We shall just wait and see." She nodded fiercely and then turned to Anne and nodded again, as if what she had said made all the sense in the world.

The ladies settled next to a roaring fire in a large withdrawing room on the second floor. Tea had been brought and poured. Her ladyship seemed to be in better spirits.

"Someone must have given Hives a good deal of money to leave his position so abruptly. Mr. Beauchamp managed to try to launch himself into the heavens again, but other than that, everyone has been remarkably tame."

"And Mr. Macready?"

"Still no sign of him. Gone in a poof. Much like Hives. And good riddance once again. Ought to bring the whole drafty castle down and start over, if you ask me. But no one does ask me." Lady Tippit stared at the walls around her, seemingly lost. Her hand drifted up to her breast, but only dangled there as if it had not the slightest idea of what to do.

"Well, I am very glad you have come to Town, madam," Anne said, refreshing their tea and setting a

343

scone on her ladyship's plate. "I could use a wise friend who knows what's what."

"Yes, I dare say you could. Before I—that is before Poppa—before I went to Ballencrieff I could spot a cully right enough. And as for the *ton's* female population, well, let us just say the spiders with their silken nets lie in every corner just waiting for an unsuspecting chit to put her foot wrong."

"Yes, I believe you will be invaluable to me, Lady Tippit." Reaching over, she squeezed the lady's chilled hand. The familiar face of Matilda Tippit had her blinking away foolish tears. She had not realized how quite alone she had felt.

"But what of you and your marquess? Why is he not seeing to your entry into society? The ball was unfortunate, too much too soon, but surely Devlin has reevaluated and is ready to sally forth again?"

A bite of scone, delayed her answer. Heavens, the thing was dry as dust. She took a swig of tea. Lady Tippit only pursed her lips and waited. No use prevaricating.

"He did take me to the opera. But since then, he has been otherwise engaged."

Like the strings on a cinched purse, Lady Tippit's mouth pulled tighter.

"He has begun a new painting for the Queen's Exhibition. It occupies much of his time, I believe."

"You believe?"

"Lady Tippit, I might have done something quite mad."

"I cannot imagine you doing anything hare-brained, Winton. You are the most right-headed person I know."

"I have taken a huge risk and might have thrown away my little bit of happiness."

"Out with it. It is best to let air into these thoughts."

What a turn of events, her ladyship parroting Anne's own directives from their days at Ballencrieff. "I have told James he must paint his countess."

Her ladyship raised her chin and narrowed her eyes. "His countess?"

"Nora Havermere"

"I see." Her ladyship set her teacup in its saucer. "I still maintain you are the sanest person I know. No flies on you, Anne Winton." Nodding her head once with such force, Anne feared her ladyship's wig might topple into her lap. Unfazed, Lady Tippit pushed it back into place. "It is well I came when I did. You will hold your head up through whatever may come your way, I promise you that. We will put things to rights."

Her ladyship patted Anne's hand. "I will have my massage now, Winton."

Chapter Thirty-Six

He had nothing.

The painting was acceptable, even good, but it was not what he wanted.

There was no time. It would have to do. Only three days left until the exhibition.

"It is good, Dev. Really." Nora was pinning up her hair.

He turned away from the painting to the window. He couldn't look at it another moment. Maybe if he got away from it for a day or two, he would gain some perspective.

But he didn't have a day or two.

His eyes felt as if glass had been shoved beneath his eyelids. His hands shook with fatigue and lack of food. "You should go, Nor. It is late and no doubt the earl will make you pay."

"He has been quite tame these days. Which is worse than when he rants. He is up to something. I just have not divined what it is."

"Have you been careful?"

"His new toady dogs me. But fortunately, the man is not very clever or does not know London very well. I can usually lose him when I visit Lady Bentley or at the Burlington Arcade." She scooped up her bonnet with its veil. "The Beadle there is a friend of mine."

"Yes, I imagine he is."

"Don't bother to walk me out. Thomas is waiting in the Rose and Thistle. I think he is sweet on a serving girl there." She touched his arm and then gave it a squeeze. "All will be well, Dev; you must have faith."

The door closed and her footsteps faded as she descended the stairs.

The tiny dark spot of a veiled Nora crossed far below him. She ducked into the tavern and emerged within a few minutes with a large man, her Thomas. A moment later a young girl, a maid's cap on her head, stood in the open doorway watching the couple climb into a hansom cab.

He rubbed his burning eyes, wishing a brilliant painting would greet him when he opened them. No such miracle.

Canvas after discarded canvas stood along the walls of the garret. Some fully realized and some only half-finished, the paint scraped off, the cast of ghostly painted-out features bleeding through.

He had not gone forward, he had regressed. These canvases stood as evidence to his mediocrity. Even this last of Nora.

Who am I if not a painter? Am I simply a title dressed up in a fine suit of clothing?

At least at Ballencrieff he had his devils to distract him. Now, he was supposed to be cured—fixed. The devils were at bay, but what did he have to replace them? The ladies scattered throughout the room raised their mute voices to echo, *Nothing.*

"Nothing." His pronouncement sounded shocking and inane in the dead quiet of the room. Is there truly nothing left inside me to give the world? To give to Anne. Other than a title—which she never wanted—and a cock.

Time to admit it, he needed his devils. Needed a bit of madness to forge ahead.

That devil still lay coiled in his pocket next to his breast where it had hid all these weeks. His heart pounded beneath it making it seem alive. It called out to him.

Release me. Just this once and I will free you.

The waxy ball rolled so smoothly between his paint-stained fingers. So simple. To feel it in his mouth, the acrid taste on his tongue. That slow, loose feeling would steal over him, allowing his frenetic mind to rest and for his passions to take over—that place of stillness and focus where magic could be born.

That place lay but a moment away from his lips. *Yes. Just once, and I will stop.*

A ship bell clanged calling him back to the window. Sea birds rose wheeling in the sky. A ballet of infinite beauty, their spread wings flashing with the light, and then, in the next instant, almost disappearing as they turned as one.

How did they know? To turn right or left? To soar up or down? Who directed them? God? What freedom to have the infinite sky as home. To be tethered to nothing except the wind.

As if in answer, the flock gathered into a thick knot. He held his breath, waiting for their next miracle. Pulsing once, then twice, they bloomed into a huge sky flower that put Vauxhall's garish fireworks display to shame.

Churning 'round again, they flew straight toward him. He didn't know if he should be frightened or push forward to meet them. Closer and closer they came.

Yes, come for me. Take me away with you so that I

may fly free!

Only a moment more and he could reach out and touch their joy.

But at the last second, they turned and flew up, a brief curtain for his window. Then they were gone.

He craned his neck, leaning far out of the casement. *Come back!* Minutes must have passed with no sign. His arms ached with the strain of holding on.

He hauled himself back inside, clawing at his stifling cravat. He nearly strangled himself jerking it off. He ripped open his silken waistcoat, the buttons flying. Next, he wrenched his shirt from his breeches and then over his head flinging it away. He rushed back to the window.

But for all his drama, his feet still were made of clay. He had sprung no wings.

I will give you wings.

The tiny pea of opium still remained clenched in his fist. Waiting.

He brought it to his lips.

So easy.

A cry had his gaze snapping toward the sky. His birds again. Farther away now, but still in sight. Again they gathered against the deepening sky, nearly disappearing as their gray melded with the clouds.

What picture were they plotting? What ephemeral delight would hatch from their close deliberation?

Their pulsing knot exploded in a burst of white.

It could not be—

He wanted to squeeze his eyes shut to get a fresh glimpse, yet he dare not waste a moment or she might be gone.

Anne. It was Anne. Her face rose with the birds.

They wheeled into the air, a swirling tide of pure white. The sun had broken through as if to baptize this vision. The birds disappeared once again, but the sun remained. Anne remained in his mind's eye. Her dark eyes so calm and steady. So very beautiful.

He imagined her hot hands on him, on his breast as they had been the first time she touched him back at Ballencrieff. The look in her eyes. Her utter fearlessness in the face of his madness. She had believed in him even then. She had not tolerated his theatrics. She had only shown him simple truth. The devils were not inside him, only poisons. He could see her now. Quietly waiting. Waiting for him to wake up. To be worthy of her. Yes. Yes.

Anne.

"I love her."

Three simple words. Yet an enormous leap to bring them from deep within his heart to his lips. "Dear God, I love her." The heaviness in his heart evaporated as if his words unlocked a tightly sealed portal. "I love Anne Winton!" he shouted at the now setting sun.

Realization dawned that he had always loved her. He'd been so focused on himself and his trials he could not see the light beyond. Could not see his own light. He *was* worthy of love, her love. He was worthy simply because he loved her with all his heart. He did not have to be an artistic genius. He only had to love her. Love was enough.

The pellet of waxy opium rolled off the tips of his fingers and fell into the world below. Gone. Finally gone.

A strong breeze blew and he sucked in a huge draft. A new beginning.

He turned, took up his pallet knife, and carved away

the old layers of Nora Havermere, exposing hidden colors beneath.

The light had gone, but he didn't need it. The picture was right there in his head, in his body. The sitter so fixed in his mind's eye. So imprinted he had no need of models and light.

Daft fool. He had circled around, trying to find a way in, but if he'd only stopped and looked, he would have seen it clear as day. So busy feinting and parrying, he had not seen what was right before him, the painting that was living in his heart.

He kept the pallet knife and picked up pure white on its edge and laid it to the canvas. Colors mounted one on top of each other as he found a rhythm and the shape. He scraped and flicked, and wiped. Brilliant color filled the canvas in bold slashes, raw with feeling and movement. Sweat rolled into his eyes. He shook his head and blinked it away. Lastly, one more color, a highlight of bright orange just at the center.

He stepped back. *By God, yes!*

Dawn's glow crept into the room as if drawn to the light within the canvas. He had worked all through the night with only a few lamps and tapers for light. The last stub of candle guttered, a kind of bow to the woman's brilliance. He tossed his pallet down and wiped his shaking hands over his chest. She stared back, luminous.

A tide of laughter hit him. He laughed as he hadn't in months and months. *Ha! Nora will be pleased. And slightly smug.*

He collapsed on his cot, every muscle, every bone, every fiber used up. Only peace remained.

For the first time in years he felt clean. Just himself, not sheltered within Anne's arms, not within the haze of brandy or drugs that gave him false comfort, but deep within his own skin.

He dared to peer into the future.

It was not a blank canvas. So many colors yet in his life. It stretched out, a long road before him. The concept was not unpleasant, just foreign.

A wife, a child—he hoped—a new home, the duchy, tenant farmers, and estates to manage. On and on. He would have balked before, wanting no part of all the responsibility. But now... Now he had Anne. She was strong enough for the both of them, but she would no longer have to be. He could be strong. Life would not always be easy, but he had just proved he could be a man worthy of her. The proof lay right before him on the canvas. Even if he never painted again, he now knew he could. His gift was not a sham, it lay within him.

He closed his eyes. He would go home in a few hours. But now he only looked for sleep.

Chapter Thirty-Seven

"Do not bother yourself, Yvette. I will fetch paper from his lordship's desk."

Lady Tippit required a full-fledged reply. No hastily scrawled missive for her ladyship.

A letter lay on the desk.

His writing.

She should not look. She should tuck it securely under the blotter and walk away. But she did not.

Nora,

The word held her as surely as if she had been snapped in a trap.

I cannot get away as planned, but you must see the portrait. After all, you bore with me through thick and thin. I think you will approve. It was painted from the heart, and I trust my love shows through. It must, for I believe it is my best work yet. I have never been so inspired.

I dare not let my Owl see. Not until it is hung and there can be no going back. It will likely be a shock to her, but I cannot help that. Indeed I am hoping it will be just the ticket to let us begin anew.

I will meet you at twelve noon tomorrow. Call me egotistical, but I want to be there when you see it.

I know you have lost your key, silly chit. I have left a new one above the doorsill on the right. I did not like the shady character I have seen lurking about. You should be careful as well. I look forward to the time when neither of us has to keep secrets.

Dev

A fat tear dropped not a hair's breadth from the salutation. She quickly moved the paper just as another fell. The letters swam before her glazed vision. She dashed her arm against her eyes and then fled from the room.

Only to collide with someone. *Margaret.*

"My dear, Anne, what has you so upset?"

She shook her head, her throat full and throbbing. She must get away.

"Oh dear, you must have found out."

A hideous sob escaped. Horrified, she covered her mouth.

"Come, my dear," Margaret ushered Anne into her bedchamber. "Higgins, you may fetch tea."

She tried to tell Margaret she needn't bother. She would surely choke.

"Sit, my dear. Heavens, your hands are ice. Now, there." Margaret settled a shawl around her shaking shoulders. "These men…well, they will be men. It is best to find out sooner than later, Anne dearest. No use deluding yourself. This way you know the way of things before you build up too many hopes."

Margaret sat heavily in the chair opposite. "Once married, we are nothing but breeding vessels. Indeed, I think Lord Austin had his—woman—installed as soon as the marriage lines were read. Most likely he never gave her up to begin with." Margaret smoothed her hand over her rounded belly. "Frankly, I am just as happy. The marriage bed is a disgusting business."

The room had a roaring fire, yet she felt as if her

bones were frozen against her skin—one move and she would break.

"I did think of telling you of the assignations, but Lord Austin forbade me. He loves his brother, and he wants him to have a bit of happi—"

Too much. The shawl fell to the floor as she lurched to her feet.

"Anne. Oh, dear, I am sorry. I do put my foot in my—"

Vessel. Yes, she was only a vessel. But she'd known that from the outset. Their marriage had been doomed the moment she lied to the old duke.

Still, she had to see. She had to see them together to make it real.

****

The next day a veiled Nora Havermere descended from her hackney cab in front of a large warehouse. Looking furtively about her, she climbed the steps and disappeared inside.

Anne alighted from her own cab and slipped in the mouth of an alleyway to wait. Only eleven-twenty. She stamped her feet, trying to keep warm. A shadow paused by a large window at the very top of the building. A glimpse of red hair as the countess leaned out. So eager to meet her lover? He must paint her up there as well as—

The figure disappeared.

"Hey there, dumplin'. Ya been waitin' 'ere fer me?" Fish and a dank musk filled her nose. Not looking back, she scurried across the street and right up to the building Nora Havermere had entered. Only three steps and through the door to safety.

And Hell.

Cold lanced through her gloved hand as she pushed down hard on the latch. Had it locked?

She turned back to see if the man had followed, but he was gone.

What had she been thinking? Like a scene from a Penny Dreadful, this madness of confronting her husband's lover. Still, she gave the latch one final yank. The door swung open.

A twisting set of iron stairs lay ahead. She set her foot on the first tread and then another, and another. Up and up she went. So silent.

The key lay just where it should. Even before she opened the door she heard the splash of water and a soft soprano.

The door thudded shut. Too loud.

"Dev? Oh dear, is it so late?"

The voice was music. Anne followed it like some pied piper, completely conscious of the danger this woman posed to her fragile world.

"Stay where you are. I will be out in a trice. You must be early, no? Heavens, how eager you are. You are never early."

Splashing like rain on a tin roof came from behind a screen. "I am sorry, I can't hear you. I always wanted to try it. Havermere will not think of modernizing. So clever, the way you have it rigged. A simple open of a tap and voila! a waterfall of delicious hot." A burble of laughter. "I just could not resist."

The water stopped, just the patter of drips now. "I cannot lie; I took a peek. I know, I do not play fair, but then you never expected me to, did you? It is magnificent, and you are a genius."

Of course Nora Havermere had looked at the

356

painting. Anyone would. Only a stupid, trusting Owl would hold fast to such an absurd promise.

Paintings lay propped against the walls. But one stood on an easel covered with a piece of cloth.

The square of canvas drew her. The fabric drape lay between her fingers. All she had to do was to lift it and see. Just one simple gesture.

"Dev, there is champagne on the table. Make yourself useful and open it, would you? I cannot stay but a few moments. Havermere will miss me soon, but I have time to toast our success for I am claiming part of it, you know."

Cut crystal held a sweating bottle on the table by the bed. Two delicate flutes stood next to the wine. So perfect, so expectant.

Anne let the fabric go. This time it was not breaking a promise that stopped her, but sheer cowardice.

Off-key singing rose from behind the screen. At least there was something not perfect about this woman.

The screen's embossed leather felt like smooth pebbles under her fingers, and the silken gown hanging over it held the countesses' spicy scent. Gritting her teeth, she peered around.

Red hair with a hundred different highlights winked at her. Several tendrils had escaped and looped about Nora Havermere's white shoulders. Swathed in a towel, the woman bent over her long leg, drying it with the edge of the cloth. Her lips were framed in a secret smile as she hummed.

James and this woman would be so stunningly perfect together. His darkness against her bright copper. Their long elegant limbs intertwined. His mouth dipping to kiss her lush, ripe lips…his hand winding in her hair…

"Dev?" The woman started to turn.

In her haste to quit the room, this building, this city, she must have made a racket on the stairs, her boots ringing against the endless treads.

Only when she was three streets away and her ribs aching did she pause to catch her breath and swipe the wet from her eyes. Her stomach heaved. Bile rose in her throat, choking her.

"Are you all right, miss?"

She tried to speak, anything to make this good Samaritan go away so she could be alone, but she only managed a nod. Footsteps started away, hesitated and then faded to nothing.

"Ugh." She jerked her skirts away just in time.

How long she huddled in a doorway, she had no idea, but the shadows had shifted and lengthened. She shivered, now in deep shade.

By God, she was no sniveling coward. She took her handkerchief from her reticule and wiped her eyes and the mess from her mouth.

****

"Norraaa!" Dev pounded up the last few stairs and burst into the garret.

Nora turned in astonishment. "Where have you been? And what has you in such an uproar? Did I get the wrong champagne?"

The room looked empty. Nothing behind the curtains. No one lurking under the cot. He raced back down the stairs. Nothing. Back up the steps to Nora.

"What has you so stirred?"

"The door was standing wide open," he said between breaths.

He whipped the cover off the painting.

There she was, in all her perfection. He sat on the bed, exhausted. "God, I just want this to be done. I just want to get on with our life."

"Be easy. Two days and this nonsense will be over. You know me, it is likely I did not shut the door properly."

"Nora, I told you to be more vigilant."

"Yes, I know. But that latch has always been tricky. You must speak to Cheswell." She buttoned the topmost button on her dress. He turned away. "I suppose I have gotten a bit lax with Havermere so indisposed. I can almost taste freedom." Her gaze caught his in the reflection of the window. "Is that terrible?"

"No, my dear. God knows I would have shot the man long ago were I you."

"Well then, it is a good thing you are not me. I would not fare well moldering in Bridewell Prison. Let us toast, shall we?"

Yes, he could use a drink, or twelve. He removed the foil and slowly twisted the cork. *Pop.* A misty breath of wine perfumed the air. Bubbles exploded into the glasses, popping and sputtering as they slid down into a pale pool.

"To our freedom." Nora's long fingers wrapped around her glass as she raised it to his.

"Yes, my countess, freedom is something I have craved for a very long time. I hope and pray this painting will be its beginning." He raised his glass to meet hers. To freedom!"

And to love.

Chapter Thirty-Eight

Anne swallowed. Despite stopping for a cup of tea, she could still taste the sour bile in her mouth.

From the street, Havermere's manse appeared cold and formidable. As she approached the front door the impression magnified and she shivered. Not one thing was out of place but it was utterly soulless.

How did one do this? Never mind, best not to think, simply knock on the door and demand to see the countess. After all, she was the Marchioness of Devlin now. It was time to behave like it.

She was admitted at once, as if she had been expected.

"Ah, Lady Devlin, what a pleasure." The earl sat very close to a roaring fire, a blanket covered his knees. He was rolling up what looked to be a canvas. He finished and tucked it away.

Lord Havermere might have been rather good looking as a younger man, but his expression was sour, and his smile looked more reptilian than genuine.

"I have been looking forward to our meeting. You must forgive me for not rising. I am somewhat incapacitated of late." He indicated the chair opposite his.

Anne stood her ground.

He cocked his head. "In truth, I thought you would come much sooner."

Several hours had passed. The countess had said she could not tarry with James and needed to be home. "I was hoping to meet your wife."

"Ah, aren't we all, Lady Devlin. Aren't we all."

She shifted her feet.

"Please sit down. You will be doing me a favor. My eyesight is not what it used to be."

Unsure what to do she sat, putting her back to the fire.

"My paramour has never been the most accessible of ladies, but these days she seems to be even more elusive. Believe me, I employ a stable of people to keep track of her, but to no avail. I fear her infamous—charm—has wheedled its way into their hearts. But, never mind, that will all change soon enough."

The heat burned her back and she rose. "I am sorry to disturb you, Lord Havermere. I really wished to speak with the countess on a personal matter."

"Yes, I would imagine you would."

The old earl's gaze gave her the sudden urge to check if the buttons at her neck were all done up. She squeezed her hands instead.

"I believe we have much to discuss, Lady Devlin. Please sit."

"I really must—"

"You seemed to enjoy the opera. I don't get out often, but the charms of Miss Lind lured me to the theater. I cannot resist true talent." This time when he indicated the chair, his fingers brushed a sheaf of papers on the table by his elbow.

About to make her apologies again, she stopped.

The topmost drawing was turned away from her, but she knew even before the earl shifted it toward her that it was of *her*. Nora Havermere.

And James.

Like stopping to witness a terrible accident, she could not look away. But instead of blood and gore, there was only heartbreaking beauty.

James must have set up a large mirror and hastily, yet so expertly, caught their ardor in just a few marks of pencil.

Her stomach clenched, still unsettled from earlier. She sat.

"Yes, I thought you might change your mind, my dear." Havermere picked up the drawing, revealing the next beneath.

James sat facing the mirror his long legs splayed wide, his sketchbook between them. Nora hovered just over his left shoulder, her hair a riot of curls as she nipped at his neck, a secret smile on her lips. One breast and a lushly-curved hip peeped out from behind James's body, a baroque frame for his austere angles.

Unable to stop, she reached for the rest of them. One by one she peeled them off. They fluttered to the floor like so many dead leaves. So many positions—another sketch—another position. She had done that one with James. It joined the others on the floor to reveal yet another—he had taken her that way as well.

These last were only very rough sketches. The mirror played no part now. No voyeuristic looking glass to peer into their deep intimacy.

Poor owlish Anne Winton could never compete with this woman. What they had together was so incredibly beautiful. As if they were made for each other. Pure art.

"I see you get the full picture now, Lady Devlin. I am sorry it is so hideously graphic, but sometimes it is better, kinder, to not have any illusions left to muddle your true and just feelings."

She stared at the papers scattered at her feet. She should gather them up, make sure they did not get destroyed, but could not make herself move.

"You need not worry my countess will dally any longer with your husband. Once I get hold of her, she will be—disciplined. I do not enjoy playing the cuckold. I will not tolerate being made a fool."

"No."

"I knew you would agree."

"You misunderstand. I mean we should not interfere. *I* will not interfere." This old bitter man and she were the interlopers. They were the ones keeping these two perfect beings from being together. "We must accept the inevitable and let them go. You must see that." She said the words as if she had memorized them long ago, like the liturgy she had intoned by rote everyday at Ardsmoore. They were only words with no meaning, strung together to put a period on this part of her dream.

"You are a little fool. He has cozened you as well. Have you fallen in love with him? Foolish woman. Do you know he has had the most elegant women in and outside of society besides my wife? You are nothing to him. Only a breeder—a means to an end. Are you increasing yet?"

Warmth flooded her cheeks that had nothing to do with the fire being so hot.

"By God, you are. Fertile ground. Well, as they say, ground nearest the dung heap always sprouts first. Do you imagine you have won with this babe? Have you never thought, once you whelp, how long he will keep you? Once he has his son you will be *de trop*, my dear lady. Make no mistake, he will pack you off to molder in the country. He might drop by in a year or two to plant a spare in you, but don't look for anything beyond that."

She could not stay to listen to this terrible man. She heaved herself onto her legs. But the drawings surrounded her, a sea of paper, trapping her against the chair.

"The marquess will be too busy trying to extricate his lover, my dear wife. He knows all too well what awaits her at Ballencrieff. That will break him. I will not have to do anything more, he will sabotage himself all on his own."

"Ballencrieff?"

"Yes, I have the documents nearly ready. She is unstable, my dear countess. She needs care and discipline. Perhaps in a few years she will see the error of her ways."

"You wouldn't."

"Oh, wouldn't I? I will not be made a fool again. By the time my lady wife gets clear of Ballencrieff, she will no longer resemble the willful shrew she is now. Her outside will finally match her black inside. And our marquess, with his—tendencies—will either be locked up with her, or will have moved on to someone else. Perhaps he might send you off to Ballencrieff as well. *Ha!* Wouldn't that be a fitting end for both of Devlin's bitches."

Dear God, she could almost forgive Nora Havermere for falling in love with James, now having met this monster.

She had never seen herself as a fool. Naïve certainly, narrowly educated, but never a fool. She supposed she must thank the *ton* for showing her that side of herself.

Yes, she had learnt a thing or two in these last few months.

How could she suppose James had ever wanted her? Oh, he was good, very good. She did not look in the mirror often, but when she did, she could not help but see her deficiencies. Nose too long, eyes too large, hair too black. These features would cause much consternation in most females. But she had made peace with her face…until James. Her eyes pricked with childish tears. Damn him for making her feel beautiful. That she could never forgive.

This new confidence was just a seedling, easily ripped out by the roots. But the notion of being a fool was not as easy to purge. The good news was she would have many hours—years—to learn to swallow it down.

****

"Where is Lady Devlin?"

"Good afternoon, your lordship. Might I be of assistance?"

Anne's maid was one of those modern beauties, her opulence put on display for all to see. She might have appealed to him in his younger days, but now he found her vulgar.

"Yes, you can tell me the whereabouts of your mistress."

The maid made a moue with her generous lips and plucked at the neckline of her bodice.

"Now."

"She is gone, sir."

"Yes, that I can see for myself. Where has she gone, and more importantly when will she return?"

The maid frowned, obviously not used to having her considerable battery of attributes ignored. "She doesn't tell me what she's about, your lordship. She keeps to herself, you know."

Halfway out the door the maid's voice stopped him. "I don't know where, but I do know she may likely be gone for a while."

"What do you mean?"

"Well, she usually goes down to the pianoforte in the afternoon, and I come up to see to her clothing at that time. I am not fond of music, I suppose. I noticed two of her gowns were missing. The gray Kerseymere and the blue serge. At first I thought she had finally followed my advice and given them to the rag and bone man, but when I investigated further, I saw some of her other things were gone as well."

"What things?"

"Well, some of her unmentionables, sir, and her brush and comb set."

He crossed to Anne's vanity. Sure enough, the silver set Lady Tippit had given her as a wedding gift was gone. He flipped open a small inlaid box. The pearls lay in a coil against the indigo lining. A bit of ribbon was wound around an object. He pulled the end and two rings rolled out onto the table. The hideous one his father had provided when they were wed, and the opal.

He slipped it on his smallest finger. It barely reached his first knuckle. The stone flashed as it caught a sliver of fading light. *Idiot,* it seemed to say. "Bloody, foolish, idiot," he agreed.

"Pardon, your lordship? You said something?"

He'd forgotten he was not alone. The maid. Still trying to get a rise out of him.

Twenty minutes later, after having quizzed his sister-in-law's maid, the cook—who he was sure was hiding something—and five footmen, he finally found Margaret at the top of the house in a room tucked between the eaves.

She was huddled in an overstuffed chair with a plate of cake on her knees, licking her fingers.

His paintings surrounded her. Dozens of faces stared back at him. Ghosts from his past. Not destroyed as he had assumed, just hidden away, much as he had been.

"Oh, dear!" Margaret began to rise and nearly lost her cake as she grabbed for a pillow next to her. "Lord Devlin. Is my husband with you?" She glanced over his shoulder.

"No. I have not seen him."

"Oh, good." She collapsed back into her nest of pillows. "How you frightened me."

"What are you doing here?" He stepped farther into the room.

"You have stumbled upon my sanctuary. No one ever comes here, you see—well, except when Lady Devlin and I found the room. That is when I started using it."

"Anne was here?"

"Oh, yes, though it was some time ago. I tried to persuade her to leave, but she had to look at every one." Margaret glanced about her. "Odd, they have become like old friends to me now."

He had never paid much mind to his brother's wife, but even he knew a woman seven or so months gone with child should have looked far more round. But she seemed to have lost her belly but gained a good three or more stone everywhere else.

"Oh, you are shocked, I see." She touched a small round pillow next to her. "Well, originally I thought to put on a few extra pounds to look as if I was still increasing. That way your brother would—well, he would leave me be. And besides, I could not bear to disappoint the duke who seemed to rally at our news."

"You are not increasing?"

Margaret bit her lip and, discovering some pastry cream, licked it. She shook her head. "No, I am not. Not anymore, at least." She shuddered. "Please, you must not tell Austin. He will be seriously displeased with me."

"Why would you indulge in this kind of subterfuge?"

"Your father was so desperate. And my husband so very—diligent. He would not stop until he got me with child. We did not anticipate you leaving Ballencrieff anytime soon."

But why would they perpetuate such a farce? Hell, that was the pot calling the kettle black. Wasn't he busy fabricating his own mythical child? Take the bloody mote out of your own eye...

At one time he would have loved revisiting these portraits. Now they no longer interested him. He'd moved beyond them. Only a reminder of what he had been, and what he no longer wanted. "Do you know where my wife is?"

"She usually practices the piano now, which is one of the reasons I found this place, being out of the way, you understand."

"Did she say anything to you about leaving?"

"Leaving? Where would she go?" Clearly Margaret could not conceive of the idea of running away, or striking out on one's own.

"Did she mention any new friends? Does she visit anyone?"

"Not that I know of. She did want to visit the British Museum, but I told her I could not countenance the idea of looking at naked bodies and heathen Egyptian deities."

And yet his sister-in-law surrounded herself with nearly naked women.

"Thank you. I will try the museum."

"Won't you stay for some tea and cake, Lord Devlin? I have plenty and the tea pot is still hot."

"No, I must find Anne."

"You really love her, don't you?"

"With all my heart." God, it felt good to say that.

Margaret nodded sadly and stuffed a bit of cake into her mouth.

Closing the door he heard a clatter. The door swung open. Margaret beamed waving her teapot. "Teapot! Lady Teapot!"

"Teapot? Lady who?"

"Now I remember, Anne mentioned a Lady Teapot once—" Her smile collapsed and the teapot drooped in her hand. "Oh, silly me, Lady Teapot. I have got it wrong. Who would be called Lady Teapot?"

"I must go now, Margaret."

"Oh, of course. And you will remember our little secret?" She smoothed her hand over her belly.

"For now, your secret is safe."

She nodded sadly again and closed the door.

Lady Teapot, indeed.

Venerable relatives lining the stairway stared down from their portraits as if to say, *What a clod this one is. Not one of us at all.* The third duke of Malvern was next to fire another insult. *Must be bad blood on the mother's side.*

Why not just heave himself over the banister as he had nearly done that fateful day at Ballencrieff.

Teapot. Tip-pit.

The second Duke of Malvern, a rather ruddy-faced man, seemed to wink at Dev.

By God, it must be Tippit.

The first, almost smiled. He must be truly barmy. The dukes of Malvern never smiled in their portraits.

Could Anne be going back to Ballencrieff? Or could Lady Tippit have finally braved coming to Town?

Ivo. Ivo would know.

****

"Devlin," Lady Tippit raised her quizzing glass. "Took you long enough."

Her ladyship had taken a good three inches off the height of her hair and triple that off her age. Dev suddenly realized she must only be in her late forties and not an unhandsome woman.

"Ivo was the ticket, your ladyship. I only needed to ask him."

"Yes, he is remarkably keen, our Ivo. Knows which end is up, don't you, dear boy?"

The giant grinned, right as rain now he was tucked up inside a house instead of battling carriages and pedestrians.

"Is she here?"

"Yes, she is, but you cannot see her."

"Lady Tippit, please—"

"She is indisposed."

"She is ill? Has a doctor been called?"

"Do sit down. Perkins,"—she waved to a rather cadaverous-looking butler—"Lord Devlin requires brandy. And give him Poppa's good stuff." The butler unlocked a cabinet and set a decanter and glass next to Dev.

"Shall I pour, my lord?" His thin reedy voice felt like spider webs, and Dev had the urge to swipe his face.

"No, thank you. I can see to myself."

"Perkins, that will be all. Take Ivo to Cook for his cider." She turned to Ivo. "And best to keep your little friend Pocket *in* your pocket. My cook does not have the best of humors. She is new, and I want to keep this one."

The walking-dead Perkins and the beefy giant made quite a pair as they left the room.

"Why can't I see her?"

"Ah, suddenly you are the knight-errant?"

He stood, the weight of the crystal glass too familiar and too comforting in his hand. He set it down.

"Could you desist in your perambulations, Devlin? You are wearing me out. You know I do not care for exercise."

"Why? Why is she here? If she is ill, she should be home, at Malvern House."

Lady Tippit shrugged. "She needed a friend. Simple as that."

What could he say? He had not taken care of her while waiting for this ridiculous business to end when he might come to her with a clean slate. But he was ready now. Anxious to tell her he was ready to be the husband she needed. That he loved her.

"In truth, I do not yet know why she is so grieved. I have given her some of Poppa's brandy as well and sent her to bed."

"Might I at least see her?"

Lady Tippit shook her head. "Drink up and then take yourself home. Give her time to calm herself. The poor mite is worn to a nub."

Lord, he had made such a hash of things. He stared at the brandy which he must have picked up again. His old friend. No, not a friend. Only something to dull his feelings. To manage himself. Once more he set the drink aside.

A piercing scream came from the back of the house.

Lady Tippit sighed. "That will be my cook. I should say former cook. Ivo cannot keep from sharing his little treasures, can he, the dear soul."

****

"You must see him sometime, Anne."

Somehow she had slipped from Winton to Anne between her third brandy and the hot soup Lady Tippit had insisted she at least try.

"The Anne Winton I know is no coward."

"Am I not? I am not sure what I am anymore." No wonder James liked brandy so well. After the initial burn it was very tasty stuff. "I was an orphan, a nobody, and now I am a somebody"—she giggled—"whatever that means. I wanted to be a healer, but it seems there is no place for that being a woman, much less a marchioness. I am not even a reasonable musician. My tutor, though very tolerant and kind, secretly despairs of me, I am sure. And I have managed to kill Mr. Hiro's Bonsai tree. I snipped where I should not have."

"You are many things, Anne Winton. But regardless of your lack of talent for music, your horticultural skills, your appalling wardrobe, and your inability to tolerate any liquor, you will hold your head up and face those bacon-faced biddies and loathsome lords."

"But I am not beautiful. I am not—her." Maybe the brandy was not such a good idea. She set it aside, her stomach at sea once again. "He doesn't want me. He never wanted me. Will never love me."

"Balderdash and poppycock. Have you seen the way the man looks at you?"

"Lady Tippit, you have only seen us in company together on perhaps three or four occasions. How can you say that?"

"First of all, you shall call me Maddy, and I will try to think of you as Anne. After all, one must dispense with social barriers when one's guest's nose is leaking all over Mama's best linen."

Horrified, Anne swiped at her nose with her sleeve.

"Secondly, believe me, when the man speaks of you, I see a man in love. Oh, I know, you say, what does she know? A dried-up old biddy whose father had to fetch her back from Gretna Green. But I know. I have felt love, and I know love when I see it."

She could well imagine a younger Maddy Tippit, a woman full of dreams and not yet so damaged by life. Anne was not alone in her trials. "But—Lady—Maddy—I saw them. I saw her... How could he not love her? She is so utterly perfect. They are perfect together. They fit."

A knock on the door interrupted their conversation.

"Come," Maddy called out.

Perkins floated in. The man seemed to hover like a ghost. "Lady Tippit, are you at home?"

"Who is calling at this hour? It is not the marquess again, is it?"

"No, madam." Perkins coughed delicately, "it is a woman."

"I am expecting Phoebe any day now." Lady Tippit took the card Perkins handed her. "Ah, yes. Put her in the south drawing room, Perkins. I will be down shortly."

The butler nodded and drifted out of the room.

"Is it Mrs. Nester? Has she brought Grace?" Anne stood, desperate for the sight of the child who was now just over three months old.

"No, my dear it is not Phoebe. It seems the Countess of Havermere has come to call."

Her stomach heaved and the room spun. She just managed to avoid her lap, but Maddy's mother's linen was now beyond redemption.

Chapter Thirty-Nine

"Devlin, where is your wife?" his sire said looking up from his breakfast of porridge. Dev did not bother with an answer, only making a note to avoid the breakfast room in the morning. The old duke was becoming a habitual early riser.

"This whole household is in chaos. Austin is ranting at Margaret. Apparently she is not increasing—merely fat." The duke flung his napkin on the table. "I swear the duchy will go to those cretins in Guernsey. Hamish Swinton, a fourth cousin twice removed, and a certifiable idiot."

"Austin wasn't any part of this sham?" Had Margaret perpetuated this pregnancy all on her own?

"Who knows what to believe. He is certainly acting as if it is news to him. He intercepted one of the maids with a tray of honey cake and found her little bower."

He needed a drink. The stopper was out of the decanter and the glass half-full before he remembered. No more.

Food. He needed something in his stomach. Beefsteak, eggs, toast, coffee. He filled a plate and then sat down.

"I have changed my mind, you know."

No, he did not know. Did not care. He cut into the rare beef.

"About the girl."

"The *girl*?"

"Your wife. Anne."

He sat up straighter, waiting.

"She will do. I did not see at first—she is such a tiny thing, but she is...very..." The old man frowned furiously as if his not being able to find the word he wanted was the greatest insult. "She is..."

Still Dev waited, not giving the duke an inch.

Suddenly, the furrows in his father's face released like a sheet being snapped taut. "Complete." He nodded once. "This woman is complete."

Complete? Yes, by heavens, that was just the word. Complete.

Staring into the eyes so much like his, he felt his own well up. Ridiculous, but this one exchange brought him closer to his father than he'd been in years.

First to break the connection, the duke delved back into his congealed porridge. "She healed me, you know."

"What did you say?"

"*Ack!* Take this pabulum away and bring me a beefsteak, Yancy." The duke swept his porridge aside. The footman leapt to take the stuff away. "She has healing within her." His father gripped the table, his gnarled fingers spreading over the white damask cloth. "Her hands are—"

"Hot." He resented his father speaking of Anne's gift. No, what he really resented was he knew nothing of this incident, so out of touch with his wife's daily life not to know of her encounter with the duke. That she had even ministered to him. The old man did look much improved. Preoccupied with his own affairs, he had not really seen his father. But more appalling, he had not seen his wife.

Well, not strictly true. He knew damn well she had no complaints with one part of their marriage. But he was ready to be a whole man now. To love her completely, as she deserved.

His father held his hands up in front of his face and slowly flexed his fingers. "Yes, burning. Extraordinary. I never felt anything like it." Yancy delivered the steak. "She has come to me several times now. Sent those quacks with their leeches and purges back to their lairs. She is all I need." His father cut into his beefsteak with relish. "She is not increasing, is she?"

He stopped mid chew.

"Your wife, Anne, is not with child."

Enough lies. He swallowed. "No."

His father nodded. "It seems you owe her a great deal, Devlin. She wanted to stay at Ballencrieff, to 'be of use,' she said."

Yet another blow, this shared confidence with her father-in-law. If only he could push her dream aside as a whim, but he could not. Not anymore. "Yes, she did. But I couldn't do without her, you see."

He could not wait to get to her. To see her. Touch her. Lady Tippit would not turn him away today.

The old man nodded slowly. "I do. See, now."

"Yes, I think you are beginning to." He laid his napkin on the table. "Child or no, I will not go back to that place. I cannot go back there."

"No. Ballencrieff was a terrible mistake. Austin did not provide a clear picture."

Easy enough to pull his shirt up and give his sire a 'clear' picture, but it seemed petty now.

His father laid down his knife and fork, wiped his mouth, and sat forward. "I honestly thought it would do you good. Get you away from your vices. Give you time for reflection. I did not know—"

"Let us not dwell on the past." He shifted in his seat, unused to this contrite father.

The old man looked as if he wanted to say more but must have thought better of it. "No, you are correct. The past is the past. Besides, you are cured. I'm sure Lady Devlin had a great deal to do with your recovery." He dug into his beef. "Speaking of moving on, Hives has decamped from Ballencrieff."

Good riddance.

"Apparently the blunt I gave him was enough for him to hie off to India where he is going to study with some heathen priest."

The coffee burned his throat. Too damned hot. The piece of beef leaching blood on the plate in front of him made his stomach heave. He pushed it aside and then jammed toast into his mouth. He could be at Lady Tippit's home in thirteen minutes or so if traffic was not a quagmire.

"Don't know where Havermere will find another doctor. He seems to go through them like a cutpurse through a crowd." His father was surprisingly talkative.

"Havermere?" Coffee sloshed onto the table linen. "What does the Earl of Havermere have to do with Ballencrieff Hall?"

"Everything. His funds run the place."

If the floor opened and swallowed him whole, he could not be more thunderstruck. "What?"

"He is the benefactor of Ballencrieff." The duke mopped up the bloody juice from his beefsteak with a bit of bread.

"But Hives said—" No, Hives had never actually

said. Dev had just assumed the place was one of his sire's charities. "Havermere? Not you?"

"Good heavens, no. Ardsmoore and Ackermoore are enough to keep my plate full."

"But who? Who was in charge? Who did Hives take his orders from?"

The old duke frowned. "Ballencrieff has always been the Earl of Havermere's pet project. Had to send one of his wives away—female hysteria, I believe." Another bite of blood-soaked bread went into his father's mouth.

Havermere? Fragments of Hives' words and deeds pricked his memory, waking him up to what had been right in front of him. The terrible abuse. Hives had never wanted to heal only to torture and break him. On Havermere's orders.

"Poor man." Oblivious, his father continued hacking away at his breakfast. "He always reminded me that *I* at least had a son to inherit. Unlucky, he was. Four wives and nothing to show for it. His heir, a poncey nephew. Queer that way, you know. Havermere thought the army would toughen the lad up, but he came back blind and lame. *Pish!* Ended up killing himself. Damned waste."

The duke's words barely registered. By all the fires of Hell, it was Havermere all along.

"The earl always took an interest in you. Always yammering on about wanting you to paint his countess. *Humph.* As if I had any sway with you," he said stabbing his beef. "Came to me directly when you were ill, said he had a place to send you. Havermere and I were at school together, you know," his sire continued as if being chums at Cambridge meant blind trust.

The duke swiped his mouth with his napkin and

pushed his mangled piece of meat away. "You must understand I did not know what to do for you. Despite Tally's best efforts in staunching any gossip, the dam broke and the Mad Marquess was born."

By God, it all began to make sense. The earl must have found out about his and Nora's affair. Havermere insinuated himself into the old duke's confidence and proposed a solution for his son and heir. So easy.

He shook his head, trying to make all the pieces line up. "I thought it was you. Hives made me believe you were behind the place."

"No, not me. But make no mistake, I signed the papers, Devlin. I thought it the best solution. But you did not improve. I wanted to see you for myself but Austin, and then my damned heart, stopped me." He closed his eyes. "I was dying, and my heir was in a madhouse. Call it vanity, but Austin…well, as you know, it is doubtful he is mine." The duke sighed heavily and his gaze found Dev's. "I hatched that betrothal to the Thornton girl out of sheer panic and promised Hives a king's ransom if he could cure you."

Yes, the tide had turned, then. The beatings and the deprivations gone, and Macready replaced by gentle Ivo. Hives must have switched his allegiance from Havermere to the duke.

Still so many questions to be answered though.

"I must go." Time to confront this fiend.

"Do not do anything you will regret, Devlin. Havermere has great influence and has always been a staunch friend."

"Trust me, sir, the Earl of Havermere is no friend of this family."

"You have the duchy and a wife to think of now.

And if you have been doing your duty, there may yet be a child."

Yes, it could be. If God were generous. But all he could focus on now was getting some answers. A terrible thought occurred to him. Did Havermere have anything to do with Anne being indisposed yesterday?

He ended up running to Upper Brook Street.

"I will see him. Now!" The ancient butler fell back.

The earl sat practically in the hearth of a huge fireplace. The blaze must surely singe the shawl shrouding the old man. Vials of medicines sat clustered on a table by his elbow.

"Ah, behold! The bridegroom cometh!"

"My wife—has she been here?"

"You have to ask? *Tush,* this is how it begins, Devlin. We must keep a close watch on these wives."

"The marchioness, was she here?"

"Calm yourself. You virile lads must always be flexing your muscles and making a show."

"By God I will kill you where you sit if I find you have hurt her." He was halfway out the door.

"Who would have thought your Owl had such fine tits."

The words slammed into him, surer than any blow.

"But she looks to have a surprising handful. Quite a wanton really, your lady wife."

"By God, if you touched her I will rip your throat out, Havermere."

"Please, kindly remove your hands from my person. So much easier to conduct business when the parties are civilized."

"When—when was my wife here?"

"Yesterday." The earl straightened his jacket and

cravat. "Rest easy, she left here fit as a fiddle and is still tucked up with the old biddy for now. According to my man, she hasn't left the place."

"If you harmed her or filled her with your lies, I will—"

"Leave off your histrionics, Mad Marquess. And please, let us not talk of deceptions." Havermere rang a bell next to his medicines. "I believe when you see what I have on offer, you will be happy enough to deceive."

He stepped back, unsure of the earl's game.

A servant's door within the paneled wall opened.

"You require assistance, your lordship?"

"Bring the marquess some brandy, Macready. I believe he is partial to Camus Frères."

"How do you know—"

Wait. Macready? He wheeled to face the man.

Tricked out in a powdered wig and livery, the servant grinned. His twisted leer transformed this trumped-up lackey into Dev's old nemesis. Another piece of the puzzle slid into place. No wonder the henchman never lost his position at Ballencrieff.

"Your old friend here has been invaluable to me. Been with me from the very beginning, haven't you Macready?"

"From nearly the time I were knee high to a grasshopper, my lord."

"You see, I needed a safe place to put my third wife. She had a terrible problem with drink, as well as with opiates. Barren, you see, and laudanum was her best friend. So Ballencrieff was born. Poor unfortunate died there, didn't she, Macready?"

"Had to scoop her brains up off the floor."

"Took a tumble, she did. Never steady on her feet."

The earl poured out two glasses of brandy. "You recall the minstrel gallery in the great hall is quite high. And the floor, stone."

The hideous picture leapt into living color in his mind's eye.

"I had to replace Doctor Oliphant after that particular incident. And then another. Much too squeamish to be of use. What was his name, Macready, I can't recall?"

"Dorson, sir, Doctor Dorson."

"Oh yes. Very dapper gent. Didn't like the cold." He carefully put the stopper back in the decanter. "Then Hives. Turns out the fellow had too much bloody conscience to finish the job. Ethics mixed with a healthy dose of greed. His bloody loyalty went right out the window when your father stepped in. Malvern could not leave well enough alone. Had to have his miracle. We had to be too damned subtle, didn't we Macready? Don't like subtlety, do we?"

"Never saw much use in it, sir. Why use a bit of poison dribbled in here and there when you can use your fists?"

Poison. He knew it. "Mercury?"

"In the porridge. Among other things. Easy enough when Mac here was your keeper. Slipped it right in." Havermere offered one of the brandies. "No?" The earl shrugged and took a long sip.

Macready danced on the balls of his feet like he had to take a wicked piss. "I should have finished you off with the dose I gave you when I offed—when that molly Cummings hung himself. A lovers' pact it were supposed to be. But you buggered it by bleeding the poison right outta yourself, by making them evil pictures on the walls."

"Yes, that did not go as planned." The earl gave Macready a quelling look. "After that incident, Hives became squeamish."

Cummings? His sire had said something about Havermere's heir being sent off to war. Major Cummings had been the earl's heir? The fiend must have sent his nephew straight from the battlefields to rot in Ballencrieff. "By God, you have much to answer for, Havermere."

"What?" The old man shrugged. "The lad hanged himself, degenerate that he was. Best thing for him, I say." He clapped his hands once. "Enough unpleasantness. I have something to show you. Macready, will you do the honors?"

The servant grinned again and started for the door.

"No, not that yet. The others first." The earl waved to a picture on the wall.

The servant crossed to a tepid painting of shepherds with their sheep and swung it open. Must be a safe behind. He pulled out a tube about two feet long.

Yet another piece of the puzzle.

Macready unrolled one of the canvases with a flourish.

Yes. By God. He squeezed his eyes shut then reopened them. The horrible empty canvas that had haunted him vanished, replaced by Anne's beauty. There she was, laid out on the fainting couch, her hair spread over pillows and brushing the floor, her mouth parted as if taking in a breath, her breasts thrust up to be cradled by one of her hands, her other tangled in her maiden's hair—

"It is mine." His nails bit into his palms stinging as

Macready's dirty fingers defiled the painting. The other roll, still tucked under his arm, must be the other portrait. "They are both mine."

"Of course." The earl smiled. "After all, what's yours is yours. I have no quarrel with that." Dev jerked the paintings from Macready. "But I will have what is mine. That seems only fair. You will get your Owl, and I will get my whore."

"What?"

"Are you sure you won't indulge?" The earl gestured to the untouched brandy.

He ignored him and rolled the nude around the other portrait as if by doing so he was somehow protecting Anne from this terrible man.

"Never thought your—Owl would be such a problem. But she botched our plans with her lies, didn't she, Mac?"

"I had to hie out of that pile of stones as if the very devil were at me."

"Was Austin—did my brother—?" He could not make himself finish the question.

"Ah, Lord Austin. Bastard younger sons are tricky. They have a lot to lose. Or gain. But Lord Austin? Alas, no. Too risky. Your brother was only inadvertently useful. Busy with his own agenda being the ever-vigilant brother who wanted to keep you down while playing the hero."

A heavy weight lifted off his heart. Austin was not the enemy. Only too trusting and foolish.

"Who is Brocket to you? I saw you with him at the opera."

The earl re-filled his glass. "He is useless to me, as it turns out. He claims to be a purveyor of art. But as usual, I have had to take matters into my own hands. Haven't I, Mac?"

The door opened.

Nora.

"Ah, the leading lady of our drama has deigned to make an entrance. We have the cuckold—a role I do not relish, by the by—the fucker, and now the harlot. We only lack the wronged little owlet to complete our play."

"What have you done?" Nora stepped forward.

"Only what is just. Punishment will finally come. No coin can atone for your sins, I realize that now, my jewel. Your punishment will require a pound of flesh." He took a long sip and set his glass aside. "The marquess and I were just discussing evening the score."

Havermere's gaze bore into Dev. "My wife has been nothing but trouble ever since I acquired her nine years ago." A large log broke and collapsed in on itself in the firebox, sending up a shower of embers. "She cost me a pretty penny. But I thought her worth it at the time. I had what every other man wanted. This stunning beauty all mine." He gestured with his glass, in a kind of toast to Nora. Brandy sloshed and spilled onto the shawl covering his legs, but he took no notice. "But we both know she wasn't, was she—all mine, that is. Eh, Devlin?"

"I do not claim to be a saint, Havermere, but your wife never strayed until you drove her to it with your cruelty. I believe the countess and I have paid enough for our sins." He turned to Nora. "Will you be well? I am anxious to see Lady Devlin."

Nora held her arms over her body as if to protect her person from her husband's vitriol. "Yes, go. He will wind down without an audience."

"But what of our business?" The old earl slammed his glass down and half rose out of his chair.

"I have no business with you. Not now. Not ever." He tucked the paintings under his arm and started for the door.

"Oh, but I think you do."

"Dear God, Havermere." Nora's cry stopped Dev cold.

The sick look on her face made him turn and draw near.

The earl held pages and pages of sketches. Nude sketches of him and Nora.

"How did you get these? They were in my private home."

Macready closed the safe and stood behind the earl.

"They may have been in your private home, but she, this whore, is mine. She is useless to me, but I will have everything that is mine."

"By God, it was you, wasn't it? It was you all along." He had never known who had brought the police that terrible night Lily died, or been the one to leak the supposed murder to the papers. In his poisoned mind, he had sometimes wondered if it had been his own brother. But, no, it had been Havermere from the first. He owed Austin a sincere apology.

"The irony is you are the only one who did her justice. You captured her beauty when no one else could." He touched the pages reverently. "Even in these crude drawings. Why should that be? Why should a whore be so beautiful and a devil so talented? It never made sense. Why should the Mad Marquess be heir to a duchy when I have nothing?" Havermere seemed lost as he lovingly caressed the drawings.

"I saw these"—the old man held the pages up—"and I wanted more. I want them all. I will have every picture you ever painted of this harlot. Then you may go off to your Owl, or whoever next catches your fancy. The countess, however, can never repay what she has stolen from me. But she will begin to. Yes, she will endure her share of hell before this is all over and I am in the grave."

"You are the madman, Havermere. If you think I would turn even one painting over to you, you are more delusional than I thought."

The earl smiled a terrible smile. "Macready, I believe the marquess is ready to see our *piece de resistance*. Could you bring it in?" Ned Macready nearly danced out of the room.

Nora's gaze caught his. Whatever had Macready so primed could only mean disaster.

"While we are in such delicious anticipation, I wanted to share some news. I have a new doctor installed at Ballencrieff. Doctor Pinnix is experimenting with lesions on the brain and inducing high fevers to burn away madness. He also believes removing the teeth may be efficacious. Very experimental." He turned to Nora. "Lord Shaftesbury and his commission on lunacy have been quite helpful in seeing your—deficiencies, my dear." He shook his head in mock sadness. "A terrible shame, as you have such perfect teeth."

"You will never get away with this, Havermere." But his words were only bravado. Shaftesbury was rumored to owe the earl a small fortune.

"Oh? You are naïve, Devlin, if you really believe that. All I have to do is release just one of these drawings to the papers and your world will collapse. So easy. Much like I did when you butchered that whore. What was the brat's name? Lily?" Nora gasped. "I don't suppose your old father's heart will survive this scandal."

He lunged for the papers, but Havermere drew a pistol from beneath his shawl. "I wouldn't. You may be heir to the Malvern duchy, but I am no two-bit child-whore who you can murder and get away with without paying a steep price." He aimed the barrel at Nora. "You are spoiling my surprise with your antics, Lord Devil."

Macready entered, carrying a covered canvas.

His gut clenched and bile rose in his throat.

"By God, Havermere," Nora said shaking her head. "You may have your revenge on me, but do not wreak havoc on innocents."

"Innocents, you say? I see no innocents here. I have been patiently waiting to unveil this masterpiece, and then we will see what these innocents have been up to. Finally I will have what is rightfully mine!"

"Husband," she was pleading now. "If you ever cared for me at all, you will stop this."

"Shut up. I will die soon enough, but you will never recover from the scandal." He turned to Dev. "So, what will it be? Will you walk away quietly and leave this whore to me, or will you ruin your life and be the death of your father? "

The door banged open, crashing against the wall. Austin burst into the room and slammed the door shut.

"Austin, stay back!"

"Nooo!" His brother charged the earl. "Never! Never again will you hurt my family!" Austin threw himself at the earl.

Dev sprang forward to intercept his brother. But an arm around his neck and then a punch to his ribs could only mean Macready.

A shot cracked, filling the air with the acrid smell of burned powder.

"Austin!" Dev twisted, frantic to get free.

Through a haze of smoke, Austin wrestled the pistol from Havermere. Thank God, the shot must have gone wide. Dev jammed the heel of his boot into his tormentor's foot. The vice around his neck slackened, and he jerked free.

A solid left to the lackey's jaw and his powdered wig slipped sideways. A right jab at the throat and Macready's oily hair shone in all its glory. Now that's the man Dev knew and loathed.

"Bloody toff, think you can fight?"

"Oh, how I have longed for this day, Macready. Let's go."

"Glad to oblige, Lord Devil." He whipped out a wicked looking blade. The light glanced off a hunting knife at least nine inches long.

"I see chivalry was never a part of your upbringing."

"My upbringing, as you put it, was cut short by one of you butcher types slicing up me mum for your science. Beings I were only seven at the time, I never got my satisfaction from that scum, but I will from you."

"Satisfaction? You have no bloody idea, Macready."

The bruiser swung, but Dev feinted, easily dodging the blade. Sounds faded to only breath and the thumping of his heart. Macready was good, but heavier and not nearly as quick. Dancing to the side Dev spun away from another swipe. Damn knife.

Springing back from yet another, he lost his footing. He dropped to the floor, playing hurt. The thug bent to finish him off. Timing was everything. Waiting until the last moment, he reared up, the top of his head cracking against Macready's chin. His skull rang and Macready reeled. The knife slipped from his hand. No time to retrieve it, instead Dev kicked it away.

Only way to beat this man was to wear him out. He feinted right and left. Back and forth. Macready repeatedly swung wide, missing his mark.

"Stand like a man, ya poncey nacker!" Already Macready was blowing hard, frustrated.

Ducking again, he set up a pattern, hoping the thug would see it soon.

A slow smile spread over the man's face. He pulled back primed to deliver a felling blow when Dev next moved to the left.

Now! Instead he threw himself to the right and caught Macready flatfooted. He drove his fist into the larger man's solar plexus. Macready staggered, bent over double.

"No!"

Havermere's cry had Dev wheeling around. The fire roared fed by the drawings which must have fallen in the scuffle. His and Nora's bodies writhed as the flames whooshed to devour them.

"No!" Havermere leapt with surprising speed to the firebox. The half-full decanter of brandy toppled to the floor, soaking the shawl he kept over his shriveled legs. Fire rushed up the wool as if a dam had broken.

"Ahhh!" The old man wailed, scrambling to get away from the flames.

Austin pulled the shawl away, casting it into the firebox. Nora hoisted her husband up by the shoulders pulling him to safety. Havermere clawed at the tablecloth where his medicine bottles and the full glass of brandy sat.

"Nora, get away!"

"You will burn with me, you witch!" Havermere yanked and everything spilled at her feet.

Nora's huge crinoline skirt acted like a bellows to the fire.

Dev dove, batting at the flames. Water hit him in the face. Austin stood with a vase upended.

Nora screamed.

Confused, he flipped her over, looking for more fire.

"The portrait!" She flailed beneath him. "He's going to destroy—"

Flames licked up the easel where the painting rested. The paisley cloth covering the portrait curled with the heat. Macready stood next to it, a twist of flaming paper in his hand.

"Ahh!" He rushed the easel colliding with Macready. The easel crashed to the floor, the painting sailing across the room.

"You bloody bastard!" The man outweighed him by nearly two stone, but vengeance was on his side. His fist smashed into the keeper's snarling lip and nose. Blood spurted.

"To your left, Macready!" the earl croaked.

The knife. In a flash Macready had it. Dev grabbed the man's wrist just as he leveled the blade at Dev's neck. Macready smiled through his smashed lips. "You're done, Mad Marquess."

He smiled back. "I think not. But one of us surely is." Bravado only went so far. He needed to be smart. The blade inched closer. Macready's grin widened.

Now, it had to be now. "Don't shoot, Austin!"

There was no second shot, but Macready turned for an instant. The pressure on the knife relaxed a fraction. Dev heaved himself sideways, and the blade struck the floor a hair's breadth from his neck.

"Why, you—"

"I never said I fought fair either." He flipped himself on top of Macready.

"Damn you to hell, you worthless cur!" Havermere's voice rasped. "Kill the bastard!"

Macready's face writhed in rage. Dev's fingers closed over the knife. Macready reared up to butt heads. The knife pulled free.

Soft muscle gave way to bone as the knife slid past his ribs and up into his heart. Macready's features loosened into slack surprise and finally to gurgling death as he slumped to the floor.

Blood. So much blood.

His hands glistened with gore. He dropped the knife and heaved himself off the body and onto his trembling legs. Blood spattered his coat and shirt front. He shook his head desperate to rid himself of this hideous scene.

"Go, Dev!" Nora's soot-streaked face pleaded. "You must go! You cannot be seen here, it will ruin you."

"But—" Merciful God, he had killed a man.

"Go! Now! Thomas will help me."

He froze.

Go. A year ago it had been him shouting at Nora to leave. Back at the Greene Street house. She had been thrashing and sobbing as he'd pulled her away from the white faced, vacant-eyed Lily. Dev swore Nora's own guts were coming out of her mouth the sound had been so piteous.

God, how had he forgotten that terrible sound? He had dragged her out of the room and thrust her into Austin's waiting arms. *Get her out of here. Her screams will bring the watch.*

Life had come full circle.

The sting of a slap snapped his mind back to the here and now. "Get hold of yourself, Devlin." Nora shook him.

Smoky air filled his lungs and he hissed as his burned and bloody hands gripped her arms.

"Dev, we must go!" This time it was Austin pulling him away, not Nora.

"Austin—I am—by God, you are hurt!" Blood soaked his brother's shoulder.

"I am well enough. But we must go *now*." Austin thrust a handkerchief into his hands. "We cannot have another scandal. Not now when you are so close to happiness."

Anne. Could Anne and he have still their chance at happiness?

A door slammed somewhere and shouts were heard.

"Listen to your brother," Nora said wiping her hands on her skirt. "You must get away from this place. I will make up something about the body."

"But the earl—"

Havermere lay on the floor, his mouth working like a beached fish. Must have suffered an apoplexy.

"I will tend to him. Only think of Anne now. Think of your Owl."

A fine rain fell, a cool balm on his hurt and pulsing hands. Fog swirled, cocooning the brothers in its heavy mist.

The portrait was safe beneath his arm, the drawings

were gone, burned in the fire, but his other two canvases were securely rolled up in his brother's hand. They stumbled down Brook Street toward Park Lane in the opposite direction of the firemen who ran toward the smoke.

Chapter Forty

The Queen's Charity Exhibition opens this afternoon. How many little dramas will hatch among our countrymen's brightest painters? This writer can think of several.

Anne's stomach was not up for more intrigue. Besides, Maddy would never know if she skipped this particular article. She continued reading farther down the page. *"'The Duchess of Monteford recently held a musical—'"*

The latest gossip rolled off her tongue while her mind spun out dire scenarios involving the Countess of Havermere and the hell Anne would inevitably have to face this afternoon.

Oh, where was her gown?

Madame Broussard had promised it would be ready this morning. Madame had been all too happy to accommodate the Marchioness of Devlin, and had listened attentively to her ideas. This gown would speak of her tastes. Not Margaret's.

Maddy had not said much of her interview with the countess the evening before last. The countess could stay but a moment. She had been grieved to have missed Anne's call, and only came to make sure she was well. Oh, and the countess wished her every happiness.

A very niggardly report. Was Maddy holding out?

At least a dozen questions pelted her brain. Didn't

Maddy think Nora Havermere the most beautiful woman she had ever seen? Why had she really come? Was she ready to give up James? And how could Anne possibly be happy with her marriage in ruins? Why hadn't James come to see her?

Better not to ask them. Not now when she was poised to put on her battle clothes and brave her majesty's Exhibition.

But where was her gown?

"Go on to *The Spectator*, Winton. *The Times* is altogether too stiff." Maddy reclined on a chaise drinking her chocolate.

She picked up the other newspaper and flicked through to the *on dit* section. *What?* She sat up straighter.

"What is it, Winton? You have stumbled on something juicy, I'll warrant." Maddy often slipped back to Winton, forgetting their new found intimacy.

"It is a blurb about the Earl of Havermere."

"Go on."

"*'A fire broke out in the Earl of Havermere's home on Upper Brook Street yesterday. Some papers and medicinal vials seemed to have been the cause. The earl was not available for comment. The countess said he was resting. But a servant was mortally injured whilst trying to save the earl. There will be an inquest, as a matter of course.'*"

Maddy raised her quizzing glass to her nose as if by doing so it would allow her to read. Impatiently, she gestured for the paper.

Anne rose to oblige her friend. No wonder the earl had been burned, he had sat so close to the flames.

"Poppa knew the earl." Maddy sniffed as she snapped the paper open. "He came to look me over, but

I did not like him one jot. Thank the gods he was still married to his second countess at the time. Let's see... Nora Havermere must be..." Maddy raised her quizzing glass once more to her eyes. "Number four."

James's portraits hinted at such deep sadness. He had not painted a merely beautiful woman he had painted Nora Havermere's truth.

"Well, apparently there will not be a chance for a fifth. Says here, the old earl is not expected to survive." Maddy slapped the paper down. "Good riddance to bad rubbish."

Anne could not say she was sorry, though it would mean Nora Havermere would finally be free.

But James would not.

A knock sounded and, at Maddy's command, Perkins entered bearing a long box. *The gown.* Her stomach, which had just begun to settle, churned anew.

The dress lay in its box on the bed. She circled it like a bee around a flower. Nancy, Lady Tippit's maid, hovered discreetly by the dressing table, arranging combs and brushes.

"Go on, girl. It's not going to leap up and bite you. Though I suspect it might stop a few dead in their tracks." Maddy rose and shook out her skirts. "Time to get you dressed. It is well to arrive late, but not too late. Nancy still has to wrangle that mass of hair into something resembling English civility. I shall be in the next room completing my toilet. Nancy, you will knock when her ladyship is dressed, and I will come in to fawn and ogle." The door clicked shut as Maddy left the room.

"Now, milady, shall we see what's what?" All thought ceased as Nancy peeled back the layers of tissue concealing the dress. Would this new gown provide the outer confidence to prop up her shaky inner self?

The maid stepped right up to the gown and then shook it out as if it were not the most exquisite confection, but merely fabric held together by thread in order to cover a body.

"A stunner, milady, if you'll pardon my forwardness." Nancy narrowed her gaze judiciously. "Best by candlelight, but I suppose one needs natural light to see all them pictures."

Nancy prattled on, but Anne was not really listening, only dutifully raising and lowering various appendages so the maid might dress her. Though this creation was made of the lightest silk, for her purposes it might as well be made of chain-mail and hammered steel, and the exhibition room, her battleground. She would stride onto the field and take her blows but remain standing. Perhaps not the victor, but she would not let one painting fell her.

The plan was to look her fill, nod regally to all the gaping hoi polloi, and then she and Maddy would get in their carriage and never look back. The waiting finally over and she could pick up the pieces of her life and begin anew. She had her child and Matilda Tippit as family. They would have to be enough.

"Sit you down, milady, while I do your hair. I've been waiting to work my magic on this lovely mass."

A bit dubious as to Nancy's talents—after all, she was in charge of Maddy's nest of hair—but as the girl worked, Anne's mind eased. No curling irons were wielded. No hair wrenched or scalp left stinging. In fact, she could have gone to sleep if her nerves weren't ratcheted up to the nth degree.

Nancy had insisted Anne not look until she was completely dressed hair and all.

"There." The maid slid something into the back of her creation—a comb of some sort—but other than the coolness against her scalp, the ornament felt light as a feather.

The girl crossed to knock on the adjoining door. "She's all dressed, your ladyship."

If she had any doubts about Madame Broussard's talents, looking in the full-length mirror now, all those worries evaporated. Madame could be counted an ally and friend. And Nancy, a bosom beau.

The dress fit her upper body like a second skin. A wide neckline highlighted her bone structure and hugged her shoulders, which were capped with tiny sleeves. The simple bodice boasted three perfect pleats tapering to her still tiny waist before fanning out to a graceful bell. The silk fabric, a rainbow of subtle colors, was the dress's real ornament. First, golden-pink, and then, when the light changed or she moved, shimmering to a silver-blue. Much like the opal he had given her. She touched her bare finger. *Never mind.*

Loathe to look away from the astonishing stranger reflected in the mirror, Maddy's verdict was more important.

Her ladyship sailed into the room decked out in full regalia and then stopped as if she had struck an iceberg.

"Turn to me." Anne did so as her ladyship raised her quizzing glass. "Now the other way. And now the back." She snapped her glass shut like a general would his scope after surveying his troops. "Perfect. Absolutely perfect. You have done wonders, Nancy. Not that I had any doubts. You have the goods, Anne Winton. You simply needed the direction of people with some sense and style." Maddy Tippit patted her hair.

"If I may, madame," Nancy offered. "The trick of it is not to overload Lady Devlin's small frame with too many gewgaws and such."

"You have the right of it, girl," her mistress added. "One must be very judicious in one's decoration."

Anne smiled. Poor Margaret had it all wrong. This gown displayed not a ruffle, not a flounce, not even a single poof.

Nancy held a hand mirror up angling it so Anne might see her shoulders and the back of her hair.

Her locks had been wound into an intricate basket-like chignon. So elaborate, yet the effect so simple and elegant. A filigree butterfly, its jewel-dusted wings quivering above, completed the coiffure. She wanted to touch it, but could not risk disturbing one strand.

"You needn't worry, Lady Devlin." Nancy assured. "It will not come tumbling down should you take it into your head to perform an Irish jig. I used to work at the docks weaving nets afore I come into service."

"Hmmm." Lady Tippit laid a boney finger against her cheek. "Do not get any ideas about poaching her, Anne. I may have her try something similar with my hair."

A knock on the door announced Perkins. "The carriage is ready, your ladyship."

"Thank you, Perkins. We shall only be a few more minutes."

"Very good, my lady."

"Are you ready?" Maddy snapped her quizzing glass against her gloved hand and gave her breast one quick squeeze.

Casting one final look in the mirror, Anne felt as if she could conquer the world. Certainly the mere upper

ten-thousand that made up the *ton*.
"Yes, Maddy, I believe I am."

Chapter Forty-One

"Certainly not a beauty, but I'll give you arresting," a long-toothed matron in an overstuffed gown said grudgingly as she lowered her quizzing glass.

"I suppose. But who wants 'arresting' when they might have beauty? For my part, I much prefer his earlier portraits." Another viper waved her fan at the painting. "Of course his subjects were often not the most upright of women—"

"My dear Lady Percy, they were not 'upright' at all but draped about as if they had just been…well, you catch my meaning."

"I wonder at her holding an orange?" A third harridan now joined the other two. "For all her quiet demeanor, it is somehow…unseemly."

Buzz, buzz, buzz. God, Dev wanted to rip his suit from his body. Where was she? He fished his watch from his waistcoat. Six minutes after five. The exhibition closed in less than thirty minutes.

"Where is this muse?" The older witch looked around.

He ducked his head. Would that he could disappear into the elaborately marbled floor.

"One would think the chit would be here to bask in her glory."

"They say she went to the country. I would imagine the Mad Marquess is quite a handful," the fan woman tittered. "Though by the looks of this portrait, he is no longer devilish but quite done in."

Gone to the country? Had she?

Lady Tippit had assured him 'all would be as it should.' Whatever that meant. And he should 'trust in his wife, let her come to him,' her ladyship advised. He shook his head trying to dislodge the fear that wedged its way into his brain. But the reality was she had stayed away.

The Queen had come and gone. She seemed well pleased. At least he thought so.

She had stood for a long while gazing at the painting and then wiped a tear from the corner of her eye. "You have employed quite a different style, Lord Devlin. Very wild, for my taste. But I see you are smitten. That is well." She nodded once quite vigorously and sniffed. "You must savor every moment, for all too soon it is lost."

He could not help but admire his Queen for her good sense and taste.

"Who was that Dutch fellow who painted the chit with the earring?" The gorgon with the fan plied it to her heaving bosom. "This lady brings to mind that portrait."

Vermeer, you feather-head. He had to get away from these harpies. He elbowed his way from the portrait toward the entry. Could she have slipped in without his noticing? The patrons crowding the floor rivaled the paintings that stood cheek by jowl on the walls. He yanked at his cravat, suffocated by the mass of humanity and richly framed art that covered the twenty-foot walls.

Austin had insisted on attending and had stood by his side through these endless hours of waiting, but Dev had finally insisted he take himself home. His arm wound was superficial, but he had suffered burns to both his arms and neck. The stifling room must have been agony for him.

Ivo stood like a fixture by the door, his huge melon bobbing above the bonnets and carefully coiffed heads of the patrons. Poor lad hated the crowds just as much as Dev and likely needed a piss. But he was a stickler when it came to obeying orders.

Dev caught Ivo's attention and then motioned for him to go relieve himself. Still the man wavered. "I will watch," he mouthed and, reluctantly, the huge man lumbered off.

My God, he could use some air as well. And a piss.

He saw the wig first. A deferential path opened to reveal a heavily rouged Lady Tippit, and—

A stunning creature in the most beautiful gown he had ever seen. Her hair so simple, so elegant, her face so outwardly calm. His wife. Anne.

His breath expelled in a rush. There she was.

****

Anne's breath expelled in a rush. There he was.

They both stood frozen to the floor, all her bravado now wavering in the face of her husband and the onlookers who crowded around him. Hushed and expectant, the audience seemed to be waiting for the players opening lines to determine if they would be watching a tragedy or a farce.

"Lord Devlin." Maddy nodded briefly to James. "Come, Anne. We will view the painting." Taking her arm firmly, she led the way through the crowd.

Bless Matilda Tippit.

Their direction was clear. The mass of bystanders peeled back to make a path to the far side of the room.

She stared straight ahead, her slightly trembling hand crooked into Maddy's elbow. It was unclear who held who up—she rather suspected Maddy Tippit kept her upright and moving. What was certain, the room appeared endless.

A curtain of patrons parted to reveal a painting.

Sudden heat flushed her entire body, her nose prickled, and she had to blink to see properly.

The sitter held an orange almost carelessly as if she were unaware it were even there.

When the mist cleared from her eyes, she saw the fruit's skin had been pierced. A glistening runnel of juice ran down its glossy skin. The woman's longest finger caught the droplet as if she did not want it to spoil her gown or, more likely, did not want to waste a drop of the sumptuous fruit. One had the impression she was just waiting patiently for the viewer to leave before she devoured it.

She knew that feeling. She knew that quiet waiting. She knew that woman. For the sitter was her own self.

"Anne—"

She waved him away wanting a private moment with this woman who sat so utterly still yet seemed poised on the precipice of some awesome experience. The sitter's eyes held a knowing wonder, and the pierced fruit only confirmed what her eyes spoke.

This woman was not beautiful—Anne Winton—for she was plain Anne Winton in this picture. But she had a grace, a confidence—perhaps even a regal quality. Yes, perhaps a bit of the marchioness she had become. No, not beautiful; luminous.

This painting was not the one she had sat for at Ballencrieff—the picture James would never let her see.

Yet this portrait had been inspired by those sittings. She remembered him asking her to roll up the sleeve of her gown. "Yes," he had said. "Yes, just there."

She saw now what he had seen, the bit of forearm now exposed, its skin slightly whiter than her hand and wrist. That bare, white arm almost made her blush.

And the orange. Her gift to him. Eyes now awash with tears, she bit her lip to stop the smile that threatened. Tears and her gap-toothed grin would not do for the Marchioness of Devlin. She stood straighter.

Now she remembered he had spent a long time turning her hands over in his after they had made love. And it had been love, she could see that now. This woman in this portrait was loved. Anne Winton, now Marchioness of Devlin, was loved.

Never taking her eyes off the picture which had begun to run and warp with the tears that gathered and finally spilled free—oh well, so much for preserving her dignity—she reached for her husband's hand.

Dashed gloves. But it didn't matter, his heat was there melding and forging to become one with hers. They were one now.

"You approve?"

She turned to him. "Not Nora Havermere." Obvious, but she was not acknowledging his choice of subject.

He smiled his pirate smile, and her breath hitched. "Not Nora. Never Nora. She is not you. She is not my little Owl. My heart."

She dashed at the tears streaming down her cheeks. Soon her nose would be dripping. This would not do.

His heart. He had painted what was in his heart.

Heavens, where was her handkerchief when she needed it? The strings of her reticule were impossibly tangled.

He pressed a square of linen into her shaking hand. "You see, I can be wise as well. It may take me longer given how inferior my wisdom is to yours, but eventually I get it."

"You are teaching me another kind of wisdom. Trust." She sniffed and turned back to the portrait. "As you say, I am no fool. I could never love an empty man."

"I am sorry I disappeared, my dears." Maddy materialized next to James. "I had to fend off Lord Rathemore who I have not seen in an age. He was excessively attentive to me. If he weren't half-way in the grave I might have spared him a moment or two, but I told him I must attend the marchioness."

Anne ducked her head and shoved the handkerchief into her bag.

"*Hmmm*...your wife looks quite spent, Devlin."

Anne cinched her reticule closed and cleared her throat. "Overwhelmed is the word, Maddy. I am overwhelmed. The marquess seems to have that effect on me. Always has."

"As well he should, Anne. You deserve nothing less." She turned to James. "I can see painting agrees with you."

"You are mistaken, Lady Tippit. Marriage agrees with me."

"About time you both sorted that out. When one is as old as I, ordering the affairs of young people can be quite taxing. I am glad to see that I shall have some leisure now." She turned back to catch the eyes of a doddering old gentleman. Did that old roué just wink at Matilda Tippit? From the giggle that escaped her ladyship, it would appear so.

"Do you mind if we depart now?" James took her hands. "I know you have only just arrived, but I have been here hours waiting and wondering, and frankly I am ready to tear my hair out."

"I have seen everything I wanted to see," she said brusquely. So important now to keep a very tight clamp on her emotions, else she might melt into a puddle at her husband's feet.

"Ivo will come home with me in my carriage, Anne." Maddy snagged his arm. "My newest cook has a fondness for giants."

Anne. How she loved her ladyship calling her Anne.

"Very well, Matilda. I am sure Ivo can be spared. He has been going on about some jam tarts he sampled at Luscombe Hall."

"Ah, yes, the gooseberry. Come along, dear boy." Following in the wide wake of Maddy and Ivo, her husband guided her through the throng.

"May I tell you how lovely you are, Anne DeVere Winton Drake, Marchioness of Devlin?"

"You may, my lord. Several people worked very hard to achieve this result."

"Ah, you speak of the gown which is very fetching—a huge improvement on Margaret's efforts. But I was not really referring to your gown. I was complimenting the woman inside."

She sniffed. Her dratted emotions kept surging to the fore. Who could blame them when she was being heaped with such praise. Thank heavens they were almost to the door.

A man stepped out of the shadows, blocking their way. Sir Charles.

"Well, you are a dark horse, Devlin. I lost a boatload

of blunt on you. Your brother assured me the Countess of Havermere was your model."

"Did he now?" He must thank Austin for that. Later. "If you'll excuse me, Sir Charles, my wife and I have a very pressing engagement." They stepped around Brocket.

"We have a pressing engagement?"

"I don't know about you, but I have something very pressing, Lady Devlin. Perhaps you'd care to step into the carriage, and we might get to the engaging part?"

"In the carriage?" An old dowager nodded to her, and she nodded back just before a hot blush flooded her cheeks. "Oh. Yes. I do think I would like to engage in a carriage." Bless Bess, the air felt delightfully cool against her heated cheeks.

"One thing I want to get quite clear." He stopped before the carriage and turned her to face him.

Now is where her entire fantasy would collapse. She steeled herself and met his gaze. "Yes?"

"Did you realize you told me you loved me in there?"

Her tongue found the gap in her teeth and pressed. "Well, yes, yes, I did."

"Ah, I thought so. I wonder, could I prevail upon you to say it again?"

"You could prevail. I love you." Her lips parted, nearly against her will, and she smiled. "I love you. Who could not love you? You are so full, full to bursting— with humor, with grace, with curiosity, with talent. You are an embarrassment of riches, Lord Devlin. I am so very lucky to have you to love."

"And I love you, my beautiful Owl." His arms came around her surrounding her in his love. "I would have discovered this great epiphany much earlier had I been wiser. If only I stopped and looked inside my heart. You were there all along, just waiting for me to see. I will be worthy of you, my love. I will make myself worthy though it takes me a lifetime. You will see."

"I do see. The evidence hung for all to behold, there in that room full of people clambering to see you fail— us fail. But instead they had to stand by and watch you soar, to witness, as I did, your love for me. You choosing me. Simple, plain Anne Winton. Pardon me, my love, if I am once again overwhelmed."

People stood about gawking at their display. She couldn't give a fig.

"Get in the carriage, madam. Now."

"Very well, you've only to say—*Ooof!"* He bodily pushed her bum into the carriage.

"I have a surprise for you."

"A gift?" She turned back to him. "I like your gifts. Especially the first one."

"Well, yes, that gift was rather special. However, this is something less awesome but more substantial." He made a motion for her to sit.

"Will I be overwhelmed?"

"I can only hope. But first things first." He rapped on the roof of the carriage and began closing the blinds.

Could they really do this in a moving conveyance? It was not nighttime. This was not her bed. He was not half foxed.

She liked these new circumstances and possibilities. Heavens, if one could make love in a carriage, what other delights lay before her? Well, one thing was certain, her husband was very creative.

John Coachman was directed to drive to Kensington

and back.
Twice.

Epilogue

Malvern Grange, May 1865

"Ellie, Grace! You must leave Ivo be. The goats will not milk themselves."

Ivo giggled and waggled his eyebrows at the girls. One goat took advantage of his distraction and nipped at his vest where he must have a treat tucked away. Anne scooped up her daughter, Eleanor, before the goat got too audacious, and then carried her to the manger full of sweet, new-mown hay. Ivo dipped into his still empty milking bucket and placed two calico kittens in Ellie's lap. Two-and-half-year-old Grace squealed and toddled after the giant man.

"An-Anne." The name had stuck when Grace had not been able to pronounce 'Aunt'. "You promised to tell Mama I am to have Spots." Grace climbed up on the fence rail and carefully used one finger to pet the larger calico kitten. Anne had a sneaking suspicion Ivo had something to do with that particular name.

She ruffled Grace's wispy golden hair. "And so I shall, but she is not yet back from Town. Remember, I told you she will come with An-Margaret, and Gran-Maddy. You must be patient." She settled Grace next to Ellie. "Now, where were we? Cristabelle was about to be eaten by the dragon."

"No, silly, An-Anne. The dragon was captured by

413

the elephant that had lost his trunk, don't you remember?"

"Ah, yes, quite right you are, Grace." Ellie nodded vigorously and touched her nose. "It is well you have been attending so. You will keep me on the right track. Now, the herd of purple rhinoceroses caused quite a ruckus as Mr. Hiro wielded his shears at Prince Dauntless—"

"Ah, there you are." James pressed a kiss fully on her lips. Grace gawped and Ellie held out her arms to her father. "The light is fading and so I have finished for the day."

"Is it going well?"

"Hello, what's this?" He took up a wriggling kitten. "How did a chicken get into the barn, Ivo?"

A look of confusion crossed his face and then he opened his mouth to answer. Poor Ivo, ever literal.

"Silly, Un-Dev, Spots is a kitten, not a chicken."

"*Hmmm*, are you quite certain?"

The tiny creature, thoroughly tired of being suspended in the air, dug its claws into her husband's hand.

"Owww!" He dropped the kitten back into the hay. "Yes, I do believe you are right, Miss Grace. It is indeed a feline."

"No silly," she said her hands on her hips, head shaking—which of course Ellie imitated. "Not a fee-lion, a kit-ten!"

"Ah, next time I shall remember." He scooped up their daughter and turned to Anne. "In answer to your question, I am quite pleased with the painting."

"Will it go into the exhibit?" Ellie's sweet dark head next to her father's, their pewter eyes smiling into each other, was a sight she would never tire of.

"Yes. I think it is just what is needed to fill the gap between the seascape and pastoral with the owl."

"Ah, my favorite—the owl. Who would have thought the devilish Lord Devlin would turn to the landscape for his muse? It still astonishes me how you hold an entire world within a simple canvas."

"You will give me a swelled head, my lady."

She smiled and then ran her tongue over the gap in her teeth, which she had begun to accept if not love. "*Hmmm...* I would like to swell your head, my lord." Her gaze fell to rest on his fall. "Oh." She jerked her eyes up to meet his. "You did remember to write the countess about the portraits?"

"*Sweet Jesu,* Owl, you go from seductress to schoolmarm in the blink of an eye. How is a fellow to keep up?" He nodded. "Yes, I did this morning. Poor Nora. The old earl, a cur to the very end, first refusing to die and then leaving Nora a pauper. Hopefully the old portraits will fetch something so she can live in relative comfort. She never wanted them displayed. Now she will have to stand by as they go under the hammer to the highest bidder. I just hope she is not stubborn about selling them."

"It is silly of her not to just accept a loan."

"We are not all as wise as you, my love." He pulled a bit of straw from her hair which Ellie grabbed and promptly put in her mouth.

Anne pried it away and dipped her hand into her pocket finding a carrot for her daughter to gnaw on. "And what of Austin? I saw you had a letter."

"He has safely reached Bombay and seems to be settling into army life. Most of his letter was about the natives and their culture. He has ridden an elephant—"

"El—font!" Ellie exclaimed with pride.

Her father tossed her in the air and she squealed. "Yes, El-an-or! It seems your uncle has become bosom beaus with Sir John, the viceroy."

Ellie squealed, so delighted with her father.

"Oh, good, I am glad he has found a calling. Margaret seems happier as well. She and Phoebe are in each other's pockets these days. Perhaps when Austin comes home they can begin anew?"

"Perhaps," was all her husband said, still busy tossing their daughter into the heavens.

The kittens wriggled out of Grace's too loving arms and dropped to the floor of the barn.

"Ivo, mind the kittens, they are headed your way!" Anne called out. Bless Bess, her skirt looked like a haystack. She shook it out. "Mrs. Ambrose came by with another cordial of elderberry wine. This time I took it gladly. There is no sense in convincing the village my healings are free."

"I told you as much, but it is well you have come to that conclusion on your own. How is young Adam?"

"Better, though I will go again this evening. I want to try some oregano oil, and perhaps if I added a poultice of—"

A peal of giggles rang out ,and two forms came barreling around the corner of the far stall. Wind milling arms and legs sorted themselves into Hester and Ava, Anne's newest charity girls.

"Oh, perfect. You ladies are just in time to relieve me." She dusted off her skirts and then turned to her husband. "Lord Devlin, I believe I feel a cold coming on."

"Indeed, my dear?" Ellie reached out a hand trying to remove her father's nose.

"Yes, I have an irresistible urge to sneeze. I am hoping you might provide some sort of relief."

"I would be most happy to be of service in any and every way I can, my lady." He pried grubby fingers from his face. "Will you relieve me of this octopus, Hester? Her ladyship is in need of my services." He deposited Ellie into Hester's waiting arms and winked at Grace who was about to correct him.

"Oh!" James swept her off her feet right then and there. "My goodness, Lord Devlin, I feel better already."

Snuggled next to her husband's breast she heard Ava say, "A trifling sneeze? Lord, old people are rather silly, aren't they, Hes? Thank heavens we shall never be so barmy."

Author's Note

Mental illness has been misunderstood for centuries. Only recently are we beginning to divine the mysteries of the brain. In 1863, these poor "unfortunates," as they were sometimes called, were subjected to terrible abuse and degradation, and were even a source of amusement for the, more or less, firm of mind. While researching *Mad for the Marquess*, I discovered many Victorian "cures" for madness. Most were too unpalatable for use in a romance novel, but I wanted the reader to get a taste of what these people had to endure, hence the cold plunges, restraints, bleeding, and cupping.

Devlin suffers from what is now known as PTSD. Today doctors can put a diagnosis to his behavior, but back then, the accepted cure-all was bleeding to "adjust the humors" of the blood. Being poisoned with mercury and arsenic exacerbated his condition and prolonged stints in the dungeon of Ballencrieff, which was rife with black mold, only added to his malaise. Certain molds are now known to cause depression and erratic behavior. I only hint at this in the book, as this theory was unknown in 1863.

I took some creative license when Queen Victoria deigns to attend the Duke of Malvern's ball and the art exhibition. In 1863, with Prince Albert dead only two years, the queen was still in deep mourning and only visited London on rare occasions.

Lastly, I so enjoyed creating my hodgepodge of secondary characters. I wanted this little tribe, with their variety of afflictions, to shed light on how those considered "abnormal" were treated in Victorian times. Horace Beauchamp is in fact very bright but has

Asperger's. In the case of Phoebe Nester and Matilda Tippit, husbands or fathers could institutionalize any wife or daughter who did not "behave" in the way deemed correct. "Female Hysteria" was a diagnosis that encompassed everything from depression to excessive sexual urges. And then there is Major Cummings, whose only crime was being a homosexual. He could have been imprisoned, but I chose to have him confined to Ballencrieff.

Humanity comes in an array of glorious color. Let us celebrate our rainbow.

Prologue

January 1864
Mayfair, London

Nora St. James, Countess of Havermere, should not have attended the burial.

Gently bred women did not go to such events. They were deemed too frail, their emotions too uncertain to withstand the ritual of consigning a body to the earth.

An equally held belief was that women, being sisters of Eve, were sinful by nature, therefore not worthy to tread upon consecrated ground. The *ton*, no doubt, would ascribe the latter to Nora.

And last, but certainly not least, the good folk of London believed she had murdered the deceased.

She went anyway.

Men in black armbands slanted looks at her beneath their stovepipe hats. Some disapproving, but most slyly coveting. Their eyes slid over her veiled face and red hair to settle on her breasts, waist, and hips.

No matter. She was used to it.

Removing her glove with two quick tugs, she bent and dug her fingers into the dark earth. Musk and pungent decay filled her nostrils. She wanted the black beneath her perfectly manicured nails. She wanted it to seep into her body and somehow make this death real.

With a fistful she rose, squeezed, and then let it fall

in a clump. It burst open, scattering over the pristinely polished ebony and rosewood casket.

Bile burned her throat at the memory of his white face turning yellow, the blood pooling in his lifeless body and the tang of urine as he finally released his brutal grip on life.

Nine years married. Just a raw, naïve girl when he'd claimed her.

Now he was gone.

Praise God.

An incredible lightness enveloped her as if she were suddenly within one of those hot-air balloons soaring over the top of the churchyard. She rose to her toes and lifted her chin higher. But she remained solidly on the frozen ground, imprisoned by mourners all huddled around the gaping hole and the black iron fence that surrounded St. Martin-in-the-Fields.

With the final benediction pronounced, she offered her own silent prayer—quite different from the Reverend Harmon's hope of eternal joy in heaven for the fifth Earl of Havermere—and then turned her back on death.

Penny press reporters, who had hung about like carrion on the edges of the churchyard, now swooped in to surround her. Their mouths formed questions, a barrage of words fired like so many shots, making her hot ears ring, their pencils poised to capture her answers, so eager to twist them into lies.

"Did you do it, Countess? Did you poison your husband, Lord Havermere?"

"No chance of the old earl sending you off to Ballencrieff Asylum now that he's conveniently dead is there, Countess?" another shouted.

"You must be relieved to have the inquest behind

you. What will you do now? Perhaps find another rich husband?"

Havermere's plan to send her to Ballencrieff Hall, a madhouse in the Scottish Highlands, had been quashed by his apoplexy. No longer able to speak or write, he had lingered, lying in bed for nearly three months while servants wiped spittle and food from his twisted lips, faithfully turning his wasting body.

Once a day Nora had made herself enter his room to endure his accusatory glare. It could not touch her. *He* could no longer touch her. Hurt her. She'd breathed in the sour smell of death and stared back, her truth deflecting his vitriol.

That last day, she'd watched as he gummed down his favorite cake, delivered each morning from Downs Bakery. He smacked his papery lips, impatiently gesturing to his nurse for more.

Disgusted, Nora had turned away. Only a moment later, a panicked gasp had her whipping around. The old man lurched, and the cake flew, the plate clattering to the floor. Nearly knocking the nurse aside in his haste to haul his lordship into a sitting position, a footman thumped on the old man's back. White froth bubbled between his blue lips.

Heedless of his peril, he seemed to use all his remaining strength to raise his arm and point an accusing finger at Nora.

Try as she might, she could not move. That boney finger and glassy gaze pinned her to the wall as if she were already imprisoned in iron shackles.

In the ensuing pandemonium, the cake had been thrown away. No evidence.

However, poison had been found in his body. Nora

would not have put it past the old reprobate to do the deed himself if only to drag her down with him. But the brief inquisition ended with the ruling, "Death by persons unknown." Still, gossip had run rampant.

And now, with the old earl's funeral, it seemed the newly widowed Countess of Havermere was still a tasty morsel for a few voracious curs, yapping to tear over the last shred of scandal.

Nora ignored them, moving steadily toward the refuge of her waiting carriage. Her heavy black lace veil lent a curtain of protection, and her coachman's hand and gaze were sure and steady as he helped her inside.

She welcomed the dark interior and sat back into the squabs, pressing her fingertips against her dry eyes. "Drive on, Thomas."

Her voice surprised her. It sounded as if it belonged to someone else.

Someone with hope.

A word about the author…

Jess Russell, best-selling, multi-award-winning writer, divides her time between New York City and the Catskill mountains.

The Dressmaker's Duke, her first novel, was a best seller, finaling as a "Best First Book" and "Best Historical" in the National Readers Choice, The Heart of Excellence, The Aspen Gold, and The Golden Leaf Awards.

Mad for the Marquess was a finalist for RWA's prestigious RITA award.

Jess is delighted to be a part of the Wild Rose family. Next in her Reluctant Hearts series is Crazy for the Countess, featuring Nora Havermere. Followed by Vexed with the Viscount, and then Daft for the Duke.

She loves to hear from her readers:
https://jessrussellromance.com